UNITED STATES OF BANANA

UNITED STATES OF BANANA

A GRAPHIC NOVEL

Written by Giannina Braschi

Illustrated by Joakim Lindengren

Edited and with an introduction by
Amanda M. Smith and Amy Sheeran

MAD CREEK BOOKS, AN IMPRINT OF
THE OHIO STATE UNIVERSITY PRESS
COLUMBUS

Published by Mad Creek Books, an imprint of The Ohio State University Press.

Library of Congress Cataloging-in-Publication Data
Names: Braschi, Giannina, author. | Lindengren, Joakim, illustrator. | Smith,
    Amanda M., 1981– editor. | Sheeran, Amy, 1986– editor.
Title: United States of Banana : a graphic novel / written by Giannina Braschi
    ; illustrated by Joakim Lindengren ; edited and with an introduction by
    Amanda M. Smith and Amy Sheeran.
Other titles: Latinographix: The Ohio State Latinx comics series.
Description: Columbus : Mad Creek Books, an imprint of The Ohio State
    University Press, [2021] | Series: Latinographix | Summary: "A graphic
    novel on terrorism, global warming, mass incarceration, US capitalism
    and imperialism, Puerto Rican independence, revolution, art, and poetry.
    Appearances by the Marx Brothers and Margaret Dumont, Antonin
    Artaud, Ruben Dario, Pablo Neruda, Fidel Castro, Munoz Marin, Barack
    Obama, Hu Jintao, Donald Trump, Shakespeare, and Walt Disney"—
    Provided by publisher.
Identifiers: LCCN 2020035298 | ISBN 9780814257869 (paperback) | ISBN
    0814257860 (paperback) | ISBN 9780814281093 (ebook) | ISBN 0814281095
    (ebook)
Subjects: LCSH: Braschi, Giannina. United States of Banana—Comic books,
    strips, etc. | Braschi, Giannina. United States of Banana—Adaptations. |
    Hispanic Americans—New York (State)—New York—Comic books, strips,
    etc. | Puerto Ricans—United States—Comic books, strips, etc. | Statue of
    Liberty National Monument (N. Y. and N. J.)—Comic books, strips, etc. |
    Graphic novels.
Classification: LCC PN6790.P93 B738 2021 | DDC 741.5/97295—dc23
LC record available at https://lccn.loc.gov/2020035298

Cover design by Christian Fuenfhausen
Text design by Juliet Williams
Type set in Serifa and Futura

PRINTED IN THE REPUBLIC OF KOREA

♾ The paper used in this publication meets the minimum requirements of the
American National Standard for Information Sciences—Permanence of Paper
for Printed Library Materials. ANSI Z39.48-1992.

CONTENTS

United States of Banana

A Graphic Revolution

AMANDA M. SMITH AND AMY SHEERAN

The graphic novel you are about to read resulted from a chance encounter between two artistic minds: the Puerto Rican poet Giannina Braschi (born 1953) and the Swedish cartoonist Joakim Lindengren (born 1962). They met in 2012 at the Gothenburg Book Fair during a presentation of the Swedish translation of Braschi's collected works. She gave him a copy of her 2011 post-modern tour de force, *United States of Banana* (*USB*), and Lindengren, unusually moved by the text, fervently sketched for months, visualizing Braschi's abstract prose with provocative, concrete images. Lindengren illustrated only a portion of *USB,* albeit a gripping one: In post-9/11 New York City, the autobiographical character Giannina,[1] along with Zarathustra (from Friedrich Nietzsche's 1883 *Thus Spoke Zarathustra*) and Hamlet (from Shakespeare's eponymous 1599 play) make their way from Manhattan to Liberty Island to liberate yet another literary character, Segismundo (from Pedro Calderón de la Barca's 1635 *Life Is a Dream [La vida es sueño]*).[2] Along the way to rescue Segismundo from imprisonment beneath the skirt of the Statue of Liberty, the trio meets a diverse cast of characters as they discuss the best way to upend the establishment and overthrow US empire. Finally, they free Segismundo, a metaphor for Puerto Rico's liberation from the US.

Though the tale is exciting and the images alluring, *United States of Banana: A Graphic Novel* is not meant to entertain. As Segismundo muses in his cell, "The representation of reality is an obstacle to the advancement of knowledge, and so is all the literature of entertainment that is impeding the advancement of thought and the blowing of minds" (Braschi 2011c, 176).[3] Averse to easy art, the graphic novel situates philosophical dialogues in oneiric landscapes in an effort to free the imagination, alongside Segismundo, and dream up new solutions to societal injustices. The following pages first offer a brief introduction to some of the most salient characters and symbols in Braschi's text so that readers may more easily access them. We then situate *USB* in Braschi's wider oeuvre and discuss critical engagements with her work. Finally, we consider what new meanings might arise when readers encounter *USB* as a graphic novel in the current political context. This introduction aims to help readers navigate a rewarding text, and we have included discussion questions at the back of the book to stimulate meaningful reflections on the graphic novel's main themes.

We would like to thank Jared Guzman for his support in editing the image files for this graphic novel. Without his technical assistance, this project would have taken much longer to come to fruition.

1. Throughout, "Giannina" refers to the character of *USB,* while "Braschi" refers to the author.

2. The graphic novel was first published in Swedish (Braschi and Lindengren 2017).

3. For consistency, all textual citations come from Braschi's 2011 *USB.*

SEGISMUNDO, HAMLET, ZARATHUSTRA, AND GIANNINA WALK INTO FULTON STREET MARKET

In the first pages, the graphic novel plunges us into a world that at first seems surreal, one that defies interpretation and meaning: Giannina finds Hamlet and Zarathustra at the Fulton Street Market in New York City; they are all carrying dead bodies on their backs. Giannina meets the two fictional characters at this real geographical location for the strange, dreamlike task of burying—along with the human corpses—a sardine. On the one hand, the scene is clearly heavy with allusions and significance, but on the other, the connections seem so enigmatic that a reader could easily assume that their meaning is unattainable. Readers who want their minds blown will have to persevere.

If this richly layered text can be said to have a single point of origin, it is an 1899 poem written by the celebrated Nicaraguan *modernista* Rubén Darío (1867–1916) and addressed to Sweden's King Oscar II (1829–1907). An epigraph to the poem taken from the French newspaper *Le Figaro* indicates that, upon arriving to Spain, the king cried out, "Vive l'Espagne!" (qtd. in Darío 2016, 401). Darío interprets Oscar's exclamation in light of the Crisis of 1898, when Spain finally lost the last vestiges of its once-vast empire—Cuba, Puerto Rico, and the Philippines—and the US became Latin America's new imperial enemy. Over the course of the poem, Darío (2016, 402, lines 28–30) thanks Oscar for reminding Spain of its glorious past:

> For Lepanto and Otumba, for Peru and Flanders;
> for Isabella who believes, for Christopher who dreams
> and Velázquez who paints and Cortés who tames
>
> por Lepanto y Otumba, por el Perú, por Flandes;

> por Isabel que cree, por Cristóbal que sueña
> y Velázquez que pinta y Cortés que domeña[4]

One line from this nostalgic reflection of former Spanish dominance was Braschi's inspiration for uniting the protagonists from two great works of early modern theater: "Si Segismundo siente pesar, Hamlet se inquieta" (Darío 2016, 401, line 11), which Braschi translates as "If Segismundo grieves, Hamlet feels it" in the front matter of *USB* (n. pag.). Segismundo, the representative of Spain's literary Golden Age, is psychically linked to the Nordic prince, who is both Oscar's fictional predecessor and the embodiment of English literary history. Darío's evocation of two characters from different imperial traditions is not accidental; indeed, they both become implicated in convoluted plots of royal succession, which makes them uniquely well-suited to Braschi's lively discussions of coloniality and empire.

The intricate, delicate web of imperial connections that the graphic novel begins to spin in the opening sardine scene, however, extends further. Outside of Sweden and Norway, King Oscar II is perhaps most well recognized as the good-natured, mustachioed logo of the King Oscar brand of canned fish, and in particular, sardines. Indeed, the very same historical king gave the company his blessing, name, and image for use on its products. In the opening panels, we see Giannina peeling back the lid of a sardine can to find a rotting fish in the tin coffin, obliquely referencing the brand. Thus, the king whom Darío praised is invoked in an entirely different register from that of the poem—but there is meaning in this connection, too. Not unlike the Spanish empire's motto, *Plus ultra* ("further beyond"), one early, official slogan of King Oscar products was "out to conquer the world" (Johnsen 2002). In other words, in this otherwise bizarre sequence, there is a hidden message about empire and a subtle parody of those with the privilege to take conquest lightly.

---

4. Unless otherwise stated, all translations are ours.

The question remains, though, why Giannina, Hamlet, and Zarathustra need to, of all things, bury the sardine. For English-language readers in particular, this action might seem puzzling. It would be readily familiar, however, to many members of the Spanish-speaking world, who would recognize it as part of the Carnival celebrations before Lent, in which the effigy of a sardine is burned to symbolically sever with the past and start anew. Our group of protagonists is out to do the same; in Giannina's words, burying the sardine suggests a need to "bury the 20th century" (Braschi 2011c, 76). Given the book's setting in post-9/11 New York City and the careful network of allusions that Braschi designs, the burial of this particular sardine recalls the fall of the Spanish empire, predicts the end of the haphazard use of imperialist discourse for product marketing, and, Giannina hopes, presages the release of the US empire's grip on Latin America, and Puerto Rico more specifically.

Braschi, who holds a PhD in early modern Spanish literature, found the personification of Puerto Rico's political status in Segismundo. To explain her choice, Braschi (qtd. in Garrigós 2004, 153) said the following:

> He interests me because he's in a dungeon, he's someone who isn't recognized; he was a prince and they haven't let him take his command. They treat him like an illegitimate son when he was legitimate. All of these things interest me: that he has been in exile in his homeland, that they call him a monster because his mother died when he was born. And to a certain extent, that has been the fate of the Latin race with the Black Legend. And it seems to me that from that poor treatment, from that abuse, something big is going to come, and Hamlet is going to save him from his dungeon.

> Me interesa porque está en un calabozo, es alguien que no está reconocido, era un príncipe y no le han dejado ejercer su mandato. Lo tratan como un ilegítimo, cuando era el hijo legítimo. Todas esas cosas me interesan: que ha estado en exilio en su propia patria, que lo llaman monstruo porque su madre murió cuando él nació. Y hasta cierto punto ése ha sido el destino de la raza latina, con la leyenda negra. Y me parece que de ese tratamiento tan malo, de ese abuso, va a salir algo grande, y Hamlet lo va a salvar del calabozo.

In Calderón's play, Segismundo, prince and heir apparent to the Polish crown, is held in captivity from birth because of a prophecy that he will bring great harm to the kingdom and be responsible for the death of his father, King Basilio. Years later, Basilio decides to give Segismundo a chance, and Segismundo learns the truth about his imprisonment when Basilio brings him to the palace in a drug-induced stupor. His behavior upon his liberation seems to confirm his father's worst fears: Segismundo throws a servant off a balcony to his death and attempts to seduce two noblewomen. His tutor drugs him again and returns him to his prison, telling him that the episode in the palace was only a dream. The people of Poland, meanwhile, have learned of the existence of their rightful heir. They free Segismundo, who then challenges his father. Following the tutor's advice that one must act according to God's laws whether awake or asleep, Segismundo decides to spare his father's life. Basilio, surprised by his son's good judgment, renounces the throne and names Segismundo king. While these actions unfold, another plotline involving a young noblewoman, the tutor's daughter, develops. Rosaura, whose narrative position Giannina occupies in *USB,* travels disguised as a man to seek revenge for a betrayal, a conflict Segismundo ultimately resolves once he assumes the throne. In his final speech, the new king remains uncertain of whether he is awake or asleep, but he resolves that, even if life is a dream, he will rule with justice and prudence.

In *Hamlet,* the prince and rightful heir likewise finds himself kept from the throne and unsure of what to believe. After Hamlet's father dies, his uncle, Claudius, quickly marries the widowed queen, Gertrude, and becomes king. The ghost of the former king tells Hamlet that Claudius poisoned him, and although Hamlet remains somewhat doubtful, he makes a plan to determine the truth that centers on leading others to believe he has lost his mind. In addition, in a sub-plotline that at first resembles Calderón's play, the daughter of the king's advisor, Ophelia, who also makes several appearances in *USB*, pursues a romantic attachment with Hamlet. Whereas all of these elements are ultimately resolved—even if problematically—in *Life Is a Dream*, in *Hamlet*, every tragic possibility comes to fruition. In one of *Hamlet*'s most famous lines, Ophelia, like Rosaura, is advised to live out her days in a nunnery; unlike Rosaura, Ophelia's story ends in suicide. Hamlet, the rightful heir, does not ascend to the throne; instead, his reasoning and machinations lead to tragedy, death, and the ascension of a foreign ruler to the throne of Denmark. Hamlet, thus, appears in *USB* as a cynical doubter of Segismundo's political project. By bringing Hamlet into the plot of *USB*, though, Braschi finds a way for him to redeem himself; with Segismundo and friends, he can help restore order to the world.

Zarathustra appears alongside these characters because, according to Braschi, Nietzsche has always been an important interlocutor for her, and she returns to *Thus Spoke Zarathustra* again and again.[5] Additionally, the presence of Nietzsche's fictional character as the sobering voice of reason and truth on the quest toward freedom provides a necessary counterweight to Giannina's unrestrained ideals, Hamlet's petulance, and Segismundo's defiance. The wandering poet-philosopher of Nietzsche's novel also resembles Giannina, the traveling poet moving through the underbelly of New York City. In the novel, Zarathustra embarks on many journeys to teach the truth that he has discovered

in the solitude of his mountain home. Along the way, he makes mistakes and learns important lessons on his quest to help others achieve the state of what Nietzsche called the overman (*Übermensch*). The overman is willing to risk everything for the betterment of humanity in this world, which contrasts with the salvation of humanity in another realm, as in Christianity, for example. In *USB*, Zarathustra believes that Segismundo has achieved this status, which is why he joins Giannina and Hamlet despite frequently finding himself annoyed by their antics. He engages Giannina in challenging dialogue as she contemplates how to achieve freedom for Segismundo, Puerto Rico, and herself, and their conversations help her define her course and clarify her mission to overthrow the power of all colonial structures. The new values that she seeks to instill beyond the framework of empire and subjugation are unmistakably of Nietzschean inspiration.

With this unlikely crew, the reader begins the pilgrimage across geography, art, and literature. This journey also draws on Braschi's previous works, which set the stage for *USB* and its interpretation in academic discourse.

CRITICAL RECEPTION OF *UNITED STATES OF BANANA* (2011)

Braschi's work, brazenly inventive and powerfully disruptive, has also been described as "obstinately opaque" (Castillo 2005, 172). The rich, erudite intertextuality described above makes her prose challenging to decipher. Making sense of a text that brings together references as diverse as the popular Spanish festival of the Burial of the Sardine, a Shakespearian tragedy, a Spanish *comedia*, Nietzschean philosophy, and Puerto Rican popular culture requires a reader with an uncommon level of intellectual curiosity who is motivated to investigate connections across genres, time periods, and geographic regions. In *USB*, a Puerto Rican pest control jin-

---

5. Interview with Braschi, New York City, October 7, 2017.

gle appears alongside glosses of Socratic dialogues, which has led one critic (González 2017, 89) to lament, "Any given reader unequipped with the decoding and reading abilities of Braschi's ideal audience will experience difficult, if not insuperable, impediments when working to co-construct a mental model of Braschi's story world." Our discussions with Braschi, however, reveal that she does not have an ideal reader in mind, nor is she interested in telling stories.[6] Rather, her work playfully flouts readers' "horizons of expectations," keeping them attentive and inquisitive while sometimes frustrating them to draw attention to interpretive complacency.[7]

As we have seen, one of Braschi's prominent techniques for questioning and undermining established categories of thought involves piecing together recognizable texts and images from a breadth of well-known archives in unexpected ways. Cristina Garrigós (2002, 17) has noted that, rather than reproducing stereotypical models for Puerto Ricans or Latinxs in New York, for example, Braschi continuously recasts questions of identity by using methods of literary collage. In fact, the author appears bored by transparent categories and, in a mode that Laura R. Loustau (2002, 119) has referred to as "nomadic consciousness," Braschi (qtd. in Sheeran and Smith 2018, 136) defiantly rejects the classification of her oeuvre because, in her words, labels "forget about the depth of [her] work. And the beauty." As a categorical nomad, Braschi is always in transition, challenging herself and pushing the limits of what language can do. What may at times sound like an inscrutably cacophonous choir is a political project to "transform new noises into new values" (Braschi 2011c, 141),

and the abundance of disparate allusions in her work invites readers to actively contribute their voices. Encountering the opaque in Braschi, then, is a signal of the limits of readers' imaginations to interpret texts in new ways, listening to what they have to say, and talking back.

Critics have also frequently praised her linguistic experimentation and innovative use of language. In Braschi, readers find linguistic multiplicity, creative uses of translation, and multiple loci of enunciation (Carrión 1996, 169) even when, as in her early collections of poetry, she writes only in Spanish.[8] In her Pulitzer prize-nominated novel *Yo-Yo Boing!* (originally published in 1998), Braschi broke out of the confines of one language to unexpectedly code-switch between English and Spanish throughout the text in what Sarah de Mojica (2002, 187) has commended as "radically heterogeneous writing, which fragments and makes porous the discourse of modernity and neocolonialism" ("una escritura radicalmente heterogénea, que fragmenta y vuelve poroso el discurso de la modernidad y el neocolonialismo"). José Torres-Padilla (2007, 292) has disparaged that same heterogeneity as a "linguistic performance, decidedly elitist and bourgeois." Christopher González, by contrast, considers this assessment an "imposition of an essentialist agenda" (2017, 93), in which Braschi's privileged background seems to disqualify her as an "authentic" writer of a group that is racialized in the United States.[9] Whether critics celebrate or condemn Braschi for her meticulous use of language, they all agree that she subverts

---

6. See Sheeran and Smith (2018).

7. "Horizon of expectations" is a phrase first coined by German literary theorist Hans Robert Jauss (1921–1997) to describe the way readers' past experiences with literature in terms of conventions of genre, style, and form determine their expectations, and, therefore, aesthetic judgment of future works of literature (Jauss 1970, 13).

8. Throughout the 1980s, Braschi published three collections of prose poetry in Spanish: *Asalto al tiempo* (1980), *La comedia profana* (1985), and *El imperio de los sueños* (1988). *El imperio de los sueños,* which includes the previous two collections, was later translated into English by Tess O'Dwyer and published as *Empire of Dreams* with Yale University Press in 1994. *Imperio* was rereleased in 2011 with the publication of *United States of Banana* by Amazon Crossing.

9. Braschi readily acknowledges that she comes from a privileged background; her grandfather brought the first automobiles to Puerto Rico and profited from the industry. See Sheeran and Smith (2018, 134).

language conventions with nearly every turn of phrase.

USB is no less linguistically experimental than Braschi's earlier works, yet it has received much less critical attention. Only a few articles have attempted to grapple with *USB,* and there has been no comprehensive study of the text.[10] Perhaps because *USB* is Braschi's first book written almost entirely in English, its linguistic multiplicity is less immediately apparent. Nonetheless, more than Braschi's previous works, *USB* is exhaustively citational, piecing together phrases from popular discourse and elite literary and artistic culture. It demonstrates the ability to use stale, ready-made language against itself to defamiliarize and resuscitate it, thus breathing creativity into cliché. Braschi's choice to conduct this experiment in English in *USB* may have displaced her too radically from literary classification for commentary. What to do with a writer who establishes herself as a Spanish-language poet (*El imperio de los sueños* [Empire of Dreams]), defiantly writes a text in Spanglish (*Yo-Yo Boing!*), and then dares to write entirely in English (*USB*)? After the publication of *Yo-Yo Boing!,* Kristian van Haesendonck (2008, 162) tentatively posited that the lack of attention to Braschi was due to the fact that she was too Puerto Rican and therefore not North American enough for US literary critics, while not being Puerto Rican or Latin American enough for Puerto Rican and Latin American critics. We suspect that Braschi's response to such an assessment would be an enthusiastic "Exactly!"—the experience of *puertorriqueñidad* that her works theatricalize corresponds to her position in literary canons. In *USB*, puertorriqueñidad is being born a prisoner in a dark dungeon beneath the skirt of the Statue of Liberty; it is to hate liberty and covet it at the same time. It is to be bound

to empire and coloniality, longing to be free without knowing what a free self looks like. When Braschi wrote *USB* in English, she drew attention to her out-of-placeness, using English not to submit to the empire of dreams, but to conquer it. She uses the language of the empire in *USB* much like she uses stock phrases: to decolonize them by removing the discursive chains that confine them.

Braschi's persistent disregard for genre distinctions is an aspect of the postmodern, and the qualities that characterize *USB*'s colonial critique—auto-reflexivity, metatextuality, intertextuality, pastiche, the erasure of the divisions between high and low culture, fragmentation, and the denial of narrative structure—also make it readily legible as a postmodern text.[11] In *USB*, character dialogue is written like a play with no stage directions in highly poetic prose in a book-length text that is not quite a novel. Though Braschi herself would prefer not to be classified as a writer of postmodern literature, her work is recognizably part of the current moment of skepticism toward established monoliths.

In describing postmodernism as a product of late capitalism, US literary critic Fredric Jameson (1998, 125) doubted whether the postmodern, which "replicates or reproduces—reinforces—the logic of consumer capitalism," could also resist that logic. *USB* passionately responds in the affirmative. If the ambiguity of Braschi's postmodern register in *Yo-Yo Boing!* once found her falsely accused of supporting "the continuing colonial status of Puerto Rico" and undermining "any desire for self-determination that might effect real change" (Torres-Padilla 2007, 292), in *USB*, Braschi uses postmodernist techniques to arm a violent poetic assault on US imperialism from a fervently Puerto Rican locus of enunciation. *USB*'s absolute rejection of consumer capitalism becomes even more apparent in the graphic novel, in which Lindengren

---

10. A much-anticipated critical volume on Braschi's work, *"Poets, Philosophers, Lovers": On the Writing of Giannina Braschi,* edited by Frederick Luis Aldama and Tess O'Dwyer, is forthcoming with Pittsburgh University Press (2020).

---

11. On Braschi as a postmodern writer, see Dessús (2001), Estill (2004), and Gonzalez (2014).

has visualized the book's insistence on the way commodities degrade societies by obliterating human creativity. For example, in one scene, the Statue of Liberty lights her Camel cigarettes with her torch while begrudgingly listening to Giannina's treatise on political liberation. Because *USB* is a postmodern text written from the perspective of a colonial subject, its marginal postmodernism works to destabilize empire, as in the book's title, which transforms the US from a producer of politically unstable, export-reliant countries into a banana republic itself.[12] This displacement of empire is not an inversion, though; on the contrary, *USB* prescribes friendship and dialogue as an antidote to empire, for *USB* is ultimately "a book about camaraderie, *compañerismo,* even the generosity of love" (Cruz-Malavé 2014, 815).

Despite Braschi's commitment to constructive dialogue across different sectors of society, some critics have mistaken the author's elite background for elitism in her works. Braschi acknowledges her wealth of knowledge of literature and the arts and winks at her social status when Giannina rubs shoulders with Darío and debates with the French avant-gardist Antonin Artaud (1896–1948). At the same time, Giannina also "attempts to identify with various different subject positions across the political spectrum, emphasizing the need for unity and understanding, and recognizing her own complicity in reifying the social structures that she condemns" (Lowry 2015, 157). *USB* imagines dialoguing with immigrants, refugees, and even terrorists in an ambitious effort to build meaning with marginalized sectors of society. Furthermore, Braschi makes frequent public appearances and often repeats her work's main convictions in easily understood vernacular. In an interview with the most widely circulating Puerto Rican newspaper, *El Nuevo Día,* Braschi (qtd. in Delgado 2012) proclaimed, "Freedom is not an option; it is a constitutional right" ("La libertad no es una opción, es un derecho constitucional"). Braschi's embrace of high culture should not automatically limit the reach of her messages beyond her immediate social circles.

Nowhere does her commitment to heterogeneous audiences become more apparent than in *USB,* a postmodern text that is also post-9/11 literature, as Elizabeth Lowry has defined it (2015). Without a doubt, much of *USB*'s fragmentation relates as much to the postmodern moment as it does to the broad-reaching trauma of 9/11—both personally for Braschi and collectively for society. Furthermore, Braschi's oeuvre makes clear that, for Puerto Ricans in New York, 9/11 was only one instance of a trauma that is, in Greg Forter's (2011, 98) words, "non-punctual"; that is, an everyday, ongoing, and insidious trauma that forms part of the fabric of colonial subjectivity. Lindengren's rich imagery in the graphic novel brings *USB* into the era of the Trump administration, further emphasizing the continuity of Puerto Rican trauma across time. The book appears to correspond to what Paul Petrovic (2015, x) has labeled a second wave of post-9/11 fiction, one that distinguishes itself from a first wave that is primarily concerned with emotional responses to the event through its focus on "the multivalent forces of empire." *USB* asserts the global reach of colonial trauma across social classes while simultaneously acknowledging its uneven spread. The text's unapologetic dismantling of empire is a communal catharsis of the shared trauma of coloniality among Puerto Ricans living on the islands or off, other immigrants in the United States, and even elite imperial subjects.

---

12. American author O. Henry (1904) first described the imaginary nation of Anchuria, based on Honduras, as a "banana republic" in his *Cabbages and Kings,* suggesting that the country's entire economy was based on the export of bananas. Today, the term more broadly describes a highly stratified and politically volatile country, usually in Latin America, whose economy is largely dependent on the export of agricultural products and other natural resources. Since the publication of *USB,* the idea of the US as a banana republic has appeared in popular media. See Gabler (2017) and Graham (2013).

A MORE GRAPHIC *UNITED STATES OF BANANA*

In part because *USB* is written as a script, its New York City setting is easily forgotten over three hundred pages of relentlessly playful and often abstract poetic prose. Braschi does little to connect characters' Socratic dialogues to specific spaces. Instead, as Sam Franzway (2016, 2) has complained, readers must "conjure their own setting" with no stage directions and "only the most cursory set-descriptions." Such a placeless text may at first seem like an odd choice for a graphic novel adaptation. A graphic novel is a visual storytelling format, and *USB* seems to be the opposite: an unremitting textual inquiry into the nature of textuality itself. And yet, in the graphic format presented here, Lindengren has anchored Braschi's purposefully challenging prose in powerfully rendered settings, showing characters navigating real spaces as they ruminate on freedom and the downfall of empire. On the first page, we see Giannina, Zarathustra, and Hamlet convene at a meticulously sketched Fulton Street Market with New York City skyscrapers hovering behind them in linear perspective. When the characters speak to the Statue of Liberty at Liberty Island, she towers over them, crouches, and steps down to sit on her pedestal. As the characters navigate the world under her skirt, they walk through a landscape that resembles M. C. Escher's *Relativity* and encounter bar scenes and jail cells. At first glance, the graphic novel's most obvious contribution to the text is the creative elaboration of the spaces the characters traverse as they speak.

Lindengren has surpassed the challenge of expanding *USB* into thought-provoking spaces with playful images worthy of the text's ludic spirit. For the Swedish artist, the task of visualizing *USB* was both easy and obvious. Lindengren (2018, 4), a well-known cartoonist in Sweden, has said that he wanted to draw the text because it "was so full of pictures. Some texts are hard as hell to illustrate, but *United States of*

Banana was reeking of pictures." For the artist, the lack of engagement with detailed settings seemed to free his imagination to conjure images that the dialogues evoke. He aimed to imitate what he described (Lindengren 2018, 4) as the text's "madness" and to parallel Braschi's cannibalization of literary history with his own cannibalization of art history. The resulting panels are rife with references to modernist art, including Picasso, Dalí, and Magritte, to name just a few. In Lindengren's rendering, Zarathustra appears as a muscular, bearded superhero complete with boots and cape, a wink at one of the translations of "Übermensch" as "Superman." Puerto Rico's three political paths—sovereignty, continued commonwealth status, and statehood, playfully described in *USB* as wishy, wishy-washy, and washy, respectively—appear as three mischievous chicks, and Donald Trump features as Oliver Exterminator, a character Braschi invented based on a popular Puerto Rican pest control jingle. Storm Troopers and the Men in Black also make surprising appearances, along with James Dean, David Bowie, Uncle Sam, Hugo Chávez, and Simón Bolívar. This visual interpretation delights and challenges while also reinvigorating the text's relevance for the current political moment.

The graphic novel is a traditionally subversive medium, and even more so in Latin American contexts, where comics and graphic novels often clamor in the face of historical silences (Catalá Carrasco, Drinot, and Scorer 2017, 15). Thus, it is ideologically well-suited to represent a text as insurrectionary as *USB*. Worldwide, the longer graphic novel format emerged after the rise of adult underground comix, which, in turn, responded to the popularity and fear surrounding the perceived negative influence of children's comics on young minds. In the early years of children's comics in the United States in the 1930s and '40s, for example, teachers, parents, journalists, and psychologists alike worried that comics posed a threat to literacy and children's intellectual development, placing "civilized" society in danger (Baetens and Frey 2015, 28). The format pays homage to its disruptive origins by taking on topics that criticize the societal status quo, and *USB*'s graphic adaptation is no exception. Lindengren's choice to illustrate in black and white adds a sinister feel to the text's political milieu; flipping through the pages, one perceives a dark universe of impending doom. The fast, dynamic quality of diagonal lines communicates both the chaos and urgency of the imperial takedown the text proposes, and repeated references to recognizable images and visual forms echo its program of reconstituting cliché as an act of liberation. These visual choices give texture to *USB*'s revolutionary impulses, bringing them into an almost tactile high relief. Thus, though this particular graphic novel is, if anything, transnational, it corresponds to a Latin American graphic tradition of conceptualizing battles between the forces of hegemonic domination and counter-hegemonic subversion. In *USB: A Graphic Novel*, Latin American readers find what they have come to expect from graphic novels: "clues for a deciphering of their situation, characters with whom to identify, and a language with which to give form and meaning to the expression of their thoughts and feelings in their new, contemporary realities" (Fernández L'Hoeste and Poblete 2009, 3).

The graphic novel is also thematically well-suited to conveying the multidimensional quality of the quest for liberation that unfolds in *USB*. Though many scholars insist that the graphic novel is a form and not a genre, some of the most famous examples share topical similarities, such as the juxtaposition of personal history with more far-reaching historical events. An entire volume of essays (Chaney, 2011) considers the question of why so many of the most celebrated graphic novels are autobiographical, and Jan Baetens and Hugo Frey (2015, 96) have posited that the pairing of text with image allows artists to situate personal feelings in broader historical contexts more clearly and directly than

a textual novel can. In *USB,* Giannina's commitment to Segismundo's liberation symbolizes her desire for Puerto Rico's political sovereignty, but her journey to free the imprisoned *comedia* character also functions as a metaphor for Braschi's personal colonial subjectivity as a Puerto Rican. As Braschi (qtd. in Sheeran and Smith 2018, 134) has suggested, Puerto Ricans "know the colonial systems will not allow their children to achieve all the things they want in life because of the way the system is. I saw that in my childhood. I saw the impotence that was imposed on me since my childhood." When Segismundo is alone in his cell, he voices similar thoughts, reflecting on how imperial forces tried to teach him helplessness. Lindengren shows him reading the *New York Times* next to a bunched-up Puerto Rican flag, references that are both universally recognizable and personal to Braschi's biography. In a scene at the wedding of Basilio and Gertrude in which Segismundo declares the liberation of Puerto Rico, Lindengren uses a classical triangular composition, placing the young prince at the center of the field of vision and inserting a dazed Giannina as a key focal point. Through such imaginative renderings, the images enhance Giannina's personal entanglement in political processes.

Because the eyes can move more quickly over Lindengren's images than Braschi's tightly packed prose, overall, the graphic novel has the effect of relieving some of the interpretive burden thrust onto readers of *USB*. In a particularly playful and challenging passage in which Giannina discusses Segismundo's upbringing in his dungeon, she describes liberating "Wishy from Washy" so that Segismundo will stop "Wishy-Washing his options away" (Braschi 2011, 106). Lindengren divides the text over three panels. In the first, three confused chicks seem to be walking in circles. In the second, two of the chicks are chained together at the neck, with the third holding a cleaver in one hand and wire cutters in the other. The final panel shows a bloody cleaver alongside a decapitated head in a pool of blood. The body rides a bicycle, and the third chick grips the chain with the wire cutters to take down the headless chick. The images dramatically gloss Braschi's dizzyingly experimental text: Puerto Ricans' perceived options pit them against each other in a murderous cycle that goes nowhere. In another section of text that describes Segismundo's treatment in the dungeon of the Statue of Liberty, Lindengren uses five panels to show the other prisoners variously ignoring Segismundo, making a spectacle of him, laughing at him, and following him like a leader. Even without considering the text, we readily see the conflicted and contradictory positions that he occupies as a prisoner of freedom, along with the motley cast of characters with whom he associates. These images gloss, interpret, and filter the text in ways that make it more accessible to a broader audience.

REREADING *USB* NOW

Aristotle (2005, 57) famously interpreted the function of the poet as one that describes "not the thing that has happened, but a kind of thing that might happen"; in other words, he signaled the prophetic potential of poetry to capture even a faint pulse, and with it, diagnose and predict the course of the future. Called the "the literary prophet of her homeland" ("profeta literaria de su tierra"; Roldán Soto 2018, n. pag.), the clairvoyant Braschi and her poetry would have pleased the Greek philosopher. *Yo-Yo Boing!* closes with an epilogue in which Hamlet, Zarathustra, and Giannina meet at a crossroads carrying dead bodies on their backs—the same scene that opens the graphic novel—and Giannina already has plans to bury the twentieth century:

> In front of me the fireman says: Fire! Fire of the People! Sudden and Fatal. Air. Dynamite. Joy. Here comes the funeral procession. The procession of dynamite.

> Delante de mí el bombero dice: ¡Fuego! ¡Fuego Popular! Fulminante. Aire. Dinamita. Alegría. Ya viene el cortejo. El cortejo de la dinamita. (Braschi 2011b, 247)

Three years after publication, the World Trade Center collapsed in lower Manhattan not far from Braschi's apartment. Her escape route from the island was a ferry to the Statue of Liberty, the very same place where the character Giannina plans to bury the twentieth century's dead body in *Yo-Yo Boing!* The fast-paced poetry of *Yo-Yo Boing!* was able to foresee such impending destruction, but it also inserts a curious noun in the midst of the funeral procession's smoke and ashes: joy (alegría). Braschi controversially associates societal destruction with a vibrant beginning. Thus, she foreshadows violence against the US as a rupture of the status quo, a dismantling of empire, a revolution of the masses, and the possibility of a new way forward, subverting the conventional meaning of the word "progress." In a cultural landscape rife with apocalyptic and postapocalyptic narratives, Braschi's capacity to envisage total annihilation with utopian rather than dystopian promise distinguishes her work among other works of literature. As *USB* now reappears in graphic novel format, its words will undoubtedly find surprising synchronicities with current and future political contexts.

Since the 2011 publication of *USB,* several of its prophecies have indeed come to pass. In *USB,* the Statue of Liberty laments her enslavement as an informant for the United States of Banana, forced "to shed [her] torchlight on all suspicious activities taking place under [her] skirt" in the dungeons of liberty (Braschi 2011c, 99). In the graphic novel, the monument appears as a silhouette on the horizon with her torch aimed at the political subversives at her feet—Giannina, Hamlet, and Zarathustra. The statue explains, "I was a monument to immigration. Now I'm a border patrol cop" (Braschi 2011c, 99). Braschi invents "liberty" as a US Customs and Border

Protection officer during President Obama's tenure at a time when immigration rights activists dubbed the former president the "deporter-in-chief" for what they saw as an undue number of deportations during his time in office. The notion has become even more eerily relevant under a Trump administration that has exacerbated the criminalization of immigration and promoted a nationalistic rhetoric. The Obama administration instigated a higher rate of removals than previous administrations, and it also deprioritized removing those with no criminal records who had established roots in the US (Chishti, Pierce, and Bolter 2017, n. pag.). Obama created the Deferred Action for Childhood Arrivals (DACA) program in 2012 to grant up to eight years of conditional permanent resident status to undocumented immigrants brought to the US as children who met certain conditions.[13] One of the program's stipulations required participants to provide the government with biometric and biographic data, creating a database that became a frightening reality for hundreds of thousands of DACA recipients when Trump announced plans to terminate the program in 2017.[14] In other words, an immigration protection measure became an immigration surveillance tool in a new political context, not unlike Braschi's Statue of Liberty, turning her torch of freedom downward to spy on those who have taken refuge at her feet. Read today, Segismundo's birth into captivity also evokes the symbolic imprisonment of undocumented immigrants living in the US who are unable to live here freely and unable to leave, either, not to mention the over two thousand children separated from their families in immigration detention centers ("Family Separation by the Numbers" n.d., n. pag.).

While *USB* promotes brotherhood among a diversity of disenfranchised people, its main theme is emphatically the political liberation of Puerto Rico and the integral role of poetry in enacting it. The residents of the islands of Puerto Rico, Vieques, and Culebra have existed under colonial status for over five hundred years, leading Puerto Rican lawyer and legal scholar José Trías Monge to call it "the oldest colony in the world" (1999). A Spanish colony until after the Spanish–American War of 1898, Puerto Rico has been a US territory ever since, and Puerto Ricans were granted US citizenship through the Jones Act of 1917. Despite their US passports, though, Puerto Ricans living on the islands do not have the right to vote in US elections, negotiate treaties with other countries, receive goods from any entity other than the United States, or determine their own tariffs. Five referenda since 1967 have indicated that Puerto Ricans are divided among independence, the status quo, and statehood.[15] Giannina insists in *USB*, "I want to liberate my island" (Braschi 2011c, 97), and she deplores the fact that the idea of liberty has imprisoned Puerto Rico by limiting the imaginative potential of Puerto Ricans. Describing Segismundo as Puerto Rico, she tells Hamlet, "He grew

13. To be eligible for DACA, immigrants must meet the following conditions: be under the age of 31 by June 15, 2012; have immigrated to the United States before the age of 16; have resided in the US continuously since June 15, 2007; be physically present in the US on June 15, 2012 and at the time of making the request for deferred action with US Citizenship and Immigration Services; no lawful status in the US on June 15, 2012; be currently enrolled in school, graduated, or obtained a high school completion certificate, or honorably discharged from the US Coast Guard or Armed Forces; and have no felony convictions, no significant misdemeanor, or three other misdemeanors, and pose no threat to national security or public safety. See "Consideration of Deferred Action for Childhood Arrivals (DACA)" (2018, n. pag.).

14. Since Trump announced the termination of the DACA program, several lawsuits have been filed against his administration. The Supreme Court heard oral arguments on November 12, 2019, and on June 18, 2020, ruled that the Trump administration could not proceed with its plan to rescind the program, citing a failure to follow proper procedure. For more on DACA status, see "DACA Litigation Timeline" (2019, n. pag.) provided by the National Immigration Law Center.

15. In 1967, 1993, and 1998, a majority of voters favored a continuation of the commonwealth status. In 2012, a slight majority cast the ballot for statehood, and in 2017, 97 percent of voters preferred statehood but due to a ballot boycott, voter turnout was only 23 percent of eligible voters. For more, see Brown (2019, n. pag.).

up thinking that he was not free—but that he could choose between three options—Wishy, Wishy-Washy, and Washy" (Braschi 2011c, 106). Therein lies the link between politics and poetry, for political imprisonment creates only a theater of choice that confines the psyche to prefabricated options. Poetry, on the other hand, can take those manufactured alternatives and combine them in surprising and innovative ways, creating otherwise unthinkable possibilities.

Puerto Rico's political status, which has been denounced by the United Nations Special Committee on Decolonization, was already urgent in 2011, when *USB* was originally published; however, when Hurricanes Irma and Maria pummeled the islands in September 2017, the political status of the islands acquired new, fatal consequences. As Puerto Rican English professor Ricia Anne Chansky (2019, 17) poignantly reported,

> What I do know is that on 20 September a category 5 hurricane devastated Puerto Rico and revealed a system of colonialism that has been just as detrimental to the people as the natural disaster itself. The care that the 3.5 million US citizens of Puerto Rico did not receive in the wake of the hurricane is a reflection and continuation of the lack of care in the months leading up to the squall.[16]

Despite the high death toll of US citizens, President Trump has consistently undermined the

---

16. Several studies have estimated the number of deaths caused by the hurricanes in their immediate aftermath. Kishore et al. estimate a 62 percent increase in mortality from September 20 to December 31, 2017, with total hurricane-related deaths at 4,645 (2018). The study's conclusions note, however, that these estimates are most likely conservative due to survivor bias and household size. Another public school-based survey of over 96,000 students (Orengo-Aguayo et al. 2019, n. pag.) found that 83.9 percent saw houses damaged; 57.8 percent had a friend or family member leave Puerto Rico; 45.7 percent had damage to their homes; 32.3 percent experienced food and/or water insecurity; 29.9 percent felt their lives were at risk; and 16.7 percent had no electricity for five to nine months following the hurricanes.

validity of reported fatalities and minimized the gravity of the aftermath of the hurricanes (Bonilla 2018, n. pag.). Only ten days after Maria hit the islands, Trump, ignoring community mobilization there, tweeted, "[Puerto Ricans] want everything to be done for them when it should be a community effort" (@realDonaldTrump 2017). Once again, Braschi's words are prescient. In *USB,* Gertrude, Segismundo's imperial stepmother, tells the imprisoned prince, "You need people to do everything for you. Why should your father have to support you at your age?" (Braschi 2011c, 149). One of the most outspoken activists in the aftermath of the hurricanes has been Puerto Rican anthropologist Yarimar Bonilla (2018, n. pag.), who, not unlike Braschi in her 9/11 poetics, finds a certain hope amid the disaster in its ability "to cast a spotlight on Puerto Rico's long-standing problems." Trump's indifference and even contempt for Puerto Rico, insists Bonilla (2017, n. pag.), do not represent a singularity but are rather part of a "long history of US policy on the island," which has resulted in issues of debt and economic crisis, income inequality, racial and social marginalization, violence, and precarity.

In the final pages of the graphic novel, Giannina and Zarathustra discuss how Segismundo's liberation will take place. First, he will be born from the Statue of Liberty. Then, the Statue will hurl her crown into the water, and all of the wealthy imperialists at the gala there will drown while Giannina, Zarathustra, Hamlet, and Segismundo sail off on the peaks of the crown (Braschi 2011c, 210). The final image is stunning: four triumphant silhouettes sailing on choppy waters toward the sun breaking through the clouds. The final line announces the end of the US imperial hold over Puerto Rico: "I liberate myself from the United States of Banana." Although Giannina makes this declaration of independence in *USB,* in the graphic novel, the text appears without a dialogue bubble—making it unattributable to an individual speaker—

thus emphasizing the collective efforts needed for the envisioned political revolution.

Such a revolution of the masses may have arrived in the wake of disaster. On August 2, 2019, Ricardo Roselló became the first Puerto Rican governor in five hundred years of governance forced to resign by popular protest. Between July 17 and July 25, three days of mass public protests brought up to 14 percent of the Puerto Rican population to the streets to decry the governor's corruption, acts of fraud, misogyny, homophobia, disrespect for Hurricane Maria victims, and threats to various prominent members of Puerto Rican society, all of which was revealed explicitly in an 889-page series of chat messages released by the Puerto Rican Center for Investigative Journalism on July 13 (Kunkel 2019, n. pag.). Braschi not only foresaw the political revolution underway in Puerto Rico, but she also participated in it. She marched in the streets and declared,

Even if Ricky Roselló goes to pray to the all-powerful one, I know that the all-powerful one is with the people. And among the people, my people, a god is dancing, and that dance of the people is the one that will triumph.

Aunque Ricky Roselló vaya a rezarle al todopoderoso, yo sé que el todopoderoso está con el pueblo. Y que dentro de este pueblo, mi pueblo, un dios está bailando, y ese baile del pueblo es el que va a triunfar. (Latinx Latinx-Culture 2019)

United States of Banana: A Graphic Novel is an astonishing visualization of the revolution underway and the one yet to come.

WORKS CITED

Aristotle. 2005. "Poetics." In *Critical Theory Since Plato,* edited by Hazard Adams and Leroy Searle, 3rd ed., 52–69. Belmont, CA: Thomson/Wadsworth.

Baetens, Jan, and Hugo Frey. 2015. *The Graphic Novel: An Introduction. Cambridge Introductions to Literature.* New York: Cambridge University Press.

Bonilla, Yarimar. 2017. "Perspective | Why Would Anyone in Puerto Rico Want a Hurricane? Because Someone Will Get Rich." *Washington Post,* September 22, 2017. https://www.washingtonpost.com/outlook/how-puerto-rican-hurricanes-devastate-many-and-enrich-a-few/2017/09/22/78e7500c-9e66-11e7-9083-fbfddf6804c2_story.html.

———. 2018. "Perspective | Trump's False Claims about Puerto Rico Are Insulting. But They Reveal a Deeper Truth." *Washington Post,* September 14, 2018. https://www.washingtonpost.com/outlook/2018/09/14/trumps-false-claims-about-puerto-rico-are-insulting-they-reveal-deeper-truth/.

Braschi, Giannina. 2011a (1988). *El imperio de los sueños.* Las Vegas, NV: Amazon Crossing.

———. 2011b (1998). *Yo-Yo Boing!* Las Vegas, NV: Amazon Crossing.

———. 2011c. *United States of Banana.* Las Vegas, NV: Amazon Crossing.

Braschi, Giannina, and Joakim Lindengren. 2017. *United States of Banana.* Sweden: Cobolt.

Brown, Beverly. 2019. "Presidential Blunders and a Path to Statehood | Harvard Political Review." August 27, 2019. http://harvardpolitics.com/united-states/puerto-rico-statehood/.

Calderón de la Barca, Pedro. 1958. *La vida es sueño.* Madrid: Ediciones Cátedra.

Carrión, María. 1996. "Geographies, (M)Other Tongues and the Role of Translation in Giannina Braschi's *El imperio de los sueños.*" *Studies in 20th Century Literature* 20 (1): 167–91.

Castillo, Debra A. 2005. *Redreaming America: Toward a Bilingual American Culture.* SUNY Series in Latin American and Iberian Thought and Culture. Albany: State University of New York Press.

Catalá Carrasco, Jorge L., Paul Drinot, and James Scorer. 2017. "Introduction: Comics and Memory in Latin America." In *Comics and Memory in Latin America,* eds. Jorge L. Catalá Carrasco, Paul Drinot, and James Scorer. 3–32. Pittsburgh: University of Pittsburgh Press.

Chaney, Michael A., ed. 2011. *Graphic Subjects: Critical Essays on Autobiography and Graphic Novels.* Wisconsin Studies in Autobiography. Madison: University of Wisconsin Press.

Chansky, Ricia Anne. 2019. "Teaching Hurricane María: Disaster Pedagogy and the Ugly Auto/Biography." *Pedagogy* 19 (1): 1–23. https://doi.org/10.1215/15314200-7173718.

Chishti, Muzaffar, Sarah Pierce, and Jessica Bolter. 2017. "The Obama Record on Deportations: Deporter in Chief or Not?" migrationpolicy.org. January 25, 2017. https://www.migrationpolicy.org/article/obama-record-deportations-deporter-chief-or-not.

"Consideration of Deferred Action for Childhood Arrivals (DACA)." 2018. US Citizenship and Immigration Services. February 14, 2018. https://www.uscis.gov/archive/consideration-deferred-action-childhood-arrivals-daca.

Cruz-Malavé, Arnaldo Manuel. 2014. "'Under the Skirt of Liberty': Giannina Braschi Rewrites Empire." *American Quarterly,* no. 3: 801–18. http://dx.doi.org/10.1353/aq.2014.0042.

"DACA Litigation Timeline." 2019. *National Immigration Law Center.* September 28, 2019. https://www.nilc.org/issues/daca/daca-litigation-timeline/.

Darío, Rubén. 2016. "Al Rey Óscar." In *Poesía Completa,* edited by Salvador Álvaro, 401–3. Madrid: Editorial Verbum.

Delgado, José A. 2012. "La libertad no es una opción, es un derecho." *El Nuevo Día; San Juan, Puerto Rico,* September 24, 2012. https://search.proquest.com/news/docview/1069216752/citation/F01BA55B55F343E4PQ/1.

Dessús, Virginia. 2001. "Identidad(es) Postmoderna(s): *Yo-Yo Boing!* De Giannina Braschi." *La Torre* 6 (22): 413–26.

Estill, Adriana. 2004. "Giannina Braschi." In *Latino and Latina Writers,* edited by Alan West, María Herrera-Sobek, and César Augusto Salgado, 841–50. New York: Charles Scribner's Sons. http://catalog.hathitrust.org/api/volumes/oclc/52631325.html.

"Family Separation by the Numbers." n.d. American Civil Liberties Union. Accessed September 26, 2019. https://www.aclu.org/issues/immigrants-rights/immigrants-rights-and-detention/family-separation.

Fernández L'Hoeste, Héctor, and Juan Poblete. 2009. Introduction. In *Redrawing the Nation: National Identity in Latin/o American Comics,* eds. Fernández L'Hoeste and Juan Poblete. 1–16. New York: Palgrave Macmillan.

Forter, Greg. 2011. *Gender, Race, and Mourning in American Modernism.* Cambridge: Cambridge University Press. http://site.ebrary.com/id/10476533.

Franzway, Sam. 2016. "United States of Banana." *Transnational Literature* 9 (1): 1–2.

Gabler, Neal. 2017. "America the Banana Republic." *BillMoyers.com.* November 29.

Garrigós, Cristina. 2002. "Bilingües, biculturales y posmodernas: Rosario Ferré y Giannina Braschi." *Ínsula* 667–68 (July): 16–18.

———. 2004. "Chicken with the Head Cut Off: Una conversación con Giannina Braschi." In *Voces de América/American Voices: Entrevistas a escritores americanos / Interviews with American Writers,* 147–63. Spain: Aduana Vieja.

González, Christopher. 2017. *Permissible Narratives: The Promise of Latino/a Literature.* Columbus: The Ohio State University Press.

Gonzalez, Madelena. 2014. "*United States of Banana* (2011), *Elizabeth Costello* (2003) and *Fury* (2001): Portrait of the Writer as the 'Bad Subject' of Globalisation." *Études Britanniques Contemporaines. Revue de La Société D'études Anglaises Contemporaines,* no. 46 (June). https://doi.org/10.4000/ebc.1279.

Graham, David. 2013. "Is the US on the Verge of Becoming a Banana Republic?" *The Atlantic.* January 10. https://www.theatlantic.com/politics/archive/2013/01/is-the-us-on-the-verge-of-becoming-a-banana-republic/267048/.

van Haesendonck, Kristian. 2008. *¿Encanto o espanto?: identitidad y nación en la novela portorriqueña actual.* Madrid: Iberoamericana.

Henry, O. 1904. *Cabbages and Kings.* Garden City, NY: Doubleday, Page & Company.

Jameson, Frederic. 1998. "Postmodernism and Consumer Society." In *The Anti-Aesthetic: Essays on Postmodern Culture,* edited by Hal Foster, 111–25. NY: The New Press.

Jauss, Hans Robert. 1970. "Literary History as a Challenge to Literary Theory." Translated by Elizabeth Benzinger. *New Literary History* 2 (1): 7–37. https://doi.org/10.2307/468585.

Johnsen, John G. 2002. *"Out to Conquer the World": King Oscar Sardiner Gjennom 100 Ar.* Norway: Stavanger Mesi.

Kishore, Nishant, Domingo Marqués, Ayesha Mahmud, Mathew V. Kiang, Irmary Rodriguez, Arlan Fuller, Peggy Ebner, et al. 2018. "Mortality in Puerto Rico after Hurricane Maria." *New England Journal of Medicine* 379 (2): 162–70. https://doi.org/10.1056/NEJMsa1803972.

Kunkel, Cathy. 2019. "Roselló Steps Down after Puerto Rico Rises." *Jacobin.* July 26, 2019. https://jacobinmag.com/2019/07/puerto-rico-protest-ricardo-rossello.

Latinx LatinxCulture. 2019. *La Revolución Puertorriqueña: Giannina Braschi En El Viejo San Juan.* https://www.youtube.com/watch?v=i7SZLM7QVeI.

Lindengren, Joakim. 2018. "Image from United States of Banana: A Comic Book." *Chiricú Journal: Latina/o Literatures, Arts, and Cultures* 2 (2): 3–4.

Loustau, Laura R. 2002. *Cuerpos errantes: Literatura latina y latinoamericana en Estados Unidos.* Argentina: Beatriz Viterbo Editora.

Lowry, Elizabeth. 2015. "The Human Barnyard: Rhetoric, Identification, and Symbolic Representation in Giannina Braschi's United States of Banana." In *Representing 9/11: Trauma, Ideology, and Nationalism in Literature, Film, and Television,* edited by Paul Petrovic, 155–64. Lanham, Maryland: Rowman & Littlefield.

de Mojica, Sarah. 2002. "Sujetos híbridos en la literatura puertorriqueña: '*Daniel Santos y Yo-Yo Boing.*' Literaturas Heterogéneas y Créoles." *Revista de Crítica Literaria Latinoamericana* 28 (56): 187–203.

Monge, José Trías. 1999. *Puerto Rico: The Trials of the Oldest Colony in the World.* New Haven, CT: Yale University Press.

Nietzsche, Friedrich Wilhelm, Adrian Del Caro, and Robert B Pippin. 2006. *Thus Spoke Zarathustra: A Book for All and None. Cambridge Texts in the History of Philosophy.* Cambridge: Cambrige University Press.

Orengo-Aguayo, Rosaura, Regan W. Stewart, Michael A. de Arellano, Joy Lynn Suárez-Kindy, and John Young. 2019. "Disaster Exposure and Mental Health Among Puerto Rican Youths After Hurricane Maria." *JAMA*

Network Open 2 (4): e192619. https://doi.org/10.1001/jamanetworkopen.2019.2619.

Petrovic, Paul, ed. 2015. "Introduction: Emergent Trends in Post-9/11 Literature and Criticism." In *Representing 9/11: Trauma, Ideology, and Nationalism in Literature, Film, and Television,* ix–xvii. Lanham, Maryland: Rowman & Littlefield.

Roldán Soto, Camile. 2018. "Giannina Braschi, profeta literaria de su tierra." *El Nuevo Dia.* July 24, 2018. https://www.elnuevodia.com/entretenimiento/cultura/nota/gianninabraschiprofetaliterariadesutierra-2437123/.

Shakespeare, William. 2006. *Hamlet.* Edited by Neil Taylor and Ann Thompson. New York: Bloomsbury.

Sheeran, Amy, and Amanda M. Smith. 2018. "A Graphic Revolution: Talking Poetry & Politics with Giannina Bra-

schi." *Chiricú Journal: Latina/o Literatures, Arts, and Cultures* 2 (2): 130–42.

Torres-Padilla, José. 2007. "When Hybridity Doesn't Resist: Giannina Braschi's *Yo-Yo Boing!*" In *Complicating Constructions: Race, Ethnicity, and Hybridity in American Texts,* edited by David S. Goldstein and Audrey B. Thacker, 290–307. Seattle: University of Washington Press.

Trump, Donald J. (@realDonaldTrump). 2017. Twitter.com. ". . . Want Everything to Be Done for Them When It Should Be a Community Effort. 10,000 Federal Workers Now on Island Doing a Fantastic Job."

UNITED STATES OF BANANA

A Graphic Novel

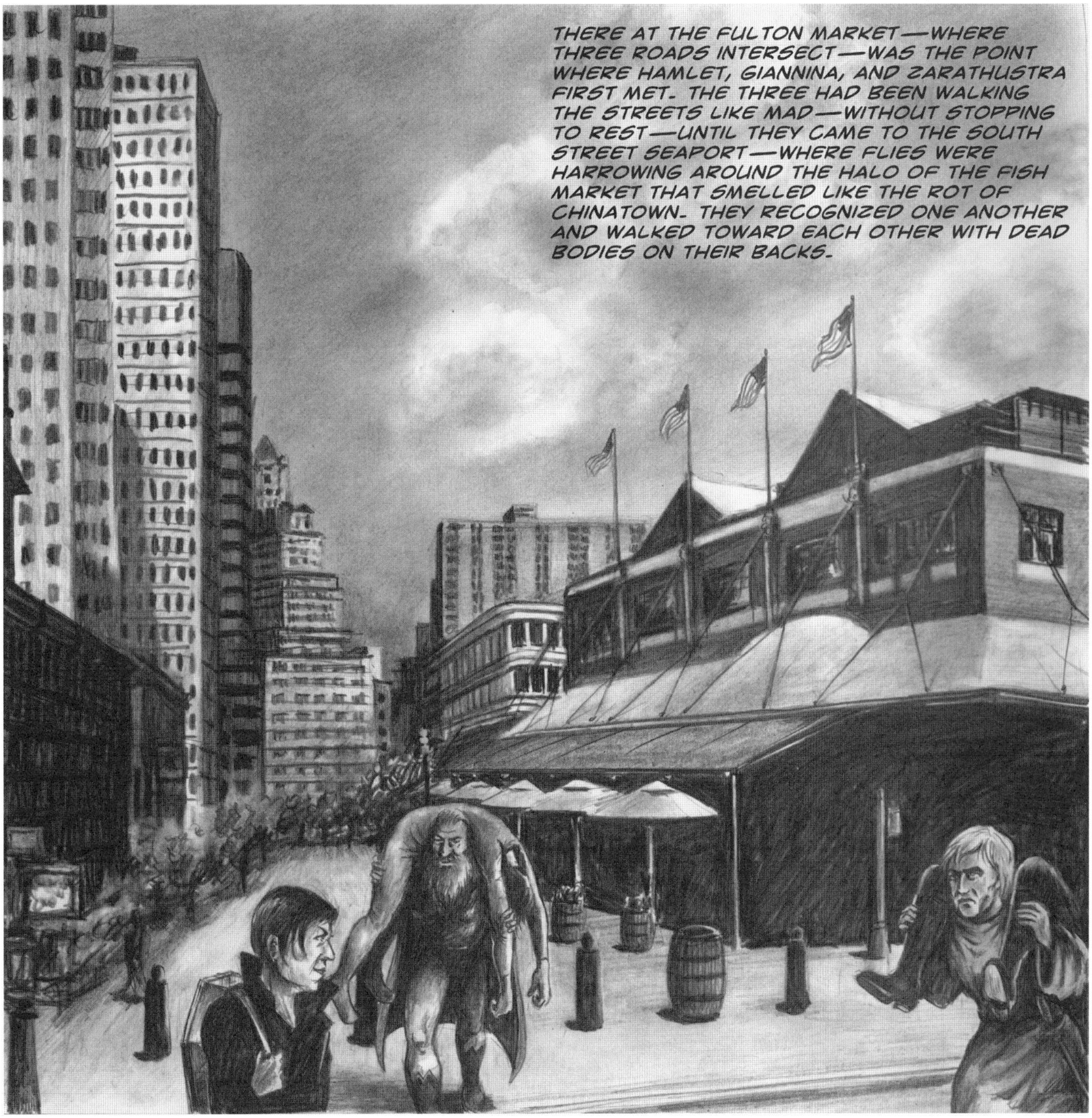
THERE AT THE FULTON MARKET—WHERE THREE ROADS INTERSECT—WAS THE POINT WHERE HAMLET, GIANNINA, AND ZARATHUSTRA FIRST MET. THE THREE HAD BEEN WALKING THE STREETS LIKE MAD—WITHOUT STOPPING TO REST—UNTIL THEY CAME TO THE SOUTH STREET SEAPORT—WHERE FLIES WERE HARROWING AROUND THE HALO OF THE FISH MARKET THAT SMELLED LIKE THE ROT OF CHINATOWN. THEY RECOGNIZED ONE ANOTHER AND WALKED TOWARD EACH OTHER WITH DEAD BODIES ON THEIR BACKS.

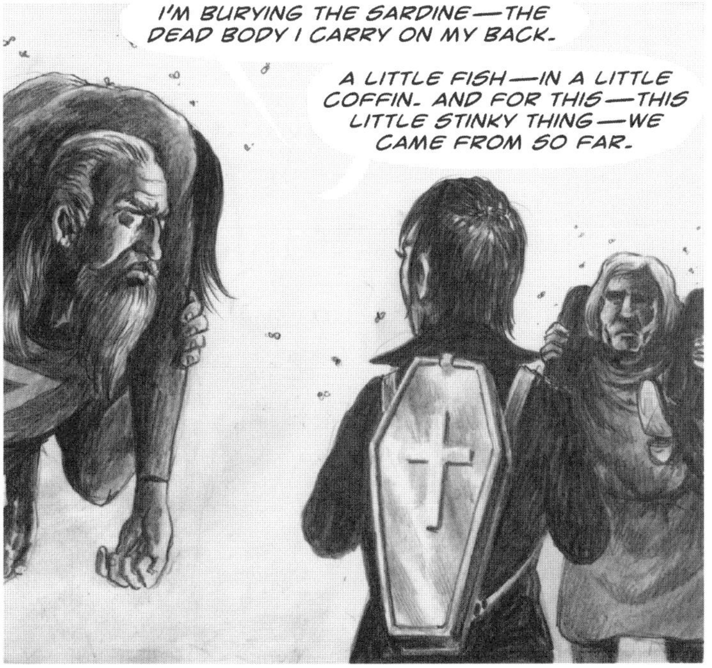
I'M BURYING THE SARDINE—THE DEAD BODY I CARRY ON MY BACK.
A LITTLE FISH—IN A LITTLE COFFIN. AND FOR THIS—THIS LITTLE STINKY THING—WE CAME FROM SO FAR.

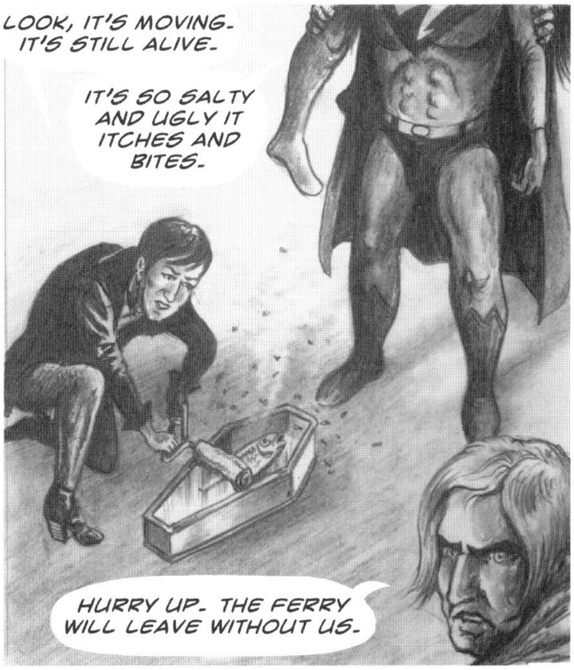
LOOK, IT'S MOVING. IT'S STILL ALIVE.
IT'S SO SALTY AND UGLY IT ITCHES AND BITES.
HURRY UP. THE FERRY WILL LEAVE WITHOUT US.

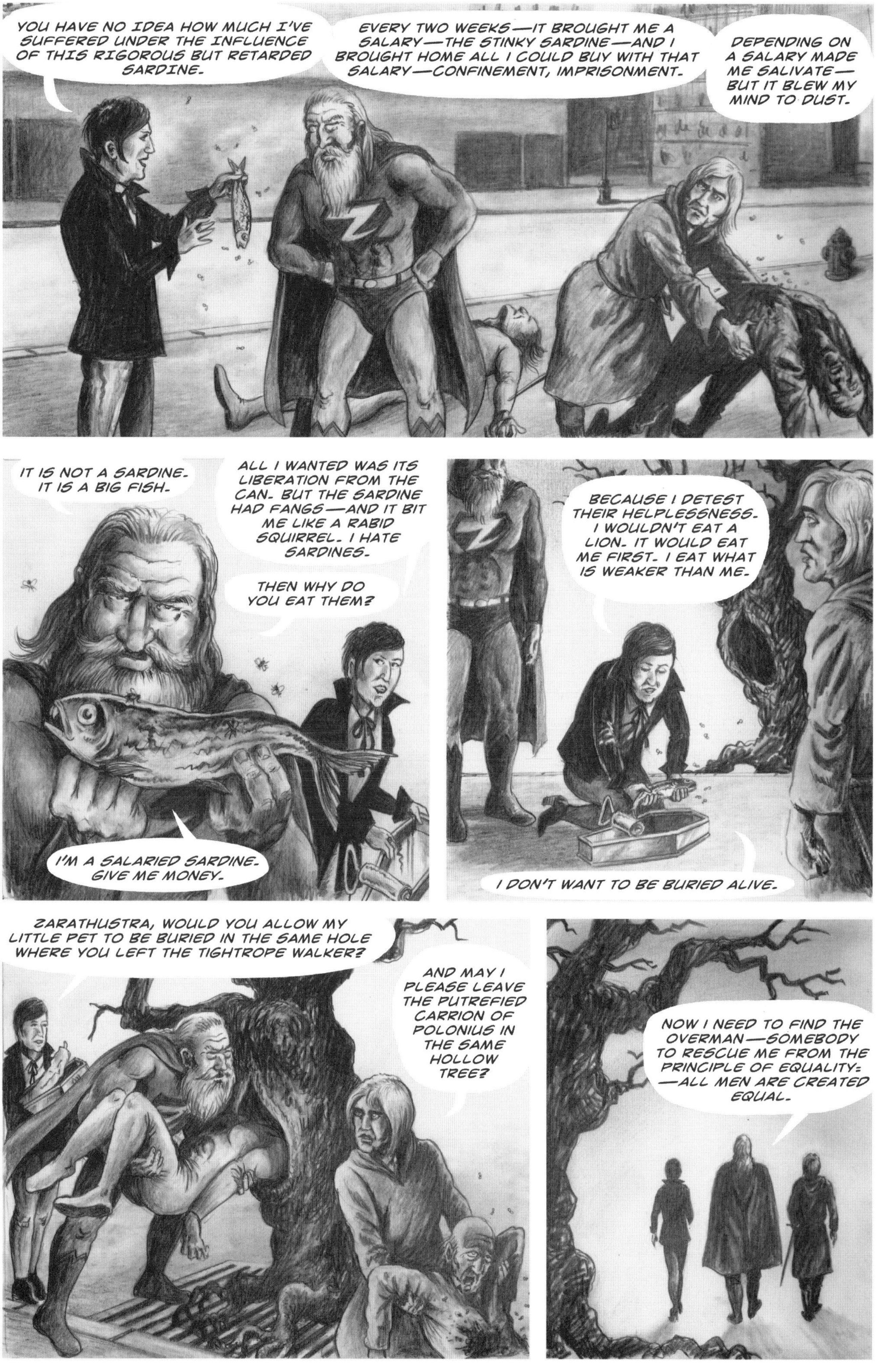
YOU HAVE NO IDEA HOW MUCH I'VE SUFFERED UNDER THE INFLUENCE OF THIS RIGOROUS BUT RETARDED SARDINE.
EVERY TWO WEEKS—IT BROUGHT ME A SALARY—THE STINKY SARDINE—AND I BROUGHT HOME ALL I COULD BUY WITH THAT SALARY—CONFINEMENT, IMPRISONMENT.
DEPENDING ON A SALARY MADE ME SALIVATE—BUT IT BLEW MY MIND TO DUST.
IT IS NOT A SARDINE. IT IS A BIG FISH.
ALL I WANTED WAS ITS LIBERATION FROM THE CAN. BUT THE SARDINE HAD FANGS—AND IT BIT ME LIKE A RABID SQUIRREL. I HATE SARDINES.
THEN WHY DO YOU EAT THEM?
I'M A SALARIED SARDINE. GIVE ME MONEY.
BECAUSE I DETEST THEIR HELPLESSNESS. I WOULDN'T EAT A LION. IT WOULD EAT ME FIRST. I EAT WHAT IS WEAKER THAN ME.
I DON'T WANT TO BE BURIED ALIVE.
ZARATHUSTRA, WOULD YOU ALLOW MY LITTLE PET TO BE BURIED IN THE SAME HOLE WHERE YOU LEFT THE TIGHTROPE WALKER?
AND MAY I PLEASE LEAVE THE PUTREFIED CARRION OF POLONIUS IN THE SAME HOLLOW TREE?
NOW I NEED TO FIND THE OVERMAN—SOMEBODY TO RESCUE ME FROM THE PRINCIPLE OF EQUALITY: —ALL MEN ARE CREATED EQUAL.

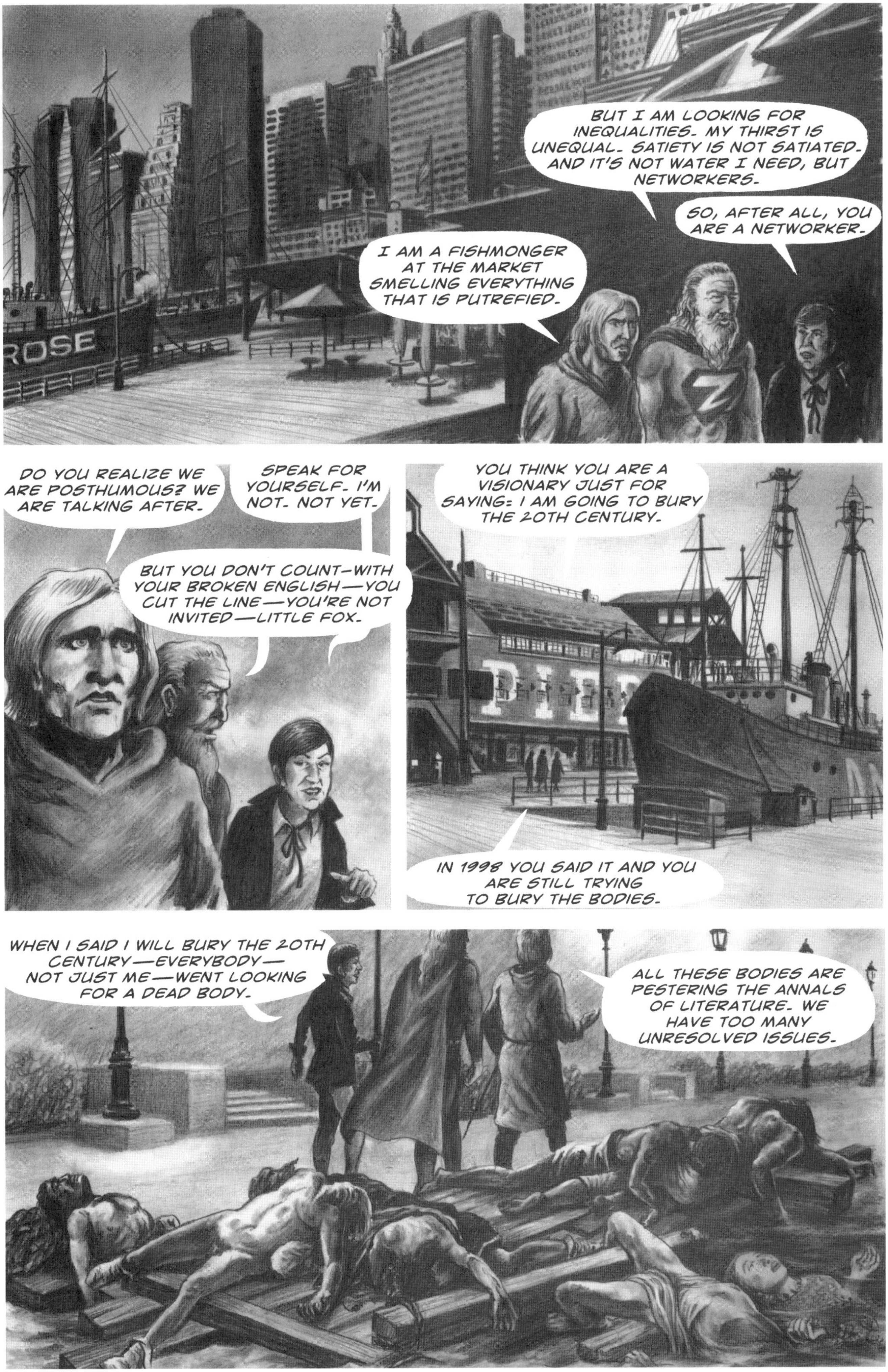
BUT I AM LOOKING FOR INEQUALITIES. MY THIRST IS UNEQUAL. SATIETY IS NOT SATIATED. AND IT'S NOT WATER I NEED, BUT NETWORKERS.
SO, AFTER ALL, YOU ARE A NETWORKER.
I AM A FISHMONGER AT THE MARKET SMELLING EVERYTHING THAT IS PUTREFIED.
DO YOU REALIZE WE ARE POSTHUMOUS? WE ARE TALKING AFTER.
SPEAK FOR YOURSELF. I'M NOT. NOT YET.
BUT YOU DON'T COUNT—WITH YOUR BROKEN ENGLISH—YOU CUT THE LINE—YOU'RE NOT INVITED—LITTLE FOX.
YOU THINK YOU ARE A VISIONARY JUST FOR SAYING: I AM GOING TO BURY THE 20TH CENTURY.
IN 1998 YOU SAID IT AND YOU ARE STILL TRYING TO BURY THE BODIES.
WHEN I SAID I WILL BURY THE 20TH CENTURY—EVERYBODY—NOT JUST ME—WENT LOOKING FOR A DEAD BODY.
ALL THESE BODIES ARE PESTERING THE ANNALS OF LITERATURE. WE HAVE TOO MANY UNRESOLVED ISSUES.

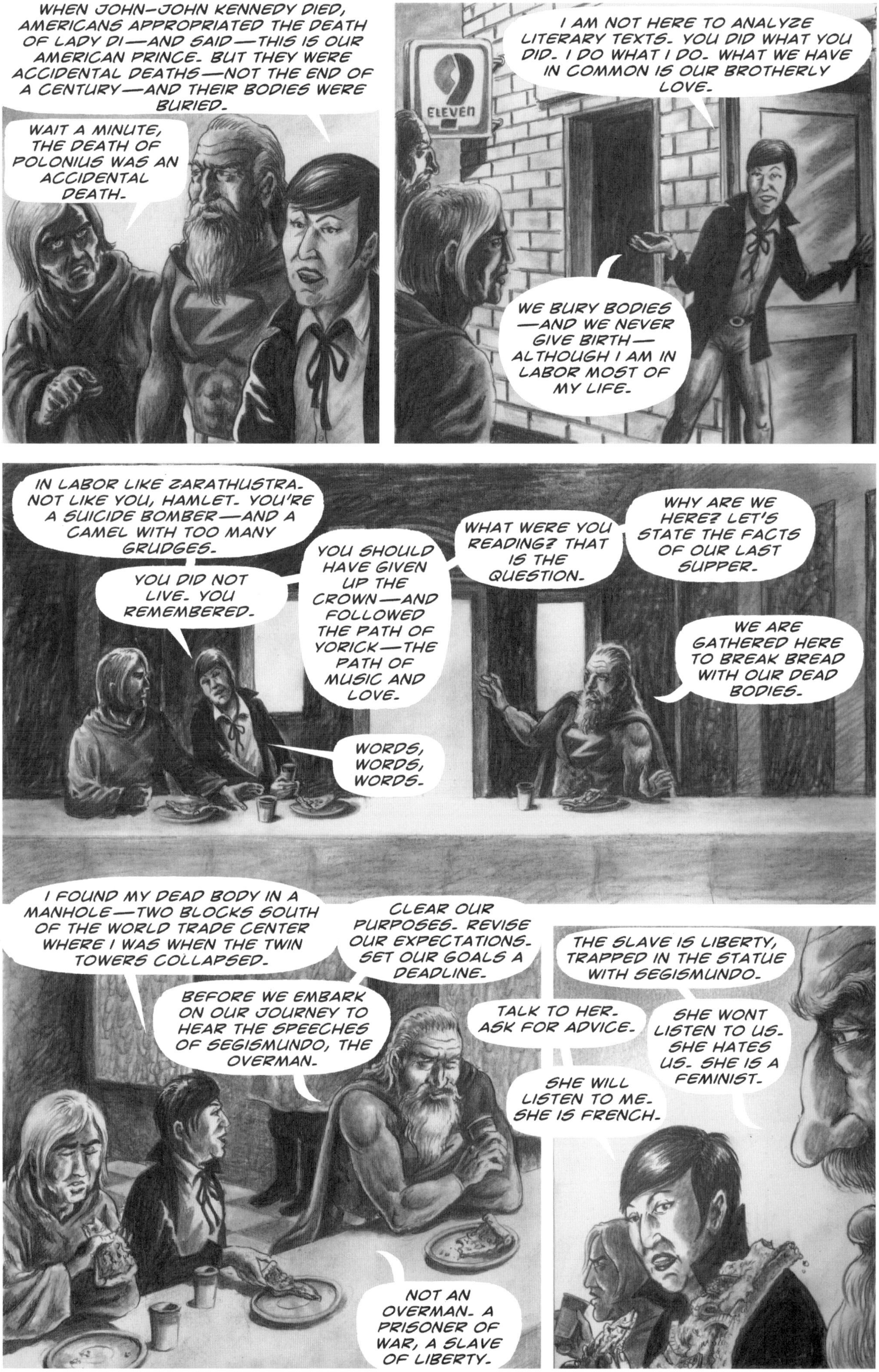
WHEN JOHN—JOHN KENNEDY DIED, AMERICANS APPROPRIATED THE DEATH OF LADY DI—AND SAID—THIS IS OUR AMERICAN PRINCE. BUT THEY WERE ACCIDENTAL DEATHS—NOT THE END OF A CENTURY—AND THEIR BODIES WERE BURIED.
WAIT A MINUTE, THE DEATH OF POLONIUS WAS AN ACCIDENTAL DEATH.
ELEVEN
I AM NOT HERE TO ANALYZE LITERARY TEXTS. YOU DID WHAT YOU DID. I DO WHAT I DO. WHAT WE HAVE IN COMMON IS OUR BROTHERLY LOVE.
WE BURY BODIES—AND WE NEVER GIVE BIRTH—ALTHOUGH I AM IN LABOR MOST OF MY LIFE.
IN LABOR LIKE ZARATHUSTRA. NOT LIKE YOU, HAMLET. YOU'RE A SUICIDE BOMBER—AND A CAMEL WITH TOO MANY GRUDGES.
YOU DID NOT LIVE. YOU REMEMBERED.
YOU SHOULD HAVE GIVEN UP THE CROWN—AND FOLLOWED THE PATH OF YORICK—THE PATH OF MUSIC AND LOVE.
WHAT WERE YOU READING? THAT IS THE QUESTION.
WHY ARE WE HERE? LET'S STATE THE FACTS OF OUR LAST SUPPER.
WE ARE GATHERED HERE TO BREAK BREAD WITH OUR DEAD BODIES.
WORDS, WORDS, WORDS.
I FOUND MY DEAD BODY IN A MANHOLE—TWO BLOCKS SOUTH OF THE WORLD TRADE CENTER WHERE I WAS WHEN THE TWIN TOWERS COLLAPSED.
CLEAR OUR PURPOSES. REVISE OUR EXPECTATIONS. SET OUR GOALS A DEADLINE.
BEFORE WE EMBARK ON OUR JOURNEY TO HEAR THE SPEECHES OF SEGISMUNDO, THE OVERMAN.
NOT AN OVERMAN. A PRISONER OF WAR, A SLAVE OF LIBERTY.
THE SLAVE IS LIBERTY, TRAPPED IN THE STATUE WITH SEGISMUNDO.
TALK TO HER. ASK FOR ADVICE.
SHE WONT LISTEN TO US. SHE HATES US. SHE IS A FEMINIST.
SHE WILL LISTEN TO ME. SHE IS FRENCH.

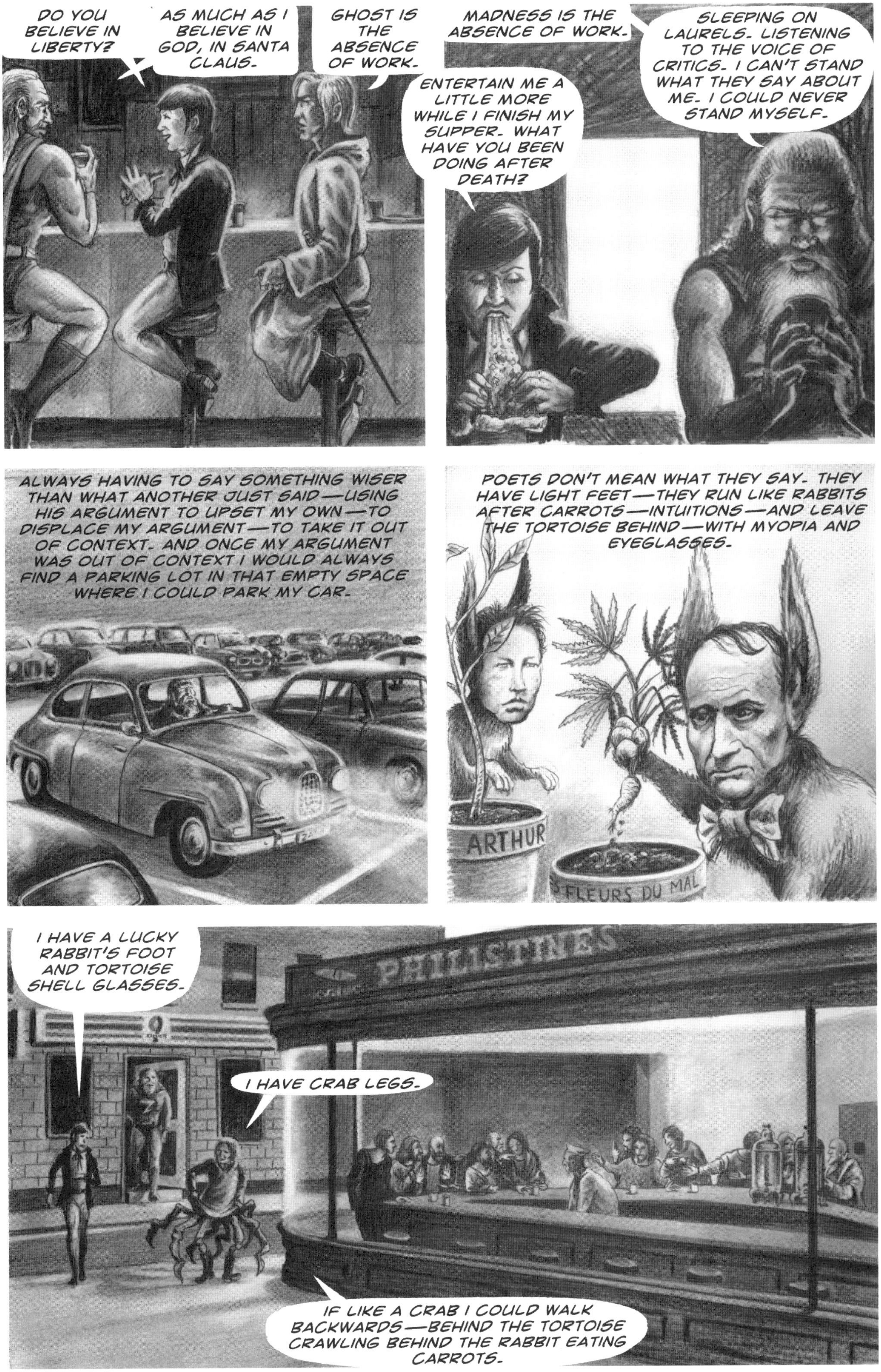
DO YOU BELIEVE IN LIBERTY?
AS MUCH AS I BELIEVE IN GOD, IN SANTA CLAUS.
GHOST IS THE ABSENCE OF WORK.
MADNESS IS THE ABSENCE OF WORK.
ENTERTAIN ME A LITTLE MORE WHILE I FINISH MY SUPPER. WHAT HAVE YOU BEEN DOING AFTER DEATH?
SLEEPING ON LAURELS. LISTENING TO THE VOICE OF CRITICS. I CAN'T STAND WHAT THEY SAY ABOUT ME. I COULD NEVER STAND MYSELF.
ALWAYS HAVING TO SAY SOMETHING WISER THAN WHAT ANOTHER JUST SAID—USING HIS ARGUMENT TO UPSET MY OWN—TO DISPLACE MY ARGUMENT—TO TAKE IT OUT OF CONTEXT. AND ONCE MY ARGUMENT WAS OUT OF CONTEXT I WOULD ALWAYS FIND A PARKING LOT IN THAT EMPTY SPACE WHERE I COULD PARK MY CAR.
POETS DON'T MEAN WHAT THEY SAY. THEY HAVE LIGHT FEET—THEY RUN LIKE RABBITS AFTER CARROTS—INTUITIONS—AND LEAVE THE TORTOISE BEHIND—WITH MYOPIA AND EYEGLASSES.
ARTHUR
FLEURS DU MAL
PHILISTINES
I HAVE A LUCKY RABBIT'S FOOT AND TORTOISE SHELL GLASSES.
I HAVE CRAB LEGS.
IF LIKE A CRAB I COULD WALK BACKWARDS—BEHIND THE TORTOISE CRAWLING BEHIND THE RABBIT EATING CARROTS.

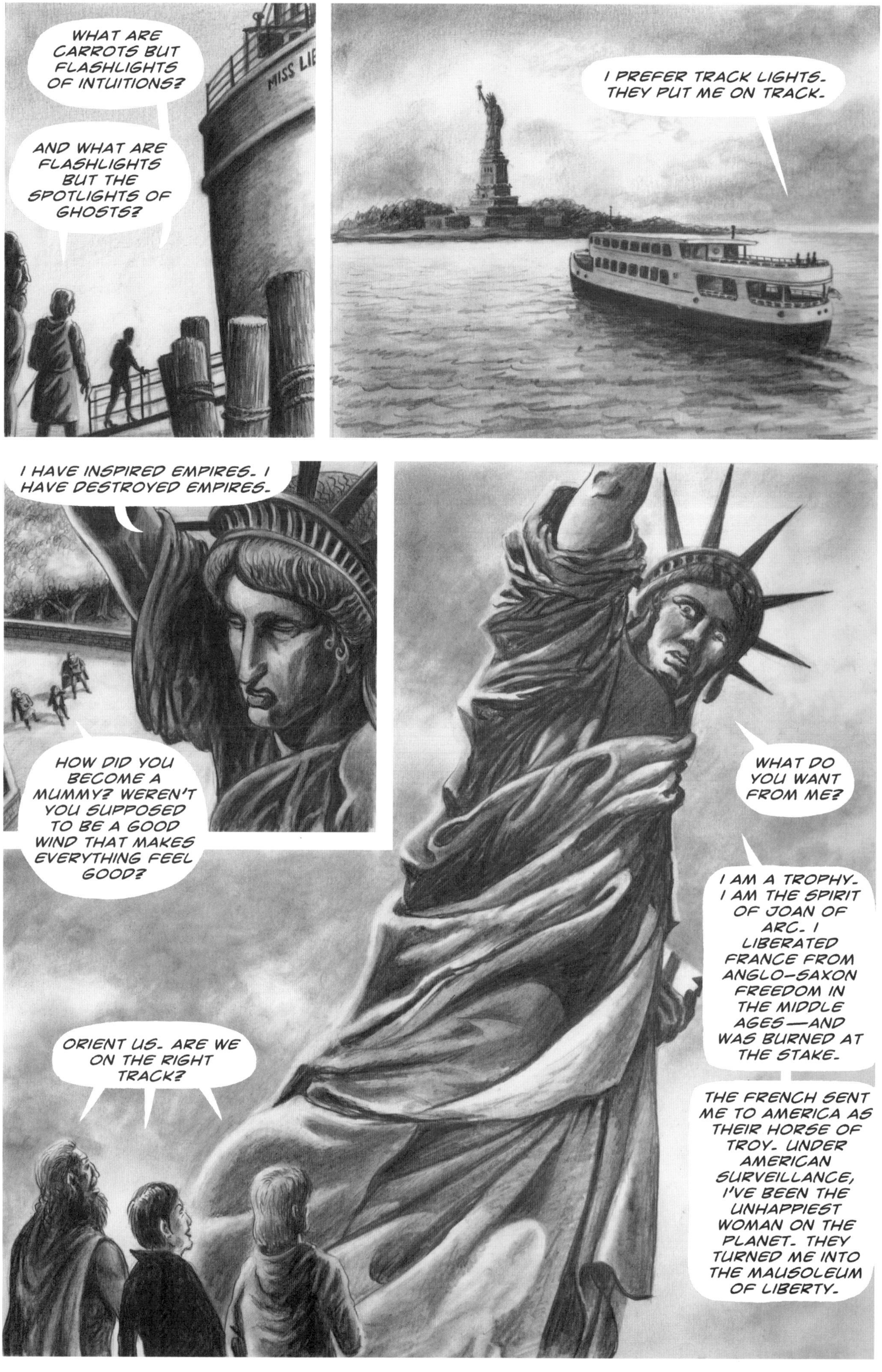
WHAT ARE CARROTS BUT FLASHLIGHTS OF INTUITIONS?
AND WHAT ARE FLASHLIGHTS BUT THE SPOTLIGHTS OF GHOSTS?
I PREFER TRACK LIGHTS. THEY PUT ME ON TRACK.
I HAVE INSPIRED EMPIRES. I HAVE DESTROYED EMPIRES.
HOW DID YOU BECOME A MUMMY? WEREN'T YOU SUPPOSED TO BE A GOOD WIND THAT MAKES EVERYTHING FEEL GOOD?
WHAT DO YOU WANT FROM ME?
I AM A TROPHY. I AM THE SPIRIT OF JOAN OF ARC. I LIBERATED FRANCE FROM ANGLO-SAXON FREEDOM IN THE MIDDLE AGES—AND WAS BURNED AT THE STAKE.
ORIENT US. ARE WE ON THE RIGHT TRACK?
THE FRENCH SENT ME TO AMERICA AS THEIR HORSE OF TROY. UNDER AMERICAN SURVEILLANCE, I'VE BEEN THE UNHAPPIEST WOMAN ON THE PLANET. THEY TURNED ME INTO THE MAUSOLEUM OF LIBERTY.

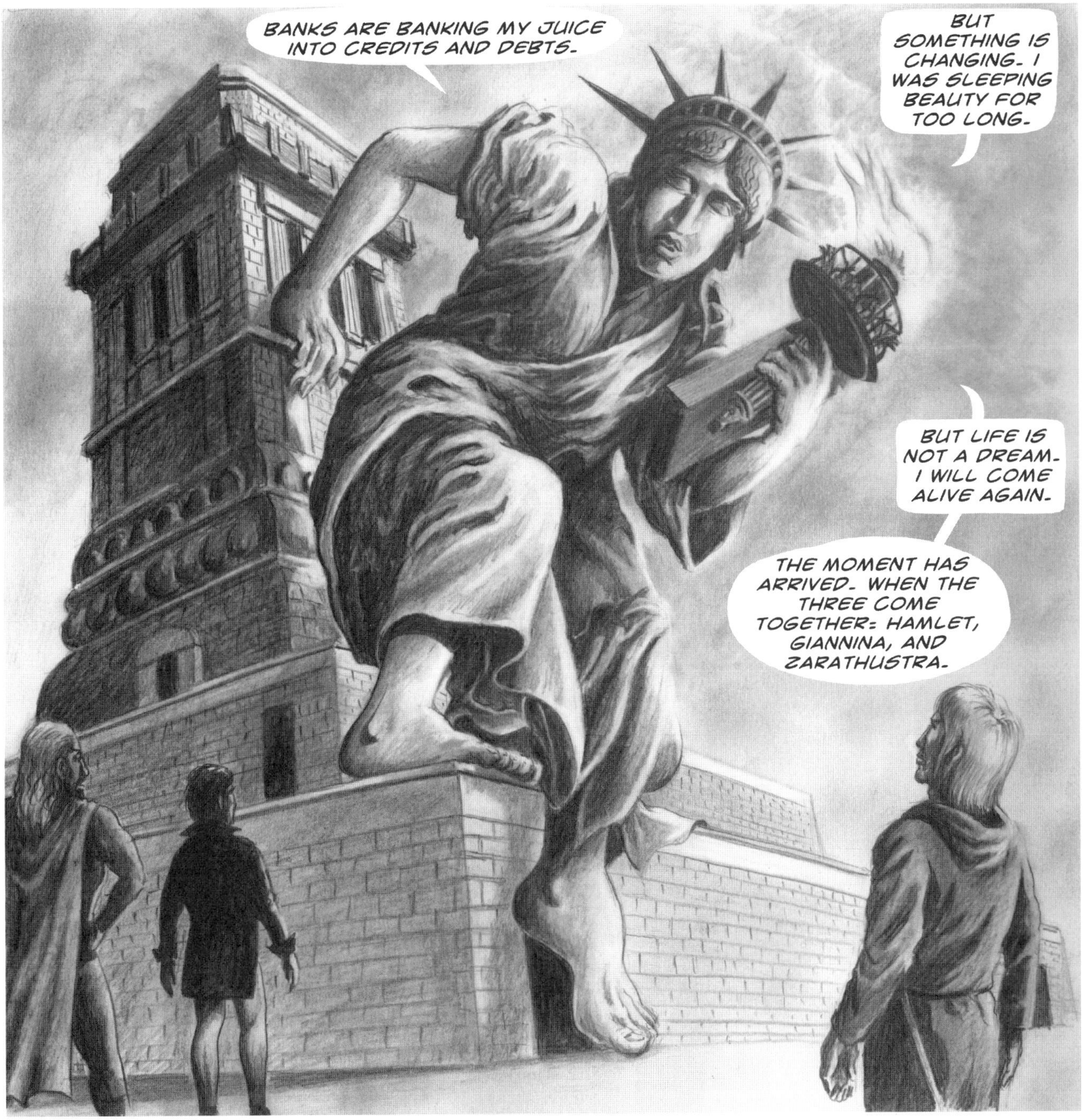

BANKS ARE BANKING MY JUICE INTO CREDITS AND DEBTS.
BUT SOMETHING IS CHANGING. I WAS SLEEPING BEAUTY FOR TOO LONG.
BUT LIFE IS NOT A DREAM. I WILL COME ALIVE AGAIN.
THE MOMENT HAS ARRIVED. WHEN THE THREE COME TOGETHER: HAMLET, GIANNINA, AND ZARATHUSTRA.

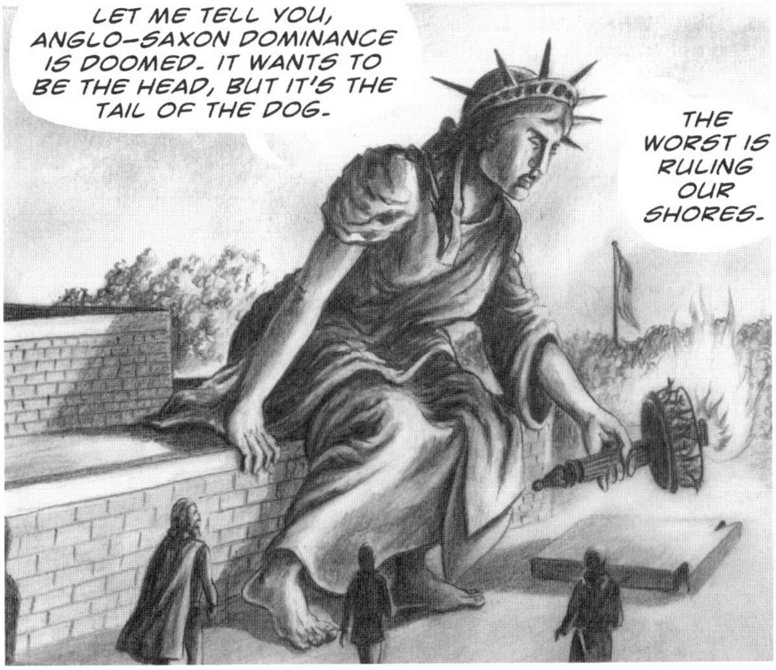

LET ME TELL YOU, ANGLO-SAXON DOMINANCE IS DOOMED. IT WANTS TO BE THE HEAD, BUT IT'S THE TAIL OF THE DOG.
THE WORST IS RULING OUR SHORES.

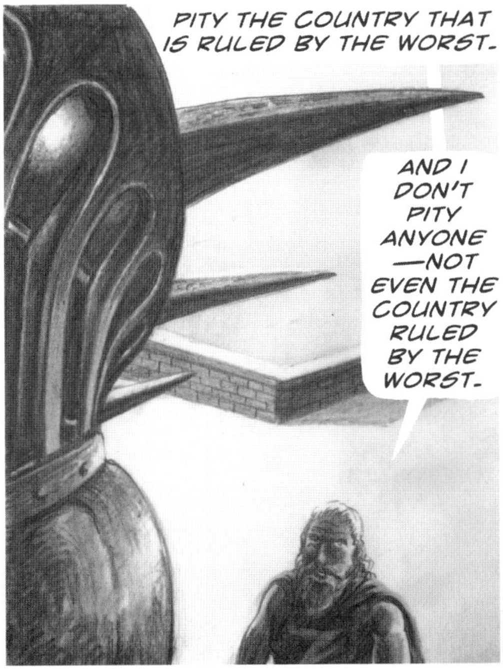

PITY THE COUNTRY THAT IS RULED BY THE WORST.
AND I DON'T PITY ANYONE —NOT EVEN THE COUNTRY RULED BY THE WORST.

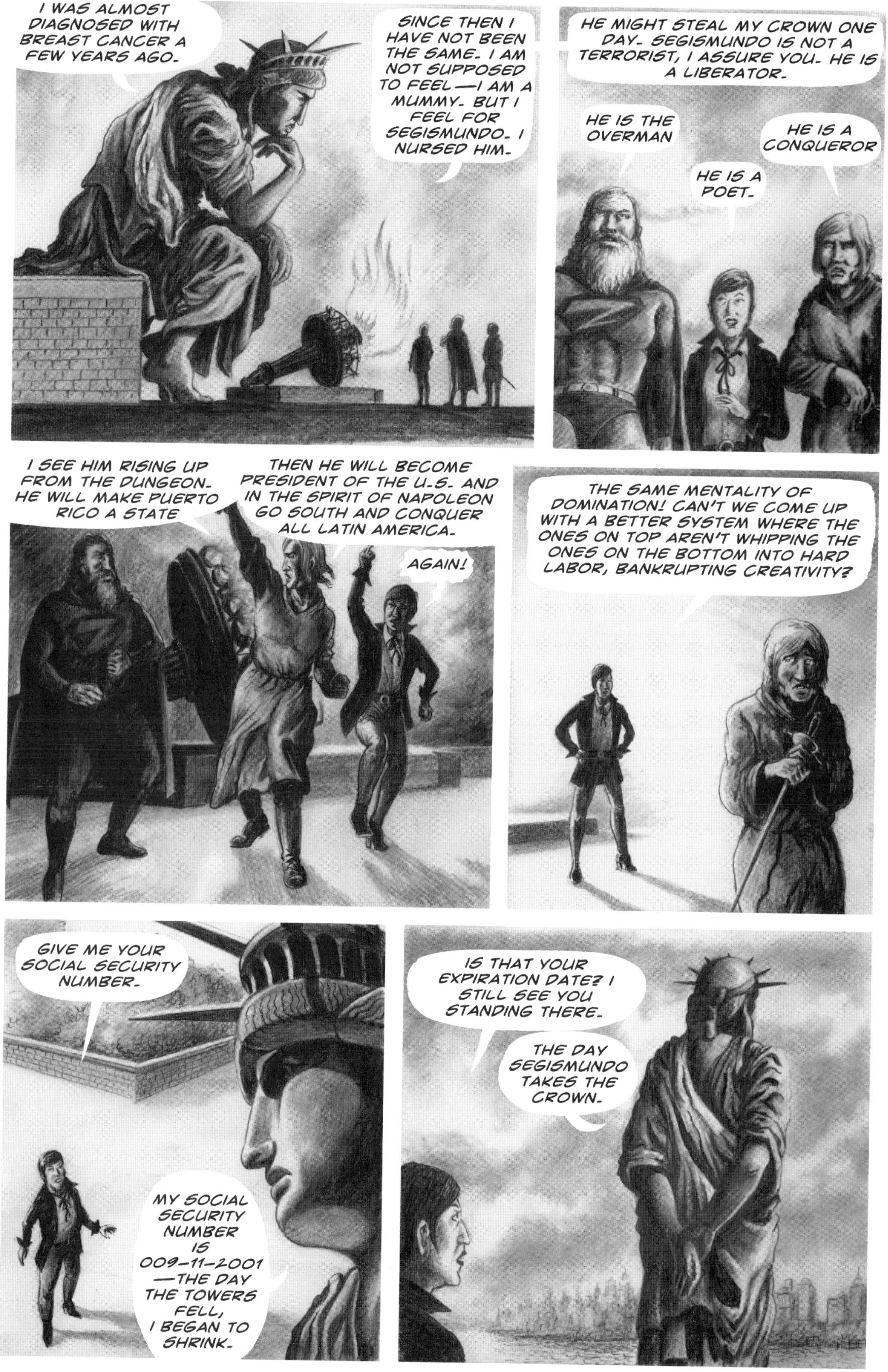
I WAS ALMOST DIAGNOSED WITH BREAST CANCER A FEW YEARS AGO.
SINCE THEN I HAVE NOT BEEN THE SAME. I AM NOT SUPPOSED TO FEEL—I AM A MUMMY. BUT I FEEL FOR SEGISMUNDO. I NURSED HIM.
HE MIGHT STEAL MY CROWN ONE DAY. SEGISMUNDO IS NOT A TERRORIST, I ASSURE YOU. HE IS A LIBERATOR.
HE IS THE OVERMAN
HE IS A POET.
HE IS A CONQUEROR
I SEE HIM RISING UP FROM THE DUNGEON. HE WILL MAKE PUERTO RICO A STATE
THEN HE WILL BECOME PRESIDENT OF THE U.S. AND IN THE SPIRIT OF NAPOLEON GO SOUTH AND CONQUER ALL LATIN AMERICA.
AGAIN!
THE SAME MENTALITY OF DOMINATION! CAN'T WE COME UP WITH A BETTER SYSTEM WHERE THE ONES ON TOP AREN'T WHIPPING THE ONES ON THE BOTTOM INTO HARD LABOR, BANKRUPTING CREATIVITY?
GIVE ME YOUR SOCIAL SECURITY NUMBER.
MY SOCIAL SECURITY NUMBER IS 009-11-2001—THE DAY THE TOWERS FELL, I BEGAN TO SHRINK.
IS THAT YOUR EXPIRATION DATE? I STILL SEE YOU STANDING THERE.
THE DAY SEGISMUNDO TAKES THE CROWN.

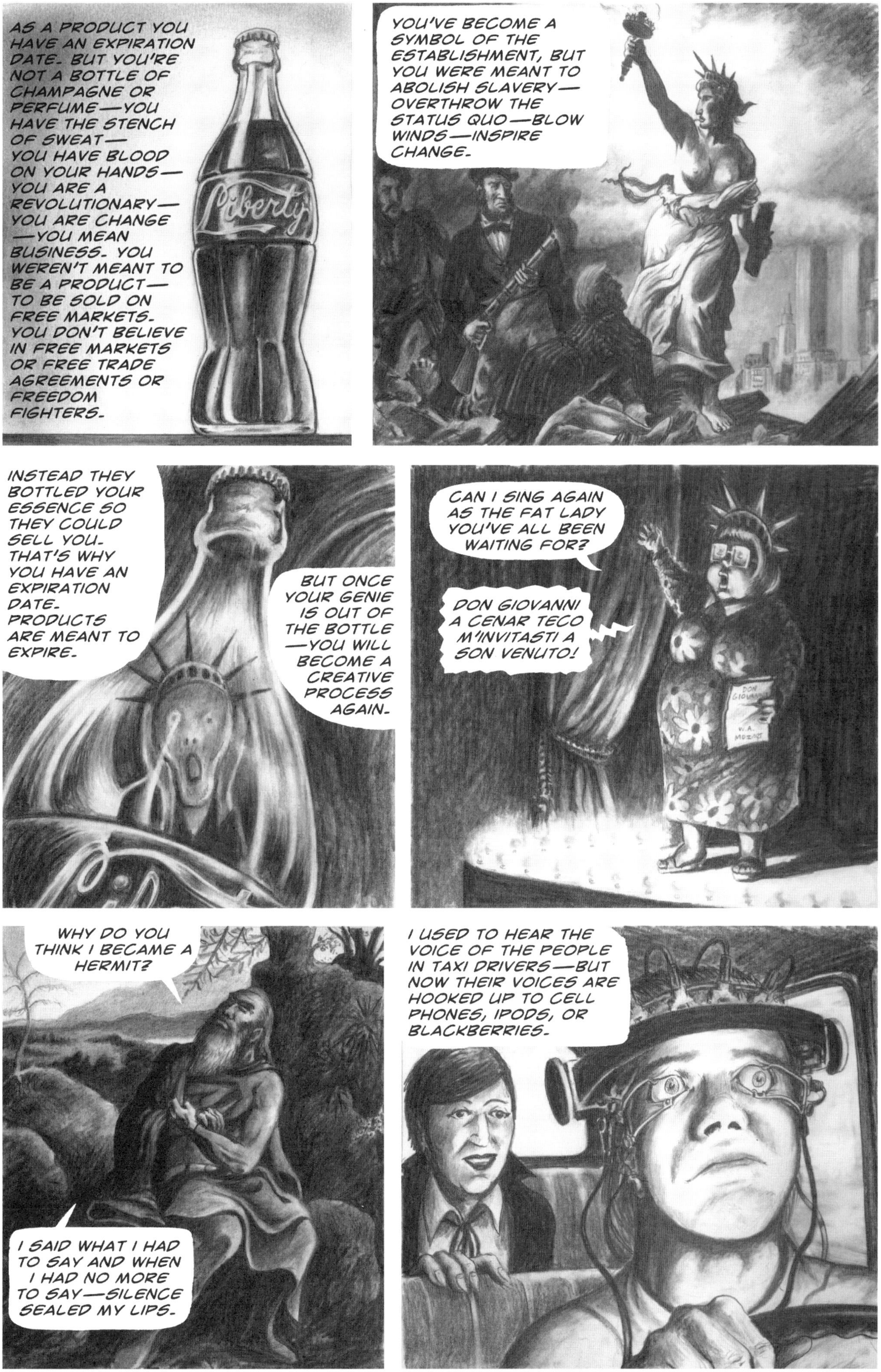
AS A PRODUCT YOU HAVE AN EXPIRATION DATE. BUT YOU'RE NOT A BOTTLE OF CHAMPAGNE OR PERFUME—YOU HAVE THE STENCH OF SWEAT—YOU HAVE BLOOD ON YOUR HANDS—YOU ARE A REVOLUTIONARY—YOU ARE CHANGE—YOU MEAN BUSINESS. YOU WEREN'T MEANT TO BE A PRODUCT—TO BE SOLD ON FREE MARKETS. YOU DON'T BELIEVE IN FREE MARKETS OR FREE TRADE AGREEMENTS OR FREEDOM FIGHTERS.
Liberty
YOU'VE BECOME A SYMBOL OF THE ESTABLISHMENT, BUT YOU WERE MEANT TO ABOLISH SLAVERY—OVERTHROW THE STATUS QUO—BLOW WINDS—INSPIRE CHANGE.
INSTEAD THEY BOTTLED YOUR ESSENCE SO THEY COULD SELL YOU. THAT'S WHY YOU HAVE AN EXPIRATION DATE. PRODUCTS ARE MEANT TO EXPIRE.
BUT ONCE YOUR GENIE IS OUT OF THE BOTTLE—YOU WILL BECOME A CREATIVE PROCESS AGAIN.
CAN I SING AGAIN AS THE FAT LADY YOU'VE ALL BEEN WAITING FOR?
DON GIOVANNI A CENAR TECO M'INVITASTI A SON VENUTO!
WHY DO YOU THINK I BECAME A HERMIT?
I SAID WHAT I HAD TO SAY AND WHEN I HAD NO MORE TO SAY—SILENCE SEALED MY LIPS.
I USED TO HEAR THE VOICE OF THE PEOPLE IN TAXI DRIVERS—BUT NOW THEIR VOICES ARE HOOKED UP TO CELL PHONES, IPODS, OR BLACKBERRIES.

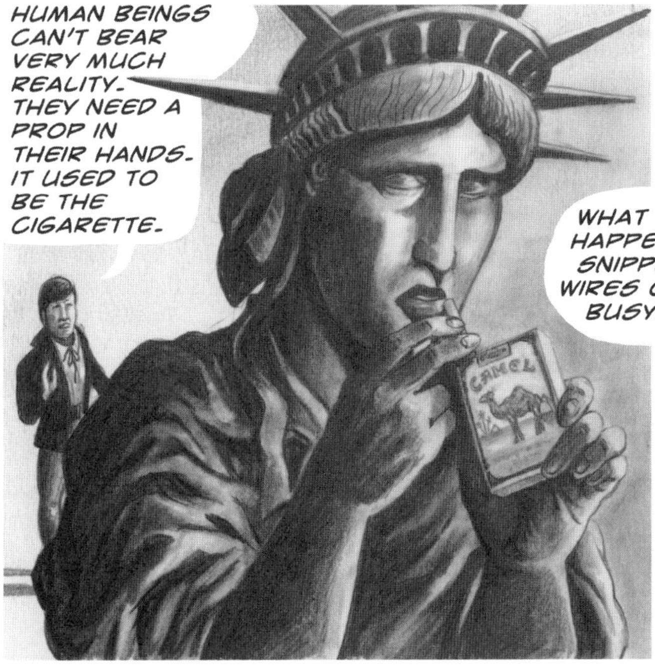
HUMAN BEINGS CAN'T BEAR VERY MUCH REALITY. THEY NEED A PROP IN THEIR HANDS. IT USED TO BE THE CIGARETTE.
CAMEL

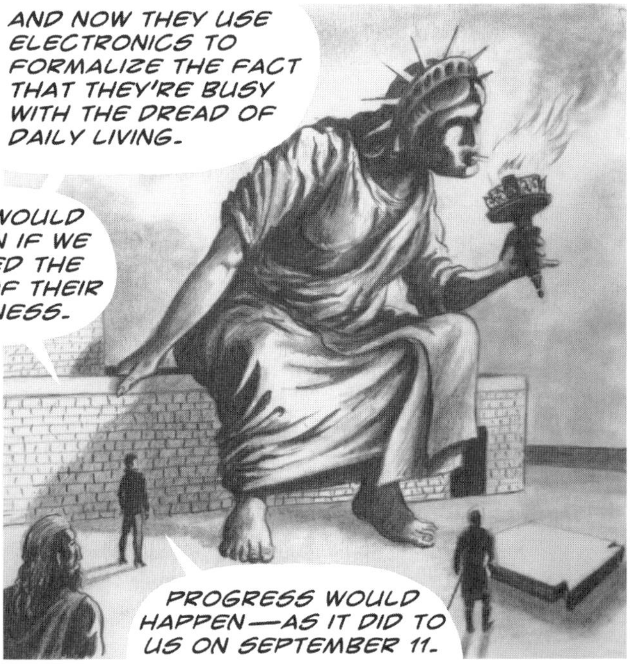
AND NOW THEY USE ELECTRONICS TO FORMALIZE THE FACT THAT THEY'RE BUSY WITH THE DREAD OF DAILY LIVING.
WHAT WOULD HAPPEN IF WE SNIPPED THE WIRES OF THEIR BUSYNESS.
PROGRESS WOULD HAPPEN—AS IT DID TO US ON SEPTEMBER 11.

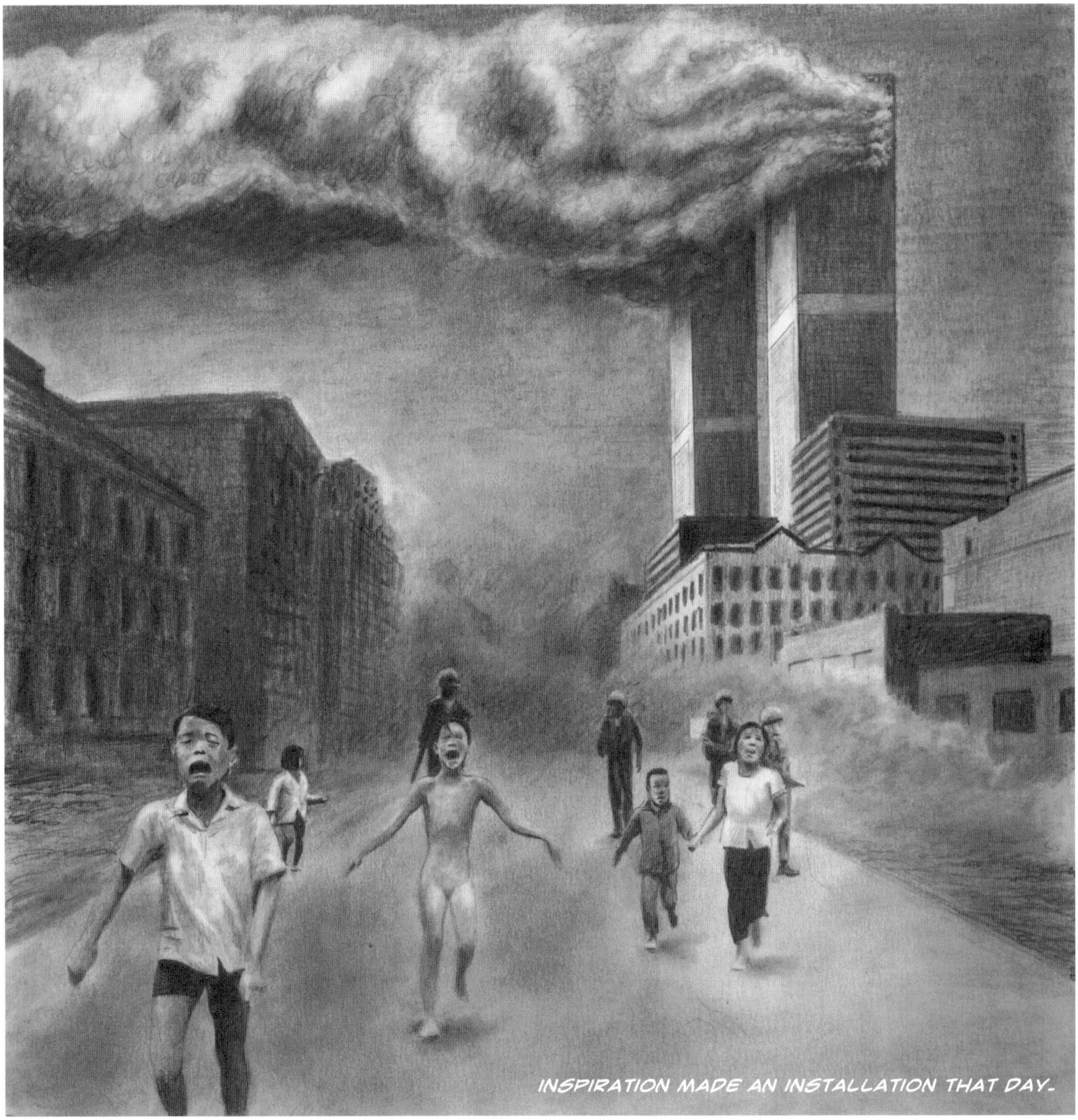
INSPIRATION MADE AN INSTALLATION THAT DAY.

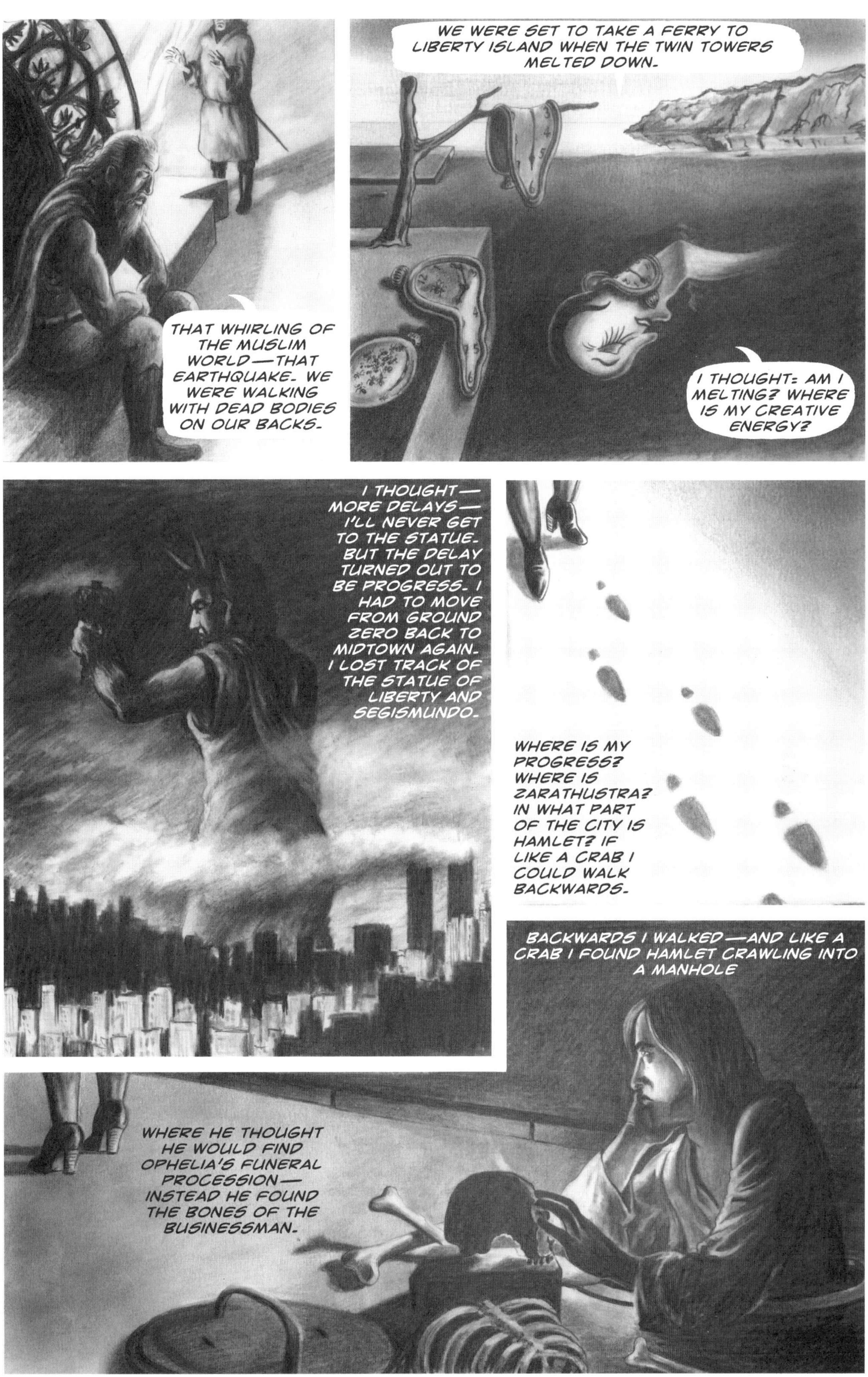
THAT WHIRLING OF THE MUSLIM WORLD—THAT EARTHQUAKE. WE WERE WALKING WITH DEAD BODIES ON OUR BACKS.
WE WERE SET TO TAKE A FERRY TO LIBERTY ISLAND WHEN THE TWIN TOWERS MELTED DOWN.
I THOUGHT: AM I MELTING? WHERE IS MY CREATIVE ENERGY?
I THOUGHT—MORE DELAYS—I'LL NEVER GET TO THE STATUE. BUT THE DELAY TURNED OUT TO BE PROGRESS. I HAD TO MOVE FROM GROUND ZERO BACK TO MIDTOWN AGAIN. I LOST TRACK OF THE STATUE OF LIBERTY AND SEGISMUNDO.
WHERE IS MY PROGRESS? WHERE IS ZARATHUSTRA? IN WHAT PART OF THE CITY IS HAMLET? IF LIKE A CRAB I COULD WALK BACKWARDS.
BACKWARDS I WALKED—AND LIKE A CRAB I FOUND HAMLET CRAWLING INTO A MANHOLE
WHERE HE THOUGHT HE WOULD FIND OPHELIA'S FUNERAL PROCESSION—INSTEAD HE FOUND THE BONES OF THE BUSINESSMAN.

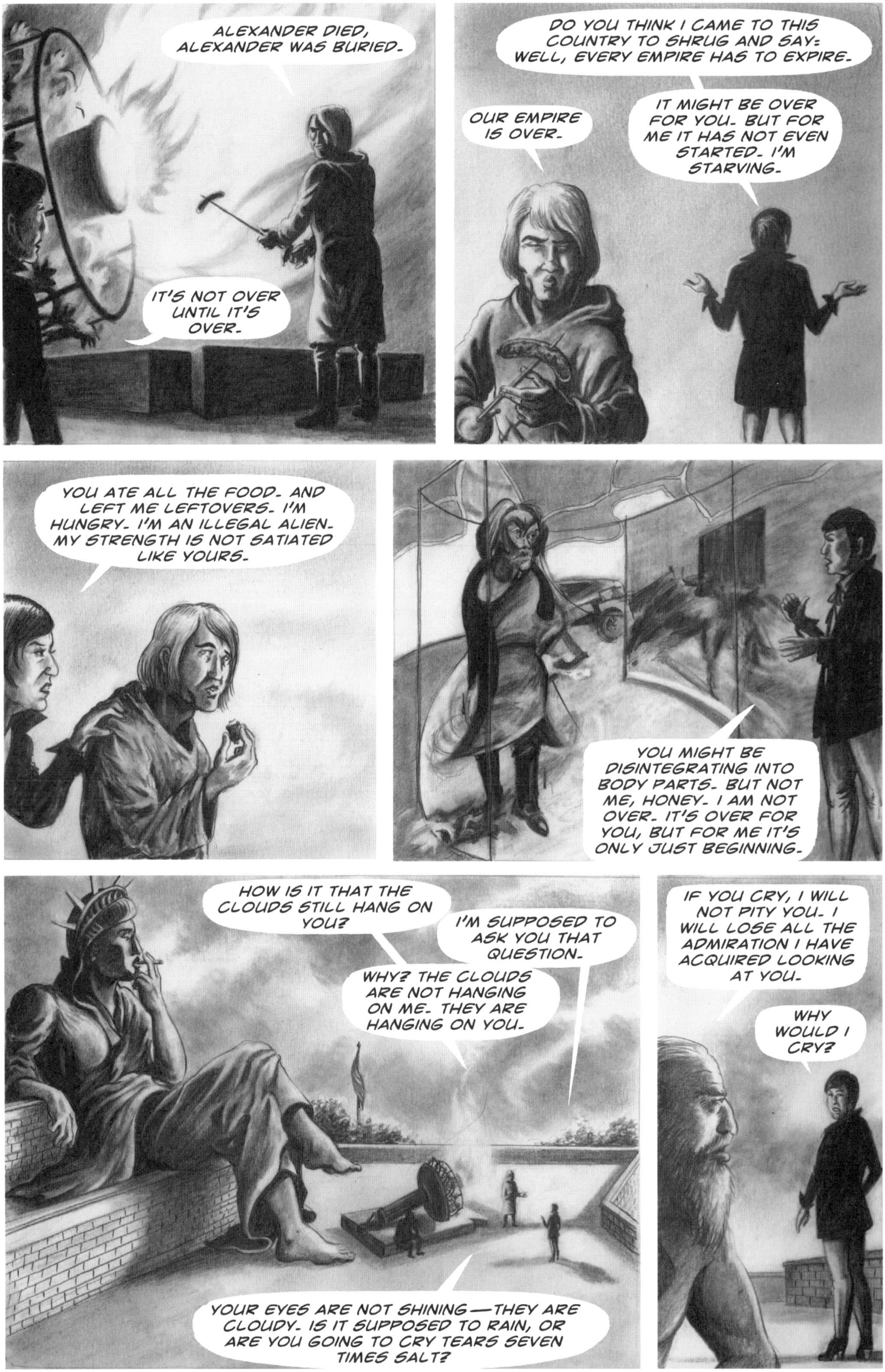
ALEXANDER DIED, ALEXANDER WAS BURIED.
IT'S NOT OVER UNTIL IT'S OVER.
DO YOU THINK I CAME TO THIS COUNTRY TO SHRUG AND SAY: WELL, EVERY EMPIRE HAS TO EXPIRE.
OUR EMPIRE IS OVER.
IT MIGHT BE OVER FOR YOU. BUT FOR ME IT HAS NOT EVEN STARTED. I'M STARVING.
YOU ATE ALL THE FOOD. AND LEFT ME LEFTOVERS. I'M HUNGRY. I'M AN ILLEGAL ALIEN. MY STRENGTH IS NOT SATIATED LIKE YOURS.
YOU MIGHT BE DISINTEGRATING INTO BODY PARTS. BUT NOT ME, HONEY. I AM NOT OVER. IT'S OVER FOR YOU, BUT FOR ME IT'S ONLY JUST BEGINNING.
HOW IS IT THAT THE CLOUDS STILL HANG ON YOU?
I'M SUPPOSED TO ASK YOU THAT QUESTION.
WHY? THE CLOUDS ARE NOT HANGING ON ME. THEY ARE HANGING ON YOU.
YOUR EYES ARE NOT SHINING—THEY ARE CLOUDY. IS IT SUPPOSED TO RAIN, OR ARE YOU GOING TO CRY TEARS SEVEN TIMES SALT?
IF YOU CRY, I WILL NOT PITY YOU. I WILL LOSE ALL THE ADMIRATION I HAVE ACQUIRED LOOKING AT YOU.
WHY WOULD I CRY?

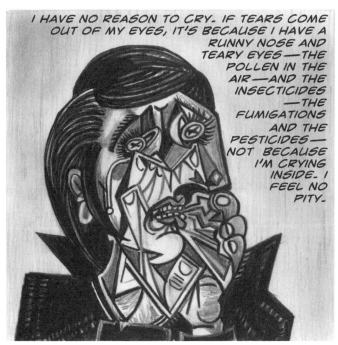

I HAVE NO REASON TO CRY. IF TEARS COME OUT OF MY EYES, IT'S BECAUSE I HAVE A RUNNY NOSE AND TEARY EYES—THE POLLEN IN THE AIR—AND THE INSECTICIDES—THE FUMIGATIONS AND THE PESTICIDES—NOT BECAUSE I'M CRYING INSIDE. I FEEL NO PITY.

LOOK HOW SHE MOVES HER EYES LIKE A SLOT MACHINE CALCULATING THE ODDS IN HER HEAD.

I CAN CONTEMPLATE LIFE FROM THE HIGHEST POINT OF VIEW—BUT RIGHT NOW I'M FEELING LOW. PEOPLE SAY I'M A SCREAMER AND A SPITTER—AND THAT IT'S DIFFICULT TO UNDERSTAND ME. ALTHOUGH I AM WRITING IN ENGLISH—THEY HEAR AND READ THE FOREIGN ACCENT.

HAMLET, YOU ARE A MINORITY AMONG US. ZARATHUSTRA AND I ARE THE MAJORITY. WE HAVE AN EXTRA VOTE. WE SPEAK ENGLISH WITH AN ACCENT—AS A SECOND LANGUAGE.

I AM NOT WORRIED.

OF COURSE YOU'RE NOT WORRIED. YOU DON'T HAVE TO WAKE UP TOMORROW.

I WAS NOT GIVEN A DEADLINE—IT COULD HAVE TAKEN A MONTH OR SO—

INSTEAD IT TOOK YEARS TO BURY WHAT IS ALREADY DEAD.

15

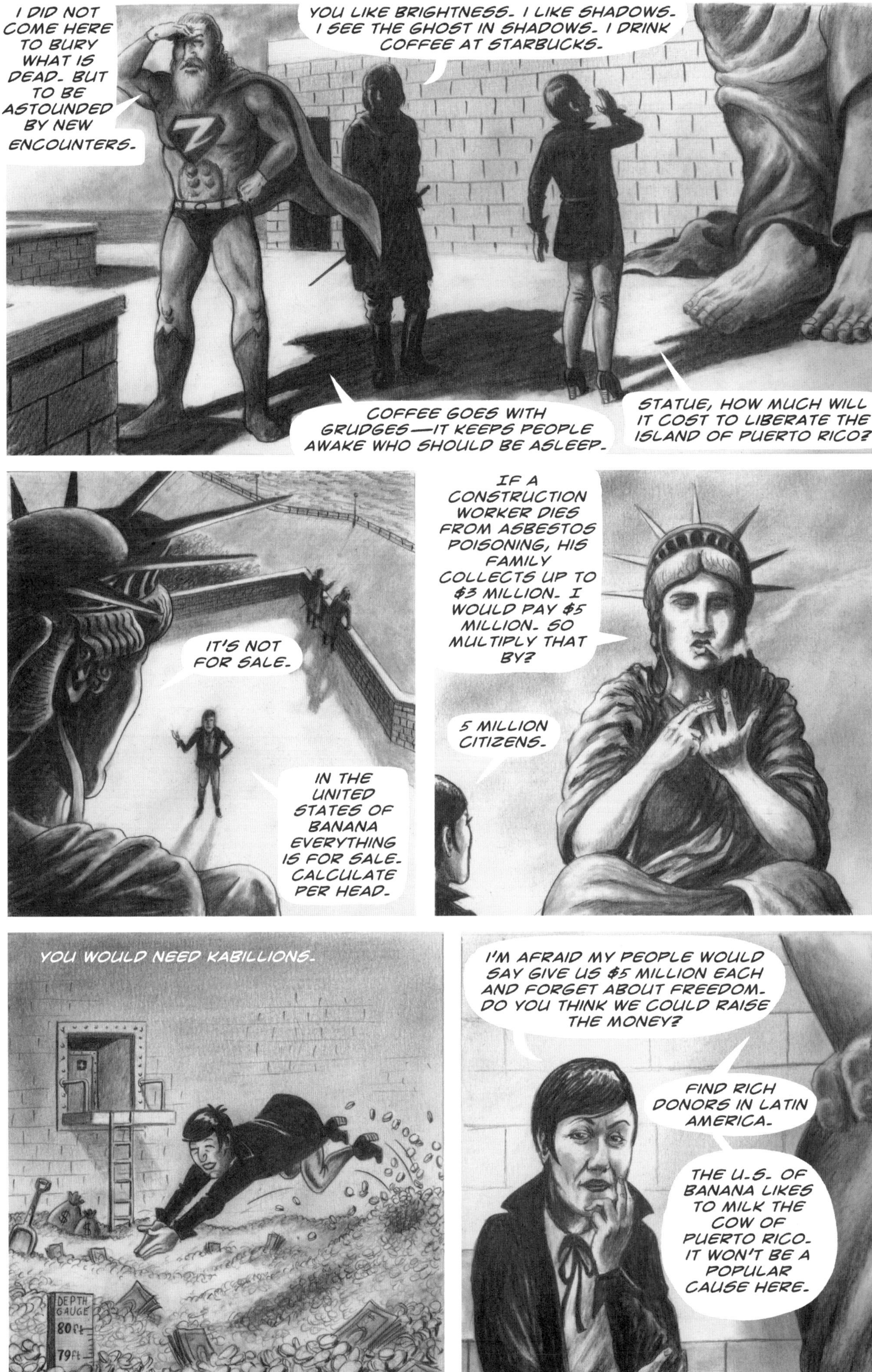
I DID NOT COME HERE TO BURY WHAT IS DEAD. BUT TO BE ASTOUNDED BY NEW ENCOUNTERS.
YOU LIKE BRIGHTNESS. I LIKE SHADOWS. I SEE THE GHOST IN SHADOWS. I DRINK COFFEE AT STARBUCKS.
COFFEE GOES WITH GRUDGES—IT KEEPS PEOPLE AWAKE WHO SHOULD BE ASLEEP.
STATUE, HOW MUCH WILL IT COST TO LIBERATE THE ISLAND OF PUERTO RICO?
IT'S NOT FOR SALE.
IN THE UNITED STATES OF BANANA EVERYTHING IS FOR SALE. CALCULATE PER HEAD.
IF A CONSTRUCTION WORKER DIES FROM ASBESTOS POISONING, HIS FAMILY COLLECTS UP TO $3 MILLION. I WOULD PAY $5 MILLION. SO MULTIPLY THAT BY?
5 MILLION CITIZENS.
YOU WOULD NEED KABILLIONS.
DEPTH GAUGE
80 Ft
79 Ft
I'M AFRAID MY PEOPLE WOULD SAY GIVE US $5 MILLION EACH AND FORGET ABOUT FREEDOM. DO YOU THINK WE COULD RAISE THE MONEY?
FIND RICH DONORS IN LATIN AMERICA.
THE U.S. OF BANANA LIKES TO MILK THE COW OF PUERTO RICO. IT WON'T BE A POPULAR CAUSE HERE.

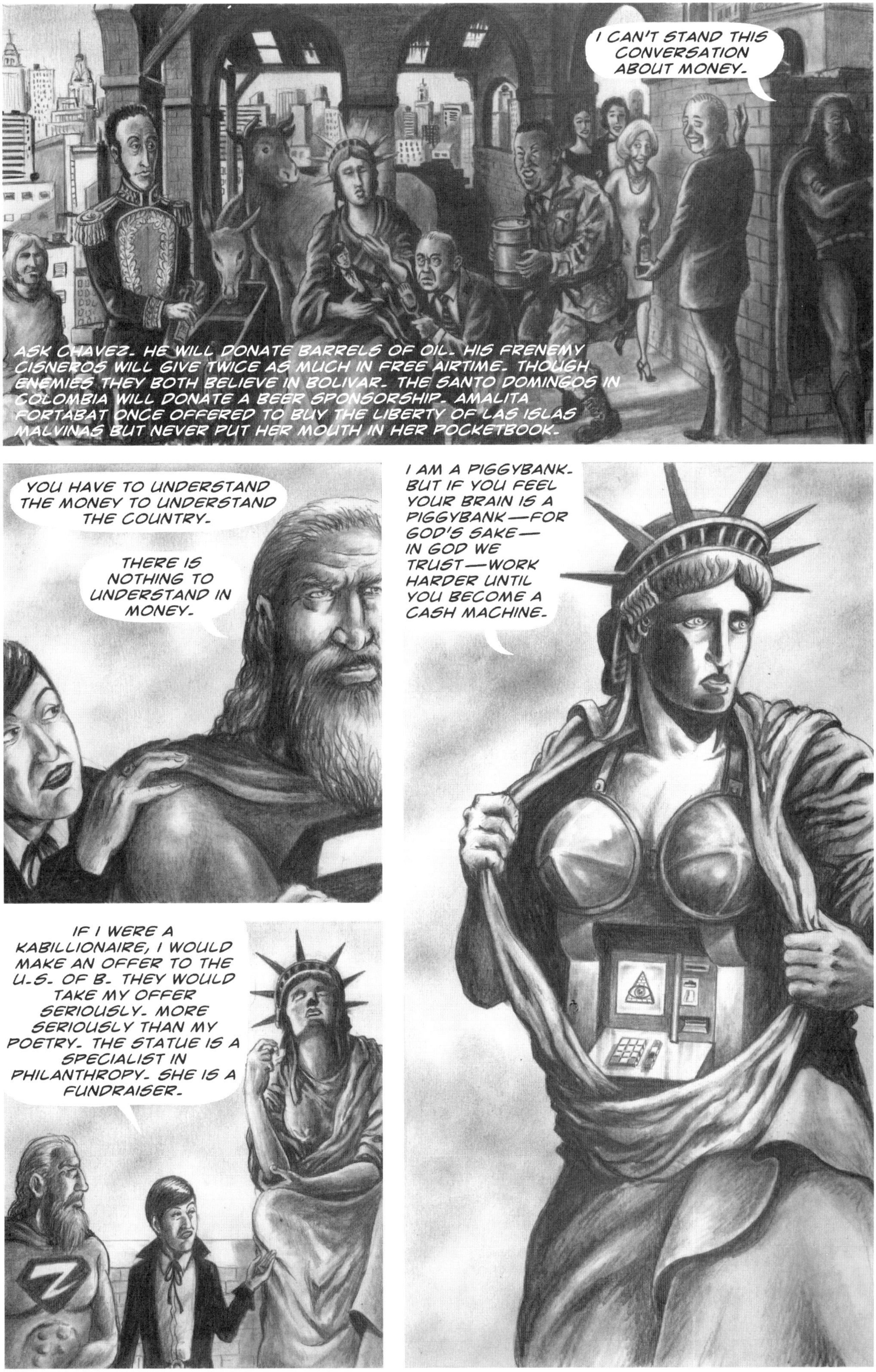
I CAN'T STAND THIS CONVERSATION ABOUT MONEY.
ASK CHAVEZ. HE WILL DONATE BARRELS OF OIL. HIS FRENEMY CISNEROS WILL GIVE TWICE AS MUCH IN FREE AIRTIME. THOUGH ENEMIES THEY BOTH BELIEVE IN BOLIVAR. THE SANTO DOMINGOS IN COLOMBIA WILL DONATE A BEER SPONSORSHIP. AMALITA FORTABAT ONCE OFFERED TO BUY THE LIBERTY OF LAS ISLAS MALVINAS BUT NEVER PUT HER MOUTH IN HER POCKETBOOK.
YOU HAVE TO UNDERSTAND THE MONEY TO UNDERSTAND THE COUNTRY.
THERE IS NOTHING TO UNDERSTAND IN MONEY.
I AM A PIGGYBANK. BUT IF YOU FEEL YOUR BRAIN IS A PIGGYBANK—FOR GOD'S SAKE—IN GOD WE TRUST—WORK HARDER UNTIL YOU BECOME A CASH MACHINE.
IF I WERE A KABILLIONAIRE, I WOULD MAKE AN OFFER TO THE U.S. OF B. THEY WOULD TAKE MY OFFER SERIOUSLY. MORE SERIOUSLY THAN MY POETRY. THE STATUE IS A SPECIALIST IN PHILANTHROPY. SHE IS A FUNDRAISER.

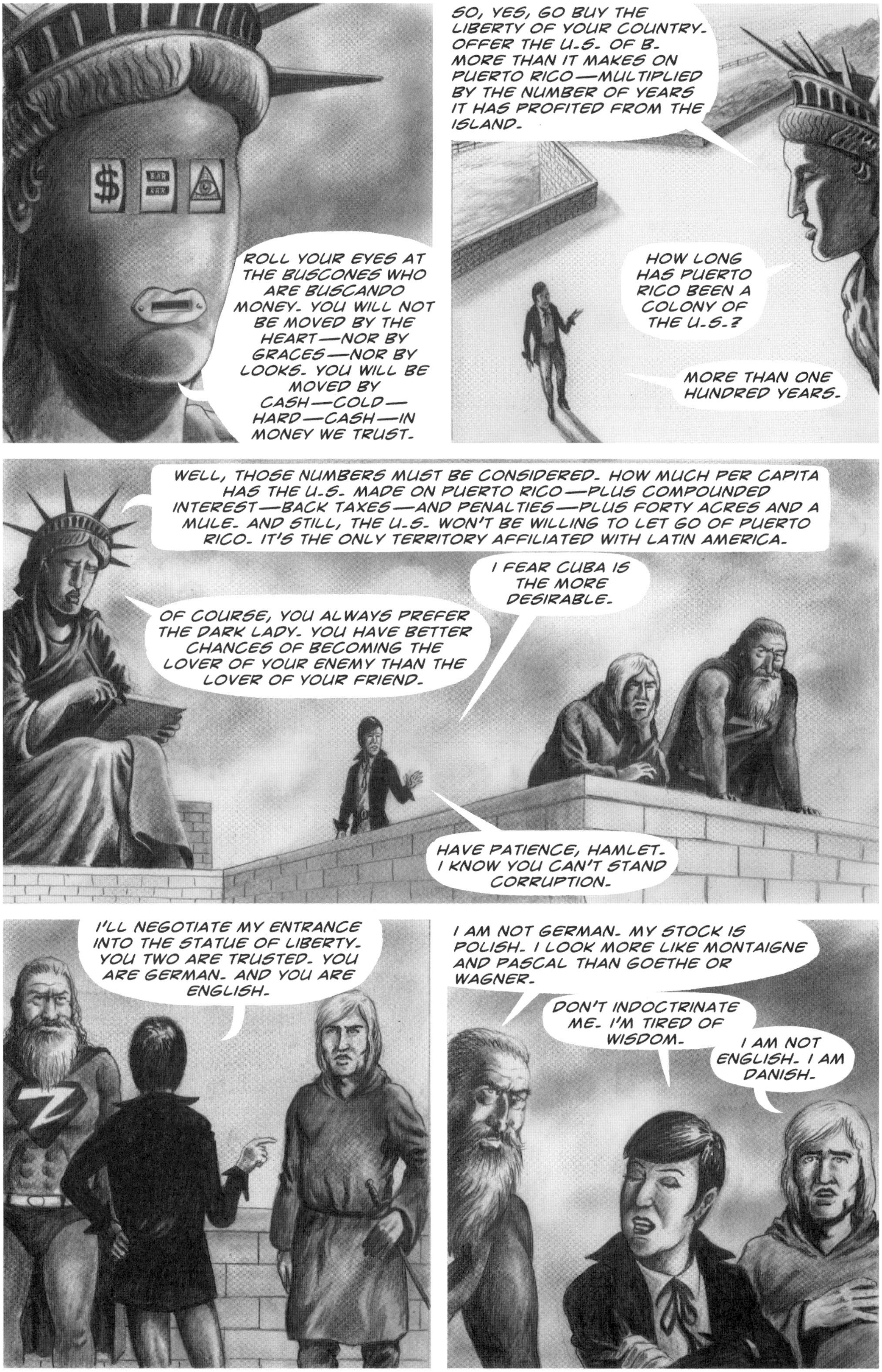
ROLL YOUR EYES AT THE BUSCONES WHO ARE BUSCANDO MONEY. YOU WILL NOT BE MOVED BY THE HEART—NOR BY GRACES—NOR BY LOOKS. YOU WILL BE MOVED BY CASH—COLD—HARD—CASH—IN MONEY WE TRUST.
SO, YES, GO BUY THE LIBERTY OF YOUR COUNTRY. OFFER THE U.S. OF B. MORE THAN IT MAKES ON PUERTO RICO—MULTIPLIED BY THE NUMBER OF YEARS IT HAS PROFITED FROM THE ISLAND.
HOW LONG HAS PUERTO RICO BEEN A COLONY OF THE U.S.?
MORE THAN ONE HUNDRED YEARS.
WELL, THOSE NUMBERS MUST BE CONSIDERED. HOW MUCH PER CAPITA HAS THE U.S. MADE ON PUERTO RICO—PLUS COMPOUNDED INTEREST—BACK TAXES—AND PENALTIES—PLUS FORTY ACRES AND A MULE. AND STILL, THE U.S. WON'T BE WILLING TO LET GO OF PUERTO RICO. IT'S THE ONLY TERRITORY AFFILIATED WITH LATIN AMERICA.
I FEAR CUBA IS THE MORE DESIRABLE.
OF COURSE, YOU ALWAYS PREFER THE DARK LADY. YOU HAVE BETTER CHANCES OF BECOMING THE LOVER OF YOUR ENEMY THAN THE LOVER OF YOUR FRIEND.
HAVE PATIENCE, HAMLET. I KNOW YOU CAN'T STAND CORRUPTION.
I'LL NEGOTIATE MY ENTRANCE INTO THE STATUE OF LIBERTY. YOU TWO ARE TRUSTED. YOU ARE GERMAN. AND YOU ARE ENGLISH.
I AM NOT GERMAN. MY STOCK IS POLISH. I LOOK MORE LIKE MONTAIGNE AND PASCAL THAN GOETHE OR WAGNER.
DON'T INDOCTRINATE ME. I'M TIRED OF WISDOM.
I AM NOT ENGLISH. I AM DANISH.

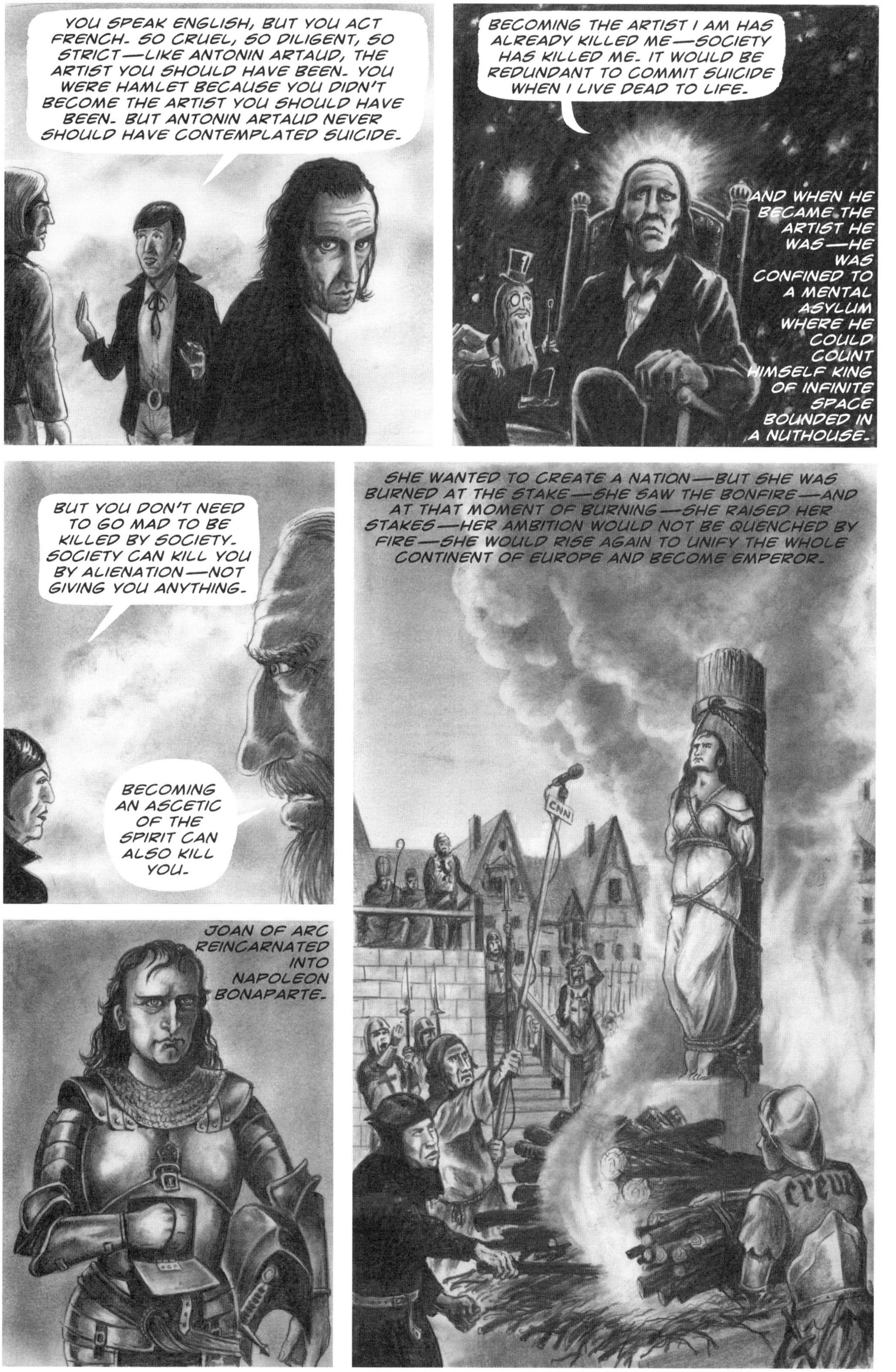
YOU SPEAK ENGLISH, BUT YOU ACT FRENCH. SO CRUEL, SO DILIGENT, SO STRICT—LIKE ANTONIN ARTAUD, THE ARTIST YOU SHOULD HAVE BEEN. YOU WERE HAMLET BECAUSE YOU DIDN'T BECOME THE ARTIST YOU SHOULD HAVE BEEN. BUT ANTONIN ARTAUD NEVER SHOULD HAVE CONTEMPLATED SUICIDE.
BECOMING THE ARTIST I AM HAS ALREADY KILLED ME—SOCIETY HAS KILLED ME. IT WOULD BE REDUNDANT TO COMMIT SUICIDE WHEN I LIVE DEAD TO LIFE.
AND WHEN HE BECAME THE ARTIST HE WAS—HE WAS CONFINED TO A MENTAL ASYLUM WHERE HE COULD COUNT HIMSELF KING OF INFINITE SPACE BOUNDED IN A NUTHOUSE.
BUT YOU DON'T NEED TO GO MAD TO BE KILLED BY SOCIETY. SOCIETY CAN KILL YOU BY ALIENATION—NOT GIVING YOU ANYTHING.
BECOMING AN ASCETIC OF THE SPIRIT CAN ALSO KILL YOU.
JOAN OF ARC REINCARNATED INTO NAPOLEON BONAPARTE.
SHE WANTED TO CREATE A NATION—BUT SHE WAS BURNED AT THE STAKE—SHE SAW THE BONFIRE—AND AT THAT MOMENT OF BURNING—SHE RAISED HER STAKES—HER AMBITION WOULD NOT BE QUENCHED BY FIRE—SHE WOULD RISE AGAIN TO UNIFY THE WHOLE CONTINENT OF EUROPE AND BECOME EMPEROR.
CNN
crew

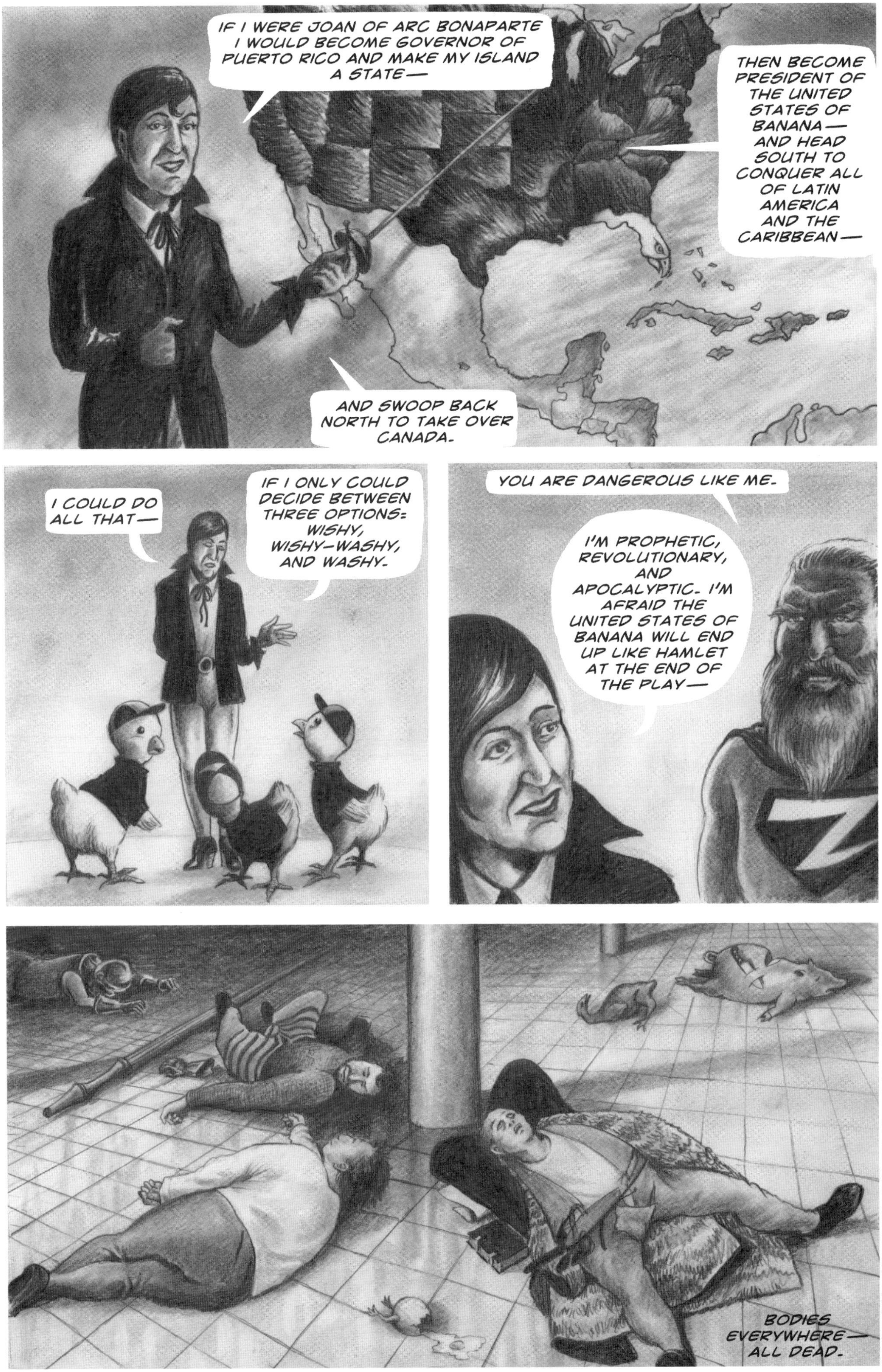
IF I WERE JOAN OF ARC BONAPARTE I WOULD BECOME GOVERNOR OF PUERTO RICO AND MAKE MY ISLAND A STATE—
THEN BECOME PRESIDENT OF THE UNITED STATES OF BANANA— AND HEAD SOUTH TO CONQUER ALL OF LATIN AMERICA AND THE CARIBBEAN—
AND SWOOP BACK NORTH TO TAKE OVER CANADA.
I COULD DO ALL THAT—
IF I ONLY COULD DECIDE BETWEEN THREE OPTIONS: WISHY, WISHY-WASHY, AND WASHY.
YOU ARE DANGEROUS LIKE ME.
I'M PROPHETIC, REVOLUTIONARY, AND APOCALYPTIC. I'M AFRAID THE UNITED STATES OF BANANA WILL END UP LIKE HAMLET AT THE END OF THE PLAY—
BODIES EVERYWHERE— ALL DEAD.

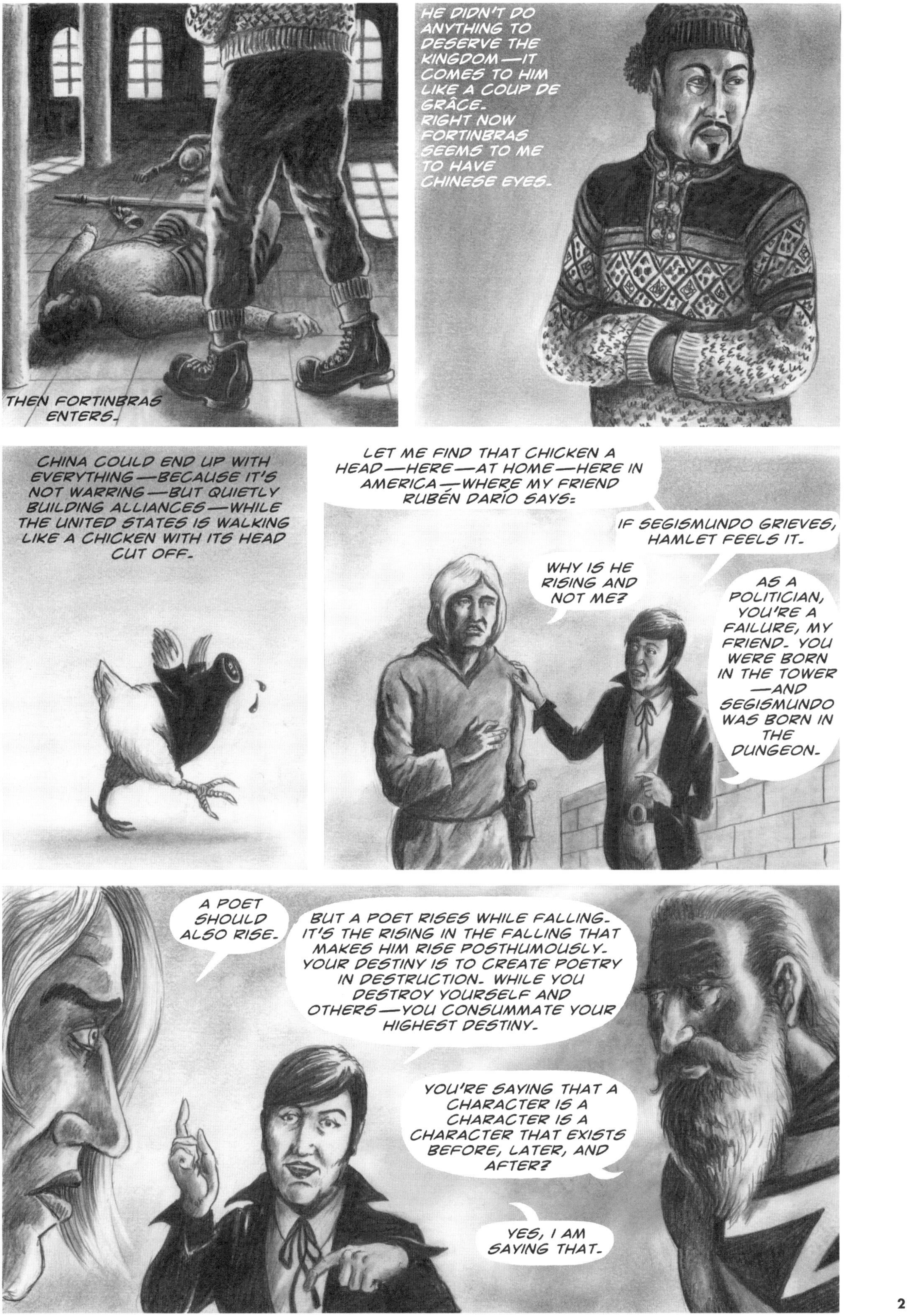
THEN FORTINBRAS ENTERS.
HE DIDN'T DO ANYTHING TO DESERVE THE KINGDOM—IT COMES TO HIM LIKE A COUP DE GRÂCE. RIGHT NOW FORTINBRAS SEEMS TO ME TO HAVE CHINESE EYES.
CHINA COULD END UP WITH EVERYTHING—BECAUSE IT'S NOT WARRING—BUT QUIETLY BUILDING ALLIANCES—WHILE THE UNITED STATES IS WALKING LIKE A CHICKEN WITH ITS HEAD CUT OFF.
LET ME FIND THAT CHICKEN A HEAD—HERE—AT HOME—HERE IN AMERICA—WHERE MY FRIEND RUBÉN DARÍO SAYS:
IF SEGISMUNDO GRIEVES, HAMLET FEELS IT.
WHY IS HE RISING AND NOT ME?
AS A POLITICIAN, YOU'RE A FAILURE, MY FRIEND. YOU WERE BORN IN THE TOWER—AND SEGISMUNDO WAS BORN IN THE DUNGEON.
A POET SHOULD ALSO RISE.
BUT A POET RISES WHILE FALLING. IT'S THE RISING IN THE FALLING THAT MAKES HIM RISE POSTHUMOUSLY. YOUR DESTINY IS TO CREATE POETRY IN DESTRUCTION. WHILE YOU DESTROY YOURSELF AND OTHERS—YOU CONSUMMATE YOUR HIGHEST DESTINY.
YOU'RE SAYING THAT A CHARACTER IS A CHARACTER IS A CHARACTER THAT EXISTS BEFORE, LATER, AND AFTER?
YES, I AM SAYING THAT.

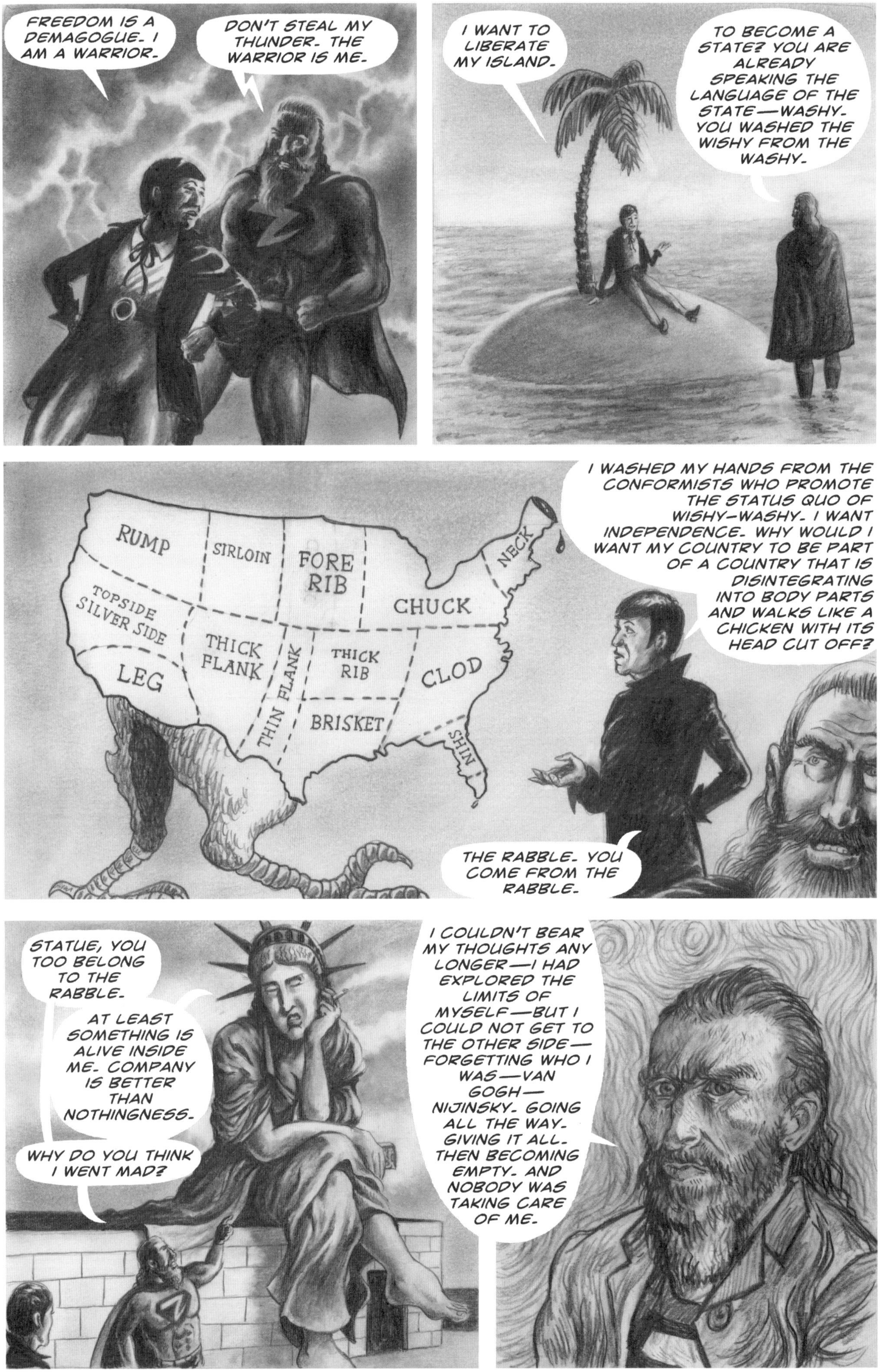
FREEDOM IS A DEMAGOGUE. I AM A WARRIOR.
DON'T STEAL MY THUNDER. THE WARRIOR IS ME.
I WANT TO LIBERATE MY ISLAND.
TO BECOME A STATE? YOU ARE ALREADY SPEAKING THE LANGUAGE OF THE STATE—WASHY. YOU WASHED THE WISHY FROM THE WASHY.
RUMP
SIRLOIN
FORE RIB
CHUCK
NECK
TOPSIDE SILVER SIDE
THICK FLANK
THIN FLANK
THICK RIB
CLOD
LEG
BRISKET
SHIN
I WASHED MY HANDS FROM THE CONFORMISTS WHO PROMOTE THE STATUS QUO OF WISHY-WASHY. I WANT INDEPENDENCE. WHY WOULD I WANT MY COUNTRY TO BE PART OF A COUNTRY THAT IS DISINTEGRATING INTO BODY PARTS AND WALKS LIKE A CHICKEN WITH ITS HEAD CUT OFF?
THE RABBLE. YOU COME FROM THE RABBLE.
STATUE, YOU TOO BELONG TO THE RABBLE.
AT LEAST SOMETHING IS ALIVE INSIDE ME. COMPANY IS BETTER THAN NOTHINGNESS.
WHY DO YOU THINK I WENT MAD?
I COULDN'T BEAR MY THOUGHTS ANY LONGER—I HAD EXPLORED THE LIMITS OF MYSELF—BUT I COULD NOT GET TO THE OTHER SIDE—FORGETTING WHO I WAS—VAN GOGH—NIJINSKY. GOING ALL THE WAY. GIVING IT ALL. THEN BECOMING EMPTY. AND NOBODY WAS TAKING CARE OF ME.

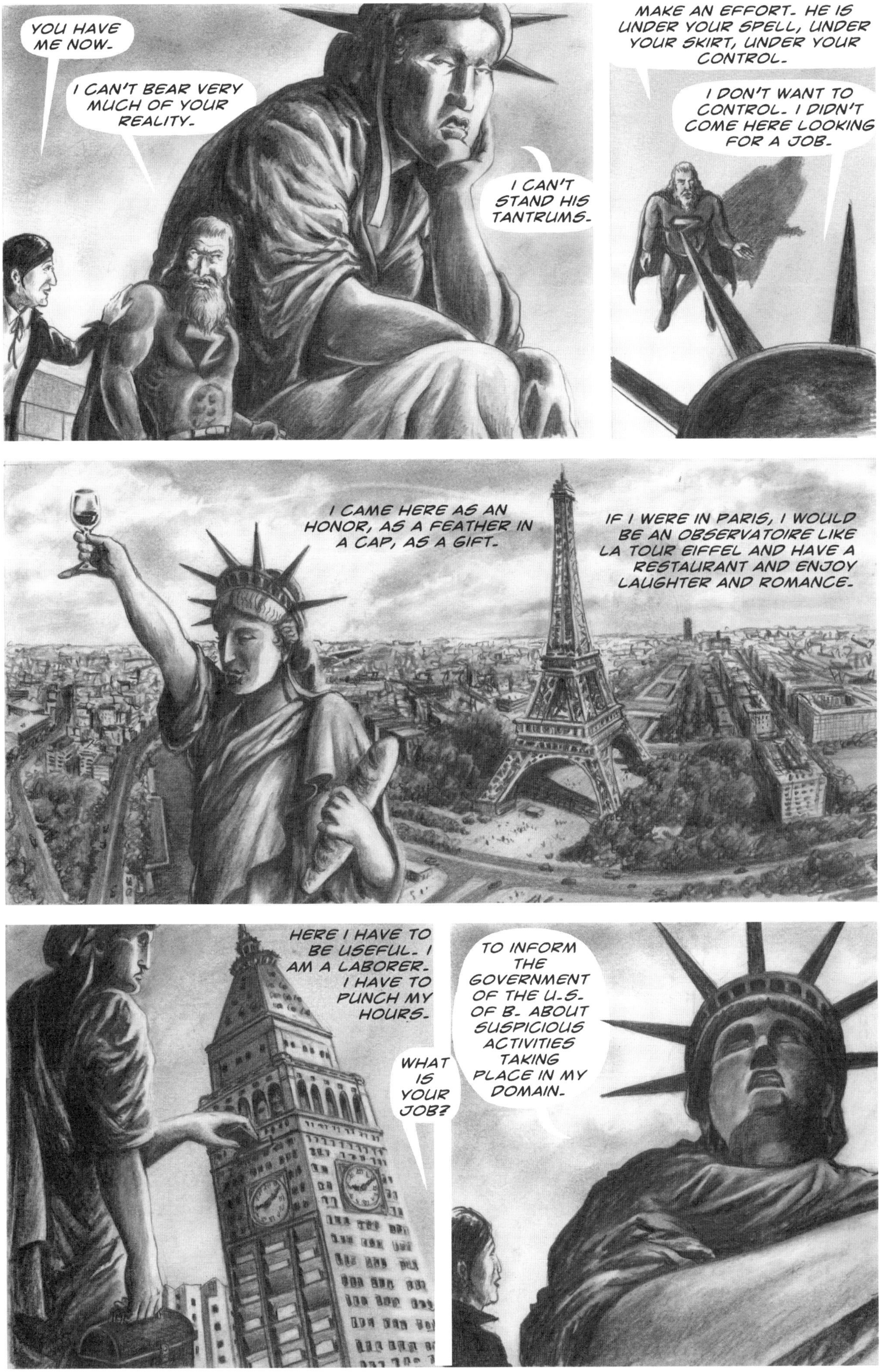
YOU HAVE ME NOW.
I CAN'T BEAR VERY MUCH OF YOUR REALITY.
I CAN'T STAND HIS TANTRUMS.
MAKE AN EFFORT. HE IS UNDER YOUR SPELL, UNDER YOUR SKIRT, UNDER YOUR CONTROL.
I DON'T WANT TO CONTROL. I DIDN'T COME HERE LOOKING FOR A JOB.
I CAME HERE AS AN HONOR, AS A FEATHER IN A CAP, AS A GIFT.
IF I WERE IN PARIS, I WOULD BE AN OBSERVATOIRE LIKE LA TOUR EIFFEL AND HAVE A RESTAURANT AND ENJOY LAUGHTER AND ROMANCE.
HERE I HAVE TO BE USEFUL. I AM A LABORER. I HAVE TO PUNCH MY HOURS.
WHAT IS YOUR JOB?
TO INFORM THE GOVERNMENT OF THE U.S. OF B. ABOUT SUSPICIOUS ACTIVITIES TAKING PLACE IN MY DOMAIN.

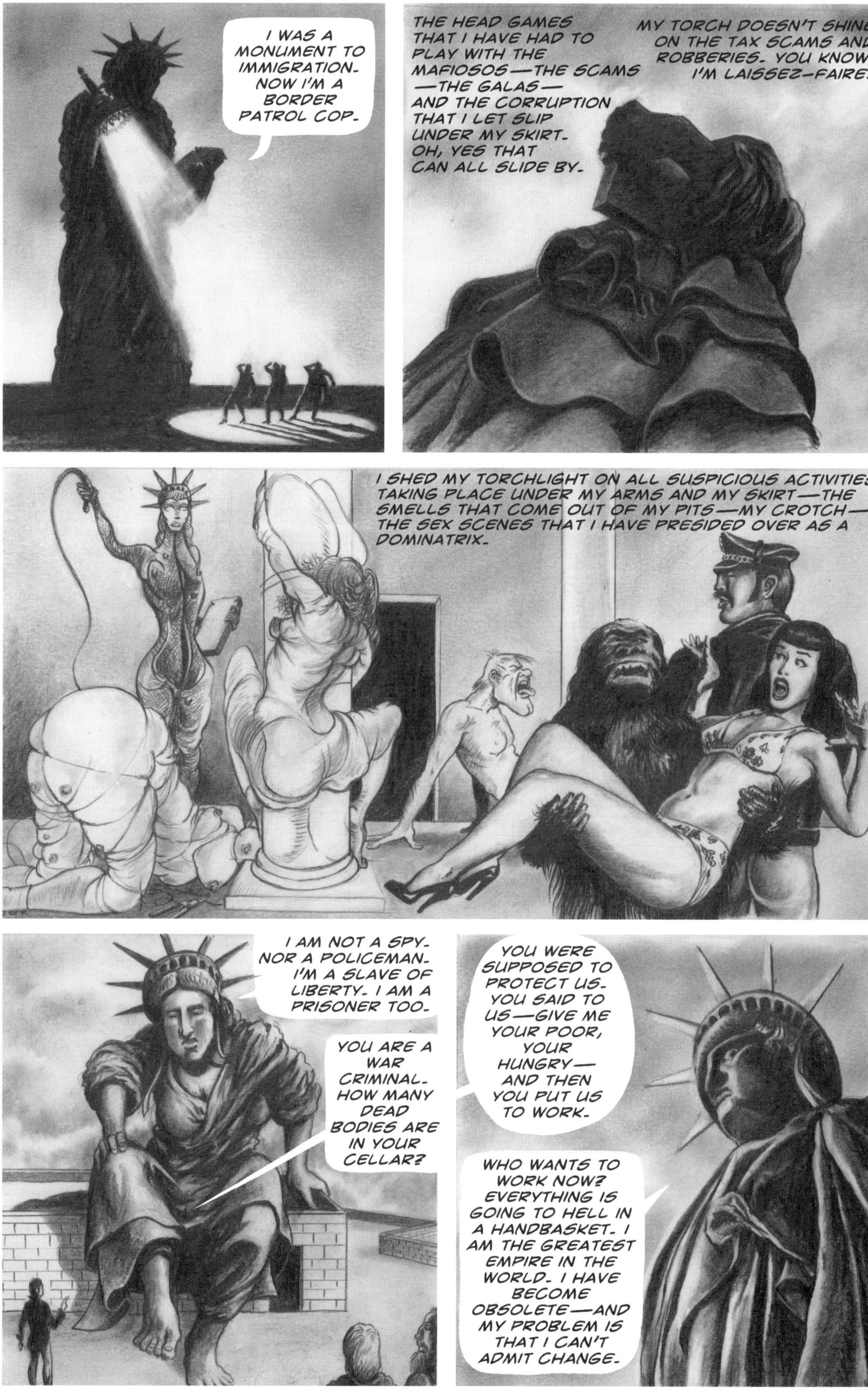
I WAS A MONUMENT TO IMMIGRATION. NOW I'M A BORDER PATROL COP.
THE HEAD GAMES THAT I HAVE HAD TO PLAY WITH THE MAFIOSOS—THE SCAMS—THE GALAS—AND THE CORRUPTION THAT I LET SLIP UNDER MY SKIRT. OH, YES THAT CAN ALL SLIDE BY.
MY TORCH DOESN'T SHINE ON THE TAX SCAMS AND ROBBERIES. YOU KNOW, I'M LAISSEZ-FAIRE.
I SHED MY TORCHLIGHT ON ALL SUSPICIOUS ACTIVITIES TAKING PLACE UNDER MY ARMS AND MY SKIRT—THE SMELLS THAT COME OUT OF MY PITS—MY CROTCH—THE SEX SCENES THAT I HAVE PRESIDED OVER AS A DOMINATRIX.
I AM NOT A SPY. NOR A POLICEMAN. I'M A SLAVE OF LIBERTY. I AM A PRISONER TOO.
YOU ARE A WAR CRIMINAL. HOW MANY DEAD BODIES ARE IN YOUR CELLAR?
YOU WERE SUPPOSED TO PROTECT US. YOU SAID TO US—GIVE ME YOUR POOR, YOUR HUNGRY—AND THEN YOU PUT US TO WORK.
WHO WANTS TO WORK NOW? EVERYTHING IS GOING TO HELL IN A HANDBASKET. I AM THE GREATEST EMPIRE IN THE WORLD. I HAVE BECOME OBSOLETE—AND MY PROBLEM IS THAT I CAN'T ADMIT CHANGE.

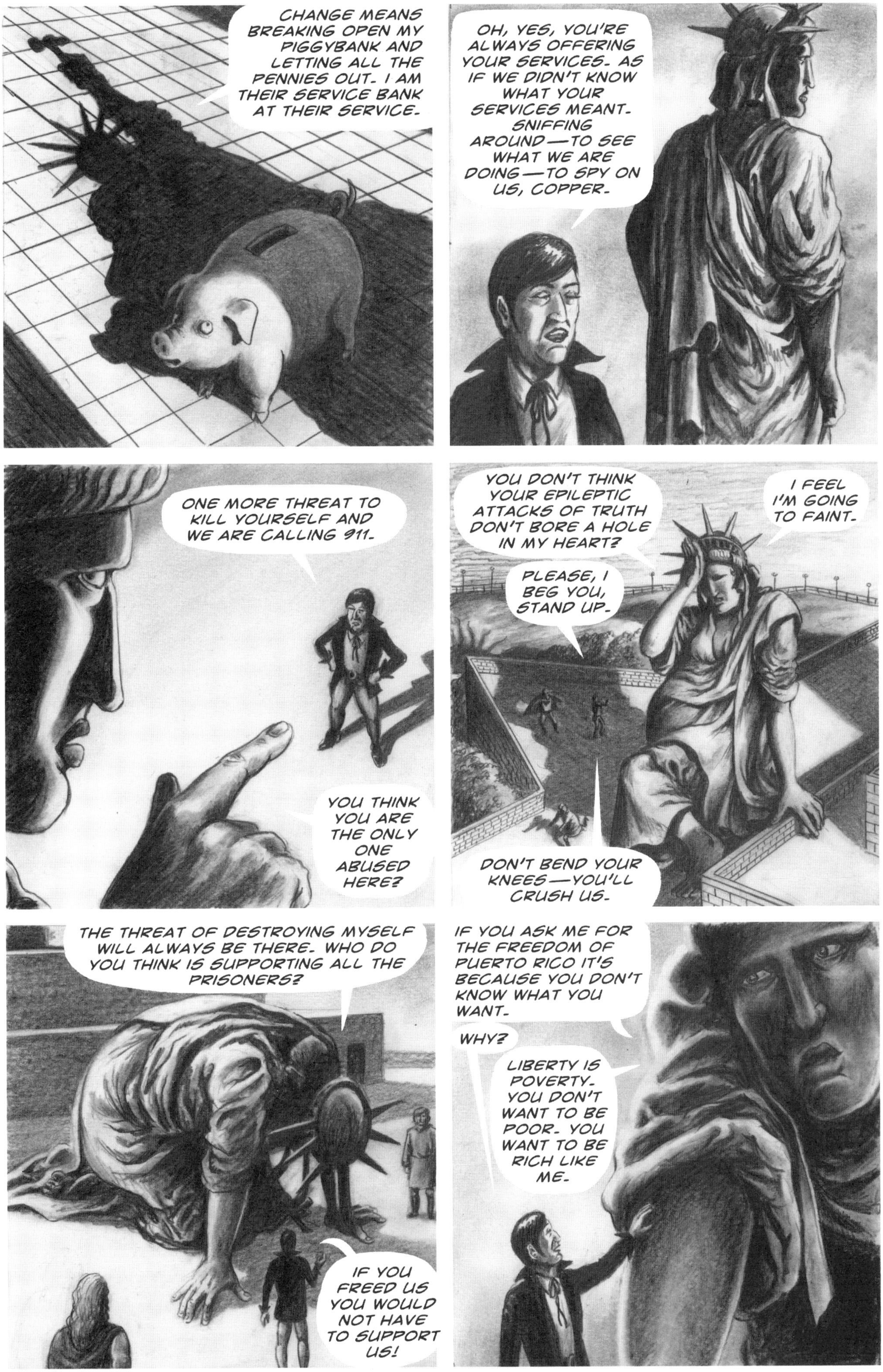
CHANGE MEANS BREAKING OPEN MY PIGGYBANK AND LETTING ALL THE PENNIES OUT. I AM THEIR SERVICE BANK AT THEIR SERVICE.
OH, YES, YOU'RE ALWAYS OFFERING YOUR SERVICES. AS IF WE DIDN'T KNOW WHAT YOUR SERVICES MEANT. SNIFFING AROUND—TO SEE WHAT WE ARE DOING—TO SPY ON US, COPPER.
ONE MORE THREAT TO KILL YOURSELF AND WE ARE CALLING 911.
YOU THINK YOU ARE THE ONLY ONE ABUSED HERE?
YOU DON'T THINK YOUR EPILEPTIC ATTACKS OF TRUTH DON'T BORE A HOLE IN MY HEART?
I FEEL I'M GOING TO FAINT.
PLEASE, I BEG YOU, STAND UP.
DON'T BEND YOUR KNEES—YOU'LL CRUSH US.
THE THREAT OF DESTROYING MYSELF WILL ALWAYS BE THERE. WHO DO YOU THINK IS SUPPORTING ALL THE PRISONERS?
IF YOU FREED US YOU WOULD NOT HAVE TO SUPPORT US!
IF YOU ASK ME FOR THE FREEDOM OF PUERTO RICO IT'S BECAUSE YOU DON'T KNOW WHAT YOU WANT.
WHY?
LIBERTY IS POVERTY. YOU DON'T WANT TO BE POOR. YOU WANT TO BE RICH LIKE ME.

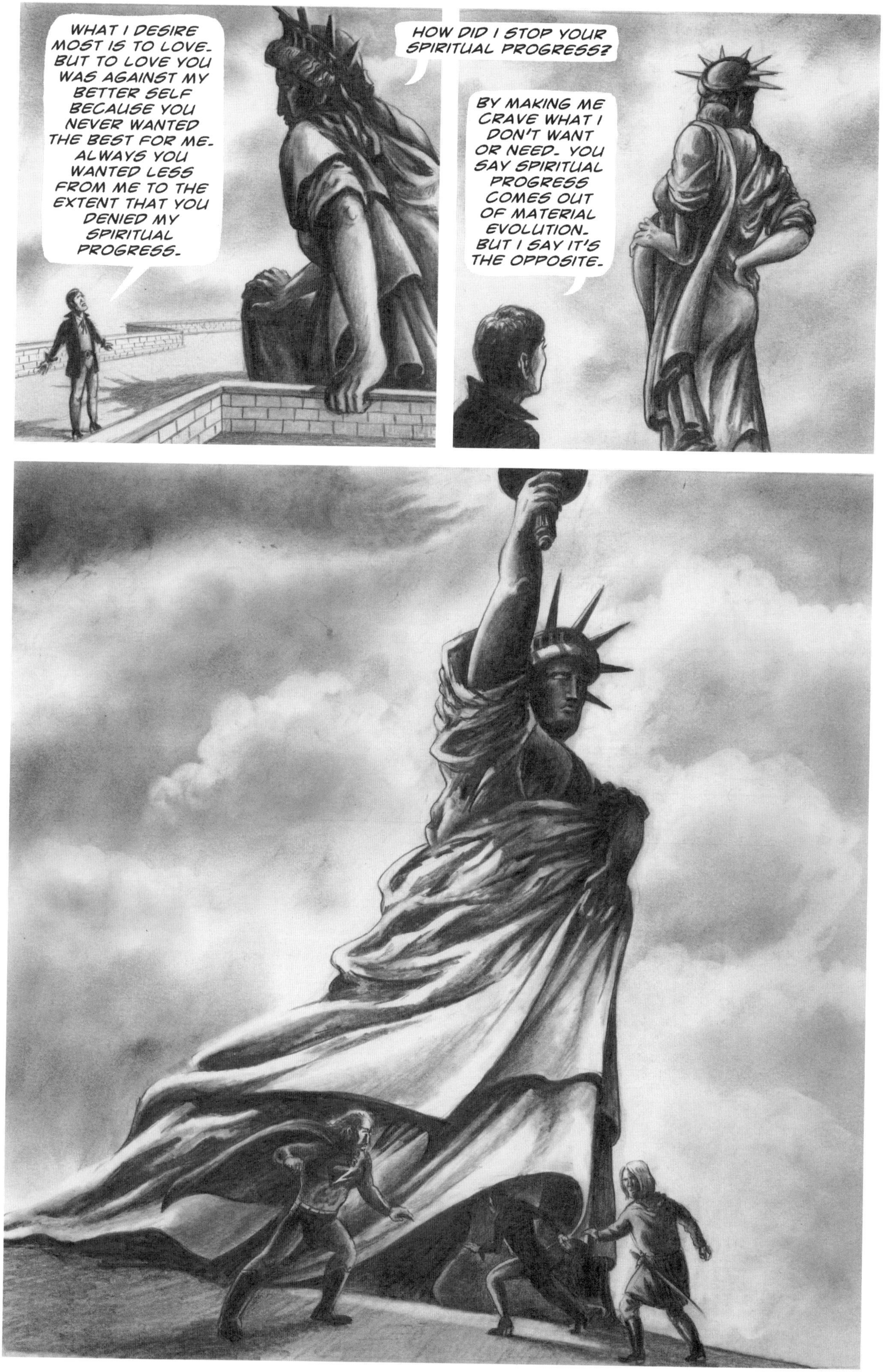
WHAT I DESIRE MOST IS TO LOVE. BUT TO LOVE YOU WAS AGAINST MY BETTER SELF BECAUSE YOU NEVER WANTED THE BEST FOR ME. ALWAYS YOU WANTED LESS FROM ME TO THE EXTENT THAT YOU DENIED MY SPIRITUAL PROGRESS.
HOW DID I STOP YOUR SPIRITUAL PROGRESS?
BY MAKING ME CRAVE WHAT I DON'T WANT OR NEED. YOU SAY SPIRITUAL PROGRESS COMES OUT OF MATERIAL EVOLUTION. BUT I SAY IT'S THE OPPOSITE.

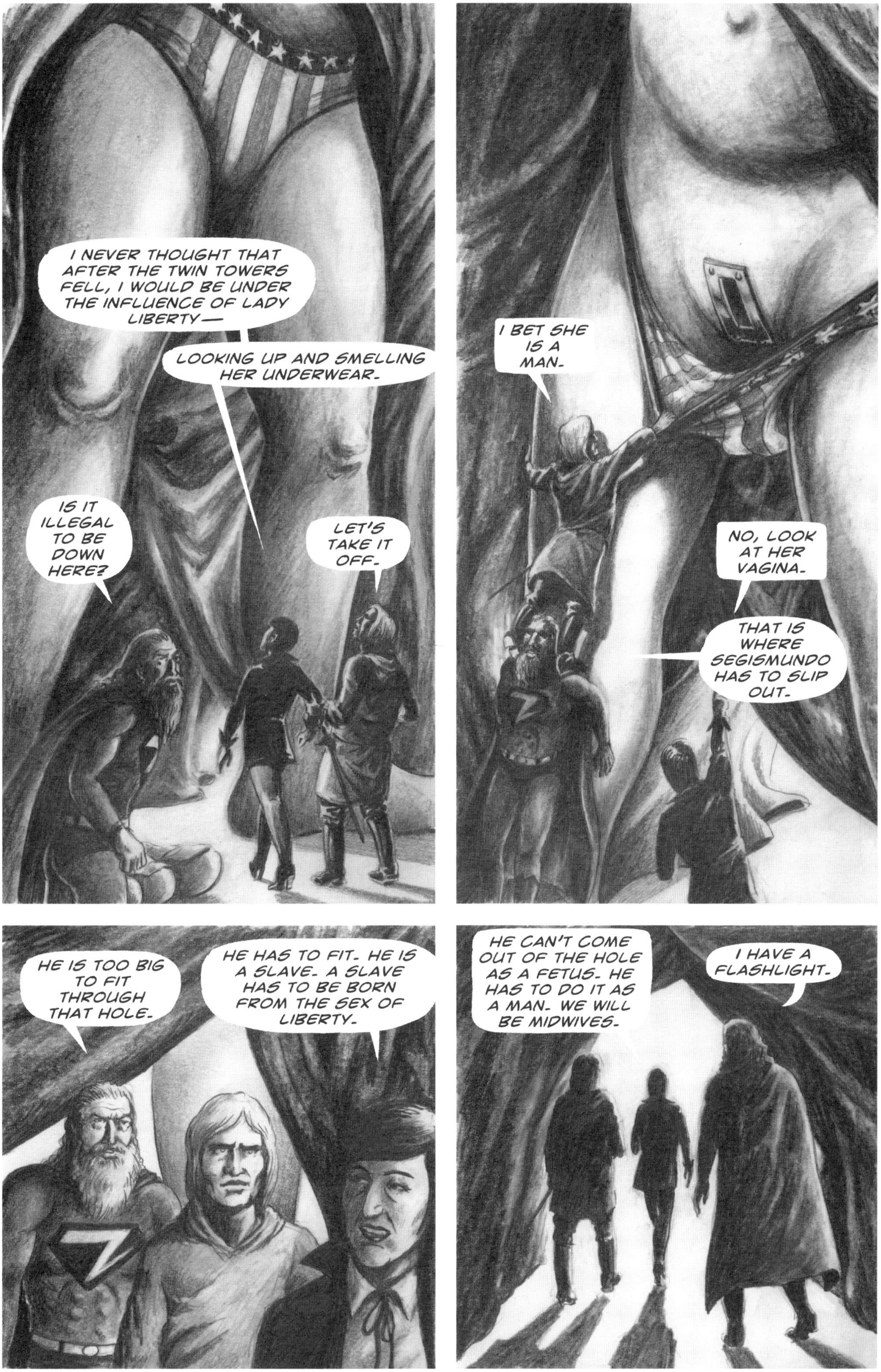
I NEVER THOUGHT THAT AFTER THE TWIN TOWERS FELL, I WOULD BE UNDER THE INFLUENCE OF LADY LIBERTY—
LOOKING UP AND SMELLING HER UNDERWEAR.
IS IT ILLEGAL TO BE DOWN HERE?
LET'S TAKE IT OFF.
I BET SHE IS A MAN.
NO, LOOK AT HER VAGINA.
THAT IS WHERE SEGISMUNDO HAS TO SLIP OUT.
HE IS TOO BIG TO FIT THROUGH THAT HOLE.
HE HAS TO FIT. HE IS A SLAVE. A SLAVE HAS TO BE BORN FROM THE SEX OF LIBERTY.
HE CAN'T COME OUT OF THE HOLE AS A FETUS. HE HAS TO DO IT AS A MAN. WE WILL BE MIDWIVES.
I HAVE A FLASHLIGHT.

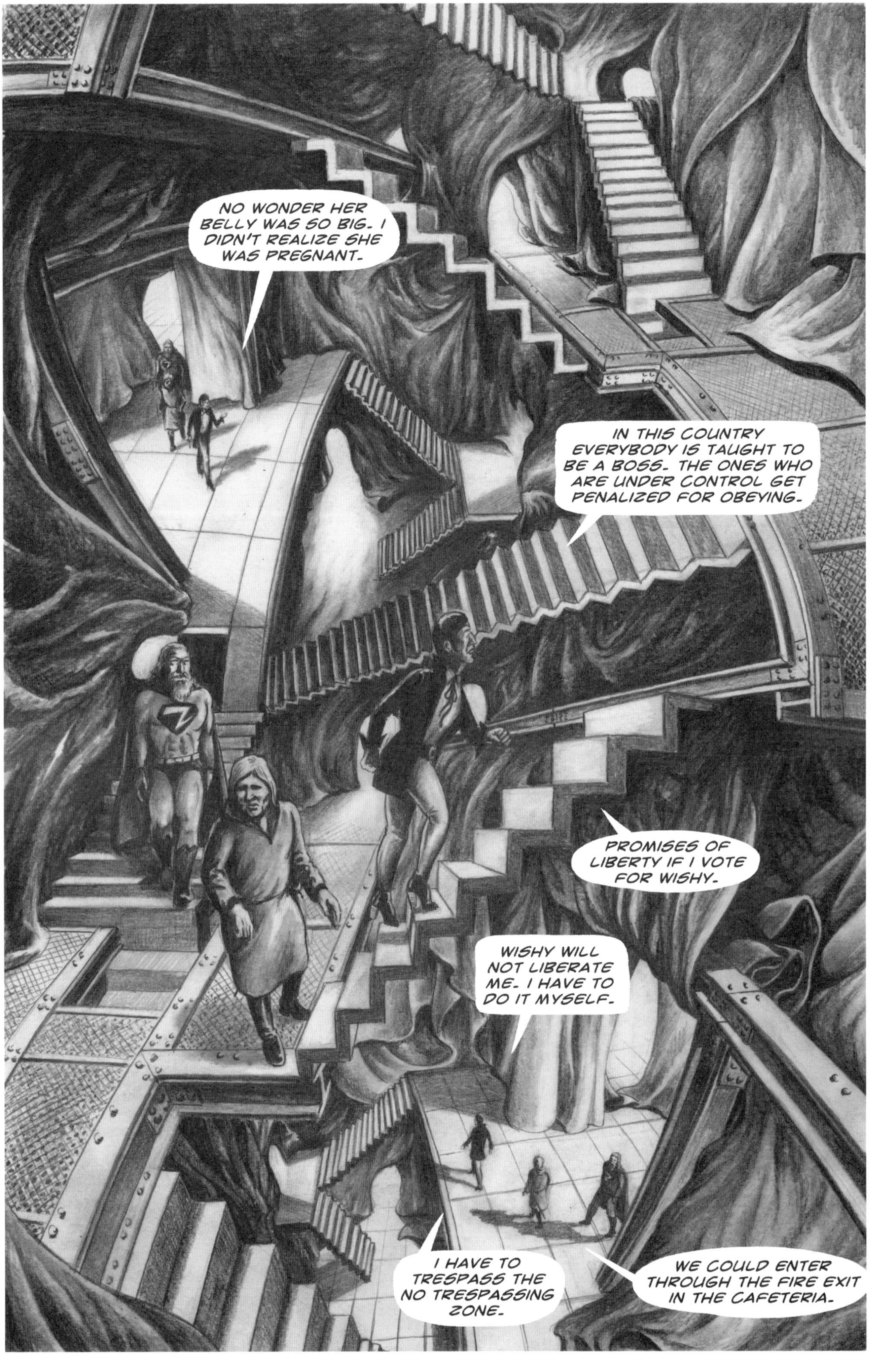
NO WONDER HER BELLY WAS SO BIG. I DIDN'T REALIZE SHE WAS PREGNANT.
IN THIS COUNTRY EVERYBODY IS TAUGHT TO BE A BOSS. THE ONES WHO ARE UNDER CONTROL GET PENALIZED FOR OBEYING.
PROMISES OF LIBERTY IF I VOTE FOR WISHY.
WISHY WILL NOT LIBERATE ME. I HAVE TO DO IT MYSELF.
I HAVE TO TRESPASS THE NO TRESPASSING ZONE.
WE COULD ENTER THROUGH THE FIRE EXIT IN THE CAFETERIA.

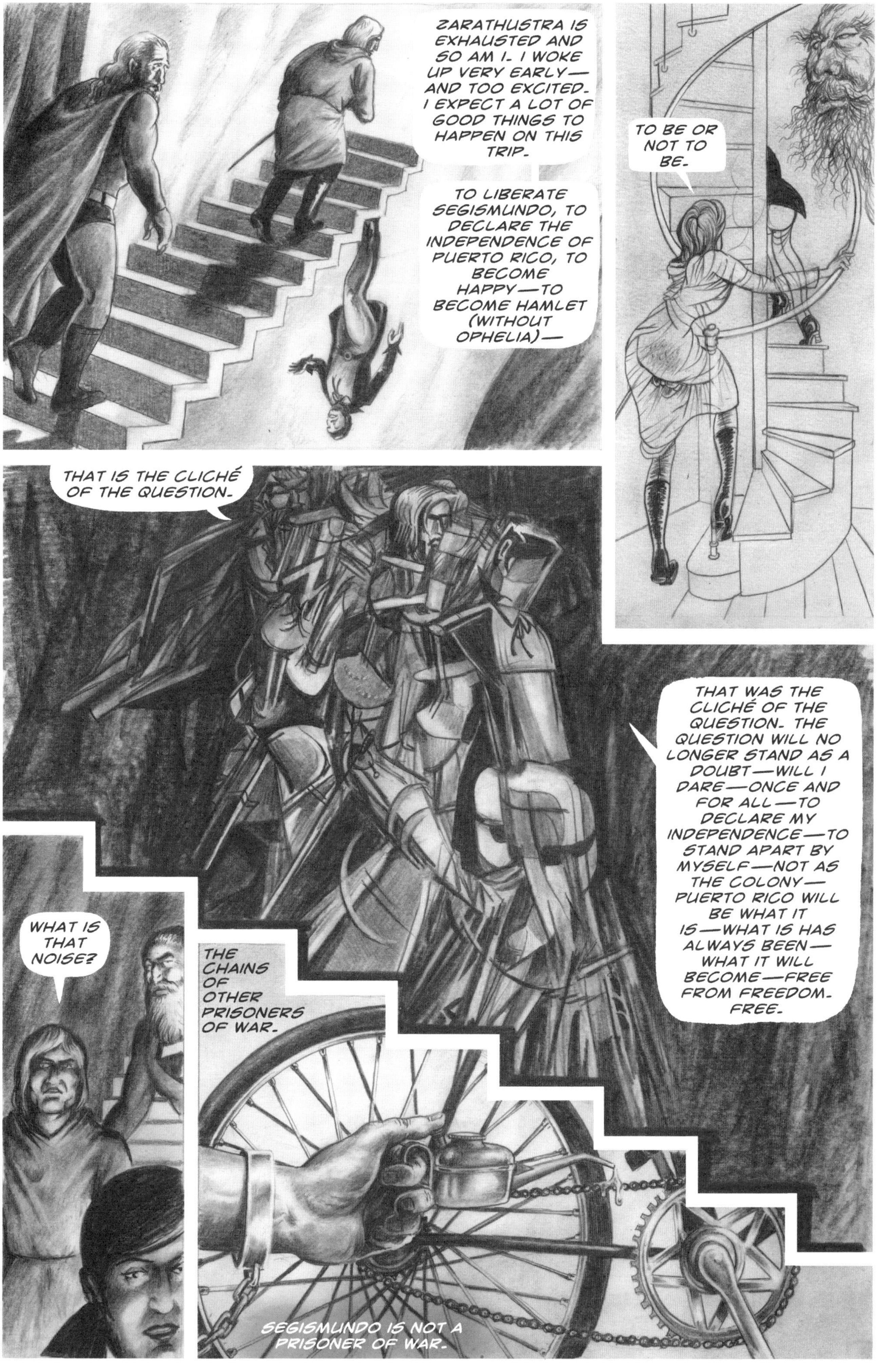
ZARATHUSTRA IS EXHAUSTED AND SO AM I. I WOKE UP VERY EARLY— AND TOO EXCITED. I EXPECT A LOT OF GOOD THINGS TO HAPPEN ON THIS TRIP.
TO LIBERATE SEGISMUNDO, TO DECLARE THE INDEPENDENCE OF PUERTO RICO, TO BECOME HAPPY—TO BECOME HAMLET (WITHOUT OPHELIA)—
TO BE OR NOT TO BE.
THAT IS THE CLICHÉ OF THE QUESTION.
THAT WAS THE CLICHÉ OF THE QUESTION. THE QUESTION WILL NO LONGER STAND AS A DOUBT—WILL I DARE—ONCE AND FOR ALL—TO DECLARE MY INDEPENDENCE—TO STAND APART BY MYSELF—NOT AS THE COLONY— PUERTO RICO WILL BE WHAT IT IS—WHAT IS HAS ALWAYS BEEN— WHAT IT WILL BECOME—FREE FROM FREEDOM. FREE.
WHAT IS THAT NOISE?
THE CHAINS OF OTHER PRISONERS OF WAR.
SEGISMUNDO IS NOT A PRISONER OF WAR.

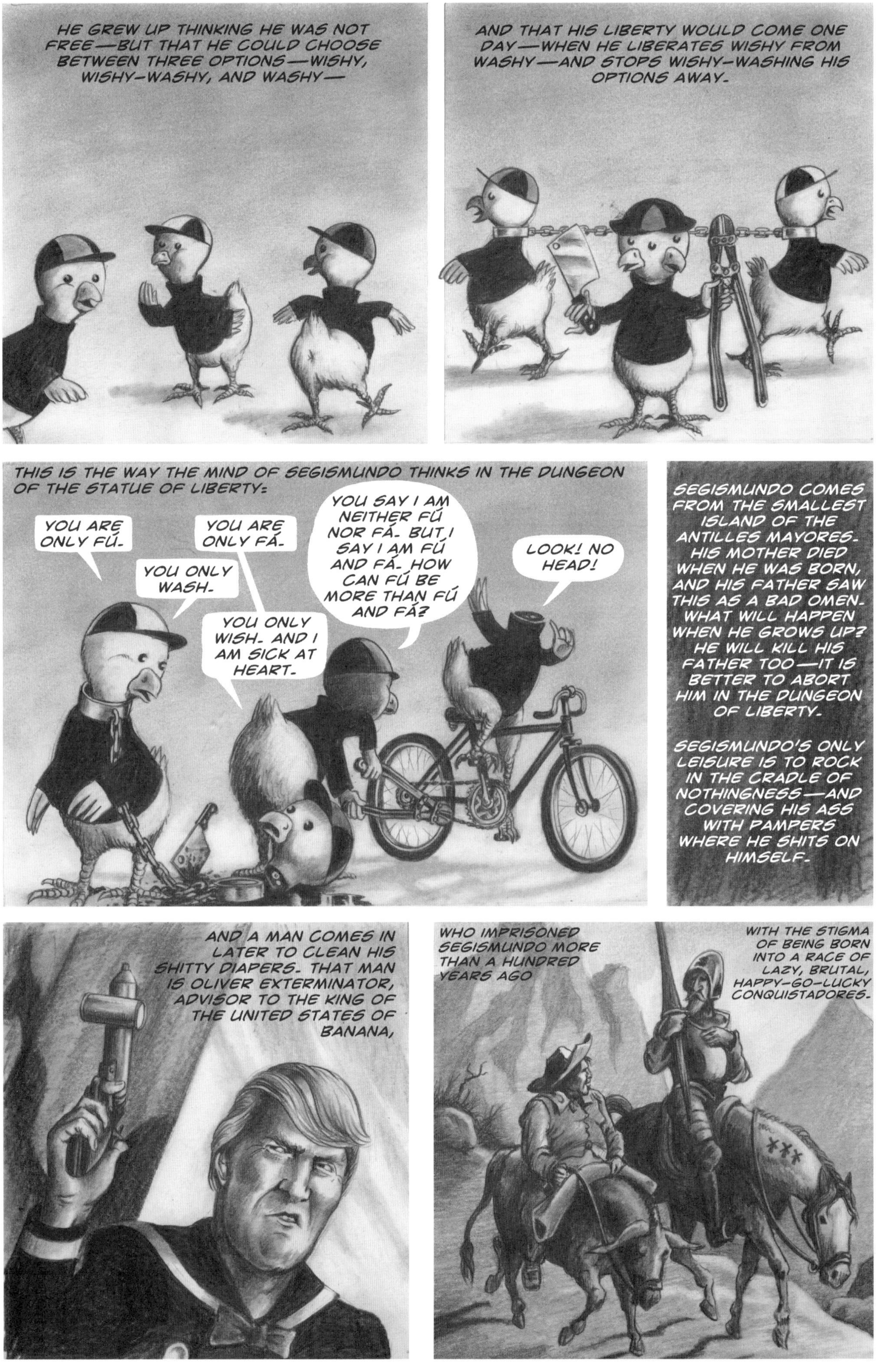
HE GREW UP THINKING HE WAS NOT FREE—BUT THAT HE COULD CHOOSE BETWEEN THREE OPTIONS—WISHY, WISHY-WASHY, AND WASHY—
AND THAT HIS LIBERTY WOULD COME ONE DAY—WHEN HE LIBERATES WISHY FROM WASHY—AND STOPS WISHY-WASHING HIS OPTIONS AWAY.
THIS IS THE WAY THE MIND OF SEGISMUNDO THINKS IN THE DUNGEON OF THE STATUE OF LIBERTY:
YOU ARE ONLY FÚ.
YOU ONLY WASH.
YOU ARE ONLY FÁ.
YOU ONLY WISH. AND I AM SICK AT HEART.
YOU SAY I AM NEITHER FÚ NOR FÁ. BUT I SAY I AM FÚ AND FÁ. HOW CAN FÚ BE MORE THAN FÚ AND FÁ?
LOOK! NO HEAD!
SEGISMUNDO COMES FROM THE SMALLEST ISLAND OF THE ANTILLES MAYORES. HIS MOTHER DIED WHEN HE WAS BORN, AND HIS FATHER SAW THIS AS A BAD OMEN. WHAT WILL HAPPEN WHEN HE GROWS UP? HE WILL KILL HIS FATHER TOO—IT IS BETTER TO ABORT HIM IN THE DUNGEON OF LIBERTY.
SEGISMUNDO'S ONLY LEISURE IS TO ROCK IN THE CRADLE OF NOTHINGNESS—AND COVERING HIS ASS WITH PAMPERS WHERE HE SHITS ON HIMSELF.
AND A MAN COMES IN LATER TO CLEAN HIS SHITTY DIAPERS. THAT MAN IS OLIVER EXTERMINATOR, ADVISOR TO THE KING OF THE UNITED STATES OF BANANA,
WHO IMPRISONED SEGISMUNDO MORE THAN A HUNDRED YEARS AGO
WITH THE STIGMA OF BEING BORN INTO A RACE OF LAZY, BRUTAL, HAPPY-GO-LUCKY CONQUISTADORES.

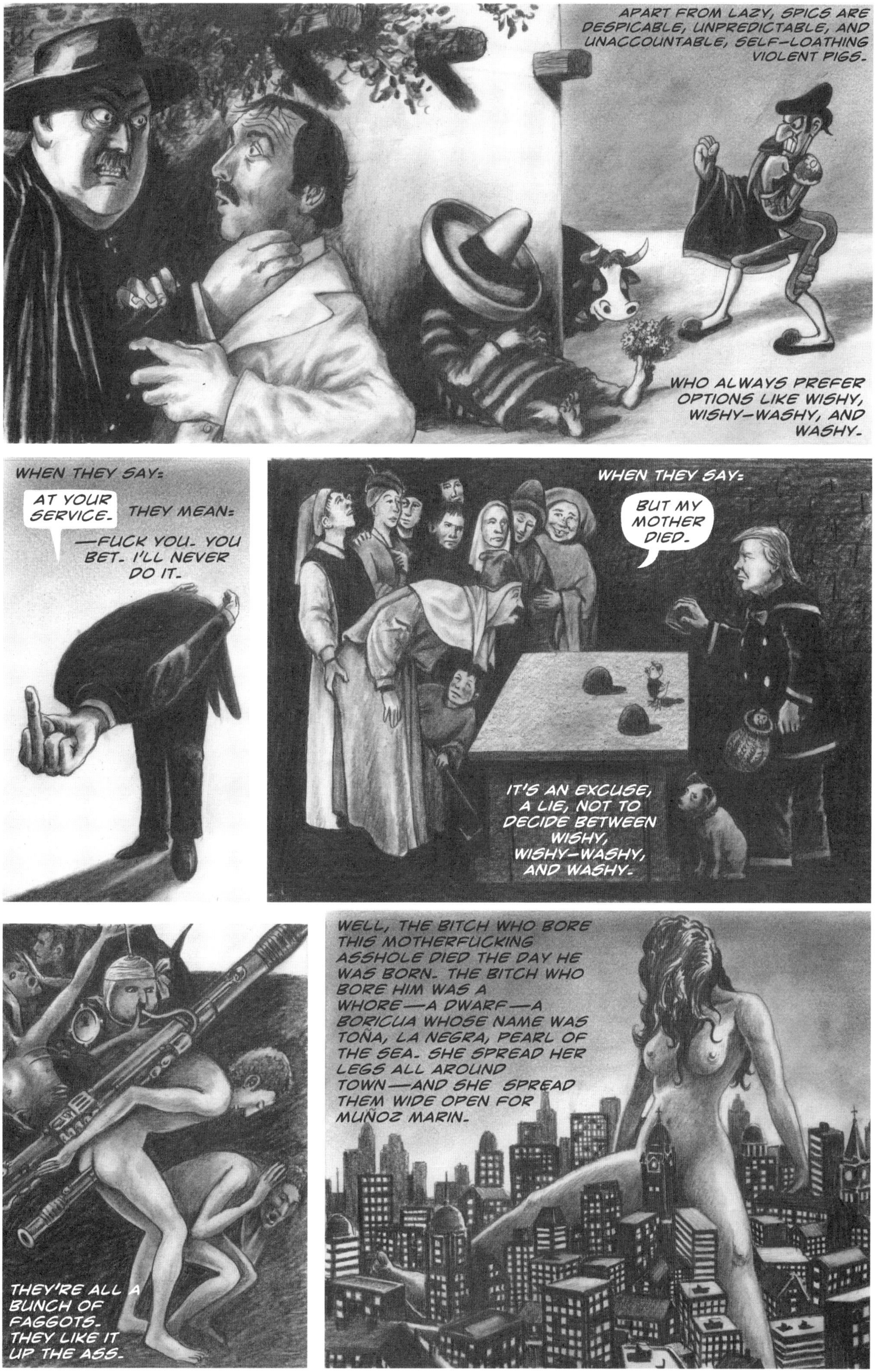

APART FROM LAZY, SPICS ARE DESPICABLE, UNPREDICTABLE, AND UNACCOUNTABLE, SELF-LOATHING VIOLENT PIGS.
WHO ALWAYS PREFER OPTIONS LIKE WISHY, WISHY-WASHY, AND WASHY.
WHEN THEY SAY:
AT YOUR SERVICE.
THEY MEAN:
—FUCK YOU. YOU BET. I'LL NEVER DO IT.
WHEN THEY SAY:
BUT MY MOTHER DIED.
IT'S AN EXCUSE, A LIE, NOT TO DECIDE BETWEEN WISHY, WISHY-WASHY, AND WASHY.
THEY'RE ALL A BUNCH OF FAGGOTS. THEY LIKE IT UP THE ASS.
WELL, THE BITCH WHO BORE THIS MOTHERFUCKING ASSHOLE DIED THE DAY HE WAS BORN. THE BITCH WHO BORE HIM WAS A WHORE—A DWARF—A BORICUA WHOSE NAME WAS TOÑA, LA NEGRA, PEARL OF THE SEA. SHE SPREAD HER LEGS ALL AROUND TOWN—AND SHE SPREAD THEM WIDE OPEN FOR MUÑOZ MARIN.

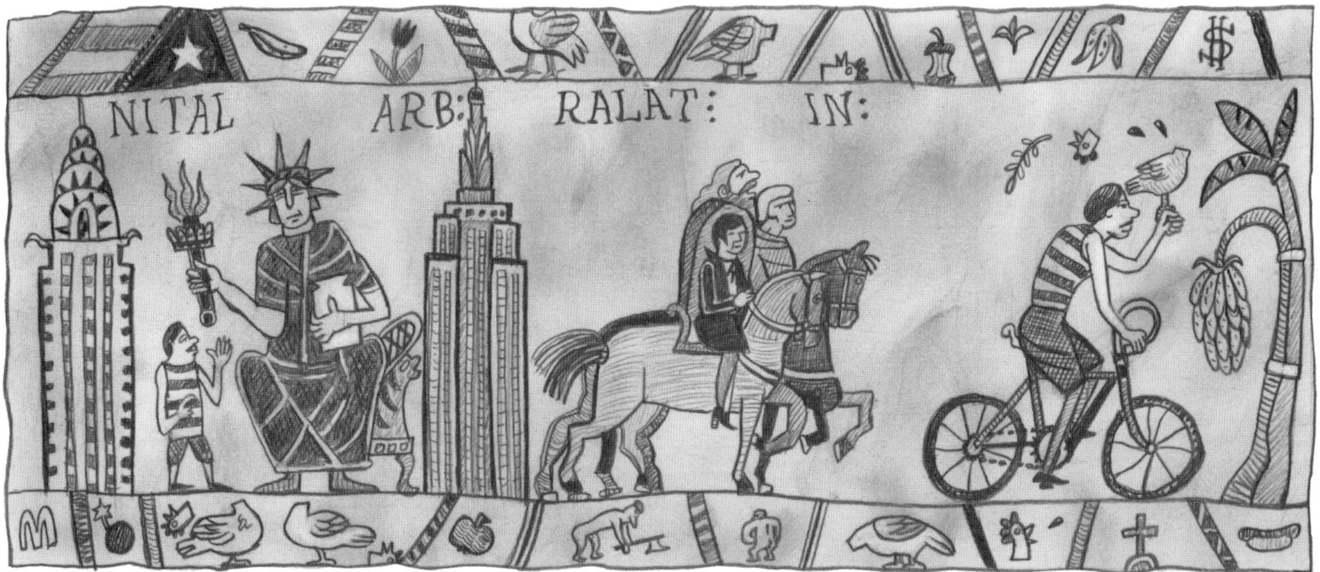
NITAL ARB: RALAT: IN:

AND THAT'S HOW SEGISMUNDO WAS BORN, BASTARD CHILD OF THE MOST BEAUTIFUL WHORE OF LA PERLA AND THE GOVERNOR OF PUERTO RICO. WITH A POUCH AROUND HIS NECK WITH A NOTE THAT SAID:

—THIS CHILD WILL MAKE THE ISLAND GREAT. THIS CHILD WILL MAKE THE WORLD CHANGE PERSPECTIVE FROM THE POINT OF VIEW OF THE COLONIZER TO THE POINT OF VIEW OF THE COLONIZED.

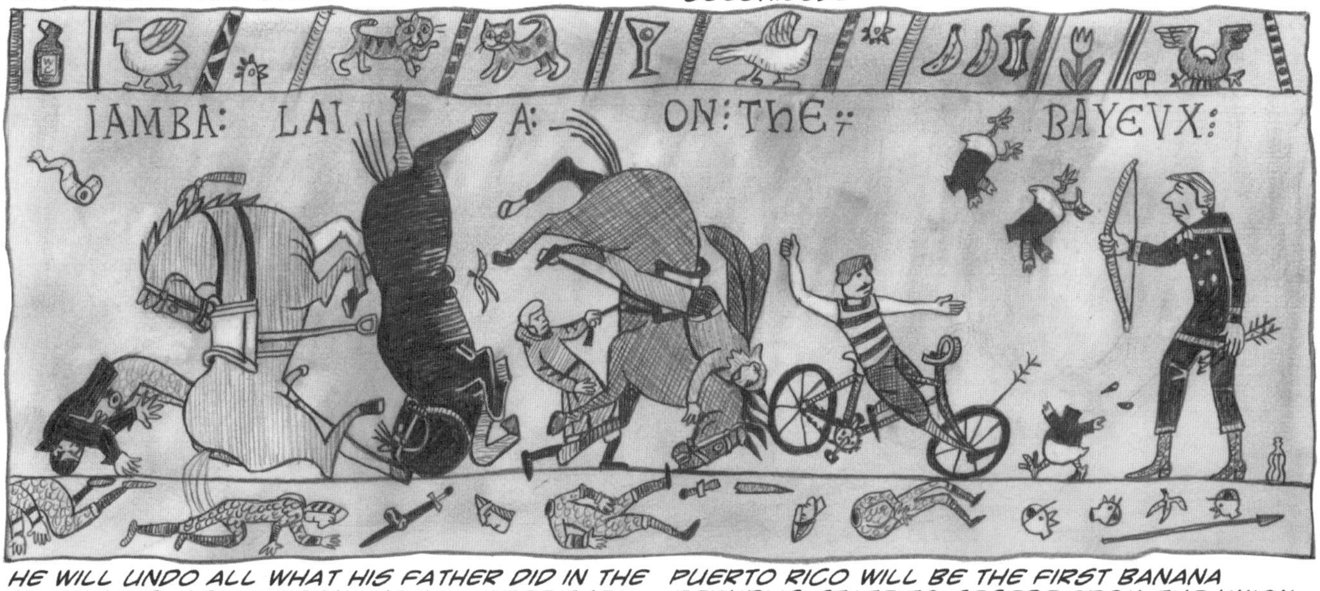
IAMBA: LAI A: ON:ThE: BAYEUX:

HE WILL UNDO ALL WHAT HIS FATHER DID IN THE NAME OF GLOBALIZATION. HE WILL FREE THE ISLAND FROM THE STATE, THE STATE FROM THE NATION, THE NATION FROM THE CONTINENT. THE UNITED STATES OF AMERICA WILL BECOME THE UNITED STATES OF BANANA.

PUERTO RICO WILL BE THE FIRST BANANA REPUBLIC STATE TO SECEDE FROM THE UNION. THEN WILL COME LIBERTY ISLAND, MISSISSIPPI BURNING, TEXAS BBQ, KENTUCKY FRIED CHICKEN, NEW YORK YANKEES, JERSEY DEVILS—YOU NAME IT—WILL WANT TO BREAK APART.

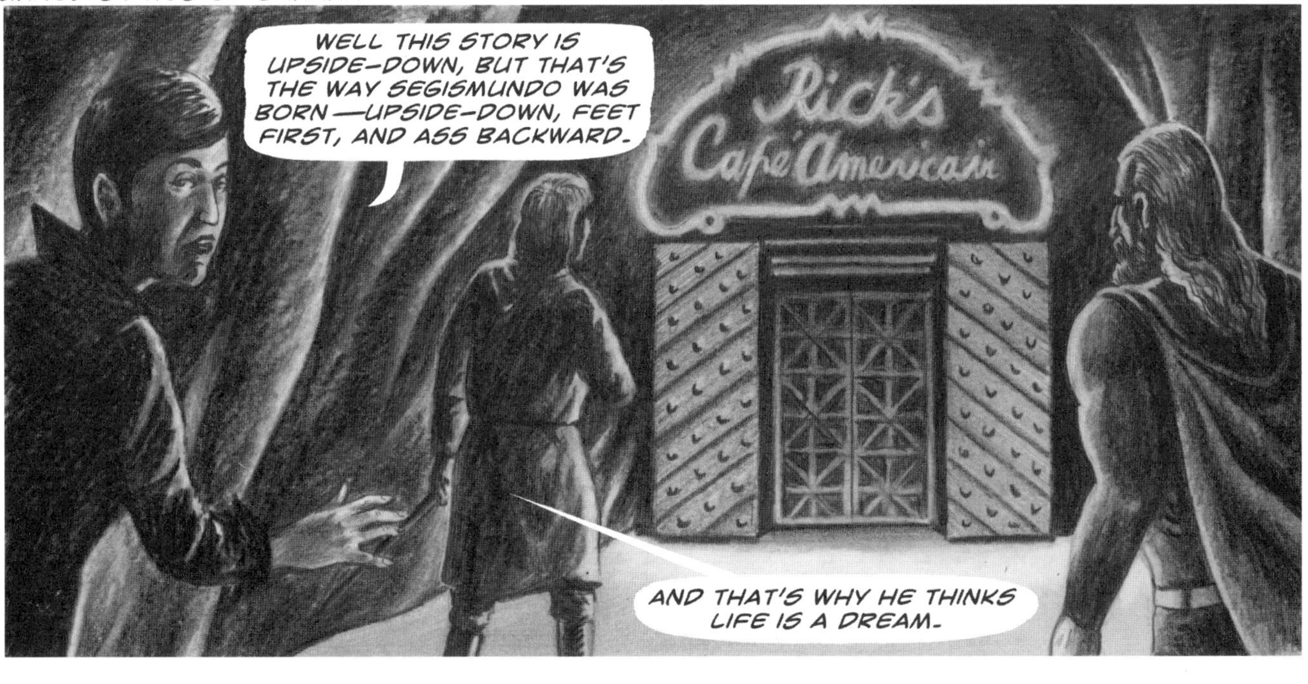
WELL THIS STORY IS UPSIDE-DOWN, BUT THAT'S THE WAY SEGISMUNDO WAS BORN—UPSIDE-DOWN, FEET FIRST, AND ASS BACKWARD.
Rick's Cafe Americain
AND THAT'S WHY HE THINKS LIFE IS A DREAM.

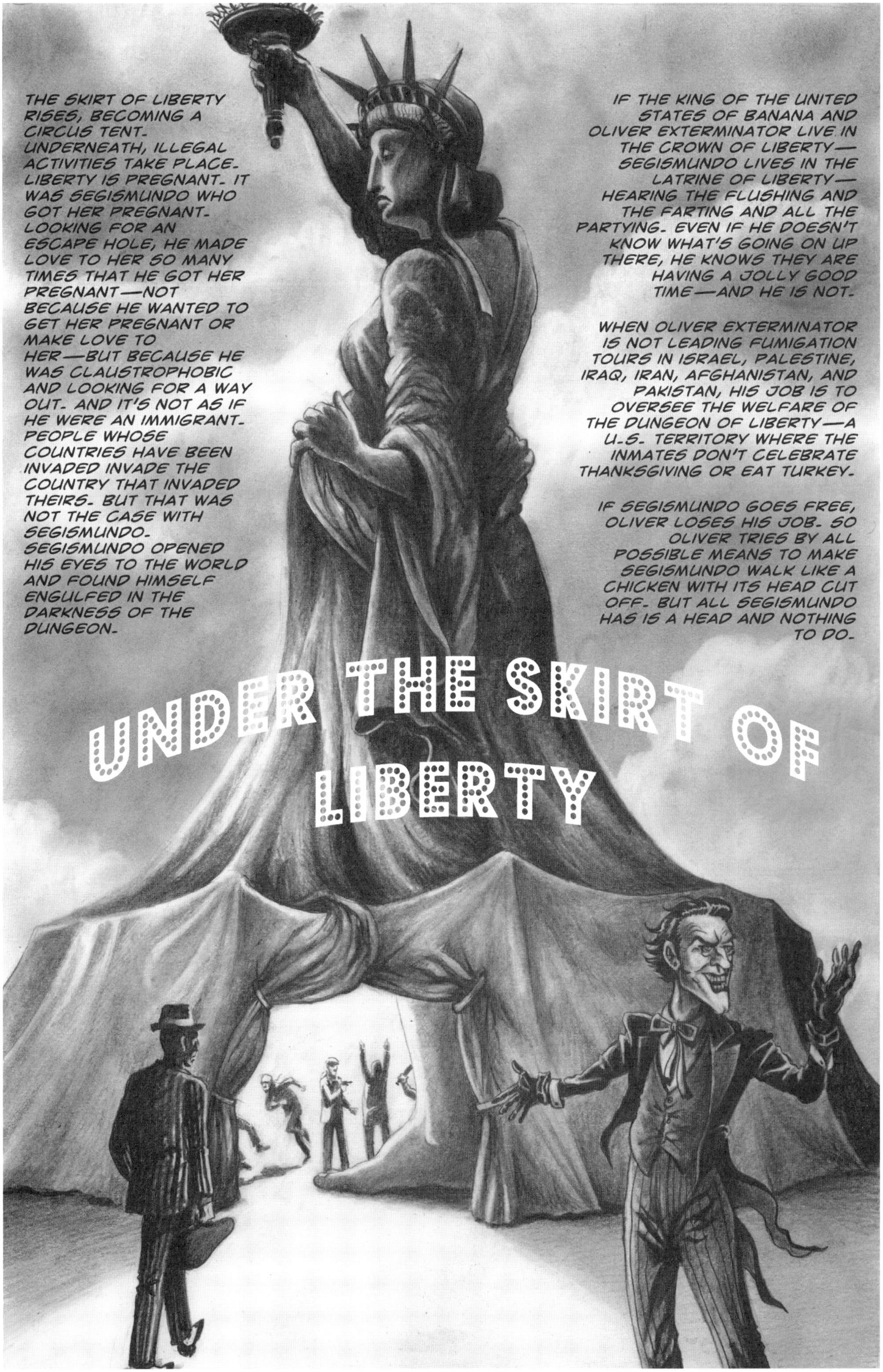
THE SKIRT OF LIBERTY RISES, BECOMING A CIRCUS TENT. UNDERNEATH, ILLEGAL ACTIVITIES TAKE PLACE. LIBERTY IS PREGNANT. IT WAS SEGISMUNDO WHO GOT HER PREGNANT. LOOKING FOR AN ESCAPE HOLE, HE MADE LOVE TO HER SO MANY TIMES THAT HE GOT HER PREGNANT—NOT BECAUSE HE WANTED TO GET HER PREGNANT OR MAKE LOVE TO HER—BUT BECAUSE HE WAS CLAUSTROPHOBIC AND LOOKING FOR A WAY OUT. AND IT'S NOT AS IF HE WERE AN IMMIGRANT. PEOPLE WHOSE COUNTRIES HAVE BEEN INVADED INVADE THE COUNTRY THAT INVADED THEIRS. BUT THAT WAS NOT THE CASE WITH SEGISMUNDO. SEGISMUNDO OPENED HIS EYES TO THE WORLD AND FOUND HIMSELF ENGULFED IN THE DARKNESS OF THE DUNGEON.
IF THE KING OF THE UNITED STATES OF BANANA AND OLIVER EXTERMINATOR LIVE IN THE CROWN OF LIBERTY—SEGISMUNDO LIVES IN THE LATRINE OF LIBERTY—HEARING THE FLUSHING AND THE FARTING AND ALL THE PARTYING. EVEN IF HE DOESN'T KNOW WHAT'S GOING ON UP THERE, HE KNOWS THEY ARE HAVING A JOLLY GOOD TIME—AND HE IS NOT.
WHEN OLIVER EXTERMINATOR IS NOT LEADING FUMIGATION TOURS IN ISRAEL, PALESTINE, IRAQ, IRAN, AFGHANISTAN, AND PAKISTAN, HIS JOB IS TO OVERSEE THE WELFARE OF THE DUNGEON OF LIBERTY—A U.S. TERRITORY WHERE THE INMATES DON'T CELEBRATE THANKSGIVING OR EAT TURKEY.
IF SEGISMUNDO GOES FREE, OLIVER LOSES HIS JOB. SO OLIVER TRIES BY ALL POSSIBLE MEANS TO MAKE SEGISMUNDO WALK LIKE A CHICKEN WITH ITS HEAD CUT OFF. BUT ALL SEGISMUNDO HAS IS A HEAD AND NOTHING TO DO.
UNDER THE SKIRT OF LIBERTY

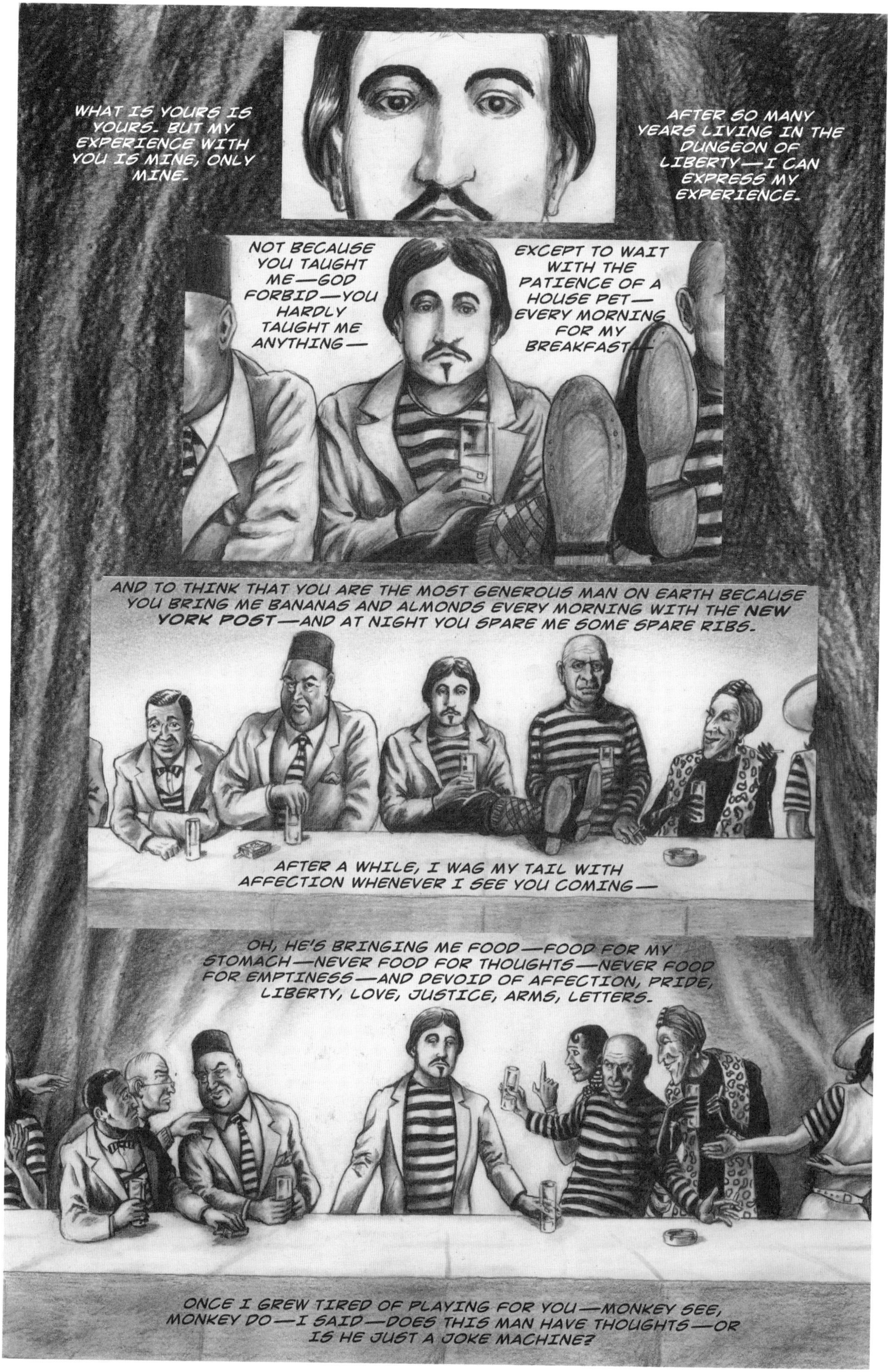
WHAT IS YOURS IS YOURS. BUT MY EXPERIENCE WITH YOU IS MINE, ONLY MINE.
AFTER SO MANY YEARS LIVING IN THE DUNGEON OF LIBERTY—I CAN EXPRESS MY EXPERIENCE.
NOT BECAUSE YOU TAUGHT ME—GOD FORBID—YOU HARDLY TAUGHT ME ANYTHING—
EXCEPT TO WAIT WITH THE PATIENCE OF A HOUSE PET—EVERY MORNING FOR MY BREAKFAST—
AND TO THINK THAT YOU ARE THE MOST GENEROUS MAN ON EARTH BECAUSE YOU BRING ME BANANAS AND ALMONDS EVERY MORNING WITH THE NEW YORK POST—AND AT NIGHT YOU SPARE ME SOME SPARE RIBS.
AFTER A WHILE, I WAG MY TAIL WITH AFFECTION WHENEVER I SEE YOU COMING—
OH, HE'S BRINGING ME FOOD—FOOD FOR MY STOMACH—NEVER FOOD FOR THOUGHTS—NEVER FOOD FOR EMPTINESS—AND DEVOID OF AFFECTION, PRIDE, LIBERTY, LOVE, JUSTICE, ARMS, LETTERS.
ONCE I GREW TIRED OF PLAYING FOR YOU—MONKEY SEE, MONKEY DO—I SAID—DOES THIS MAN HAVE THOUGHTS—OR IS HE JUST A JOKE MACHINE?

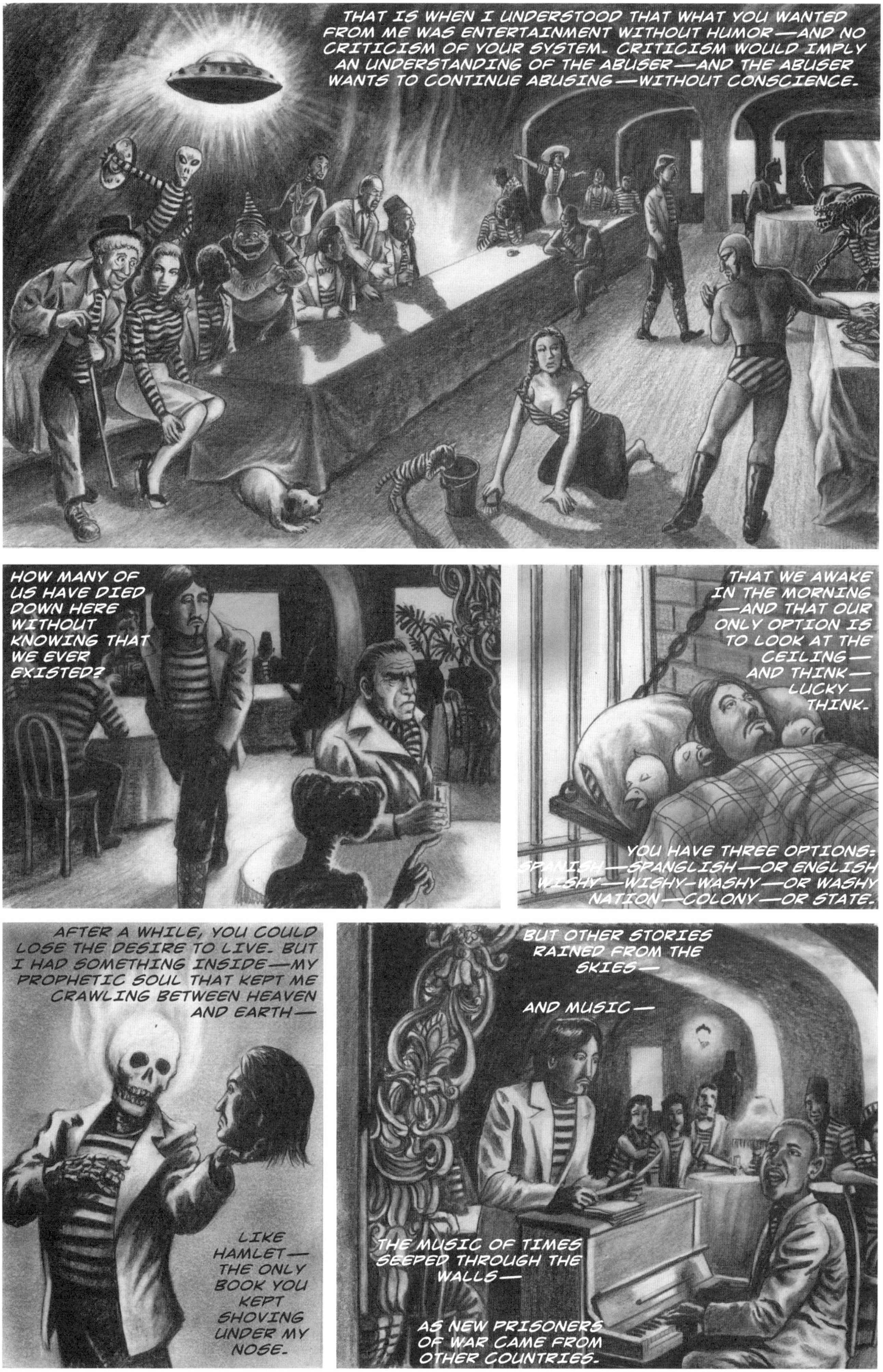
THAT IS WHEN I UNDERSTOOD THAT WHAT YOU WANTED FROM ME WAS ENTERTAINMENT WITHOUT HUMOR—AND NO CRITICISM OF YOUR SYSTEM. CRITICISM WOULD IMPLY AN UNDERSTANDING OF THE ABUSER—AND THE ABUSER WANTS TO CONTINUE ABUSING—WITHOUT CONSCIENCE.
HOW MANY OF US HAVE DIED DOWN HERE WITHOUT KNOWING THAT WE EVER EXISTED?
THAT WE AWAKE IN THE MORNING—AND THAT OUR ONLY OPTION IS TO LOOK AT THE CEILING—AND THINK—LUCKY—THINK.
YOU HAVE THREE OPTIONS: SPANISH—SPANGLISH—OR ENGLISH WISHY—WISHY-WASHY—OR WASHY NATION—COLONY—OR STATE.
AFTER A WHILE, YOU COULD LOSE THE DESIRE TO LIVE. BUT I HAD SOMETHING INSIDE—MY PROPHETIC SOUL THAT KEPT ME CRAWLING BETWEEN HEAVEN AND EARTH—
LIKE HAMLET—THE ONLY BOOK YOU KEPT SHOVING UNDER MY NOSE.
BUT OTHER STORIES RAINED FROM THE SKIES—
AND MUSIC—
THE MUSIC OF TIMES SEEPED THROUGH THE WALLS—
AS NEW PRISONERS OF WAR CAME FROM OTHER COUNTRIES.

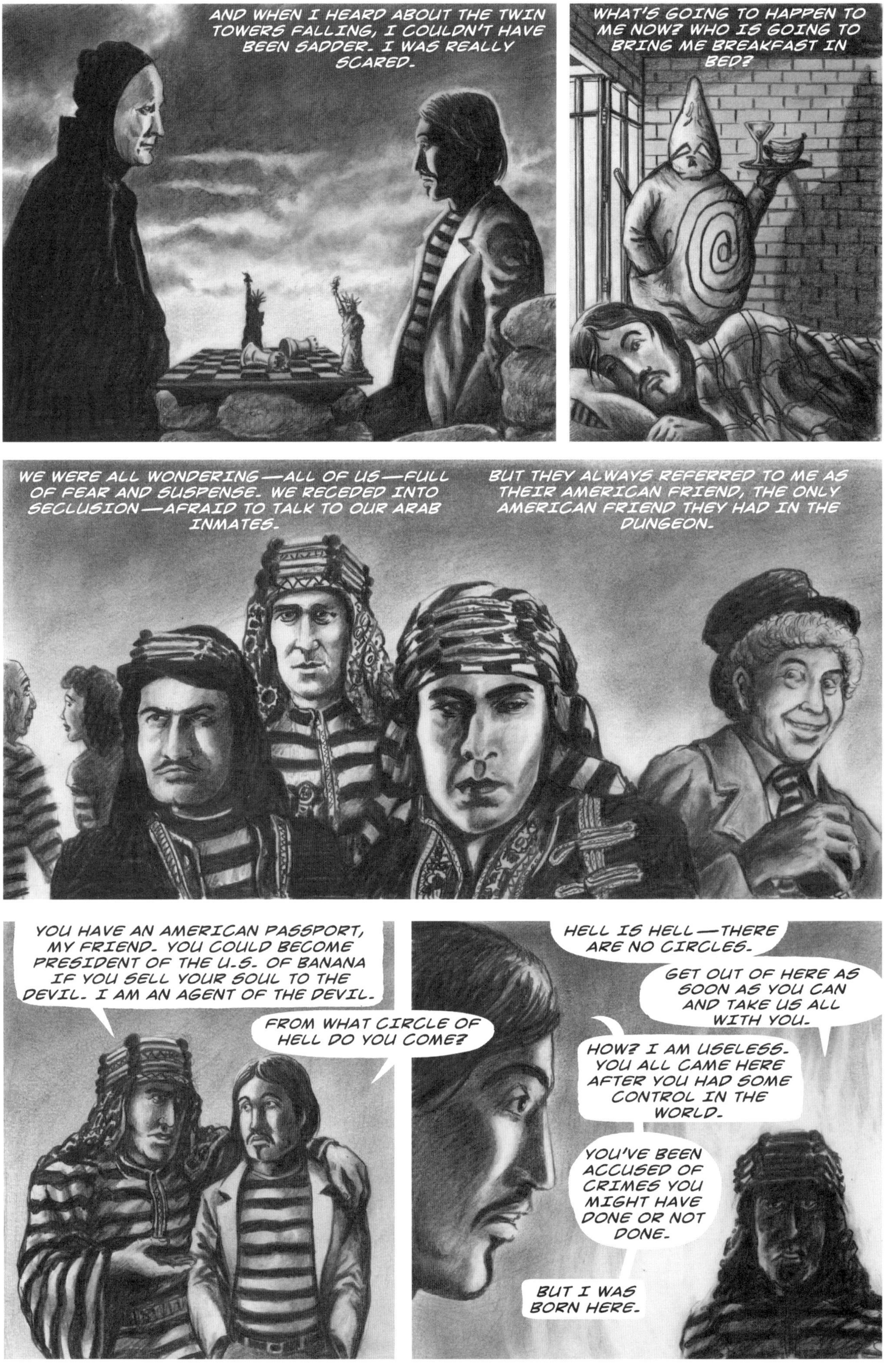
AND WHEN I HEARD ABOUT THE TWIN TOWERS FALLING, I COULDN'T HAVE BEEN SADDER. I WAS REALLY SCARED.
WHAT'S GOING TO HAPPEN TO ME NOW? WHO IS GOING TO BRING ME BREAKFAST IN BED?
WE WERE ALL WONDERING—ALL OF US—FULL OF FEAR AND SUSPENSE. WE RECEDED INTO SECLUSION—AFRAID TO TALK TO OUR ARAB INMATES.
BUT THEY ALWAYS REFERRED TO ME AS THEIR AMERICAN FRIEND, THE ONLY AMERICAN FRIEND THEY HAD IN THE DUNGEON.
YOU HAVE AN AMERICAN PASSPORT, MY FRIEND. YOU COULD BECOME PRESIDENT OF THE U.S. OF BANANA IF YOU SELL YOUR SOUL TO THE DEVIL. I AM AN AGENT OF THE DEVIL.
FROM WHAT CIRCLE OF HELL DO YOU COME?
HELL IS HELL—THERE ARE NO CIRCLES.
GET OUT OF HERE AS SOON AS YOU CAN AND TAKE US ALL WITH YOU.
HOW? I AM USELESS. YOU ALL CAME HERE AFTER YOU HAD SOME CONTROL IN THE WORLD.
YOU'VE BEEN ACCUSED OF CRIMES YOU MIGHT HAVE DONE OR NOT DONE.
BUT I WAS BORN HERE.

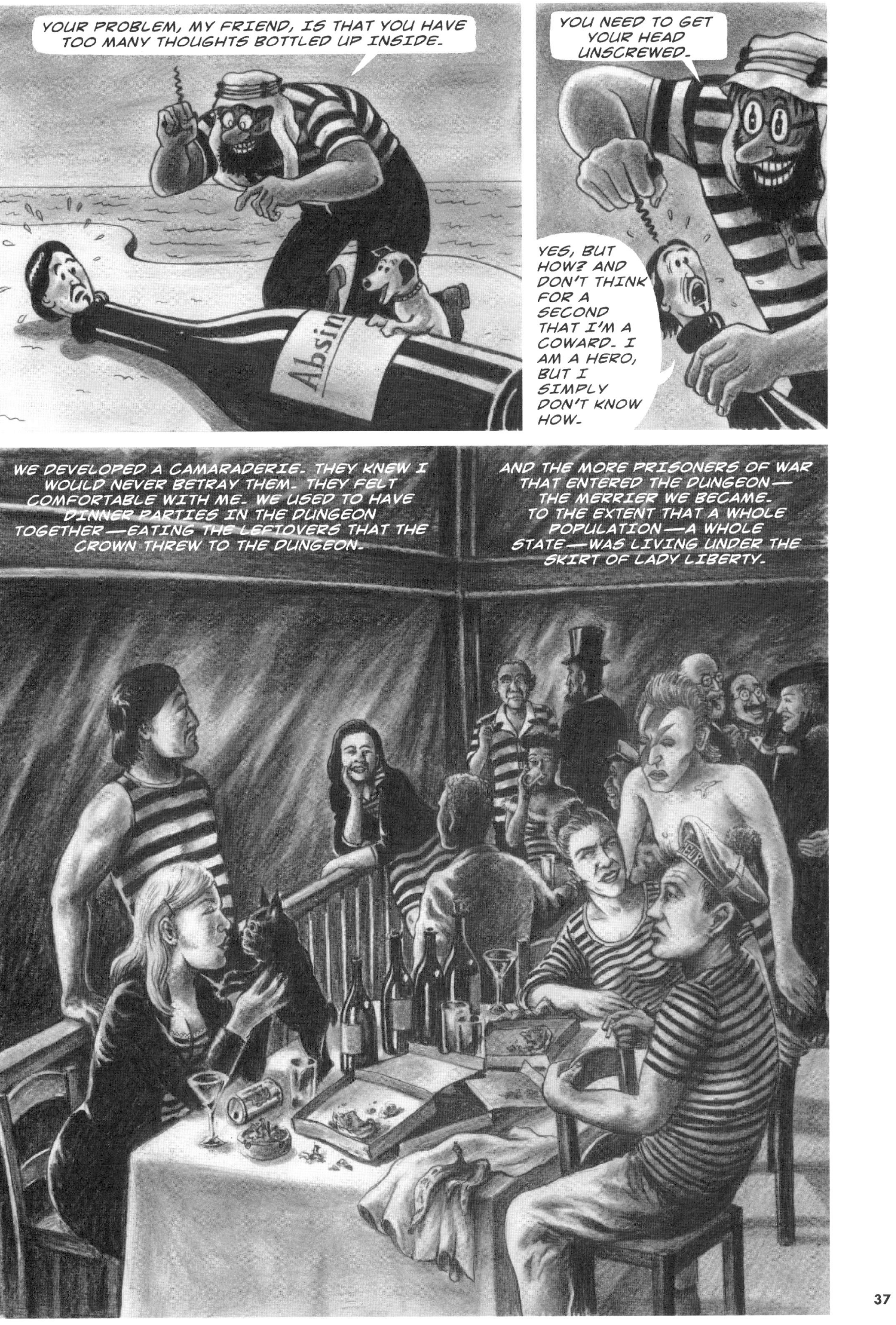
YOUR PROBLEM, MY FRIEND, IS THAT YOU HAVE TOO MANY THOUGHTS BOTTLED UP INSIDE.
YOU NEED TO GET YOUR HEAD UNSCREWED.
YES, BUT HOW? AND DON'T THINK FOR A SECOND THAT I'M A COWARD. I AM A HERO, BUT I SIMPLY DON'T KNOW HOW.
WE DEVELOPED A CAMARADERIE. THEY KNEW I WOULD NEVER BETRAY THEM. THEY FELT COMFORTABLE WITH ME. WE USED TO HAVE DINNER PARTIES IN THE DUNGEON TOGETHER—EATING THE LEFTOVERS THAT THE CROWN THREW TO THE DUNGEON.
AND THE MORE PRISONERS OF WAR THAT ENTERED THE DUNGEON—THE MERRIER WE BECAME. TO THE EXTENT THAT A WHOLE POPULATION—A WHOLE STATE—WAS LIVING UNDER THE SKIRT OF LADY LIBERTY.

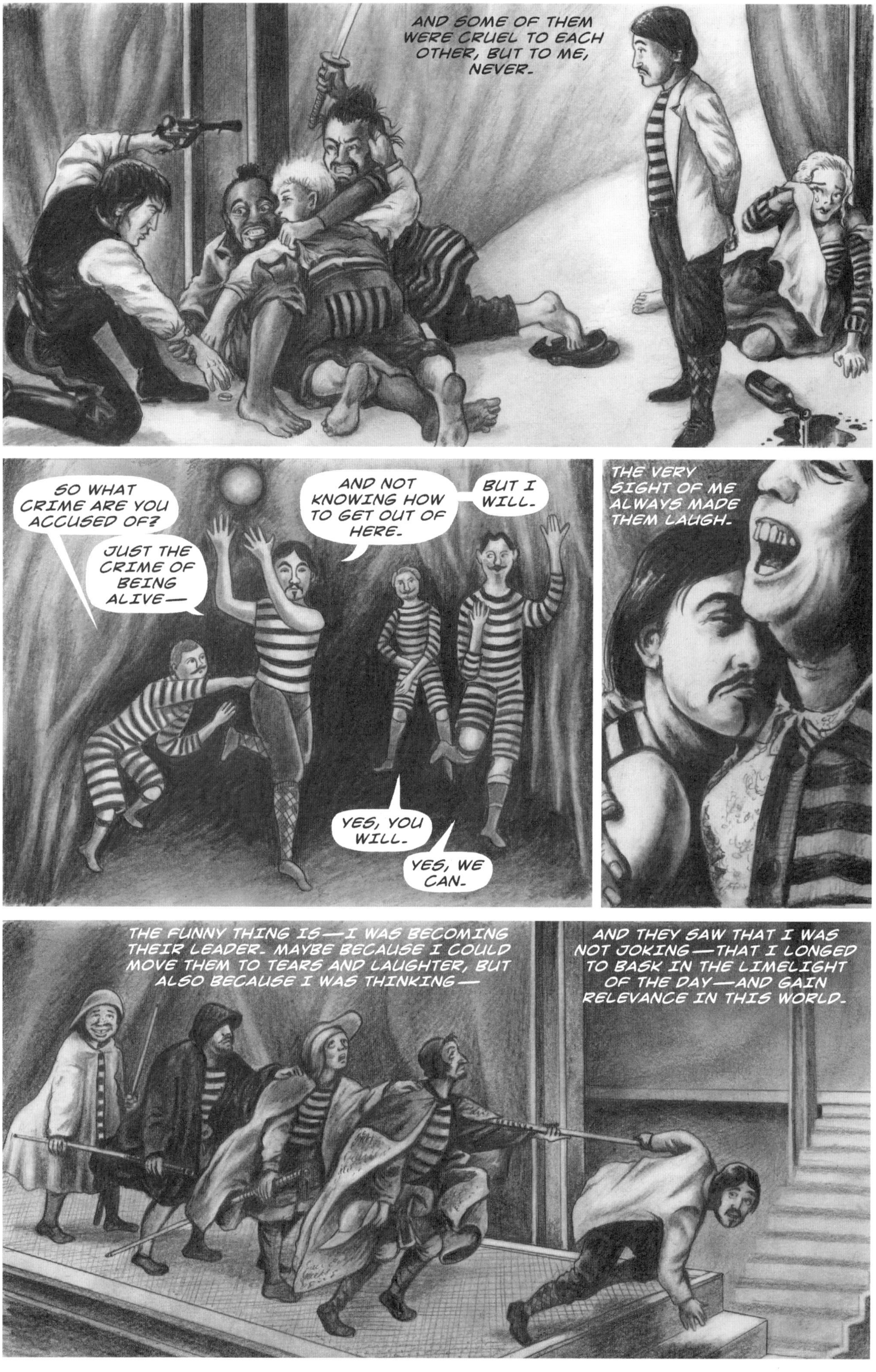
AND SOME OF THEM WERE CRUEL TO EACH OTHER, BUT TO ME, NEVER.
SO WHAT CRIME ARE YOU ACCUSED OF?
JUST THE CRIME OF BEING ALIVE—
AND NOT KNOWING HOW TO GET OUT OF HERE.
BUT I WILL.
YES, YOU WILL.
YES, WE CAN.
THE VERY SIGHT OF ME ALWAYS MADE THEM LAUGH.
THE FUNNY THING IS—I WAS BECOMING THEIR LEADER. MAYBE BECAUSE I COULD MOVE THEM TO TEARS AND LAUGHTER, BUT ALSO BECAUSE I WAS THINKING—
AND THEY SAW THAT I WAS NOT JOKING—THAT I LONGED TO BASK IN THE LIMELIGHT OF THE DAY—AND GAIN RELEVANCE IN THIS WORLD.

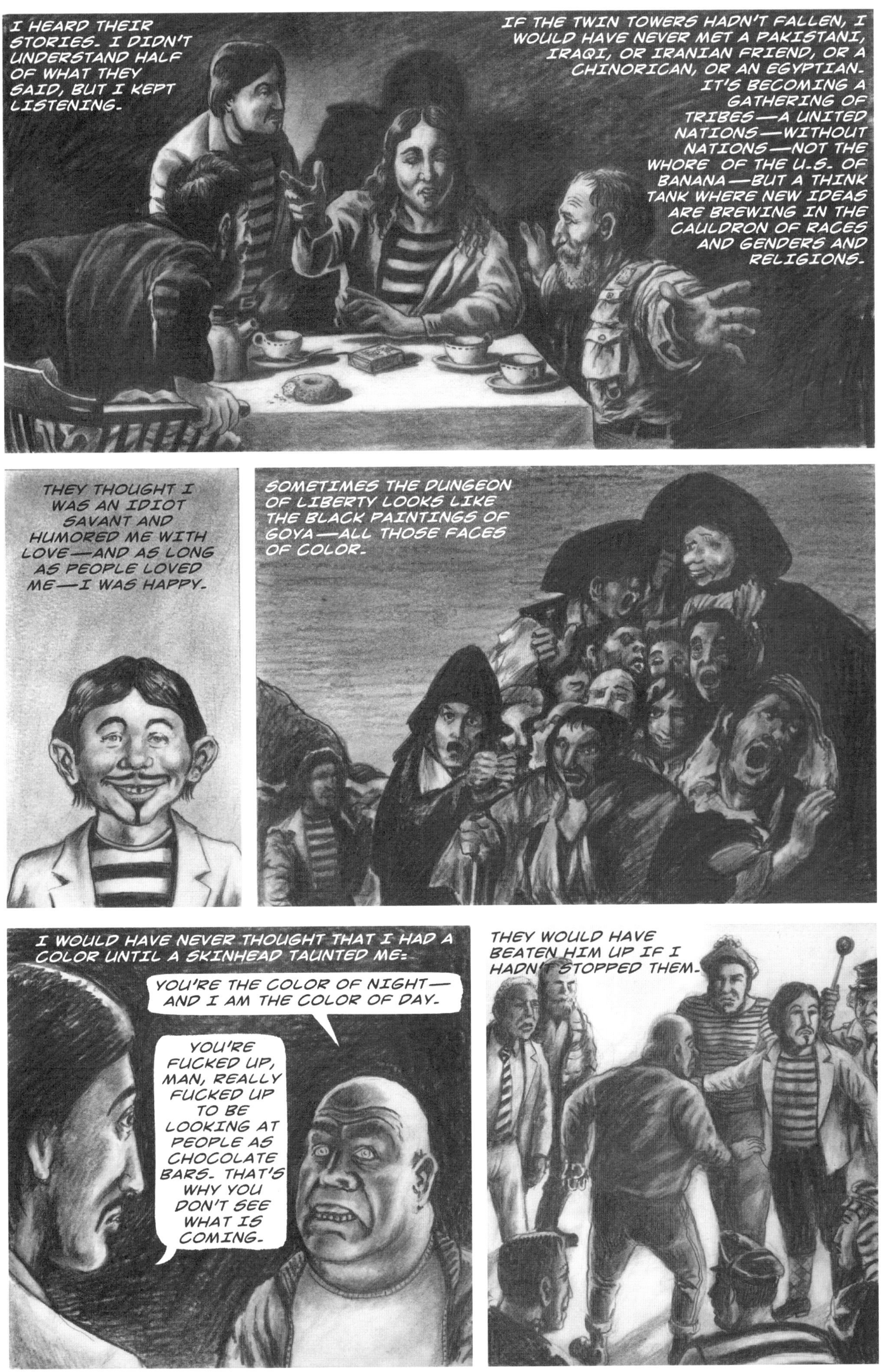

I HEARD THEIR STORIES. I DIDN'T UNDERSTAND HALF OF WHAT THEY SAID, BUT I KEPT LISTENING.
IF THE TWIN TOWERS HADN'T FALLEN, I WOULD HAVE NEVER MET A PAKISTANI, IRAQI, OR IRANIAN FRIEND, OR A CHINORICAN, OR AN EGYPTIAN. IT'S BECOMING A GATHERING OF TRIBES—A UNITED NATIONS—WITHOUT NATIONS—NOT THE WHORE OF THE U.S. OF BANANA—BUT A THINK TANK WHERE NEW IDEAS ARE BREWING IN THE CAULDRON OF RACES AND GENDERS AND RELIGIONS.
THEY THOUGHT I WAS AN IDIOT SAVANT AND HUMORED ME WITH LOVE—AND AS LONG AS PEOPLE LOVED ME—I WAS HAPPY.
SOMETIMES THE DUNGEON OF LIBERTY LOOKS LIKE THE BLACK PAINTINGS OF GOYA—ALL THOSE FACES OF COLOR.
I WOULD HAVE NEVER THOUGHT THAT I HAD A COLOR UNTIL A SKINHEAD TAUNTED ME:
YOU'RE THE COLOR OF NIGHT—AND I AM THE COLOR OF DAY.
YOU'RE FUCKED UP, MAN, REALLY FUCKED UP TO BE LOOKING AT PEOPLE AS CHOCOLATE BARS. THAT'S WHY YOU DON'T SEE WHAT IS COMING.
THEY WOULD HAVE BEATEN HIM UP IF I HADN'T STOPPED THEM.

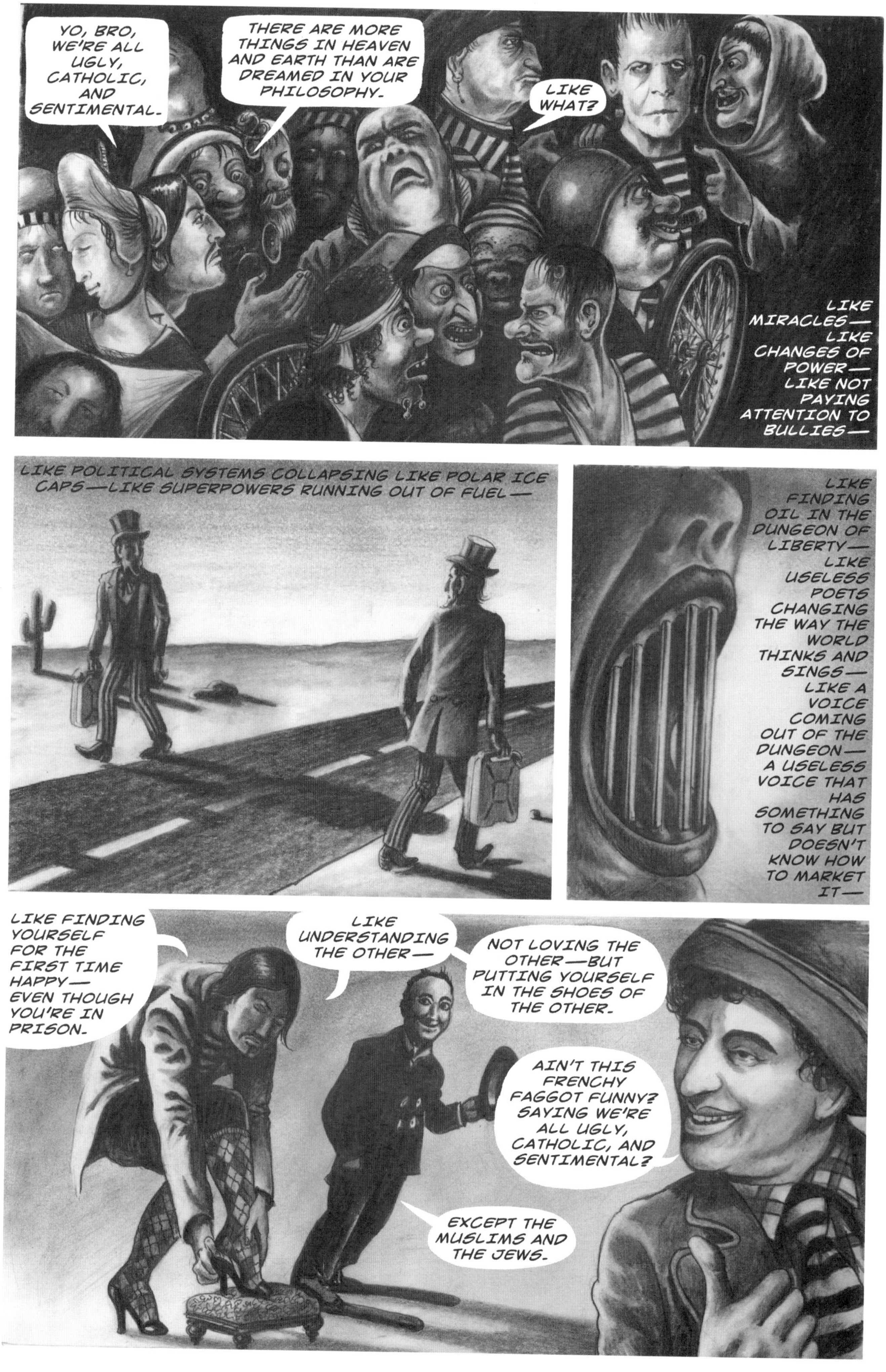
YO, BRO, WE'RE ALL UGLY, CATHOLIC, AND SENTIMENTAL.
THERE ARE MORE THINGS IN HEAVEN AND EARTH THAN ARE DREAMED IN YOUR PHILOSOPHY.
LIKE WHAT?
LIKE MIRACLES—LIKE CHANGES OF POWER—LIKE NOT PAYING ATTENTION TO BULLIES—
LIKE POLITICAL SYSTEMS COLLAPSING LIKE POLAR ICE CAPS—LIKE SUPERPOWERS RUNNING OUT OF FUEL—
LIKE FINDING OIL IN THE DUNGEON OF LIBERTY—LIKE USELESS POETS CHANGING THE WAY THE WORLD THINKS AND SINGS—LIKE A VOICE COMING OUT OF THE DUNGEON—A USELESS VOICE THAT HAS SOMETHING TO SAY BUT DOESN'T KNOW HOW TO MARKET IT—
LIKE FINDING YOURSELF FOR THE FIRST TIME HAPPY—EVEN THOUGH YOU'RE IN PRISON.
LIKE UNDERSTANDING THE OTHER—
NOT LOVING THE OTHER—BUT PUTTING YOURSELF IN THE SHOES OF THE OTHER.
AIN'T THIS FRENCHY FAGGOT FUNNY? SAYING WE'RE ALL UGLY, CATHOLIC, AND SENTIMENTAL?
EXCEPT THE MUSLIMS AND THE JEWS.

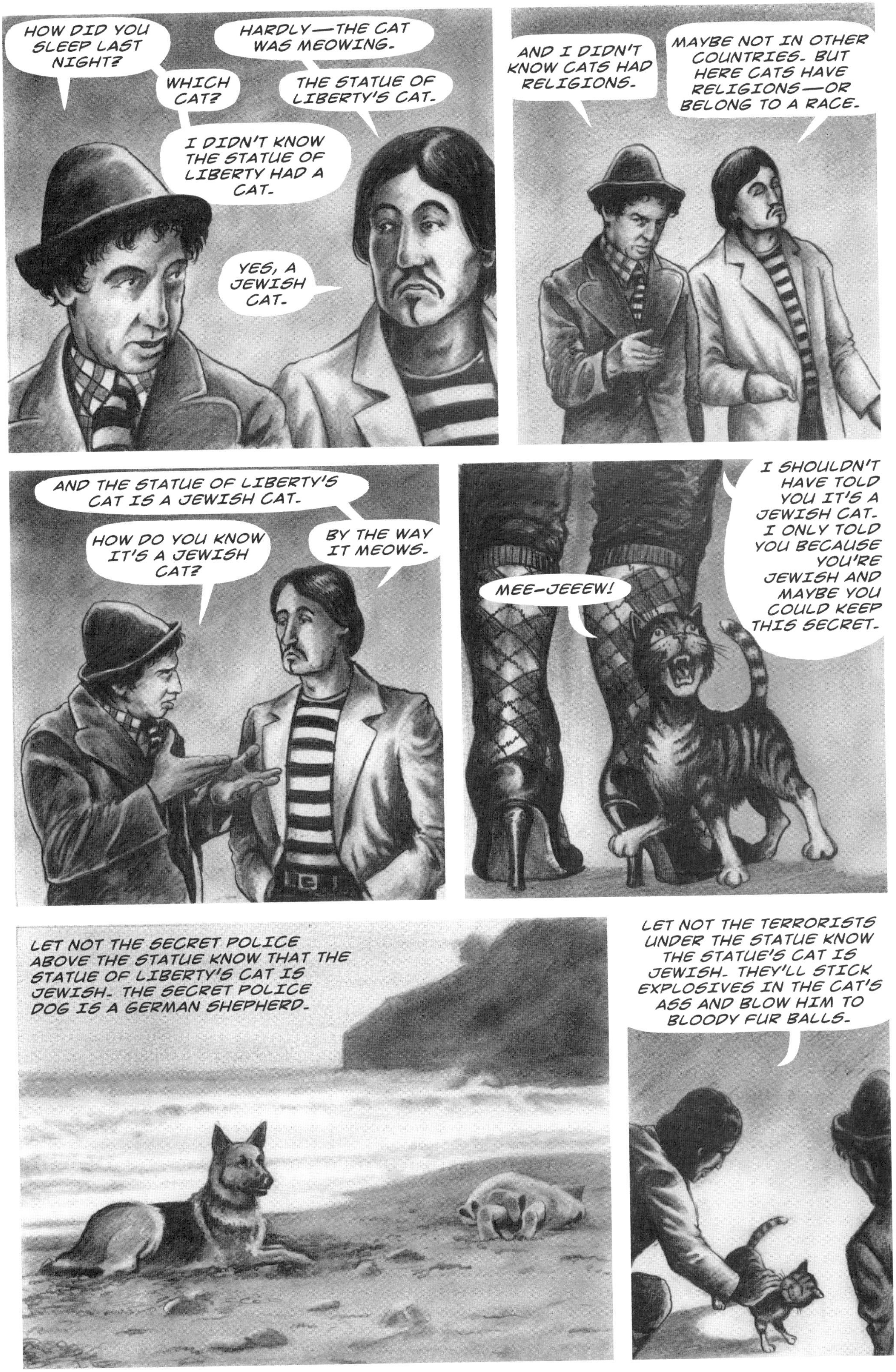

HOW DID YOU SLEEP LAST NIGHT?
HARDLY—THE CAT WAS MEOWING.
WHICH CAT?
THE STATUE OF LIBERTY'S CAT.
I DIDN'T KNOW THE STATUE OF LIBERTY HAD A CAT.
YES, A JEWISH CAT.
AND I DIDN'T KNOW CATS HAD RELIGIONS.
MAYBE NOT IN OTHER COUNTRIES. BUT HERE CATS HAVE RELIGIONS—OR BELONG TO A RACE.
AND THE STATUE OF LIBERTY'S CAT IS A JEWISH CAT.
HOW DO YOU KNOW IT'S A JEWISH CAT?
BY THE WAY IT MEOWS.
MEE-JEEEW!
I SHOULDN'T HAVE TOLD YOU IT'S A JEWISH CAT. I ONLY TOLD YOU BECAUSE YOU'RE JEWISH AND MAYBE YOU COULD KEEP THIS SECRET.
LET NOT THE SECRET POLICE ABOVE THE STATUE KNOW THAT THE STATUE OF LIBERTY'S CAT IS JEWISH. THE SECRET POLICE DOG IS A GERMAN SHEPHERD.
LET NOT THE TERRORISTS UNDER THE STATUE KNOW THE STATUE'S CAT IS JEWISH. THEY'LL STICK EXPLOSIVES IN THE CAT'S ASS AND BLOW HIM TO BLOODY FUR BALLS.

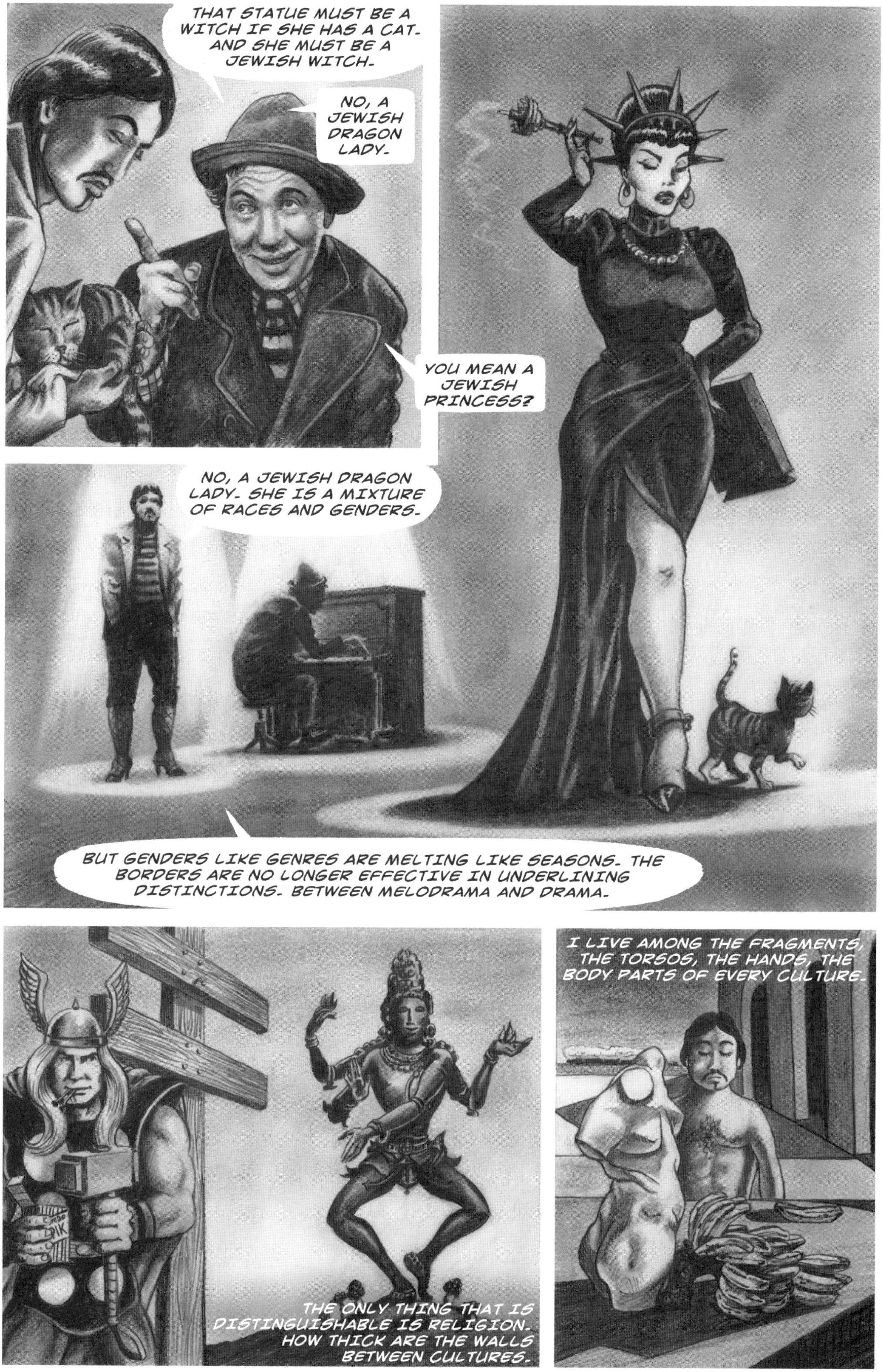
THAT STATUE MUST BE A WITCH IF SHE HAS A CAT. AND SHE MUST BE A JEWISH WITCH.
NO, A JEWISH DRAGON LADY.
YOU MEAN A JEWISH PRINCESS?
NO, A JEWISH DRAGON LADY. SHE IS A MIXTURE OF RACES AND GENDERS.
BUT GENDERS LIKE GENRES ARE MELTING LIKE SEASONS. THE BORDERS ARE NO LONGER EFFECTIVE IN UNDERLINING DISTINCTIONS. BETWEEN MELODRAMA AND DRAMA.
THE ONLY THING THAT IS DISTINGUISHABLE IS RELIGION. HOW THICK ARE THE WALLS BETWEEN CULTURES.
I LIVE AMONG THE FRAGMENTS, THE TORSOS, THE HANDS, THE BODY PARTS OF EVERY CULTURE.

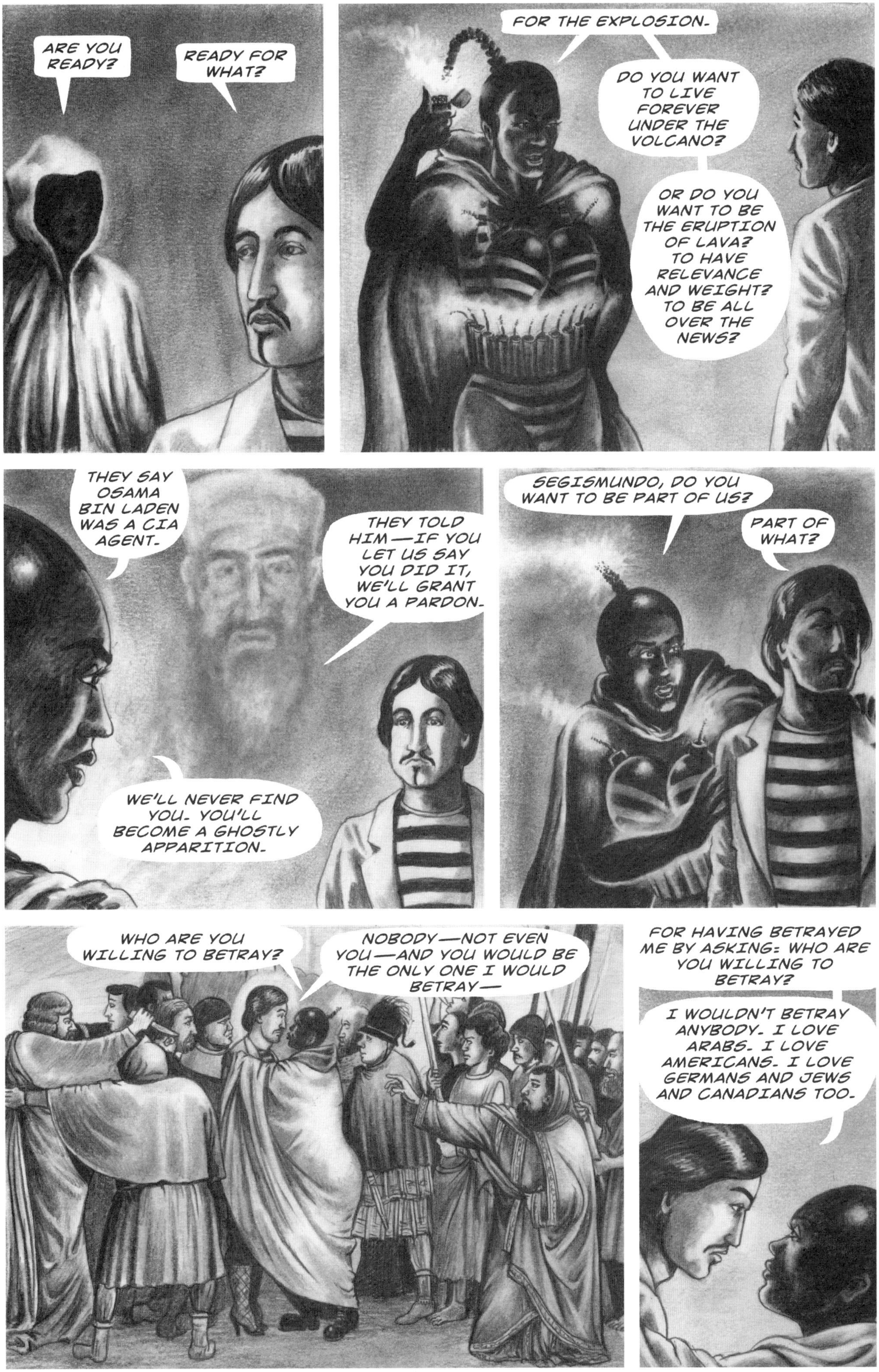
ARE YOU READY?
READY FOR WHAT?
FOR THE EXPLOSION.
DO YOU WANT TO LIVE FOREVER UNDER THE VOLCANO?
OR DO YOU WANT TO BE THE ERUPTION OF LAVA? TO HAVE RELEVANCE AND WEIGHT? TO BE ALL OVER THE NEWS?
THEY SAY OSAMA BIN LADEN WAS A CIA AGENT.
THEY TOLD HIM—IF YOU LET US SAY YOU DID IT, WE'LL GRANT YOU A PARDON.
WE'LL NEVER FIND YOU. YOU'LL BECOME A GHOSTLY APPARITION.
SEGISMUNDO, DO YOU WANT TO BE PART OF US?
PART OF WHAT?
WHO ARE YOU WILLING TO BETRAY?
NOBODY—NOT EVEN YOU—AND YOU WOULD BE THE ONLY ONE I WOULD BETRAY—
FOR HAVING BETRAYED ME BY ASKING: WHO ARE YOU WILLING TO BETRAY?
I WOULDN'T BETRAY ANYBODY. I LOVE ARABS. I LOVE AMERICANS. I LOVE GERMANS AND JEWS AND CANADIANS TOO.

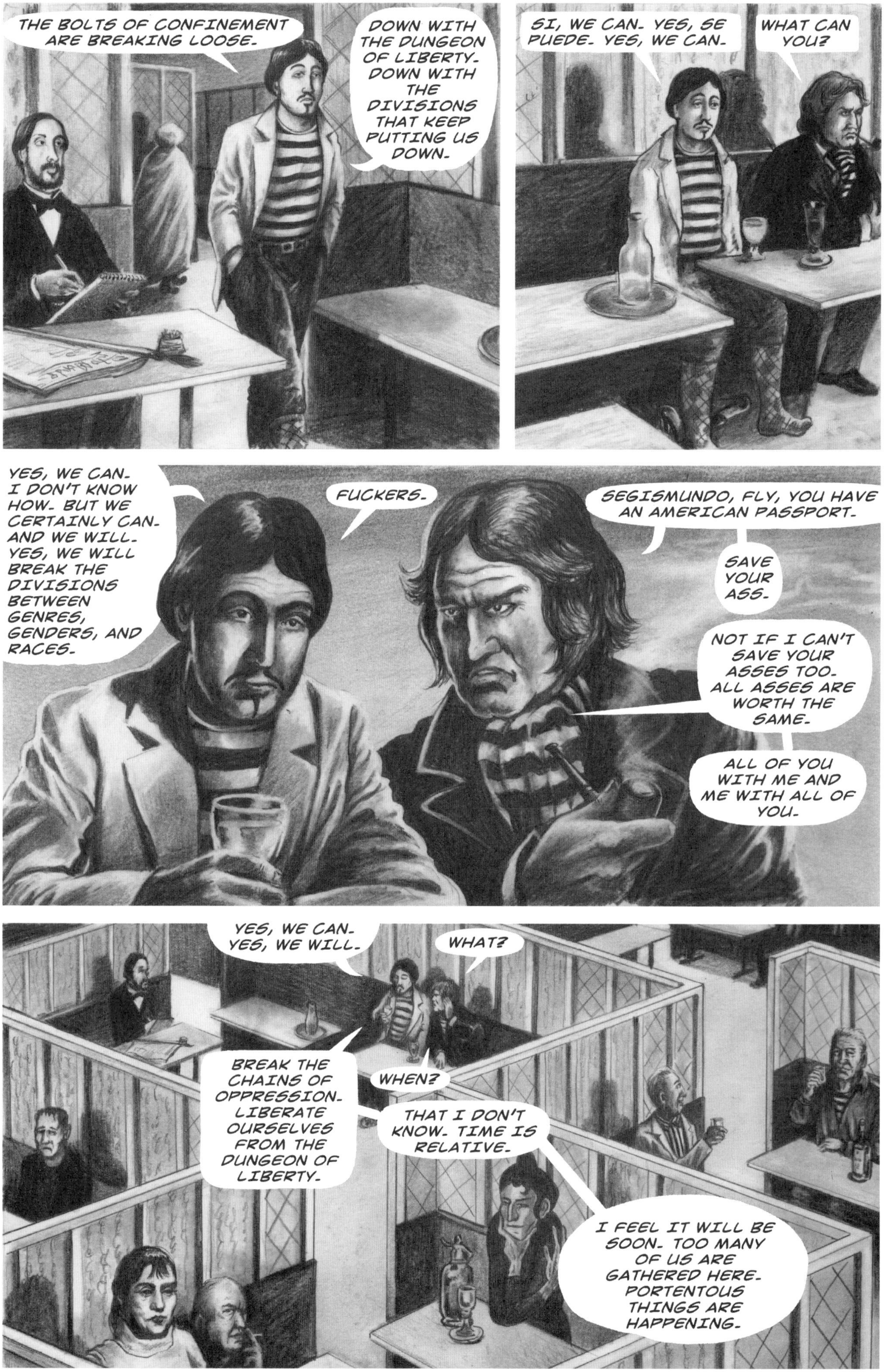
THE BOLTS OF CONFINEMENT ARE BREAKING LOOSE.
DOWN WITH THE DUNGEON OF LIBERTY. DOWN WITH THE DIVISIONS THAT KEEP PUTTING US DOWN.
SI, WE CAN. YES, SE PUEDE. YES, WE CAN.
WHAT CAN YOU?
YES, WE CAN. I DON'T KNOW HOW. BUT WE CERTAINLY CAN. AND WE WILL. YES, WE WILL BREAK THE DIVISIONS BETWEEN GENRES, GENDERS, AND RACES.
FUCKERS.
SEGISMUNDO, FLY, YOU HAVE AN AMERICAN PASSPORT.
SAVE YOUR ASS.
NOT IF I CAN'T SAVE YOUR ASSES TOO. ALL ASSES ARE WORTH THE SAME.
ALL OF YOU WITH ME AND ME WITH ALL OF YOU.
YES, WE CAN. YES, WE WILL.
WHAT?
BREAK THE CHAINS OF OPPRESSION. LIBERATE OURSELVES FROM THE DUNGEON OF LIBERTY.
WHEN?
THAT I DON'T KNOW. TIME IS RELATIVE.
I FEEL IT WILL BE SOON. TOO MANY OF US ARE GATHERED HERE. PORTENTOUS THINGS ARE HAPPENING.

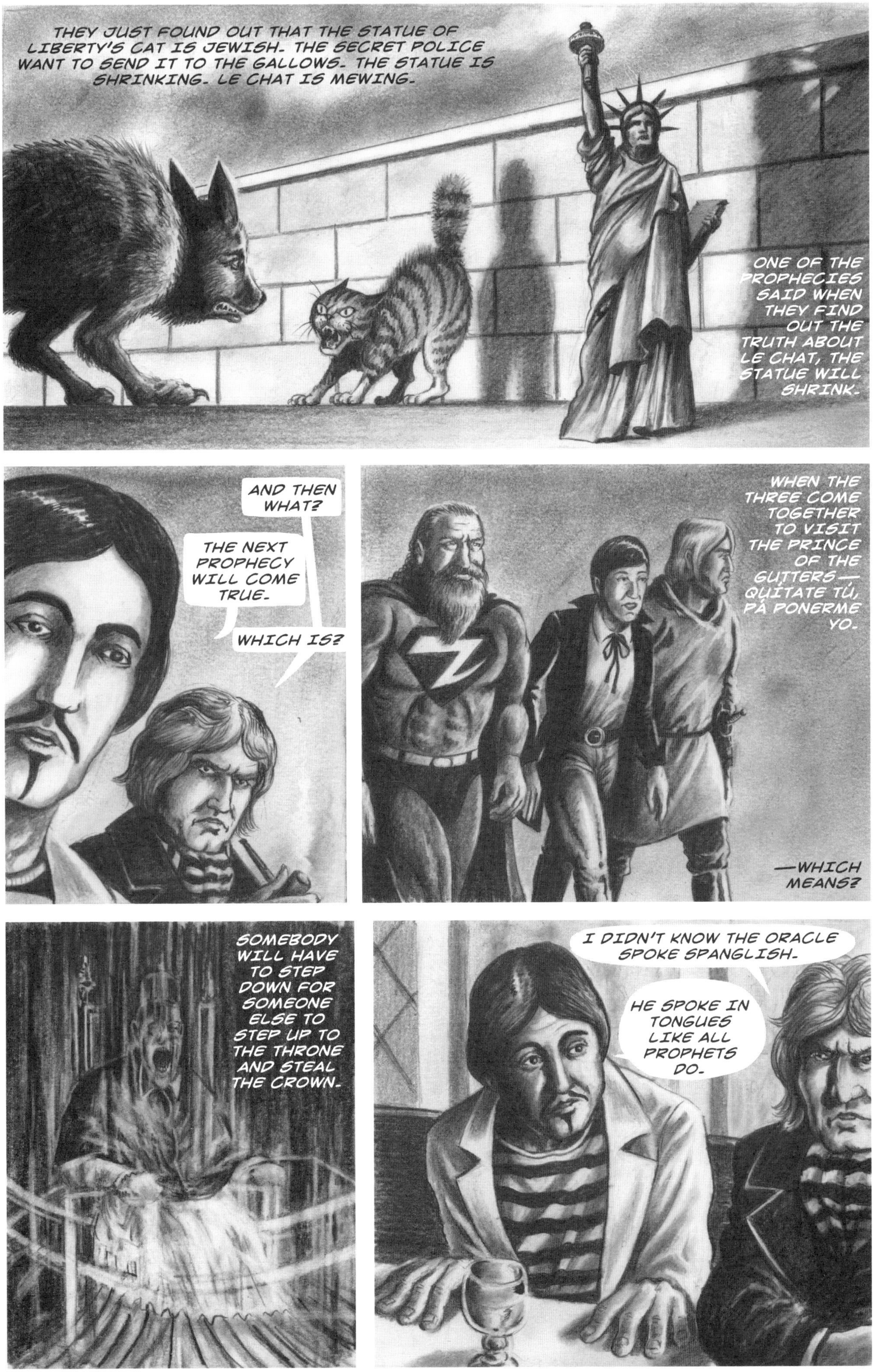
THEY JUST FOUND OUT THAT THE STATUE OF LIBERTY'S CAT IS JEWISH. THE SECRET POLICE WANT TO SEND IT TO THE GALLOWS. THE STATUE IS SHRINKING. LE CHAT IS MEWING.
ONE OF THE PROPHECIES SAID WHEN THEY FIND OUT THE TRUTH ABOUT LE CHAT, THE STATUE WILL SHRINK.
AND THEN WHAT?
THE NEXT PROPHECY WILL COME TRUE.
WHICH IS?
WHEN THE THREE COME TOGETHER TO VISIT THE PRINCE OF THE GUTTERS— QUÍTATE TÚ, PÁ PONERME YO.
—WHICH MEANS?
SOMEBODY WILL HAVE TO STEP DOWN FOR SOMEONE ELSE TO STEP UP TO THE THRONE AND STEAL THE CROWN.
I DIDN'T KNOW THE ORACLE SPOKE SPANGLISH.
HE SPOKE IN TONGUES LIKE ALL PROPHETS DO.

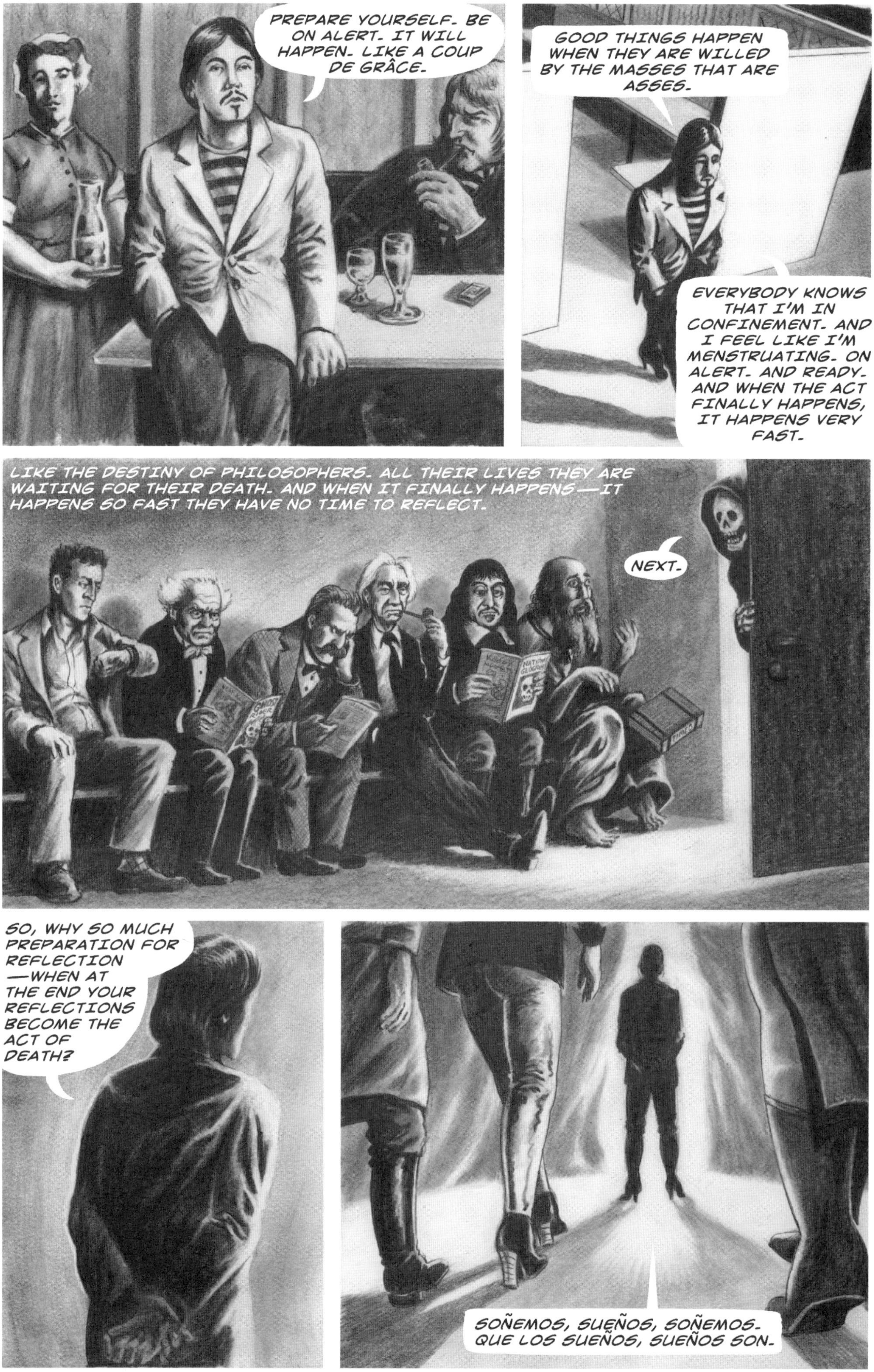
PREPARE YOURSELF. BE ON ALERT. IT WILL HAPPEN. LIKE A COUP DE GRÂCE.
GOOD THINGS HAPPEN WHEN THEY ARE WILLED BY THE MASSES THAT ARE ASSES.
EVERYBODY KNOWS THAT I'M IN CONFINEMENT. AND I FEEL LIKE I'M MENSTRUATING. ON ALERT. AND READY. AND WHEN THE ACT FINALLY HAPPENS, IT HAPPENS VERY FAST.
LIKE THE DESTINY OF PHILOSOPHERS. ALL THEIR LIVES THEY ARE WAITING FOR THEIR DEATH. AND WHEN IT FINALLY HAPPENS—IT HAPPENS SO FAST THEY HAVE NO TIME TO REFLECT.
NEXT.
SO, WHY SO MUCH PREPARATION FOR REFLECTION —WHEN AT THE END YOUR REFLECTIONS BECOME THE ACT OF DEATH?
SOÑEMOS, SUEÑOS, SOÑEMOS. QUE LOS SUEÑOS, SUEÑOS SON.

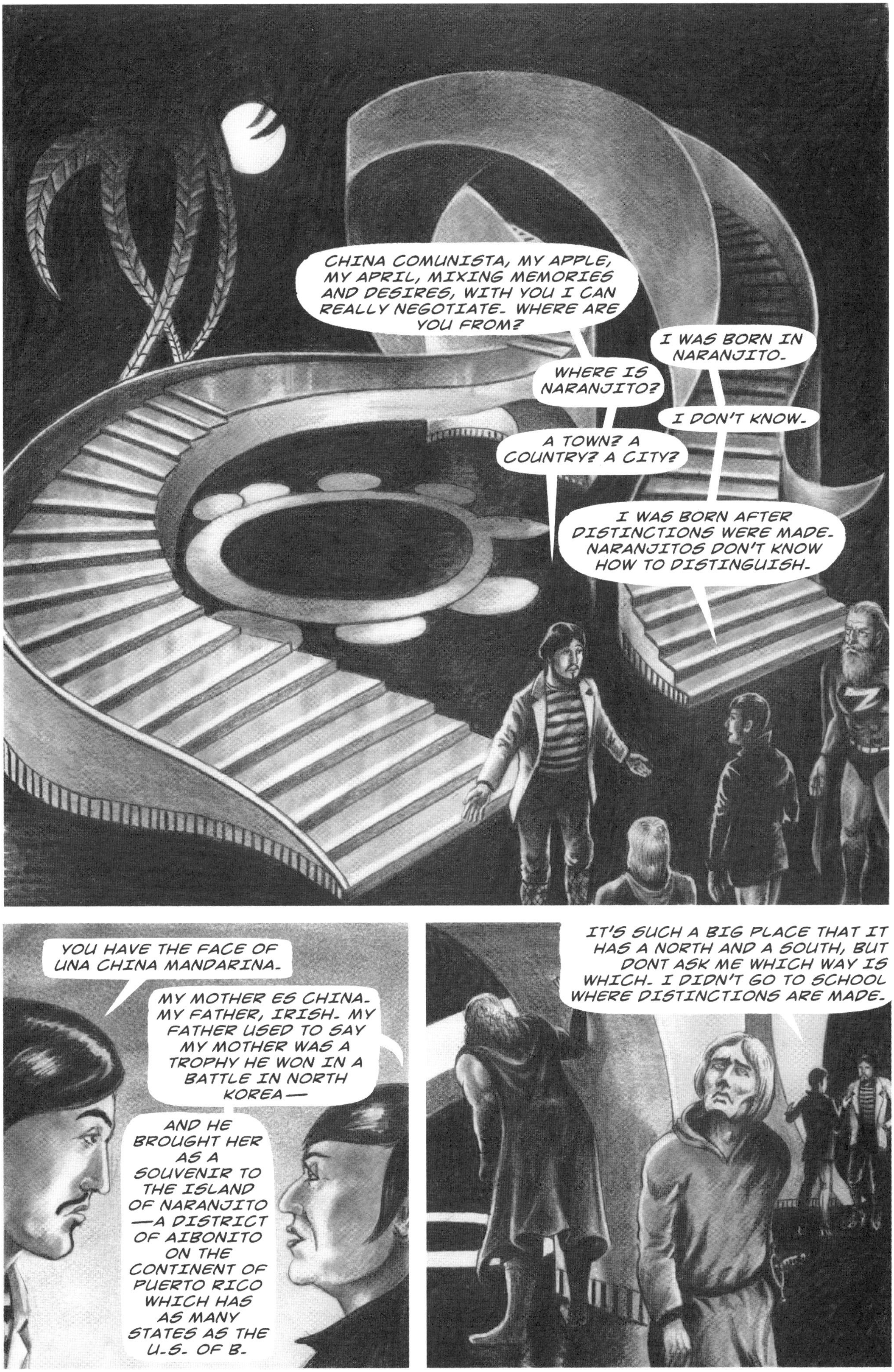
CHINA COMUNISTA, MY APPLE, MY APRIL, MIXING MEMORIES AND DESIRES, WITH YOU I CAN REALLY NEGOTIATE. WHERE ARE YOU FROM?
I WAS BORN IN NARANJITO.
WHERE IS NARANJITO?
I DON'T KNOW.
A TOWN? A COUNTRY? A CITY?
I WAS BORN AFTER DISTINCTIONS WERE MADE. NARANJITOS DON'T KNOW HOW TO DISTINGUISH.
YOU HAVE THE FACE OF UNA CHINA MANDARINA.
MY MOTHER ES CHINA. MY FATHER, IRISH. MY FATHER USED TO SAY MY MOTHER WAS A TROPHY HE WON IN A BATTLE IN NORTH KOREA—
AND HE BROUGHT HER AS A SOUVENIR TO THE ISLAND OF NARANJITO —A DISTRICT OF AIBONITO ON THE CONTINENT OF PUERTO RICO WHICH HAS AS MANY STATES AS THE U.S. OF B.
IT'S SUCH A BIG PLACE THAT IT HAS A NORTH AND A SOUTH, BUT DONT ASK ME WHICH WAY IS WHICH. I DIDN'T GO TO SCHOOL WHERE DISTINCTIONS ARE MADE.

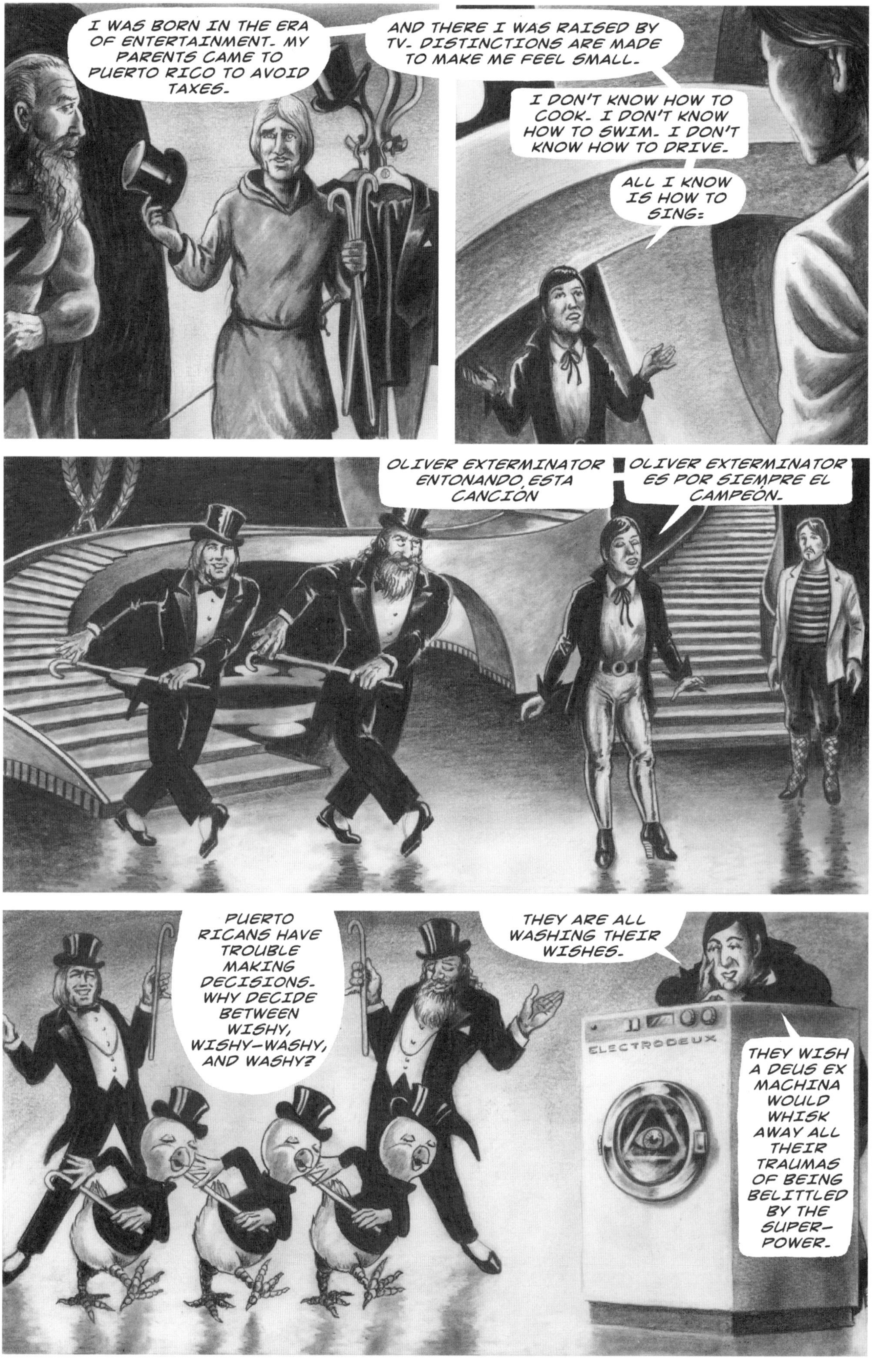

I WAS BORN IN THE ERA OF ENTERTAINMENT. MY PARENTS CAME TO PUERTO RICO TO AVOID TAXES.
AND THERE I WAS RAISED BY TV. DISTINCTIONS ARE MADE TO MAKE ME FEEL SMALL.
I DON'T KNOW HOW TO COOK. I DON'T KNOW HOW TO SWIM. I DON'T KNOW HOW TO DRIVE.
ALL I KNOW IS HOW TO SING:
OLIVER EXTERMINATOR ENTONANDO, ESTA CANCIÓN
OLIVER EXTERMINATOR ES POR SIEMPRE EL CAMPEÓN.
PUERTO RICANS HAVE TROUBLE MAKING DECISIONS. WHY DECIDE BETWEEN WISHY, WISHY-WASHY, AND WASHY?
THEY ARE ALL WASHING THEIR WISHES.
ELECTRODEUX
THEY WISH A DEUS EX MACHINA WOULD WHISK AWAY ALL THEIR TRAUMAS OF BEING BELITTLED BY THE SUPER-POWER.

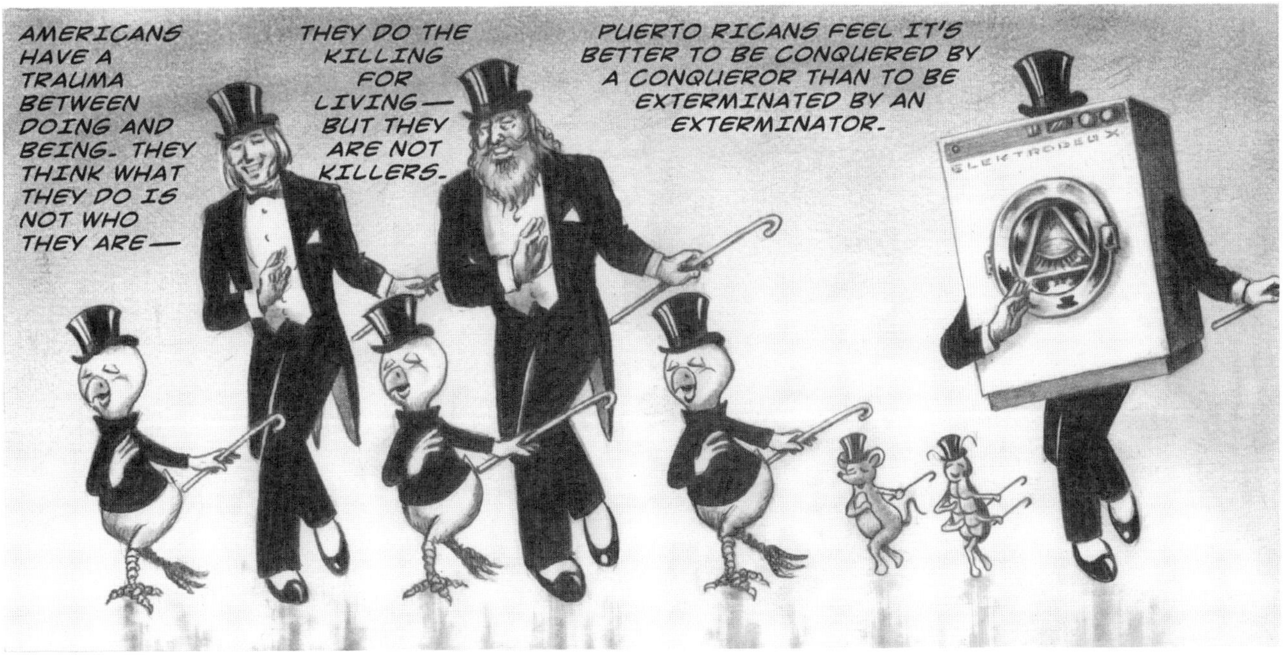
AMERICANS HAVE A TRAUMA BETWEEN DOING AND BEING. THEY THINK WHAT THEY DO IS NOT WHO THEY ARE—
THEY DO THE KILLING FOR LIVING—BUT THEY ARE NOT KILLERS.
PUERTO RICANS FEEL IT'S BETTER TO BE CONQUERED BY A CONQUEROR THAN TO BE EXTERMINATED BY AN EXTERMINATOR.
ELEKTRODEUX

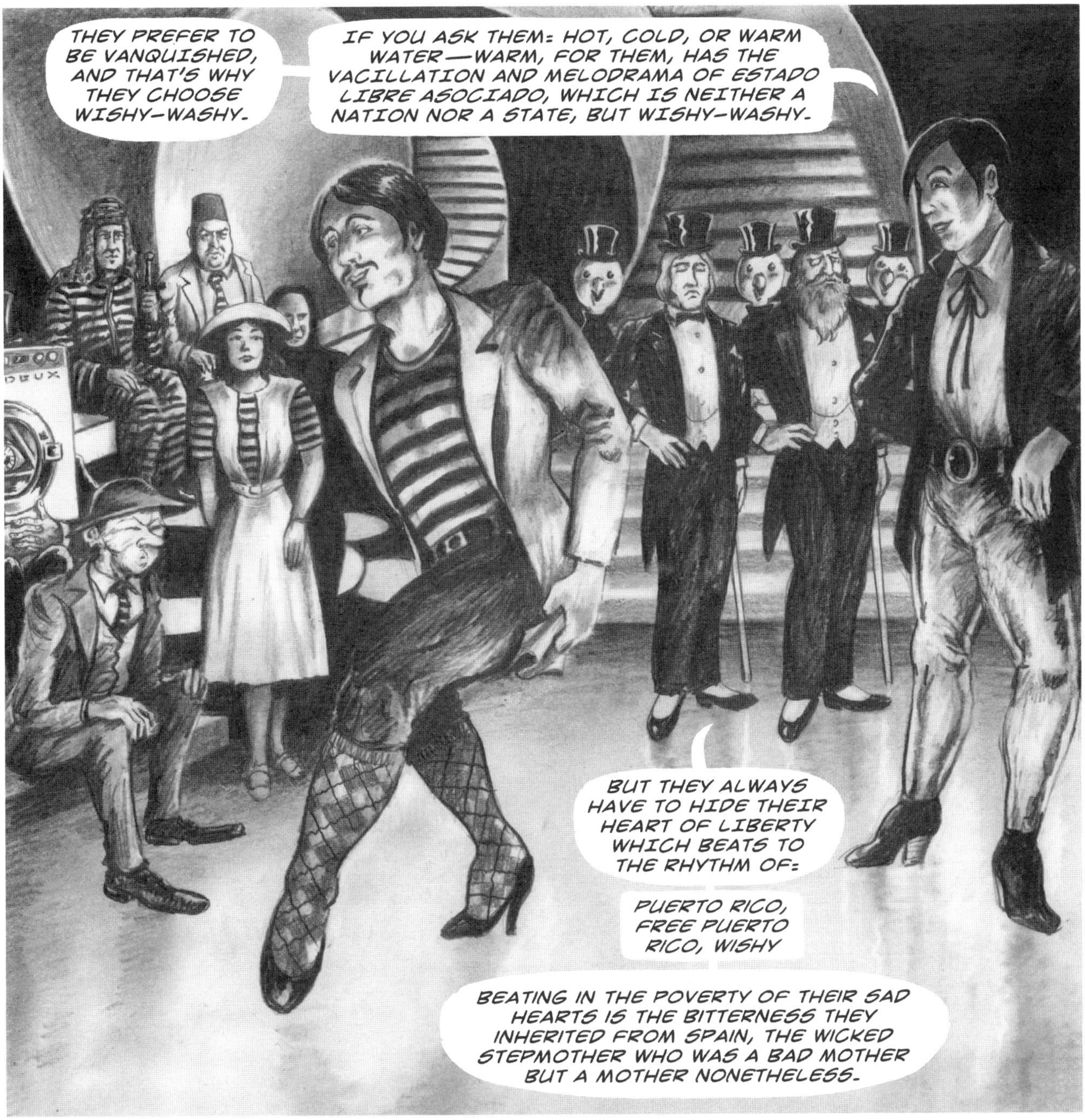
THEY PREFER TO BE VANQUISHED, AND THAT'S WHY THEY CHOOSE WISHY-WASHY.
IF YOU ASK THEM: HOT, COLD, OR WARM WATER—WARM, FOR THEM, HAS THE VACILLATION AND MELODRAMA OF ESTADO LIBRE ASOCIADO, WHICH IS NEITHER A NATION NOR A STATE, BUT WISHY-WASHY.
BUT THEY ALWAYS HAVE TO HIDE THEIR HEART OF LIBERTY WHICH BEATS TO THE RHYTHM OF:
PUERTO RICO, FREE PUERTO RICO, WISHY
BEATING IN THE POVERTY OF THEIR SAD HEARTS IS THE BITTERNESS THEY INHERITED FROM SPAIN, THE WICKED STEPMOTHER WHO WAS A BAD MOTHER BUT A MOTHER NONETHELESS.

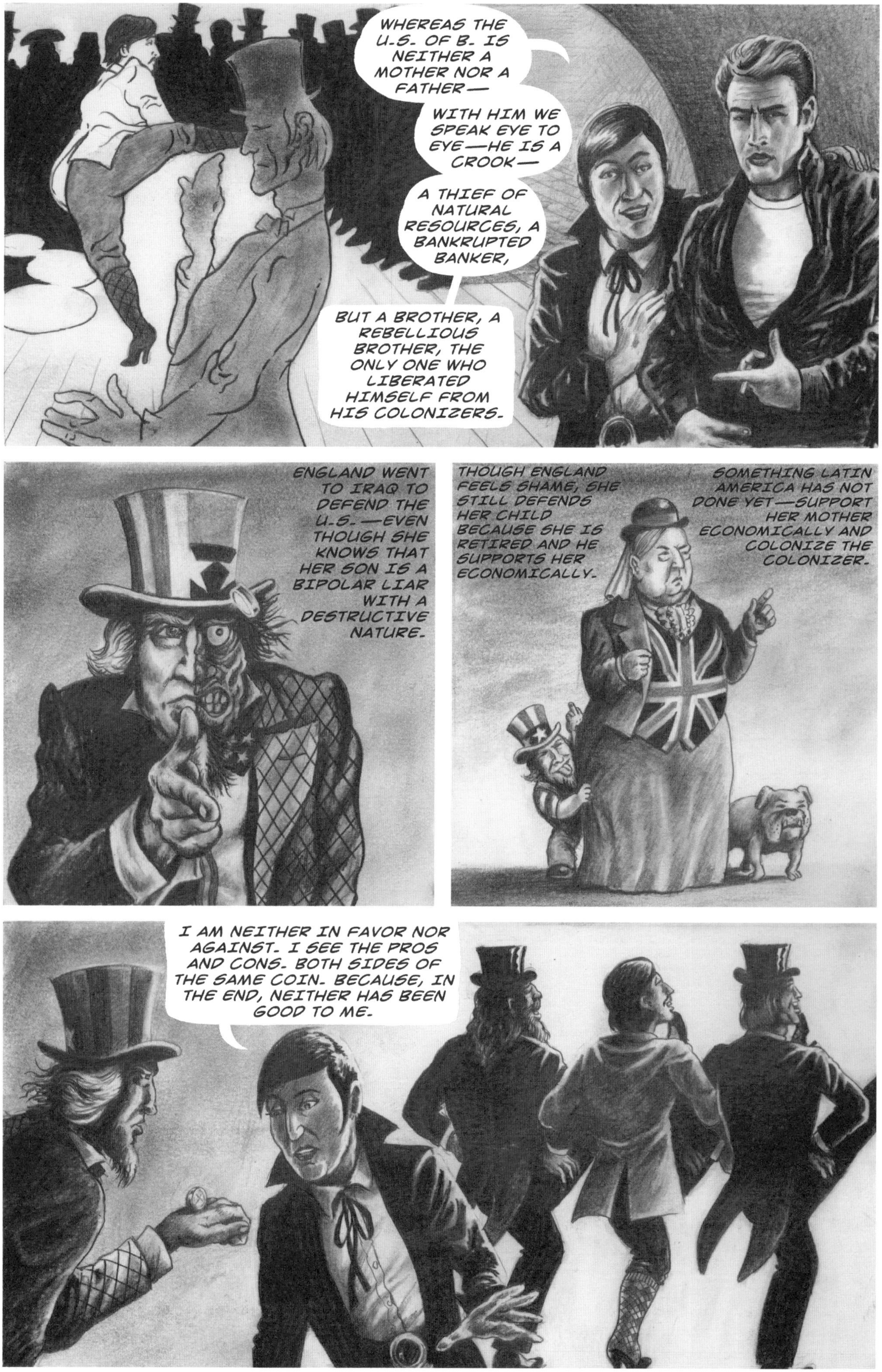
WHEREAS THE U.S. OF B. IS NEITHER A MOTHER NOR A FATHER—
WITH HIM WE SPEAK EYE TO EYE—HE IS A CROOK—
A THIEF OF NATURAL RESOURCES, A BANKRUPTED BANKER,
BUT A BROTHER, A REBELLIOUS BROTHER, THE ONLY ONE WHO LIBERATED HIMSELF FROM HIS COLONIZERS.
ENGLAND WENT TO IRAQ TO DEFEND THE U.S.—EVEN THOUGH SHE KNOWS THAT HER SON IS A BIPOLAR LIAR WITH A DESTRUCTIVE NATURE.
THOUGH ENGLAND FEELS SHAME, SHE STILL DEFENDS HER CHILD BECAUSE SHE IS RETIRED AND HE SUPPORTS HER ECONOMICALLY.
SOMETHING LATIN AMERICA HAS NOT DONE YET—SUPPORT HER MOTHER ECONOMICALLY AND COLONIZE THE COLONIZER.
I AM NEITHER IN FAVOR NOR AGAINST. I SEE THE PROS AND CONS. BOTH SIDES OF THE SAME COIN. BECAUSE, IN THE END, NEITHER HAS BEEN GOOD TO ME.

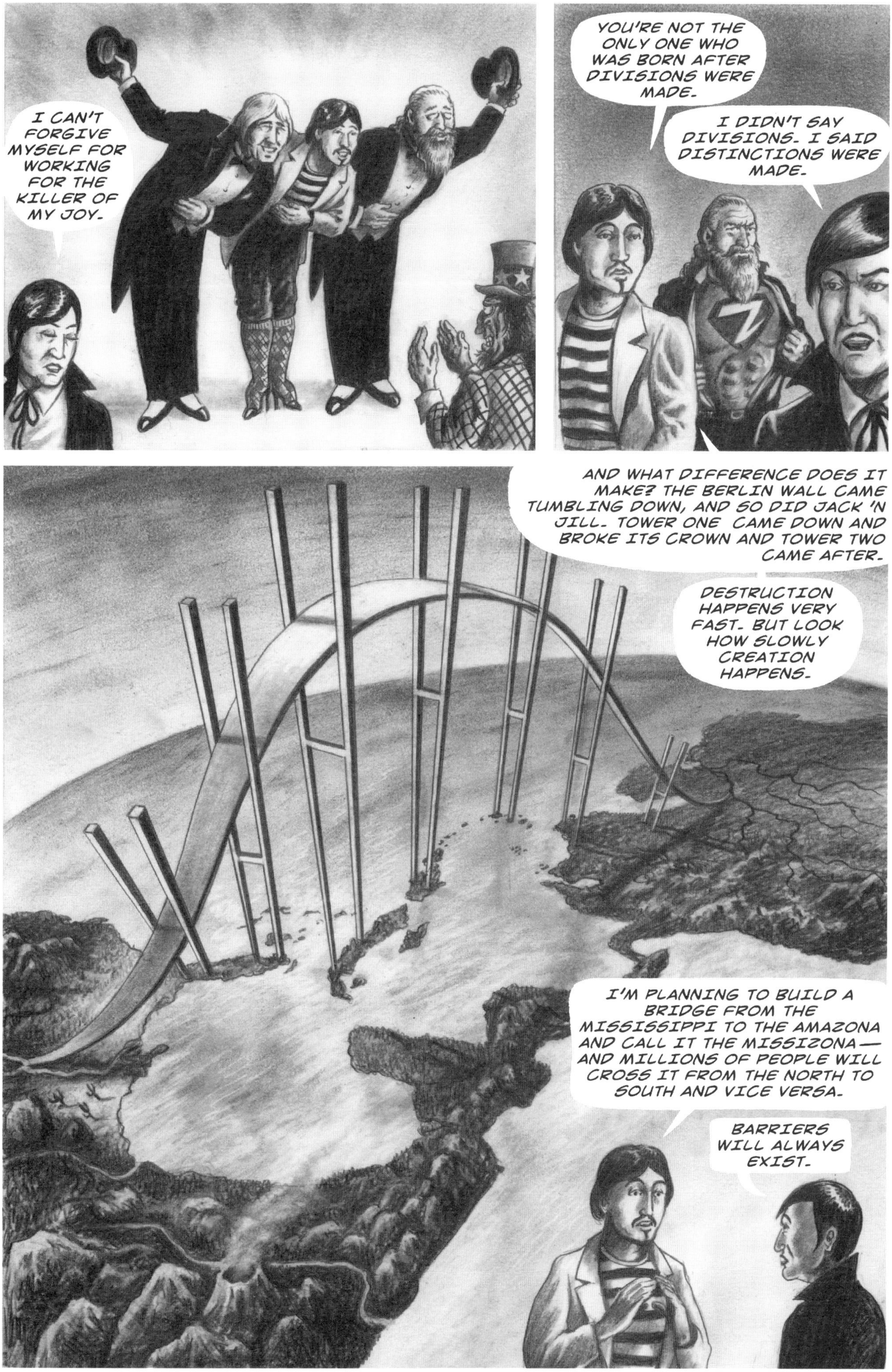
I CAN'T FORGIVE MYSELF FOR WORKING FOR THE KILLER OF MY JOY.
YOU'RE NOT THE ONLY ONE WHO WAS BORN AFTER DIVISIONS WERE MADE.
I DIDN'T SAY DIVISIONS. I SAID DISTINCTIONS WERE MADE.
AND WHAT DIFFERENCE DOES IT MAKE? THE BERLIN WALL CAME TUMBLING DOWN, AND SO DID JACK 'N JILL. TOWER ONE CAME DOWN AND BROKE ITS CROWN AND TOWER TWO CAME AFTER.
DESTRUCTION HAPPENS VERY FAST. BUT LOOK HOW SLOWLY CREATION HAPPENS.
I'M PLANNING TO BUILD A BRIDGE FROM THE MISSISSIPPI TO THE AMAZONA AND CALL IT THE MISSIZONA— AND MILLIONS OF PEOPLE WILL CROSS IT FROM THE NORTH TO SOUTH AND VICE VERSA.
BARRIERS WILL ALWAYS EXIST.

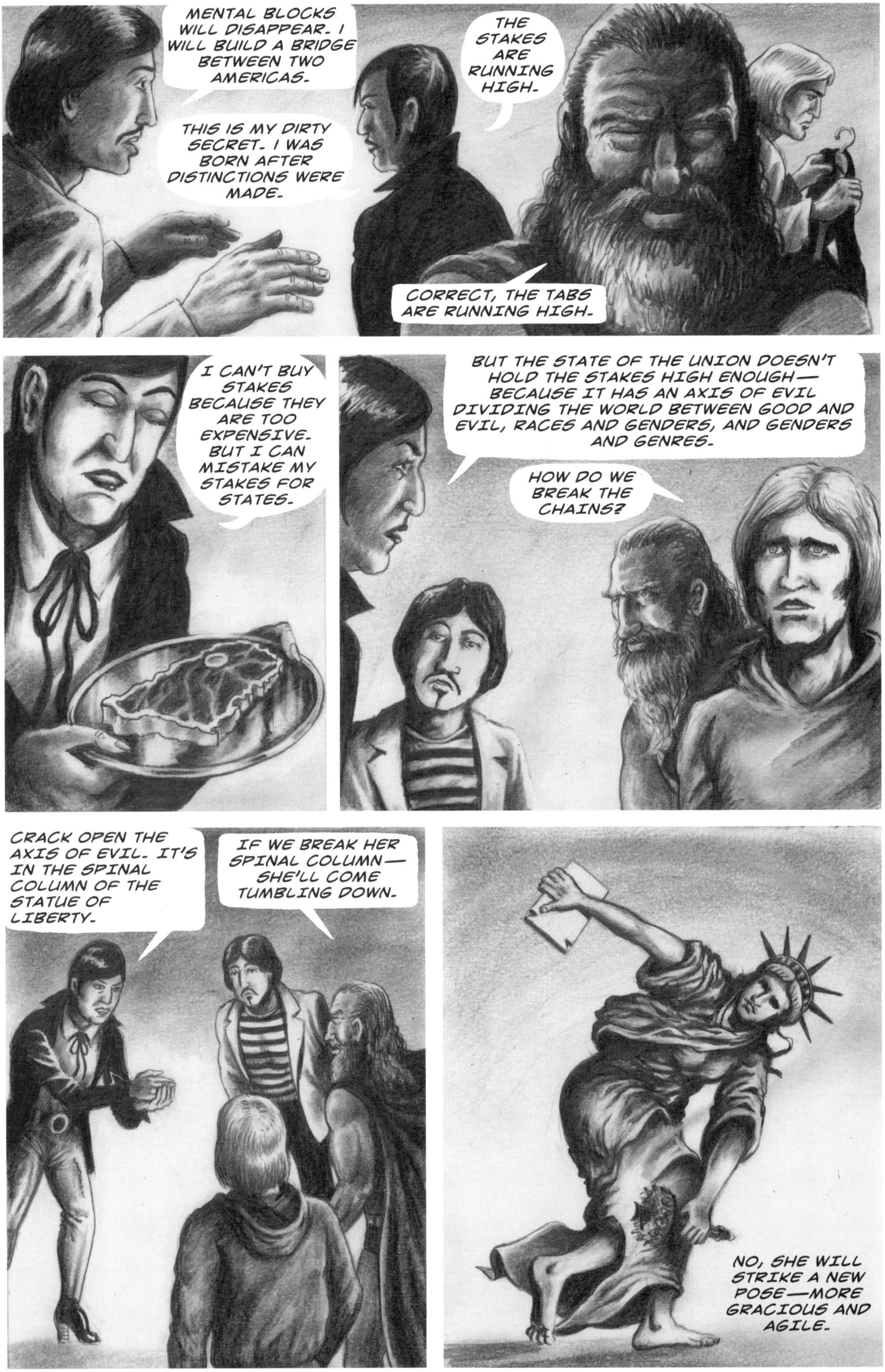
MENTAL BLOCKS WILL DISAPPEAR. I WILL BUILD A BRIDGE BETWEEN TWO AMERICAS.
THIS IS MY DIRTY SECRET. I WAS BORN AFTER DISTINCTIONS WERE MADE.
THE STAKES ARE RUNNING HIGH.
CORRECT, THE TABS ARE RUNNING HIGH.
I CAN'T BUY STAKES BECAUSE THEY ARE TOO EXPENSIVE. BUT I CAN MISTAKE MY STAKES FOR STATES.
BUT THE STATE OF THE UNION DOESN'T HOLD THE STAKES HIGH ENOUGH—BECAUSE IT HAS AN AXIS OF EVIL DIVIDING THE WORLD BETWEEN GOOD AND EVIL, RACES AND GENDERS, AND GENDERS AND GENRES.
HOW DO WE BREAK THE CHAINS?
CRACK OPEN THE AXIS OF EVIL. IT'S IN THE SPINAL COLUMN OF THE STATUE OF LIBERTY.
IF WE BREAK HER SPINAL COLUMN—SHE'LL COME TUMBLING DOWN.
NO, SHE WILL STRIKE A NEW POSE—MORE GRACIOUS AND AGILE.

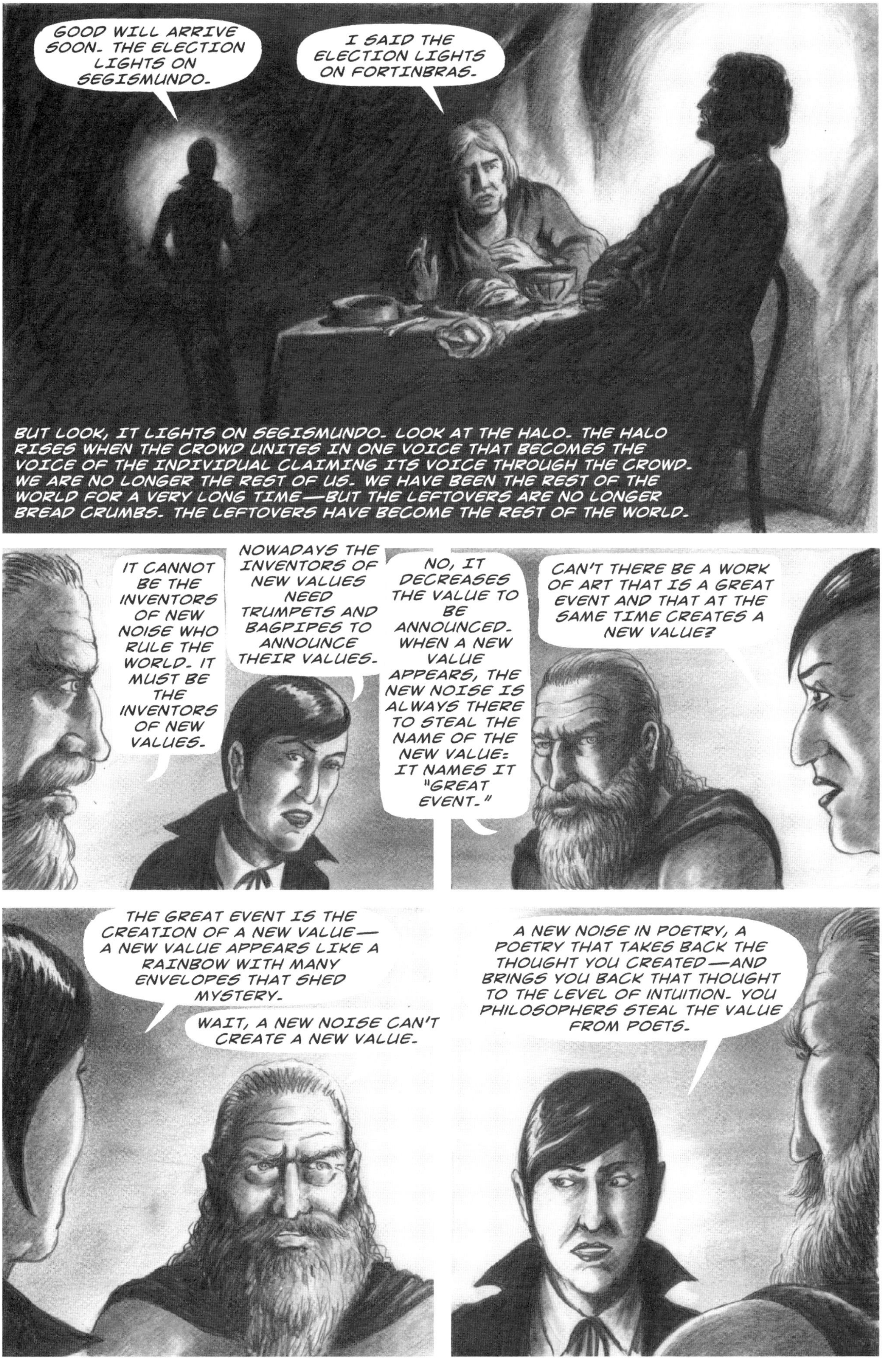
GOOD WILL ARRIVE SOON. THE ELECTION LIGHTS ON SEGISMUNDO.
I SAID THE ELECTION LIGHTS ON FORTINBRAS.
BUT LOOK, IT LIGHTS ON SEGISMUNDO. LOOK AT THE HALO. THE HALO RISES WHEN THE CROWD UNITES IN ONE VOICE THAT BECOMES THE VOICE OF THE INDIVIDUAL CLAIMING ITS VOICE THROUGH THE CROWD. WE ARE NO LONGER THE REST OF US. WE HAVE BEEN THE REST OF THE WORLD FOR A VERY LONG TIME—BUT THE LEFTOVERS ARE NO LONGER BREAD CRUMBS. THE LEFTOVERS HAVE BECOME THE REST OF THE WORLD.
IT CANNOT BE THE INVENTORS OF NEW NOISE WHO RULE THE WORLD. IT MUST BE THE INVENTORS OF NEW VALUES.
NOWADAYS THE INVENTORS OF NEW VALUES NEED TRUMPETS AND BAGPIPES TO ANNOUNCE THEIR VALUES.
NO, IT DECREASES THE VALUE TO BE ANNOUNCED. WHEN A NEW VALUE APPEARS, THE NEW NOISE IS ALWAYS THERE TO STEAL THE NAME OF THE NEW VALUE: IT NAMES IT "GREAT EVENT."
CAN'T THERE BE A WORK OF ART THAT IS A GREAT EVENT AND THAT AT THE SAME TIME CREATES A NEW VALUE?
THE GREAT EVENT IS THE CREATION OF A NEW VALUE—A NEW VALUE APPEARS LIKE A RAINBOW WITH MANY ENVELOPES THAT SHED MYSTERY.
WAIT, A NEW NOISE CAN'T CREATE A NEW VALUE.
A NEW NOISE IN POETRY, A POETRY THAT TAKES BACK THE THOUGHT YOU CREATED—AND BRINGS YOU BACK THAT THOUGHT TO THE LEVEL OF INTUITION. YOU PHILOSOPHERS STEAL THE VALUE FROM POETS.

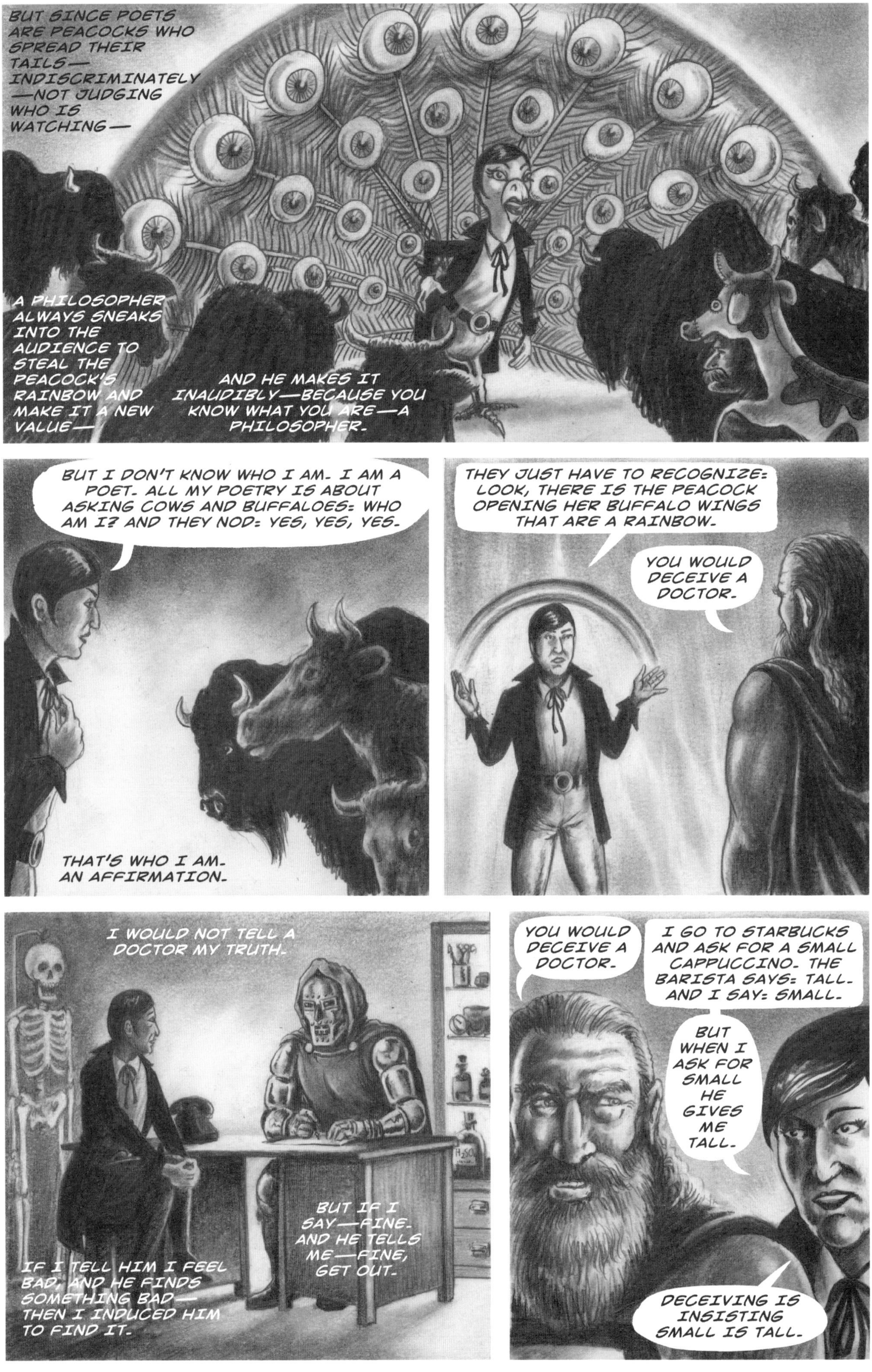
BUT SINCE POETS ARE PEACOCKS WHO SPREAD THEIR TAILS— INDISCRIMINATELY —NOT JUDGING WHO IS WATCHING—
A PHILOSOPHER ALWAYS SNEAKS INTO THE AUDIENCE TO STEAL THE PEACOCK'S RAINBOW AND MAKE IT A NEW VALUE—
AND HE MAKES IT INAUDIBLY—BECAUSE YOU KNOW WHAT YOU ARE—A PHILOSOPHER.
BUT I DON'T KNOW WHO I AM. I AM A POET. ALL MY POETRY IS ABOUT ASKING COWS AND BUFFALOES: WHO AM I? AND THEY NOD: YES, YES, YES.
THAT'S WHO I AM. AN AFFIRMATION.
THEY JUST HAVE TO RECOGNIZE: LOOK, THERE IS THE PEACOCK OPENING HER BUFFALO WINGS THAT ARE A RAINBOW.
YOU WOULD DECEIVE A DOCTOR.
I WOULD NOT TELL A DOCTOR MY TRUTH.
IF I TELL HIM I FEEL BAD, AND HE FINDS SOMETHING BAD— THEN I INDUCED HIM TO FIND IT.
BUT IF I SAY—FINE. AND HE TELLS ME—FINE, GET OUT.
YOU WOULD DECEIVE A DOCTOR.
I GO TO STARBUCKS AND ASK FOR A SMALL CAPPUCCINO. THE BARISTA SAYS: TALL. AND I SAY: SMALL.
BUT WHEN I ASK FOR SMALL HE GIVES ME TALL.
DECEIVING IS INSISTING SMALL IS TALL.

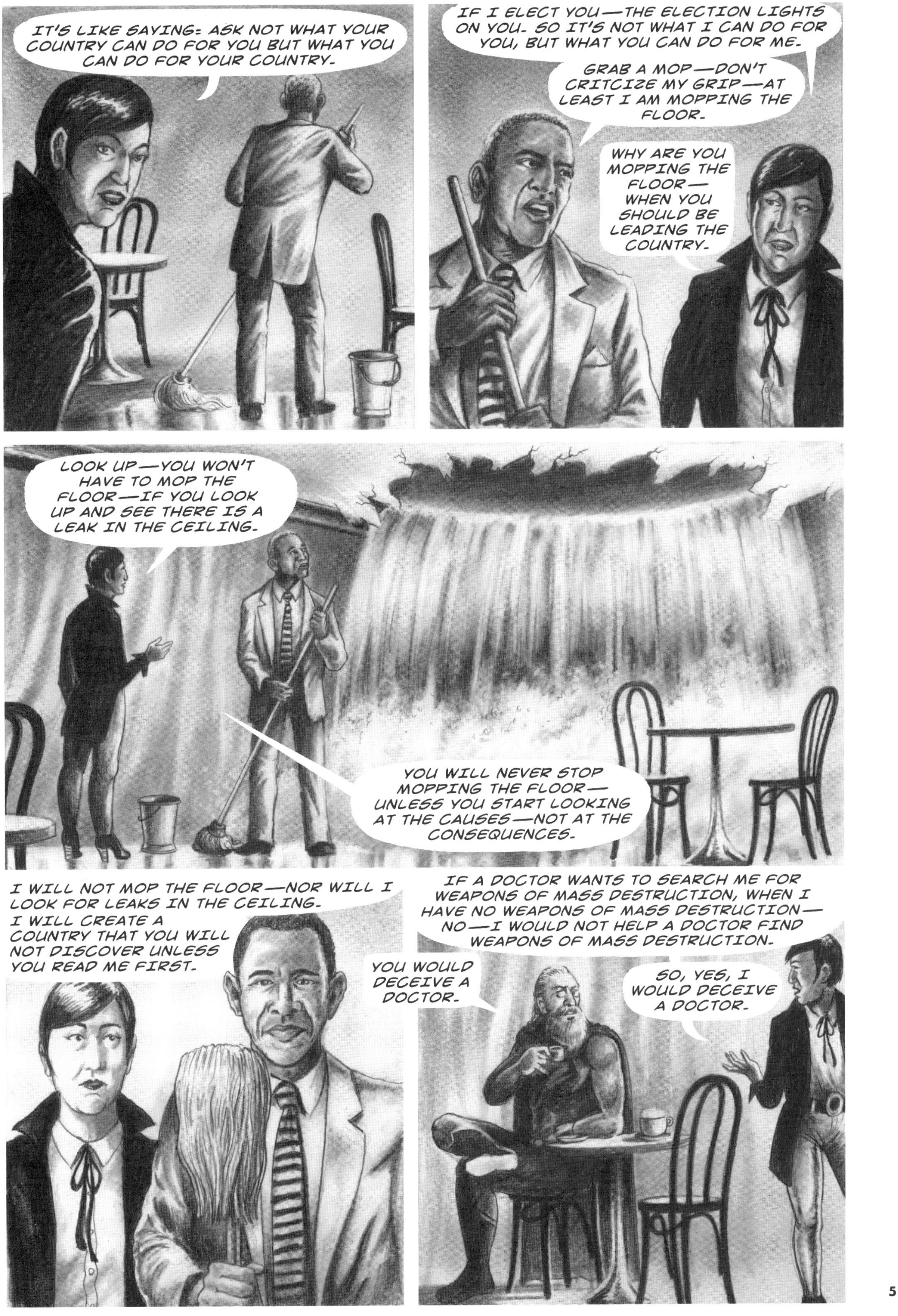
IT'S LIKE SAYING: ASK NOT WHAT YOUR COUNTRY CAN DO FOR YOU BUT WHAT YOU CAN DO FOR YOUR COUNTRY.
IF I ELECT YOU—THE ELECTION LIGHTS ON YOU. SO IT'S NOT WHAT I CAN DO FOR YOU, BUT WHAT YOU CAN DO FOR ME.
GRAB A MOP—DON'T CRITCIZE MY GRIP—AT LEAST I AM MOPPING THE FLOOR.
WHY ARE YOU MOPPING THE FLOOR—WHEN YOU SHOULD BE LEADING THE COUNTRY.
LOOK UP—YOU WON'T HAVE TO MOP THE FLOOR—IF YOU LOOK UP AND SEE THERE IS A LEAK IN THE CEILING.
YOU WILL NEVER STOP MOPPING THE FLOOR—UNLESS YOU START LOOKING AT THE CAUSES—NOT AT THE CONSEQUENCES.
I WILL NOT MOP THE FLOOR—NOR WILL I LOOK FOR LEAKS IN THE CEILING. I WILL CREATE A COUNTRY THAT YOU WILL NOT DISCOVER UNLESS YOU READ ME FIRST.
IF A DOCTOR WANTS TO SEARCH ME FOR WEAPONS OF MASS DESTRUCTION, WHEN I HAVE NO WEAPONS OF MASS DESTRUCTION—NO—I WOULD NOT HELP A DOCTOR FIND WEAPONS OF MASS DESTRUCTION.
YOU WOULD DECEIVE A DOCTOR.
SO, YES, I WOULD DECEIVE A DOCTOR.

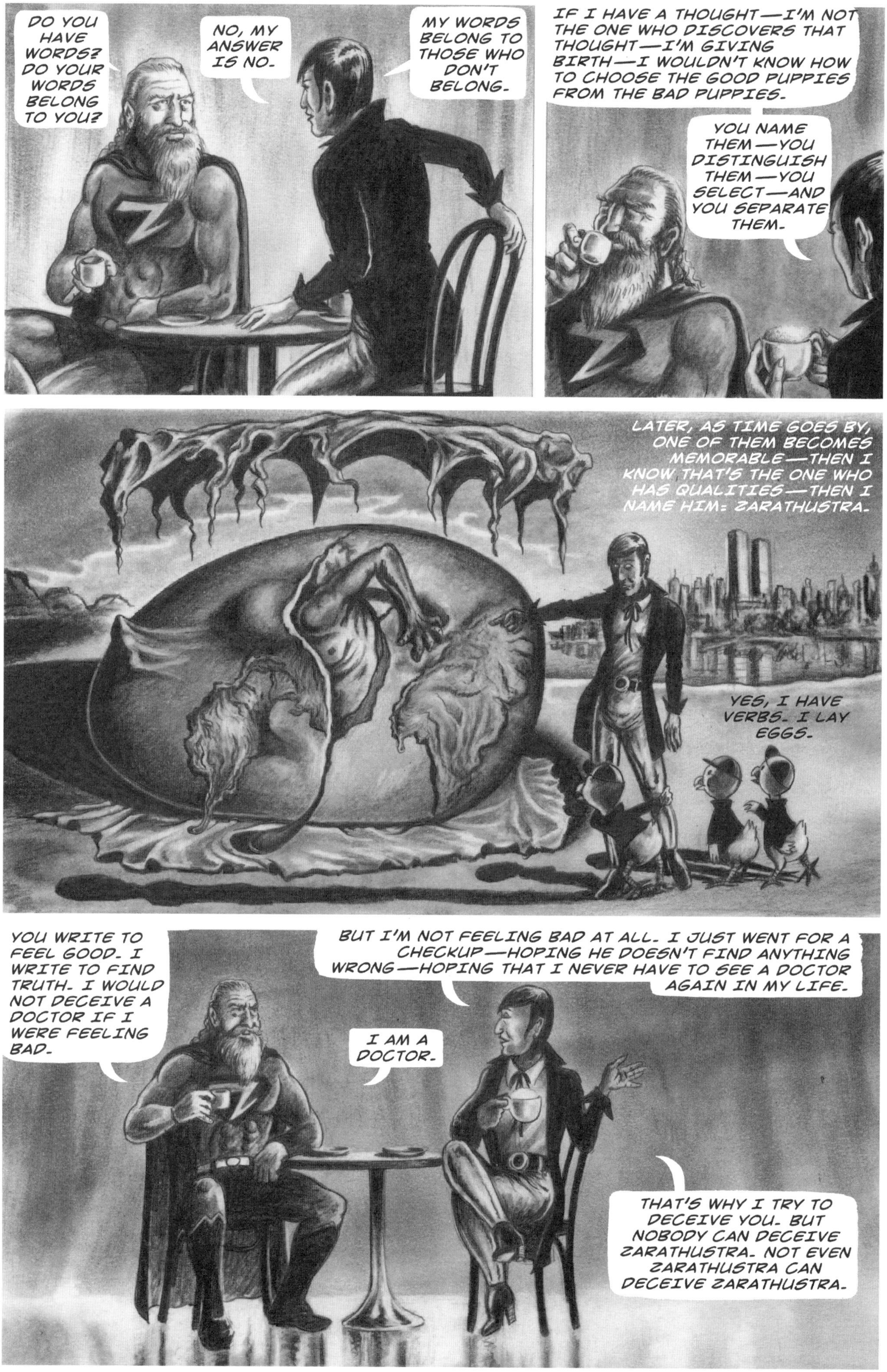
DO YOU HAVE WORDS? DO YOUR WORDS BELONG TO YOU?
NO, MY ANSWER IS NO.
MY WORDS BELONG TO THOSE WHO DON'T BELONG.
IF I HAVE A THOUGHT—I'M NOT THE ONE WHO DISCOVERS THAT THOUGHT—I'M GIVING BIRTH—I WOULDN'T KNOW HOW TO CHOOSE THE GOOD PUPPIES FROM THE BAD PUPPIES.
YOU NAME THEM—YOU DISTINGUISH THEM—YOU SELECT—AND YOU SEPARATE THEM.
LATER, AS TIME GOES BY, ONE OF THEM BECOMES MEMORABLE—THEN I KNOW THAT'S THE ONE WHO HAS QUALITIES—THEN I NAME HIM: ZARATHUSTRA.
YES, I HAVE VERBS. I LAY EGGS.
YOU WRITE TO FEEL GOOD. I WRITE TO FIND TRUTH. I WOULD NOT DECEIVE A DOCTOR IF I WERE FEELING BAD.
BUT I'M NOT FEELING BAD AT ALL. I JUST WENT FOR A CHECKUP—HOPING HE DOESN'T FIND ANYTHING WRONG—HOPING THAT I NEVER HAVE TO SEE A DOCTOR AGAIN IN MY LIFE.
I AM A DOCTOR.
THAT'S WHY I TRY TO DECEIVE YOU. BUT NOBODY CAN DECEIVE ZARATHUSTRA. NOT EVEN ZARATHUSTRA CAN DECEIVE ZARATHUSTRA.

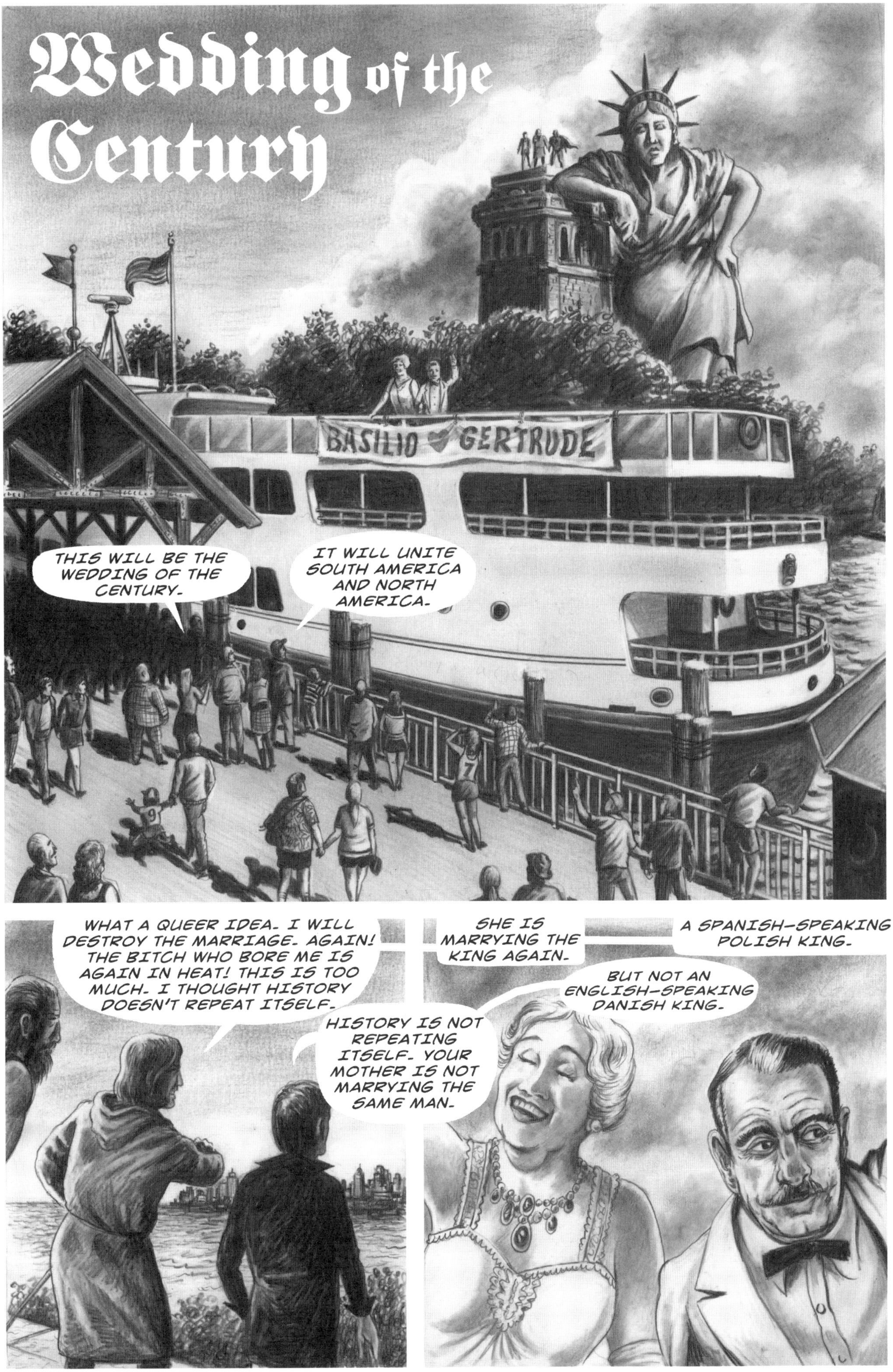
Wedding of the Century
BASILIO GERTRUDE
THIS WILL BE THE WEDDING OF THE CENTURY.
IT WILL UNITE SOUTH AMERICA AND NORTH AMERICA.
WHAT A QUEER IDEA. I WILL DESTROY THE MARRIAGE. AGAIN! THE BITCH WHO BORE ME IS AGAIN IN HEAT! THIS IS TOO MUCH. I THOUGHT HISTORY DOESN'T REPEAT ITSELF.
HISTORY IS NOT REPEATING ITSELF. YOUR MOTHER IS NOT MARRYING THE SAME MAN.
SHE IS MARRYING THE KING AGAIN.
A SPANISH-SPEAKING POLISH KING.
BUT NOT AN ENGLISH-SPEAKING DANISH KING.

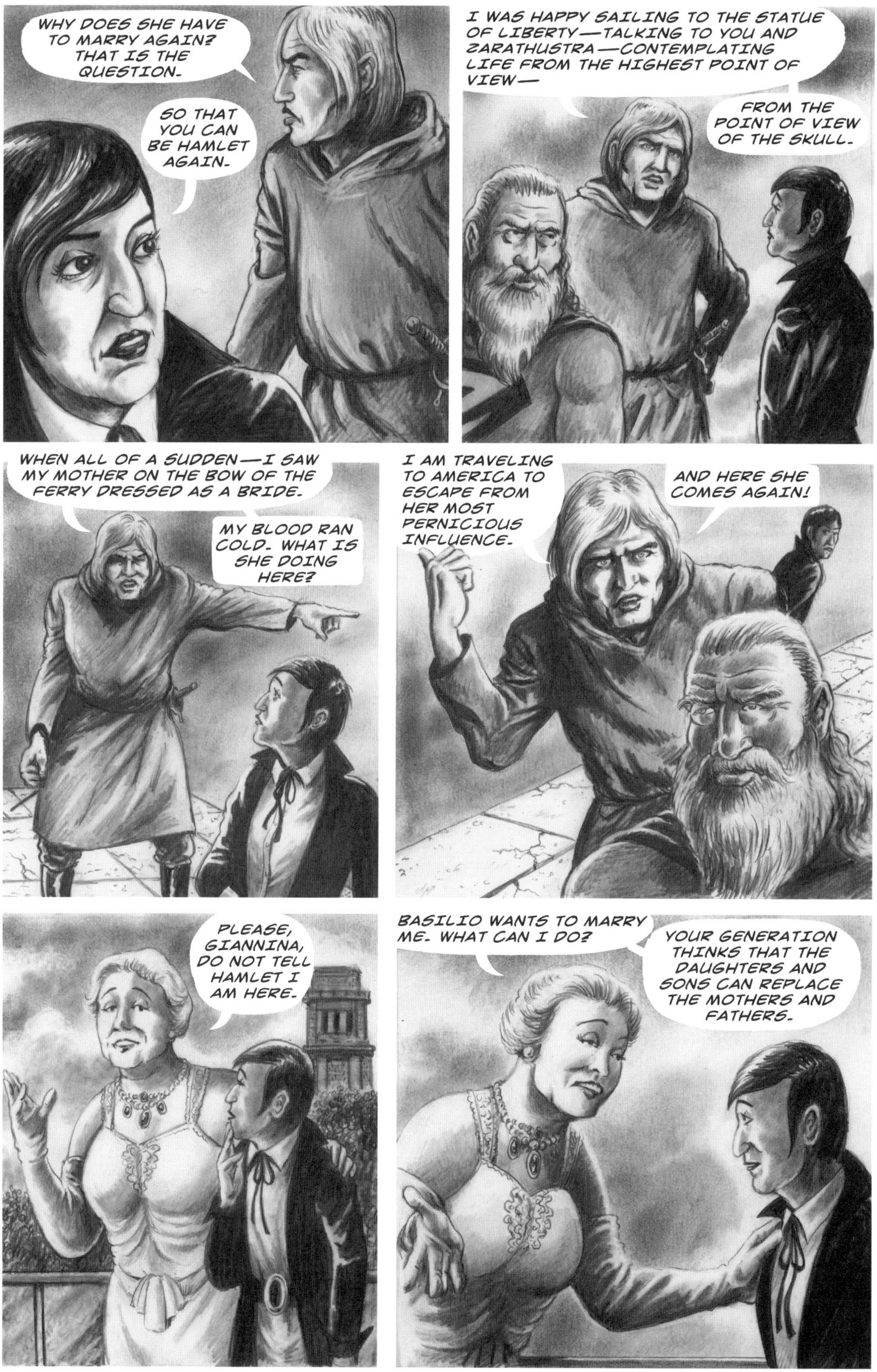
WHY DOES SHE HAVE TO MARRY AGAIN? THAT IS THE QUESTION.
SO THAT YOU CAN BE HAMLET AGAIN.
I WAS HAPPY SAILING TO THE STATUE OF LIBERTY—TALKING TO YOU AND ZARATHUSTRA—CONTEMPLATING LIFE FROM THE HIGHEST POINT OF VIEW—
FROM THE POINT OF VIEW OF THE SKULL.
WHEN ALL OF A SUDDEN—I SAW MY MOTHER ON THE BOW OF THE FERRY DRESSED AS A BRIDE.
MY BLOOD RAN COLD. WHAT IS SHE DOING HERE?
I AM TRAVELING TO AMERICA TO ESCAPE FROM HER MOST PERNICIOUS INFLUENCE.
AND HERE SHE COMES AGAIN!
PLEASE, GIANNINA, DO NOT TELL HAMLET I AM HERE.
BASILIO WANTS TO MARRY ME. WHAT CAN I DO?
YOUR GENERATION THINKS THAT THE DAUGHTERS AND SONS CAN REPLACE THE MOTHERS AND FATHERS.

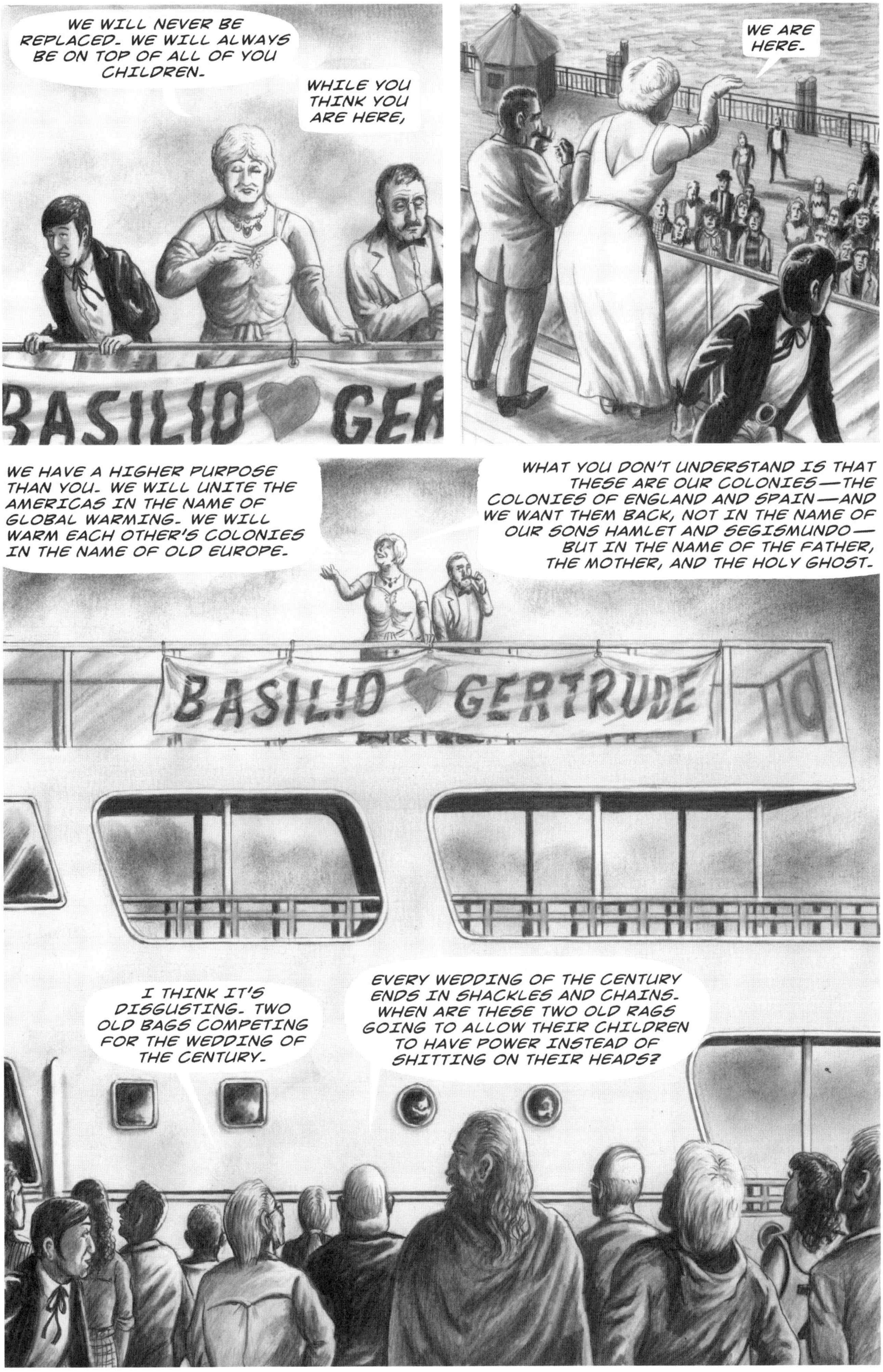
WE WILL NEVER BE REPLACED. WE WILL ALWAYS BE ON TOP OF ALL OF YOU CHILDREN.
WHILE YOU THINK YOU ARE HERE,
BASILIO GER
WE ARE HERE.
WE HAVE A HIGHER PURPOSE THAN YOU. WE WILL UNITE THE AMERICAS IN THE NAME OF GLOBAL WARMING. WE WILL WARM EACH OTHER'S COLONIES IN THE NAME OF OLD EUROPE.
WHAT YOU DON'T UNDERSTAND IS THAT THESE ARE OUR COLONIES—THE COLONIES OF ENGLAND AND SPAIN—AND WE WANT THEM BACK, NOT IN THE NAME OF OUR SONS HAMLET AND SEGISMUNDO—BUT IN THE NAME OF THE FATHER, THE MOTHER, AND THE HOLY GHOST.
BASILIO GERTRUDE
I THINK IT'S DISGUSTING. TWO OLD BAGS COMPETING FOR THE WEDDING OF THE CENTURY.
EVERY WEDDING OF THE CENTURY ENDS IN SHACKLES AND CHAINS. WHEN ARE THESE TWO OLD RAGS GOING TO ALLOW THEIR CHILDREN TO HAVE POWER INSTEAD OF SHITTING ON THEIR HEADS?

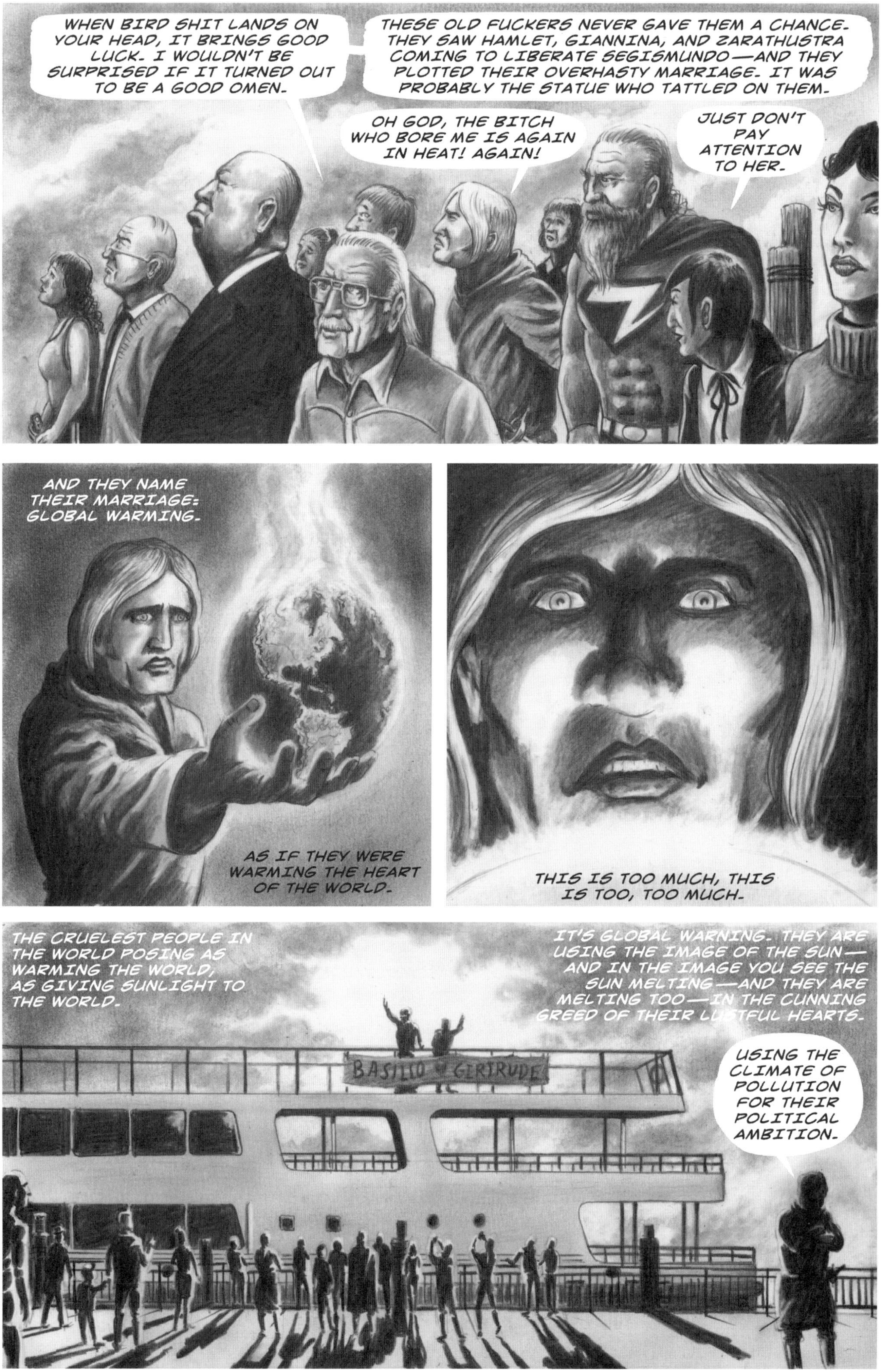
WHEN BIRD SHIT LANDS ON YOUR HEAD, IT BRINGS GOOD LUCK. I WOULDN'T BE SURPRISED IF IT TURNED OUT TO BE A GOOD OMEN.
THESE OLD FUCKERS NEVER GAVE THEM A CHANCE. THEY SAW HAMLET, GIANNINA, AND ZARATHUSTRA COMING TO LIBERATE SEGISMUNDO—AND THEY PLOTTED THEIR OVERHASTY MARRIAGE. IT WAS PROBABLY THE STATUE WHO TATTLED ON THEM.
OH GOD, THE BITCH WHO BORE ME IS AGAIN IN HEAT! AGAIN!
JUST DON'T PAY ATTENTION TO HER.
AND THEY NAME THEIR MARRIAGE: GLOBAL WARMING.
AS IF THEY WERE WARMING THE HEART OF THE WORLD.
THIS IS TOO MUCH, THIS IS TOO, TOO MUCH.
THE CRUELEST PEOPLE IN THE WORLD POSING AS WARMING THE WORLD, AS GIVING SUNLIGHT TO THE WORLD.
IT'S GLOBAL WARNING. THEY ARE USING THE IMAGE OF THE SUN—AND IN THE IMAGE YOU SEE THE SUN MELTING—AND THEY ARE MELTING TOO—IN THE CUNNING GREED OF THEIR LUSTFUL HEARTS.
BASILIO GERTRUDE
USING THE CLIMATE OF POLLUTION FOR THEIR POLITICAL AMBITION.

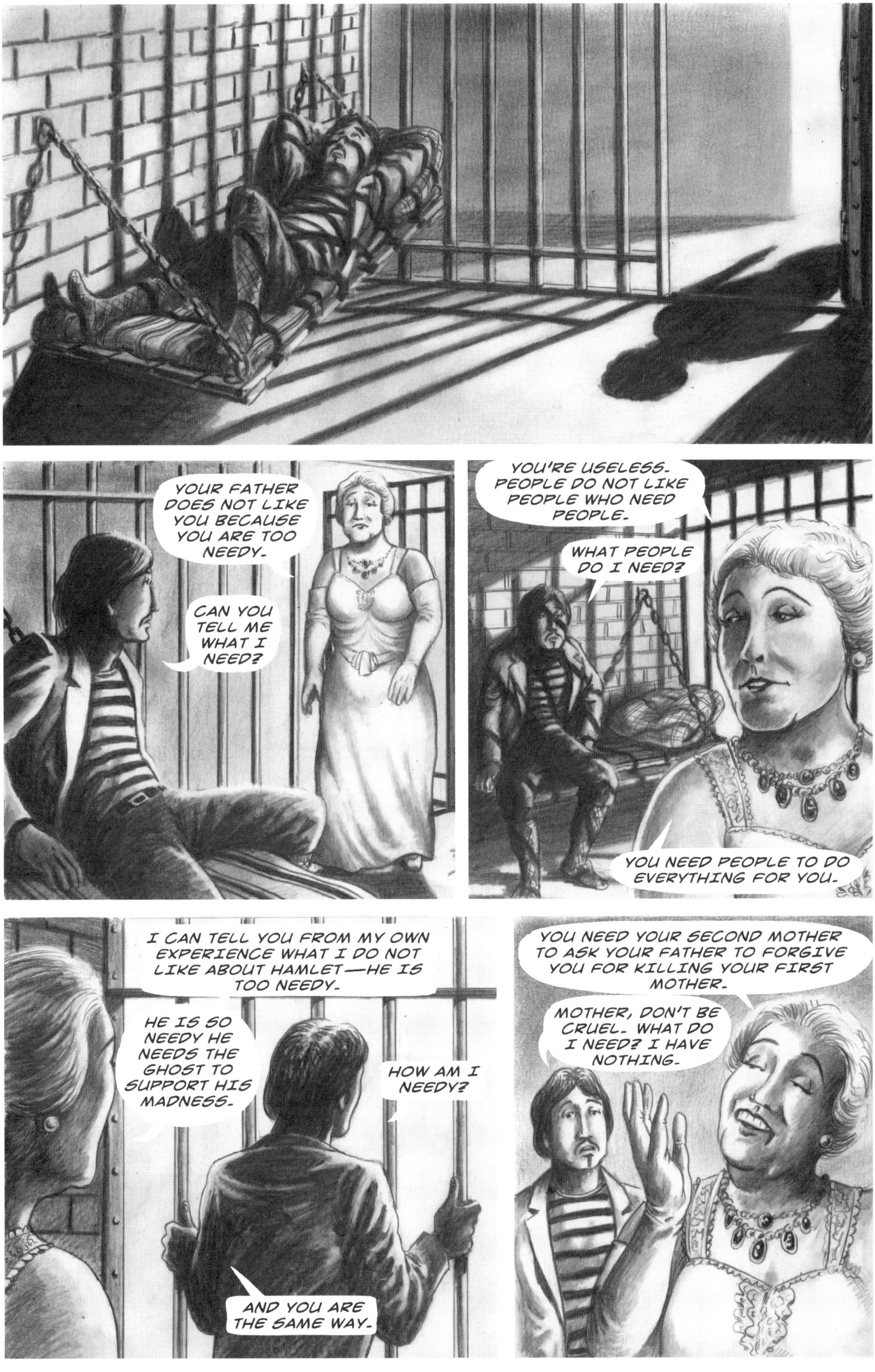
YOUR FATHER DOES NOT LIKE YOU BECAUSE YOU ARE TOO NEEDY.
CAN YOU TELL ME WHAT I NEED?
YOU'RE USELESS. PEOPLE DO NOT LIKE PEOPLE WHO NEED PEOPLE.
WHAT PEOPLE DO I NEED?
YOU NEED PEOPLE TO DO EVERYTHING FOR YOU.
I CAN TELL YOU FROM MY OWN EXPERIENCE WHAT I DO NOT LIKE ABOUT HAMLET—HE IS TOO NEEDY.
HE IS SO NEEDY HE NEEDS THE GHOST TO SUPPORT HIS MADNESS.
HOW AM I NEEDY?
AND YOU ARE THE SAME WAY.
YOU NEED YOUR SECOND MOTHER TO ASK YOUR FATHER TO FORGIVE YOU FOR KILLING YOUR FIRST MOTHER.
MOTHER, DON'T BE CRUEL. WHAT DO I NEED? I HAVE NOTHING.

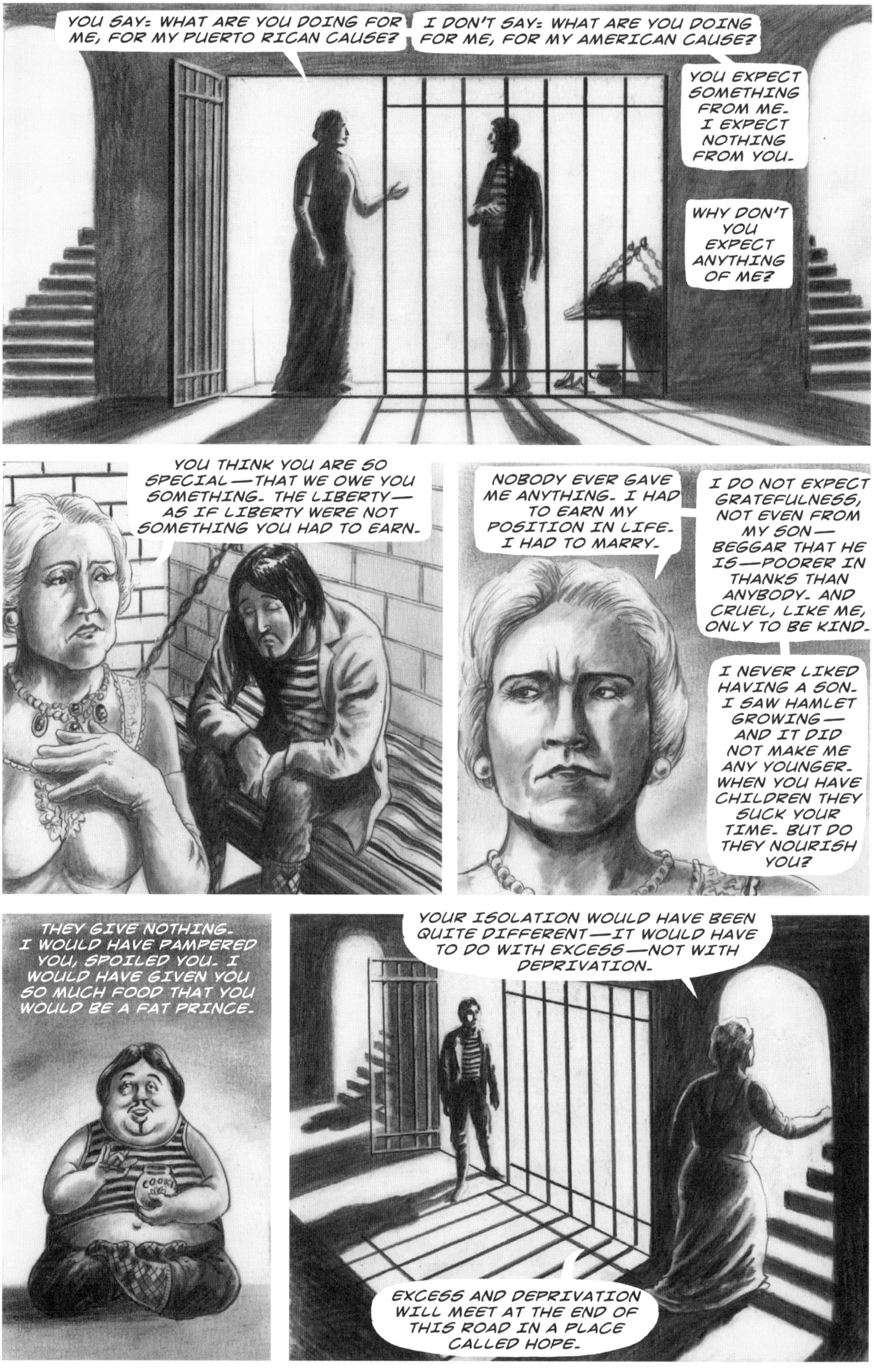
YOU SAY: WHAT ARE YOU DOING FOR ME, FOR MY PUERTO RICAN CAUSE?
I DON'T SAY: WHAT ARE YOU DOING FOR ME, FOR MY AMERICAN CAUSE?
YOU EXPECT SOMETHING FROM ME. I EXPECT NOTHING FROM YOU.
WHY DON'T YOU EXPECT ANYTHING OF ME?
YOU THINK YOU ARE SO SPECIAL—THAT WE OWE YOU SOMETHING. THE LIBERTY—AS IF LIBERTY WERE NOT SOMETHING YOU HAD TO EARN.
NOBODY EVER GAVE ME ANYTHING. I HAD TO EARN MY POSITION IN LIFE. I HAD TO MARRY.
I DO NOT EXPECT GRATEFULNESS, NOT EVEN FROM MY SON—BEGGAR THAT HE IS—POORER IN THANKS THAN ANYBODY. AND CRUEL, LIKE ME, ONLY TO BE KIND.
I NEVER LIKED HAVING A SON. I SAW HAMLET GROWING—AND IT DID NOT MAKE ME ANY YOUNGER. WHEN YOU HAVE CHILDREN THEY SUCK YOUR TIME. BUT DO THEY NOURISH YOU?
THEY GIVE NOTHING. I WOULD HAVE PAMPERED YOU, SPOILED YOU. I WOULD HAVE GIVEN YOU SO MUCH FOOD THAT YOU WOULD BE A FAT PRINCE.
COOKIES
YOUR ISOLATION WOULD HAVE BEEN QUITE DIFFERENT—IT WOULD HAVE TO DO WITH EXCESS—NOT WITH DEPRIVATION.
EXCESS AND DEPRIVATION WILL MEET AT THE END OF THIS ROAD IN A PLACE CALLED HOPE.

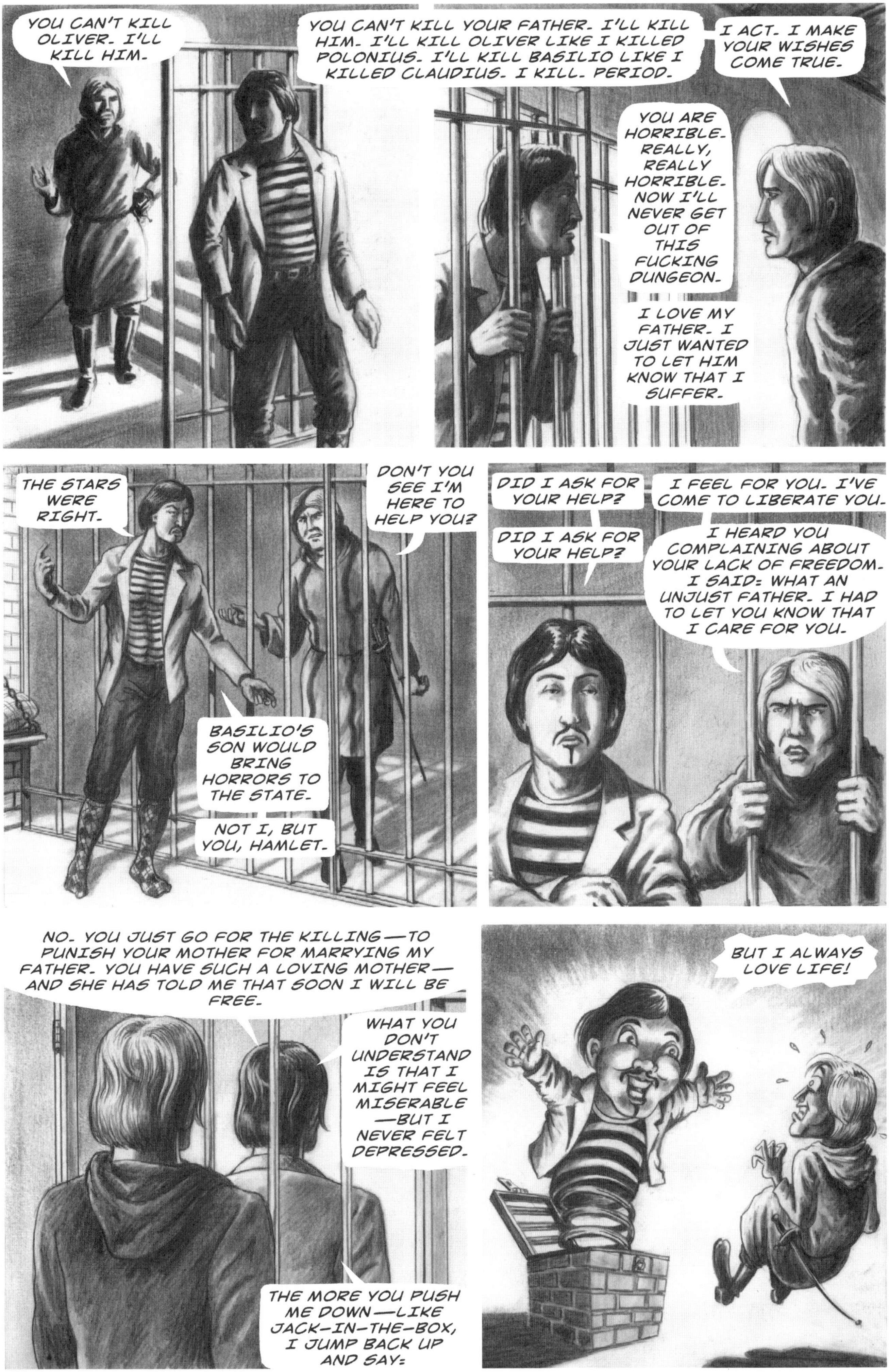

YOU CAN'T KILL OLIVER. I'LL KILL HIM.
YOU CAN'T KILL YOUR FATHER. I'LL KILL HIM. I'LL KILL OLIVER LIKE I KILLED POLONIUS. I'LL KILL BASILIO LIKE I KILLED CLAUDIUS. I KILL. PERIOD.
I ACT. I MAKE YOUR WISHES COME TRUE.
YOU ARE HORRIBLE. REALLY, REALLY HORRIBLE. NOW I'LL NEVER GET OUT OF THIS FUCKING DUNGEON.
I LOVE MY FATHER. I JUST WANTED TO LET HIM KNOW THAT I SUFFER.
THE STARS WERE RIGHT.
DON'T YOU SEE I'M HERE TO HELP YOU?
BASILIO'S SON WOULD BRING HORRORS TO THE STATE.
NOT I, BUT YOU, HAMLET.
DID I ASK FOR YOUR HELP?
DID I ASK FOR YOUR HELP?
I FEEL FOR YOU. I'VE COME TO LIBERATE YOU.
I HEARD YOU COMPLAINING ABOUT YOUR LACK OF FREEDOM. I SAID: WHAT AN UNJUST FATHER. I HAD TO LET YOU KNOW THAT I CARE FOR YOU.
NO. YOU JUST GO FOR THE KILLING—TO PUNISH YOUR MOTHER FOR MARRYING MY FATHER. YOU HAVE SUCH A LOVING MOTHER—AND SHE HAS TOLD ME THAT SOON I WILL BE FREE.
WHAT YOU DON'T UNDERSTAND IS THAT I MIGHT FEEL MISERABLE—BUT I NEVER FELT DEPRESSED.
THE MORE YOU PUSH ME DOWN—LIKE JACK-IN-THE-BOX, I JUMP BACK UP AND SAY:
BUT I ALWAYS LOVE LIFE!

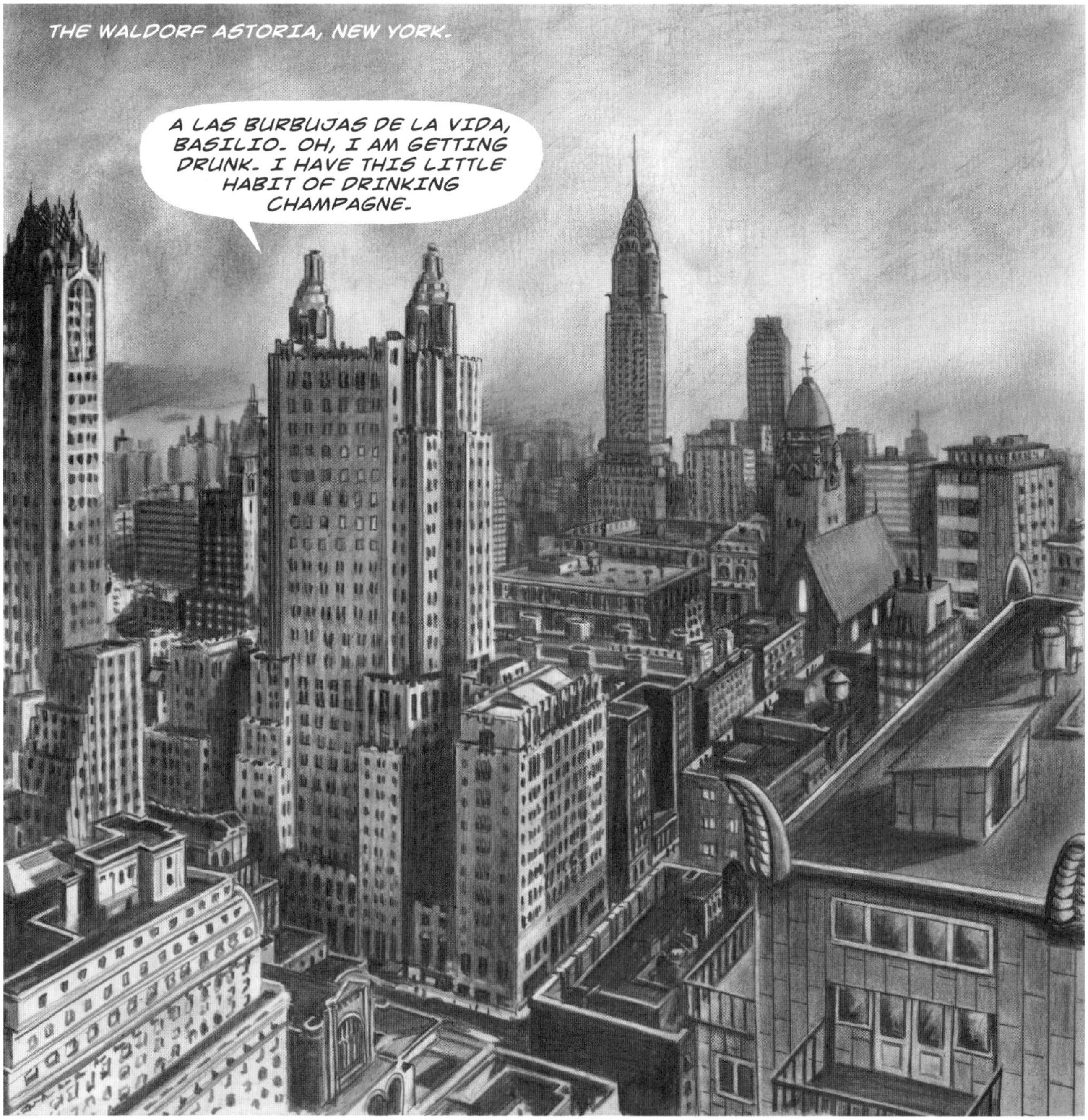
THE WALDORF ASTORIA, NEW YORK.
A LAS BURBUJAS DE LA VIDA, BASILIO. OH, I AM GETTING DRUNK. I HAVE THIS LITTLE HABIT OF DRINKING CHAMPAGNE.

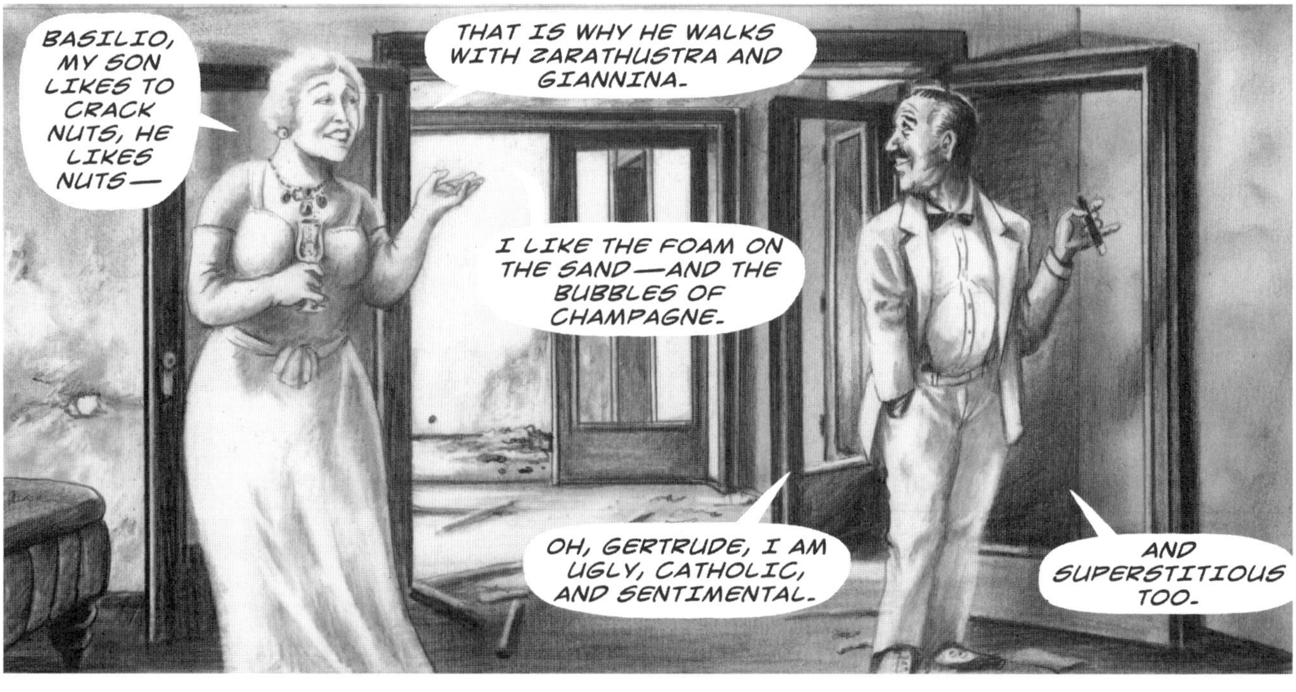
BASILIO, MY SON LIKES TO CRACK NUTS, HE LIKES NUTS—
THAT IS WHY HE WALKS WITH ZARATHUSTRA AND GIANNINA.
I LIKE THE FOAM ON THE SAND—AND THE BUBBLES OF CHAMPAGNE.
OH, GERTRUDE, I AM UGLY, CATHOLIC, AND SENTIMENTAL.
AND SUPERSTITIOUS TOO.

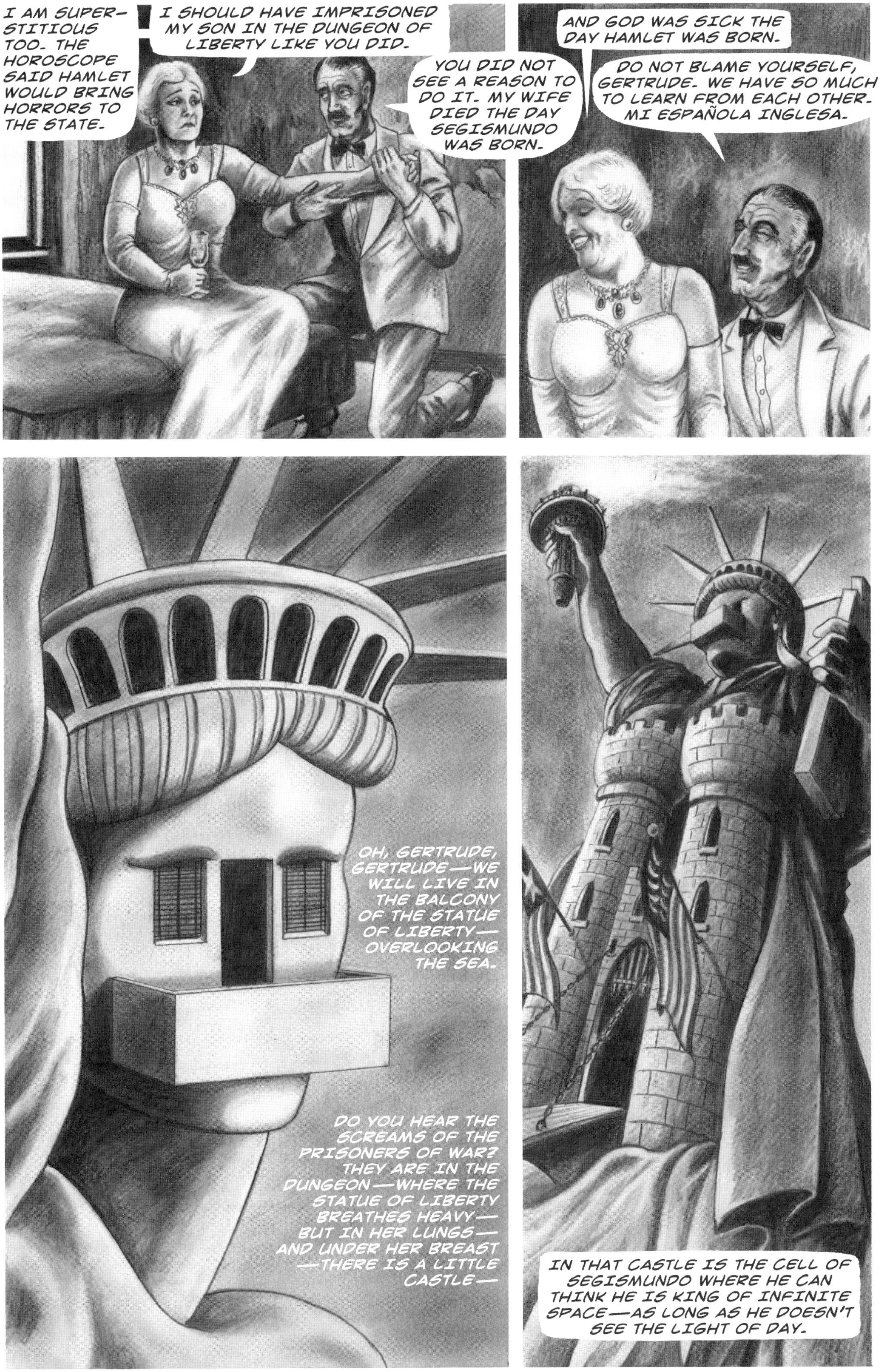
I AM SUPER-STITIOUS TOO. THE HOROSCOPE SAID HAMLET WOULD BRING HORRORS TO THE STATE.
I SHOULD HAVE IMPRISONED MY SON IN THE DUNGEON OF LIBERTY LIKE YOU DID.
YOU DID NOT SEE A REASON TO DO IT. MY WIFE DIED THE DAY SEGISMUNDO WAS BORN.
AND GOD WAS SICK THE DAY HAMLET WAS BORN.
DO NOT BLAME YOURSELF, GERTRUDE. WE HAVE SO MUCH TO LEARN FROM EACH OTHER. MI ESPAÑOLA INGLESA.
OH, GERTRUDE, GERTRUDE—WE WILL LIVE IN THE BALCONY OF THE STATUE OF LIBERTY—OVERLOOKING THE SEA.
DO YOU HEAR THE SCREAMS OF THE PRISONERS OF WAR? THEY ARE IN THE DUNGEON—WHERE THE STATUE OF LIBERTY BREATHES HEAVY—BUT IN HER LUNGS—AND UNDER HER BREAST—THERE IS A LITTLE CASTLE—
IN THAT CASTLE IS THE CELL OF SEGISMUNDO WHERE HE CAN THINK HE IS KING OF INFINITE SPACE—AS LONG AS HE DOESN'T SEE THE LIGHT OF DAY.

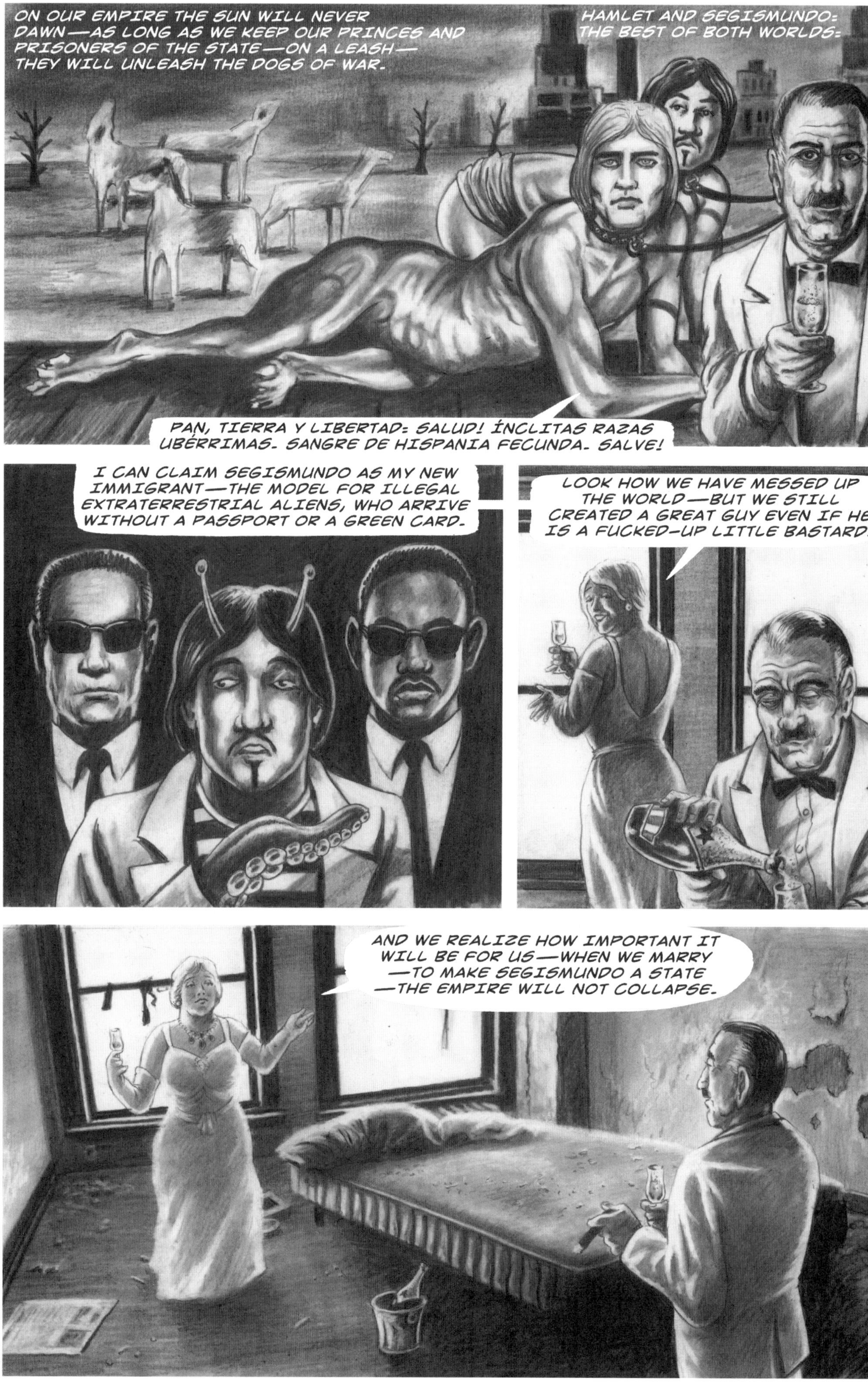
ON OUR EMPIRE THE SUN WILL NEVER DAWN—AS LONG AS WE KEEP OUR PRINCES AND PRISONERS OF THE STATE—ON A LEASH—THEY WILL UNLEASH THE DOGS OF WAR.
HAMLET AND SEGISMUNDO: THE BEST OF BOTH WORLDS:
PAN, TIERRA Y LIBERTAD: SALUD! ÍNCLITAS RAZAS UBÉRRIMAS. SANGRE DE HISPANIA FECUNDA. SALVE!
I CAN CLAIM SEGISMUNDO AS MY NEW IMMIGRANT—THE MODEL FOR ILLEGAL EXTRATERRESTRIAL ALIENS, WHO ARRIVE WITHOUT A PASSPORT OR A GREEN CARD.
LOOK HOW WE HAVE MESSED UP THE WORLD—BUT WE STILL CREATED A GREAT GUY EVEN IF HE IS A FUCKED-UP LITTLE BASTARD.
AND WE REALIZE HOW IMPORTANT IT WILL BE FOR US—WHEN WE MARRY—TO MAKE SEGISMUNDO A STATE—THE EMPIRE WILL NOT COLLAPSE.

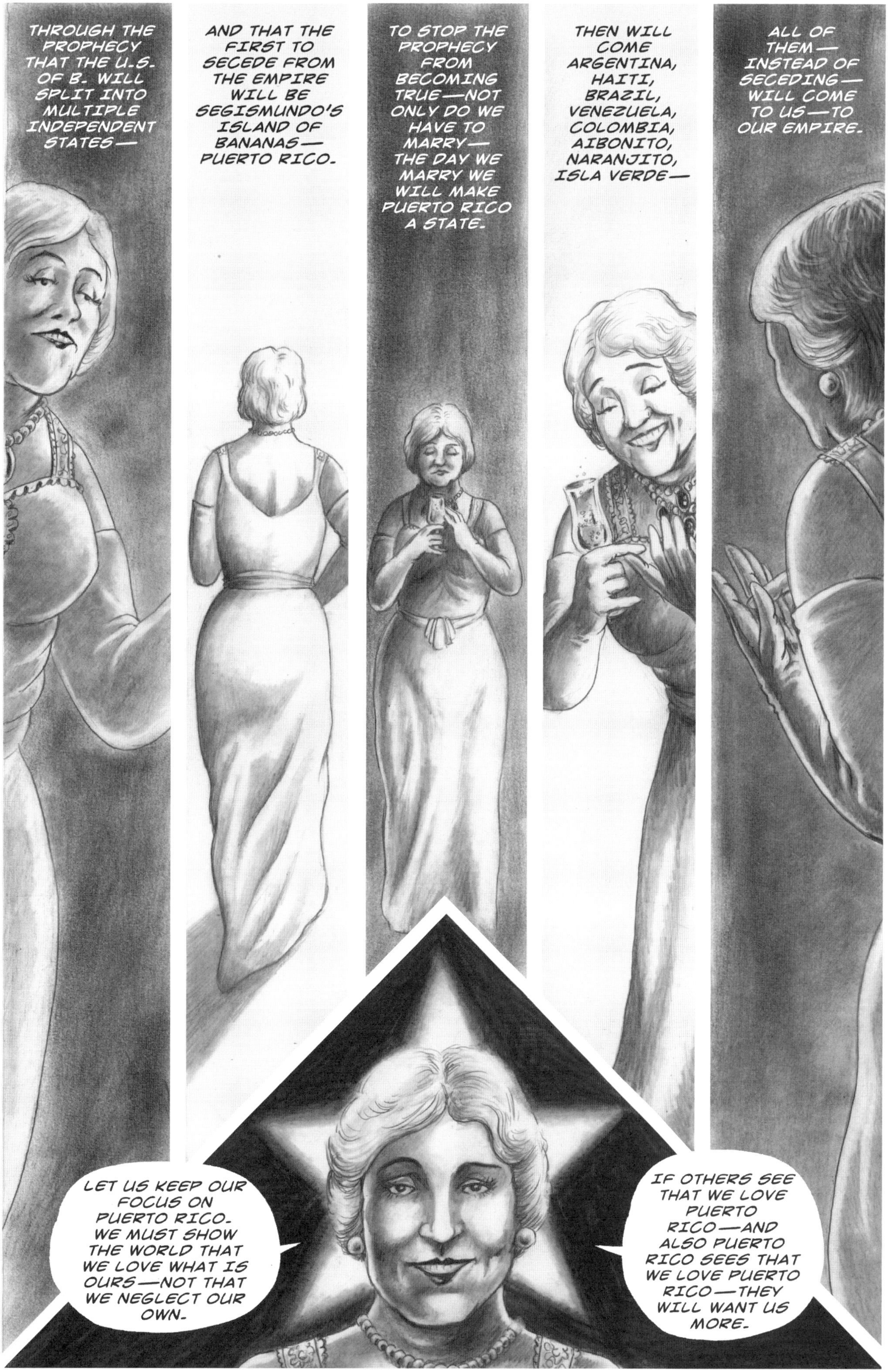
THROUGH THE PROPHECY THAT THE U.S. OF B. WILL SPLIT INTO MULTIPLE INDEPENDENT STATES—
AND THAT THE FIRST TO SECEDE FROM THE EMPIRE WILL BE SEGISMUNDO'S ISLAND OF BANANAS—PUERTO RICO.
TO STOP THE PROPHECY FROM BECOMING TRUE—NOT ONLY DO WE HAVE TO MARRY—THE DAY WE MARRY WE WILL MAKE PUERTO RICO A STATE.
THEN WILL COME ARGENTINA, HAITI, BRAZIL, VENEZUELA, COLOMBIA, AIBONITO, NARANJITO, ISLA VERDE—
ALL OF THEM—INSTEAD OF SECEDING—WILL COME TO US—TO OUR EMPIRE.
LET US KEEP OUR FOCUS ON PUERTO RICO. WE MUST SHOW THE WORLD THAT WE LOVE WHAT IS OURS—NOT THAT WE NEGLECT OUR OWN.
IF OTHERS SEE THAT WE LOVE PUERTO RICO—AND ALSO PUERTO RICO SEES THAT WE LOVE PUERTO RICO—THEY WILL WANT US MORE.

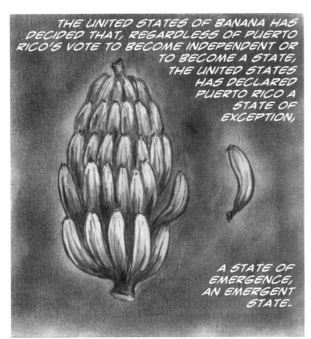

THE UNITED STATES OF BANANA HAS DECIDED THAT, REGARDLESS OF PUERTO RICO'S VOTE TO BECOME INDEPENDENT OR TO BECOME A STATE, THE UNITED STATES HAS DECLARED PUERTO RICO A STATE OF EXCEPTION,

A STATE OF EMERGENCE, AN EMERGENT STATE.

AND THIS I SAY WITHOUT CARING A HOOT ABOUT THE DECISION THAT THE ISLAND MAKES OR DOES NOT MAKE. THE PEOPLE HAVE HAD ENOUGH TIME TO DECIDE—AND THEY DID NOT.

NOW WE HAVE TO MAKE THE TOUGH DECISION FOR THEM—AS A GIFT.

WE WILL GRANT STATEHOOD TO THE ISLAND OF PUERTO RICO-IMPERATIVE—TO PROVE THAT WE ARE NOT RACISTS—

THAT WE WANT PUERTO RICO TO BE THE FIRST LATIN AMERICAN COUNTRY TO BECOME A STATE OF THE UNION.

THEN WILL COME MEXICO, NICARAGUA, SURINAME, COSTA RICA, ECUADOR, SANTO DOMINGO, MARTINIQUE...

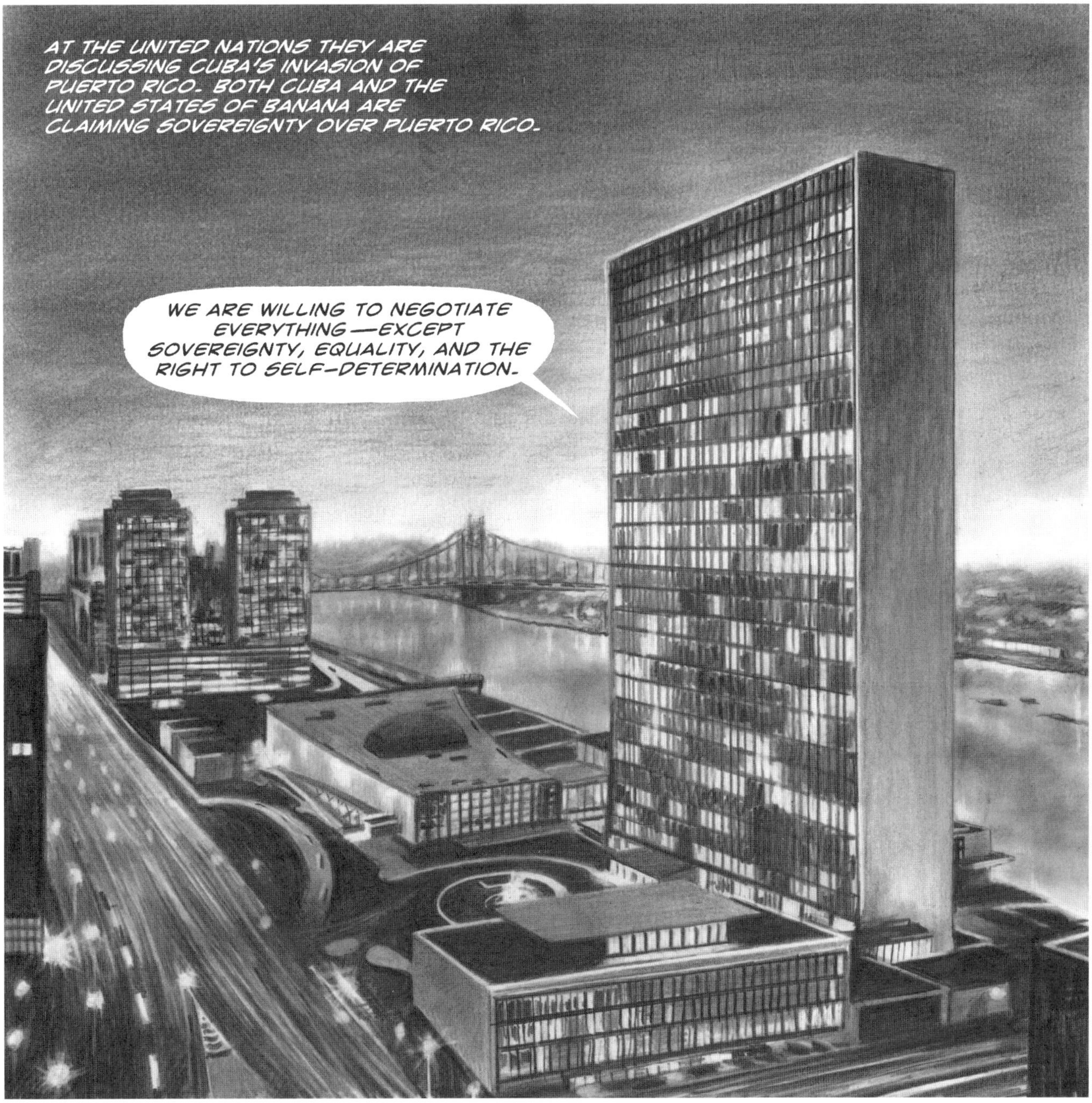
AT THE UNITED NATIONS THEY ARE DISCUSSING CUBA'S INVASION OF PUERTO RICO. BOTH CUBA AND THE UNITED STATES OF BANANA ARE CLAIMING SOVEREIGNTY OVER PUERTO RICO.
WE ARE WILLING TO NEGOTIATE EVERYTHING—EXCEPT SOVEREIGNTY, EQUALITY, AND THE RIGHT TO SELF-DETERMINATION.

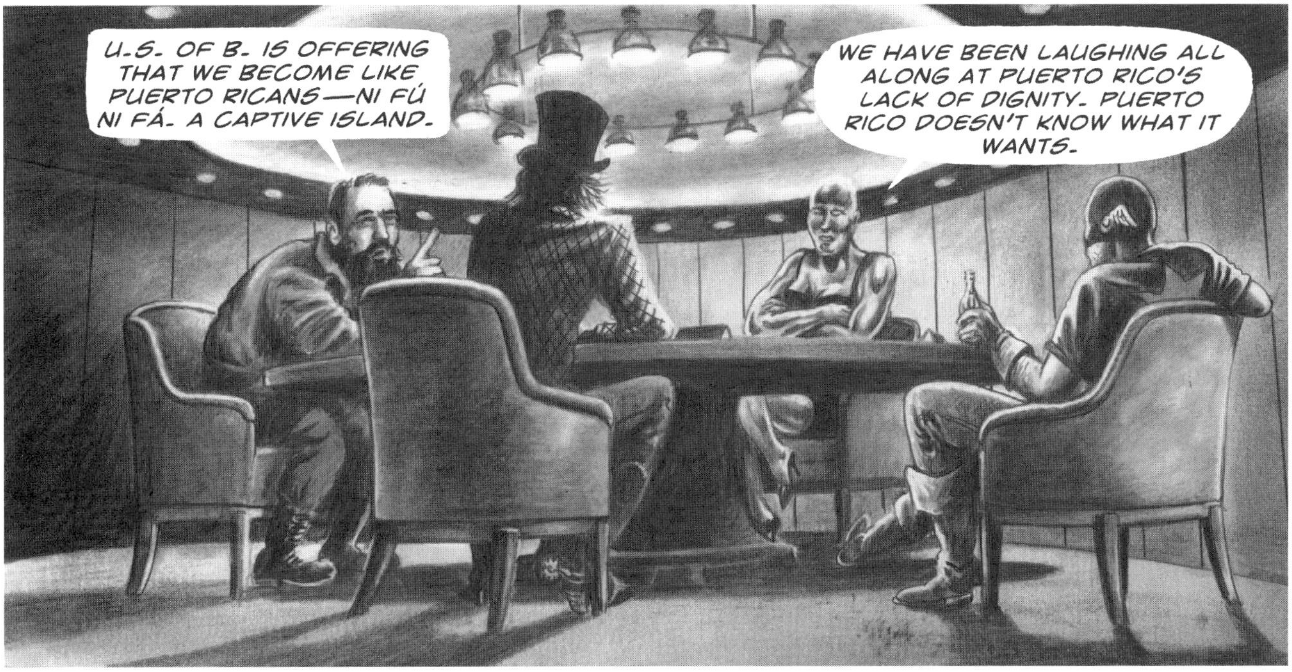
U.S. OF B. IS OFFERING THAT WE BECOME LIKE PUERTO RICANS—NI FÚ NI FÁ. A CAPTIVE ISLAND.
WE HAVE BEEN LAUGHING ALL ALONG AT PUERTO RICO'S LACK OF DIGNITY. PUERTO RICO DOESN'T KNOW WHAT IT WANTS.

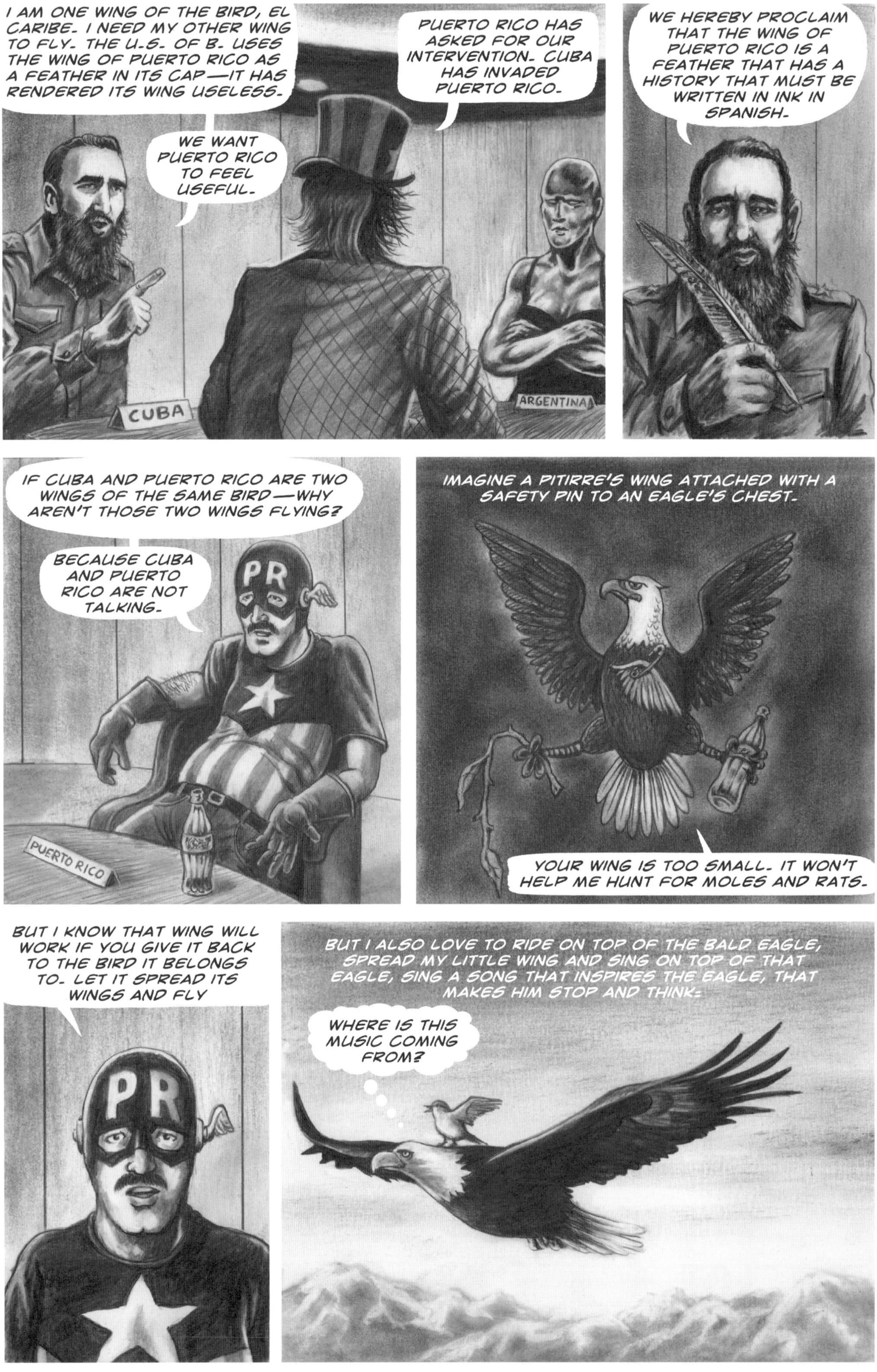
I AM ONE WING OF THE BIRD, EL CARIBE. I NEED MY OTHER WING TO FLY. THE U.S. OF B. USES THE WING OF PUERTO RICO AS A FEATHER IN ITS CAP—IT HAS RENDERED ITS WING USELESS.
WE WANT PUERTO RICO TO FEEL USEFUL.
PUERTO RICO HAS ASKED FOR OUR INTERVENTION. CUBA HAS INVADED PUERTO RICO.
CUBA
ARGENTINA
WE HEREBY PROCLAIM THAT THE WING OF PUERTO RICO IS A FEATHER THAT HAS A HISTORY THAT MUST BE WRITTEN IN INK IN SPANISH.
IF CUBA AND PUERTO RICO ARE TWO WINGS OF THE SAME BIRD—WHY AREN'T THOSE TWO WINGS FLYING?
BECAUSE CUBA AND PUERTO RICO ARE NOT TALKING.
PR
PUERTO RICO
IMAGINE A PITIRRE'S WING ATTACHED WITH A SAFETY PIN TO AN EAGLE'S CHEST.
YOUR WING IS TOO SMALL. IT WON'T HELP ME HUNT FOR MOLES AND RATS.
BUT I KNOW THAT WING WILL WORK IF YOU GIVE IT BACK TO THE BIRD IT BELONGS TO. LET IT SPREAD ITS WINGS AND FLY
PR
BUT I ALSO LOVE TO RIDE ON TOP OF THE BALD EAGLE, SPREAD MY LITTLE WING AND SING ON TOP OF THAT EAGLE, SING A SONG THAT INSPIRES THE EAGLE, THAT MAKES HIM STOP AND THINK:
WHERE IS THIS MUSIC COMING FROM?

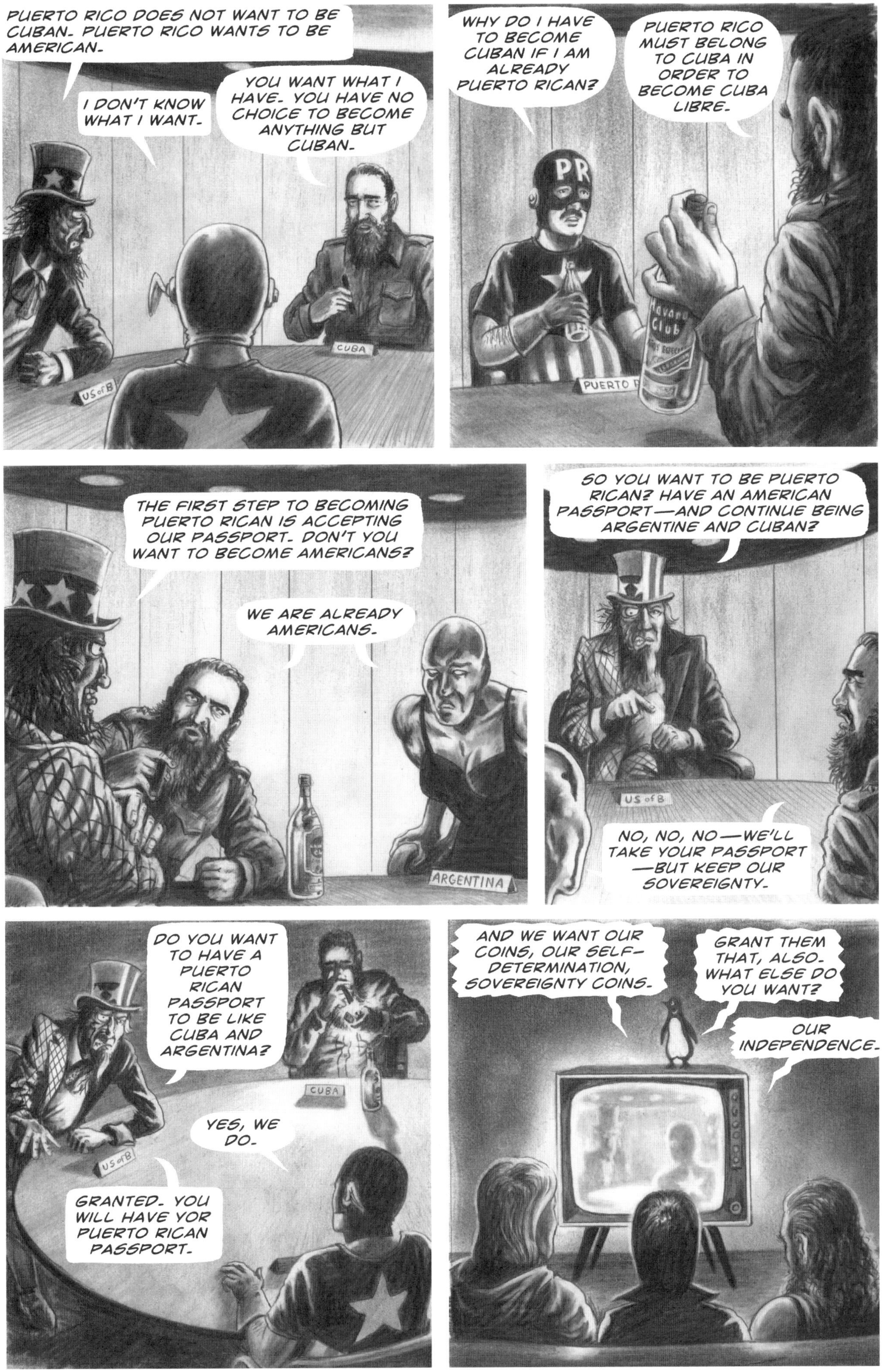
PUERTO RICO DOES NOT WANT TO BE CUBAN. PUERTO RICO WANTS TO BE AMERICAN.
I DON'T KNOW WHAT I WANT.
YOU WANT WHAT I HAVE. YOU HAVE NO CHOICE TO BECOME ANYTHING BUT CUBAN.
US of B
CUBA
WHY DO I HAVE TO BECOME CUBAN IF I AM ALREADY PUERTO RICAN?
PUERTO RICO MUST BELONG TO CUBA IN ORDER TO BECOME CUBA LIBRE.
PR
Havana Club
PUERTO R
THE FIRST STEP TO BECOMING PUERTO RICAN IS ACCEPTING OUR PASSPORT. DON'T YOU WANT TO BECOME AMERICANS?
WE ARE ALREADY AMERICANS.
ARGENTINA
SO YOU WANT TO BE PUERTO RICAN? HAVE AN AMERICAN PASSPORT—AND CONTINUE BEING ARGENTINE AND CUBAN?
US of B
NO, NO, NO—WE'LL TAKE YOUR PASSPORT—BUT KEEP OUR SOVEREIGNTY.
DO YOU WANT TO HAVE A PUERTO RICAN PASSPORT TO BE LIKE CUBA AND ARGENTINA?
CUBA
YES, WE DO.
US of B
GRANTED. YOU WILL HAVE YOR PUERTO RICAN PASSPORT.
AND WE WANT OUR COINS, OUR SELF-DETERMINATION, SOVEREIGNTY COINS.
GRANT THEM THAT, ALSO. WHAT ELSE DO YOU WANT?
OUR INDEPENDENCE.

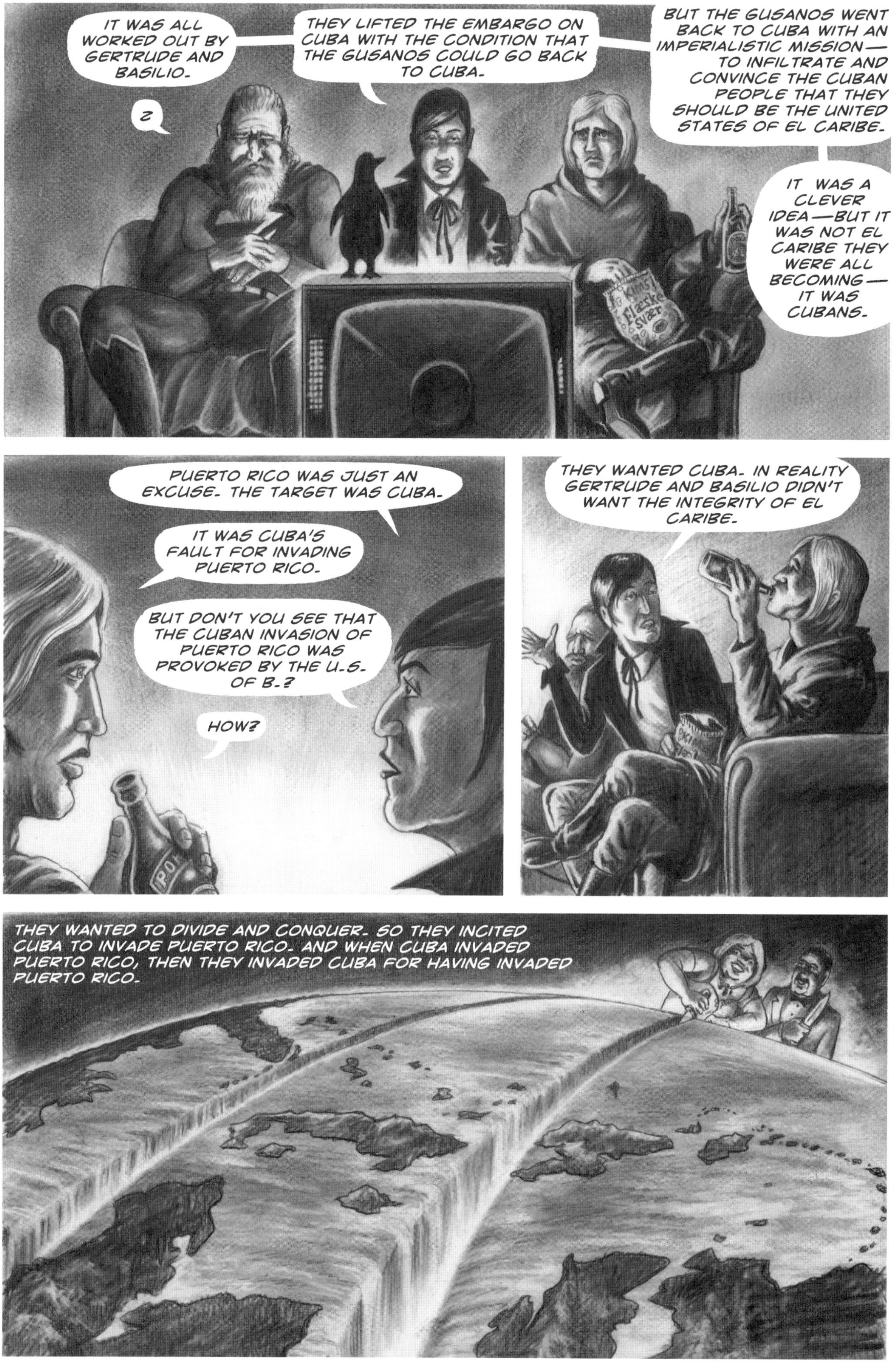
IT WAS ALL WORKED OUT BY GERTRUDE AND BASILIO.
?
THEY LIFTED THE EMBARGO ON CUBA WITH THE CONDITION THAT THE GUSANOS COULD GO BACK TO CUBA.
BUT THE GUSANOS WENT BACK TO CUBA WITH AN IMPERIALISTIC MISSION—TO INFILTRATE AND CONVINCE THE CUBAN PEOPLE THAT THEY SHOULD BE THE UNITED STATES OF EL CARIBE.
IT WAS A CLEVER IDEA—BUT IT WAS NOT EL CARIBE THEY WERE ALL BECOMING—IT WAS CUBANS.
KIMS! Flæske svær
PUERTO RICO WAS JUST AN EXCUSE. THE TARGET WAS CUBA.
IT WAS CUBA'S FAULT FOR INVADING PUERTO RICO.
BUT DON'T YOU SEE THAT THE CUBAN INVASION OF PUERTO RICO WAS PROVOKED BY THE U.S. OF B.?
HOW?
THEY WANTED CUBA. IN REALITY GERTRUDE AND BASILIO DIDN'T WANT THE INTEGRITY OF EL CARIBE.
THEY WANTED TO DIVIDE AND CONQUER. SO THEY INCITED CUBA TO INVADE PUERTO RICO. AND WHEN CUBA INVADED PUERTO RICO, THEN THEY INVADED CUBA FOR HAVING INVADED PUERTO RICO.

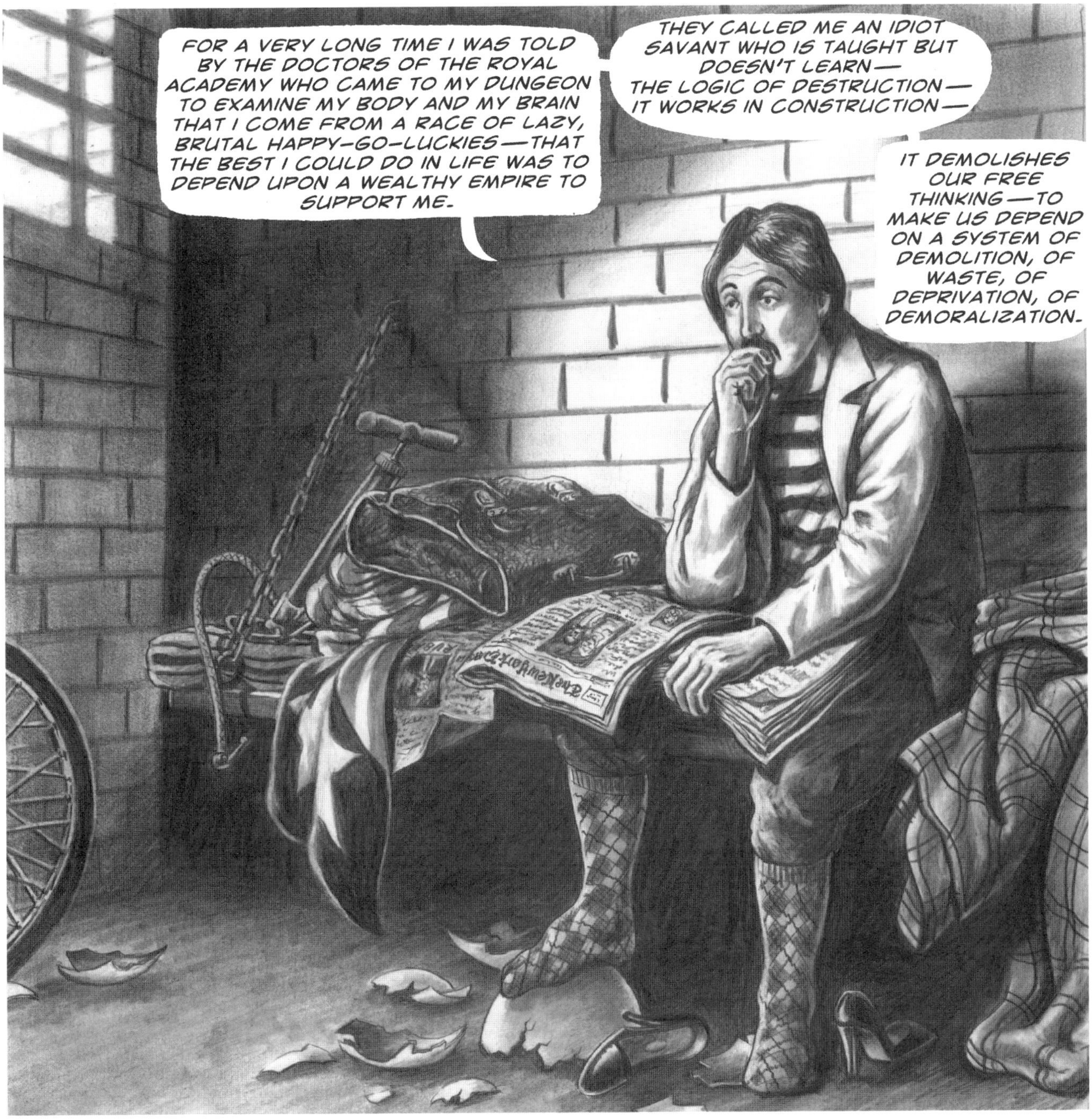
FOR A VERY LONG TIME I WAS TOLD BY THE DOCTORS OF THE ROYAL ACADEMY WHO CAME TO MY DUNGEON TO EXAMINE MY BODY AND MY BRAIN THAT I COME FROM A RACE OF LAZY, BRUTAL HAPPY-GO-LUCKIES—THAT THE BEST I COULD DO IN LIFE WAS TO DEPEND UPON A WEALTHY EMPIRE TO SUPPORT ME.
THEY CALLED ME AN IDIOT SAVANT WHO IS TAUGHT BUT DOESN'T LEARN—THE LOGIC OF DESTRUCTION—IT WORKS IN CONSTRUCTION—
IT DEMOLISHES OUR FREE THINKING—TO MAKE US DEPEND ON A SYSTEM OF DEMOLITION, OF WASTE, OF DEPRIVATION, OF DEMORALIZATION.

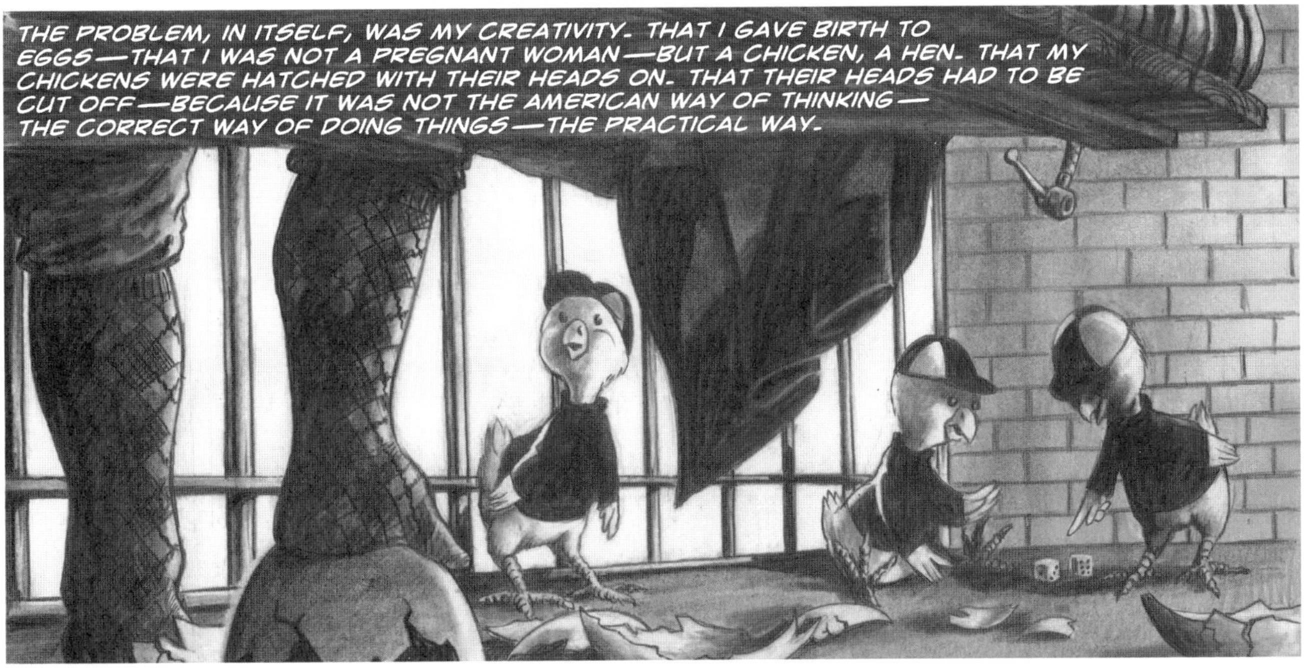
THE PROBLEM, IN ITSELF, WAS MY CREATIVITY. THAT I GAVE BIRTH TO EGGS—THAT I WAS NOT A PREGNANT WOMAN—BUT A CHICKEN, A HEN. THAT MY CHICKENS WERE HATCHED WITH THEIR HEADS ON. THAT THEIR HEADS HAD TO BE CUT OFF—BECAUSE IT WAS NOT THE AMERICAN WAY OF THINKING—THE CORRECT WAY OF DOING THINGS—THE PRACTICAL WAY.

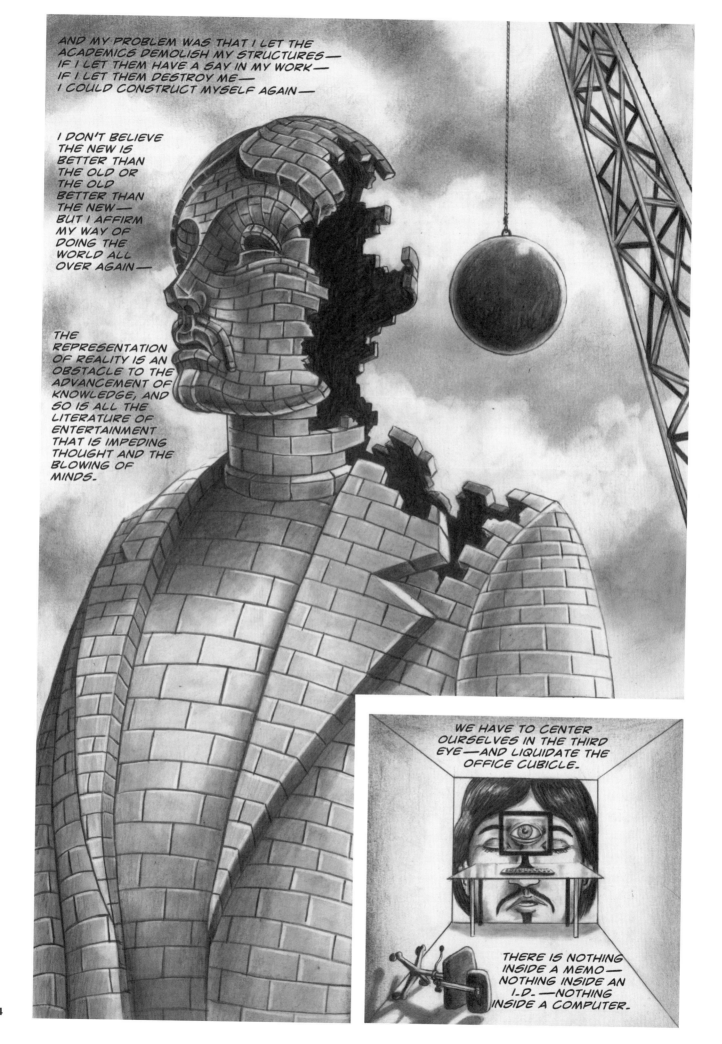

AND MY PROBLEM WAS THAT I LET THE
ACADEMICS DEMOLISH MY STRUCTURES—
IF I LET THEM HAVE A SAY IN MY WORK—
IF I LET THEM DESTROY ME—
I COULD CONSTRUCT MYSELF AGAIN—

I DON'T BELIEVE
THE NEW IS
BETTER THAN
THE OLD OR
THE OLD
BETTER THAN
THE NEW—
BUT I AFFIRM
MY WAY OF
DOING THE
WORLD ALL
OVER AGAIN—

THE
REPRESENTATION
OF REALITY IS AN
OBSTACLE TO THE
ADVANCEMENT OF
KNOWLEDGE, AND
SO IS ALL THE
LITERATURE OF
ENTERTAINMENT
THAT IS IMPEDING
THOUGHT AND THE
BLOWING OF
MINDS.

WE HAVE TO CENTER
OURSELVES IN THE THIRD
EYE—AND LIQUIDATE THE
OFFICE CUBICLE.

THERE IS NOTHING
INSIDE A MEMO—
NOTHING INSIDE AN
I.D.—NOTHING
INSIDE A COMPUTER.

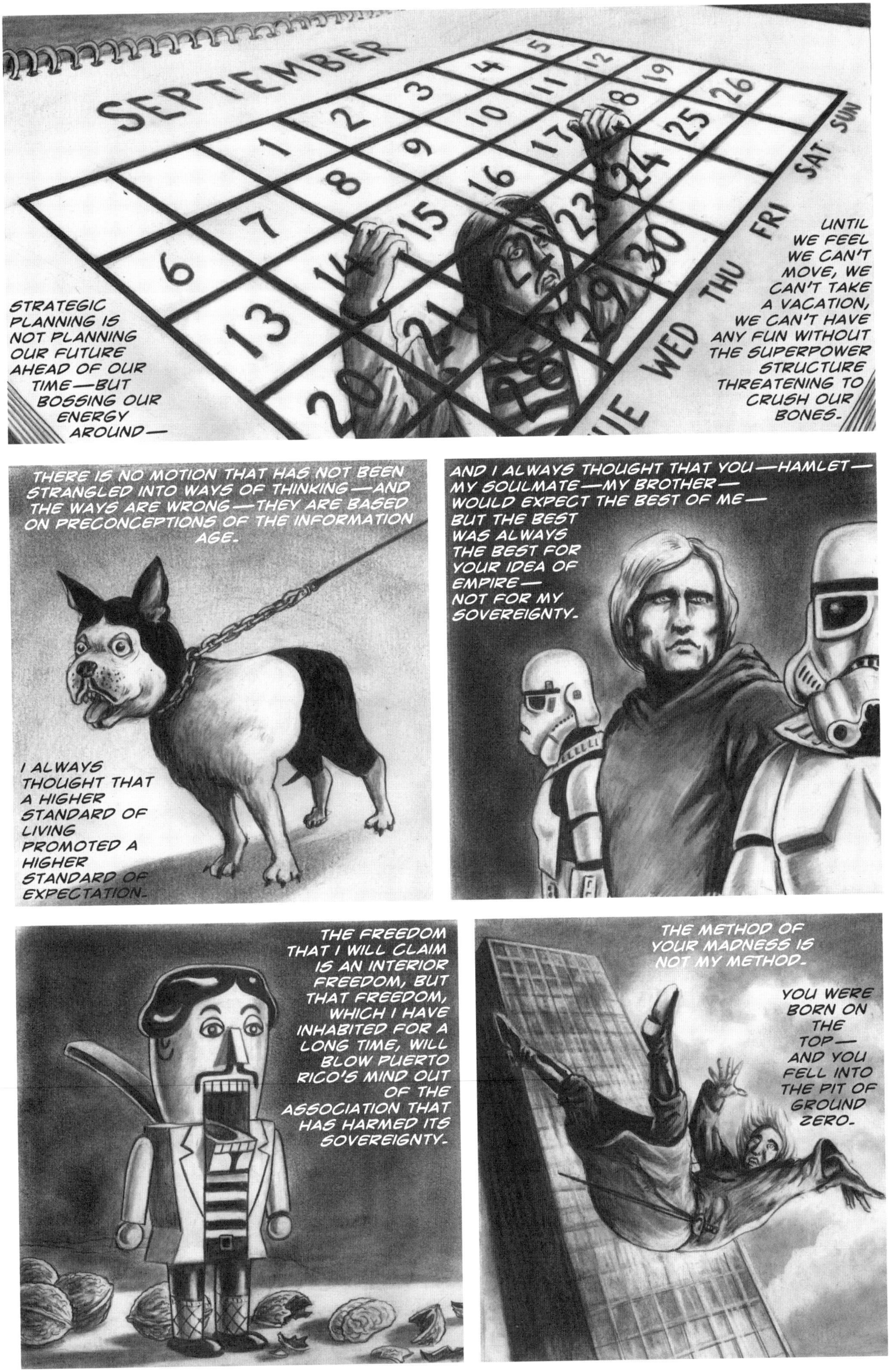
SEPTEMBER
TUE
WED
THU
FRI
SAT
SUN
STRATEGIC PLANNING IS NOT PLANNING OUR FUTURE AHEAD OF OUR TIME—BUT BOSSING OUR ENERGY AROUND—
UNTIL WE FEEL WE CAN'T MOVE, WE CAN'T TAKE A VACATION, WE CAN'T HAVE ANY FUN WITHOUT THE SUPERPOWER STRUCTURE THREATENING TO CRUSH OUR BONES.
THERE IS NO MOTION THAT HAS NOT BEEN STRANGLED INTO WAYS OF THINKING—AND THE WAYS ARE WRONG—THEY ARE BASED ON PRECONCEPTIONS OF THE INFORMATION AGE.
I ALWAYS THOUGHT THAT A HIGHER STANDARD OF LIVING PROMOTED A HIGHER STANDARD OF EXPECTATION.
AND I ALWAYS THOUGHT THAT YOU—HAMLET—MY SOULMATE—MY BROTHER—WOULD EXPECT THE BEST OF ME—
BUT THE BEST WAS ALWAYS THE BEST FOR YOUR IDEA OF EMPIRE—NOT FOR MY SOVEREIGNTY.
THE FREEDOM THAT I WILL CLAIM IS AN INTERIOR FREEDOM, BUT THAT FREEDOM, WHICH I HAVE INHABITED FOR A LONG TIME, WILL BLOW PUERTO RICO'S MIND OUT OF THE ASSOCIATION THAT HAS HARMED ITS SOVEREIGNTY.
THE METHOD OF YOUR MADNESS IS NOT MY METHOD.
YOU WERE BORN ON THE TOP—AND YOU FELL INTO THE PIT OF GROUND ZERO.

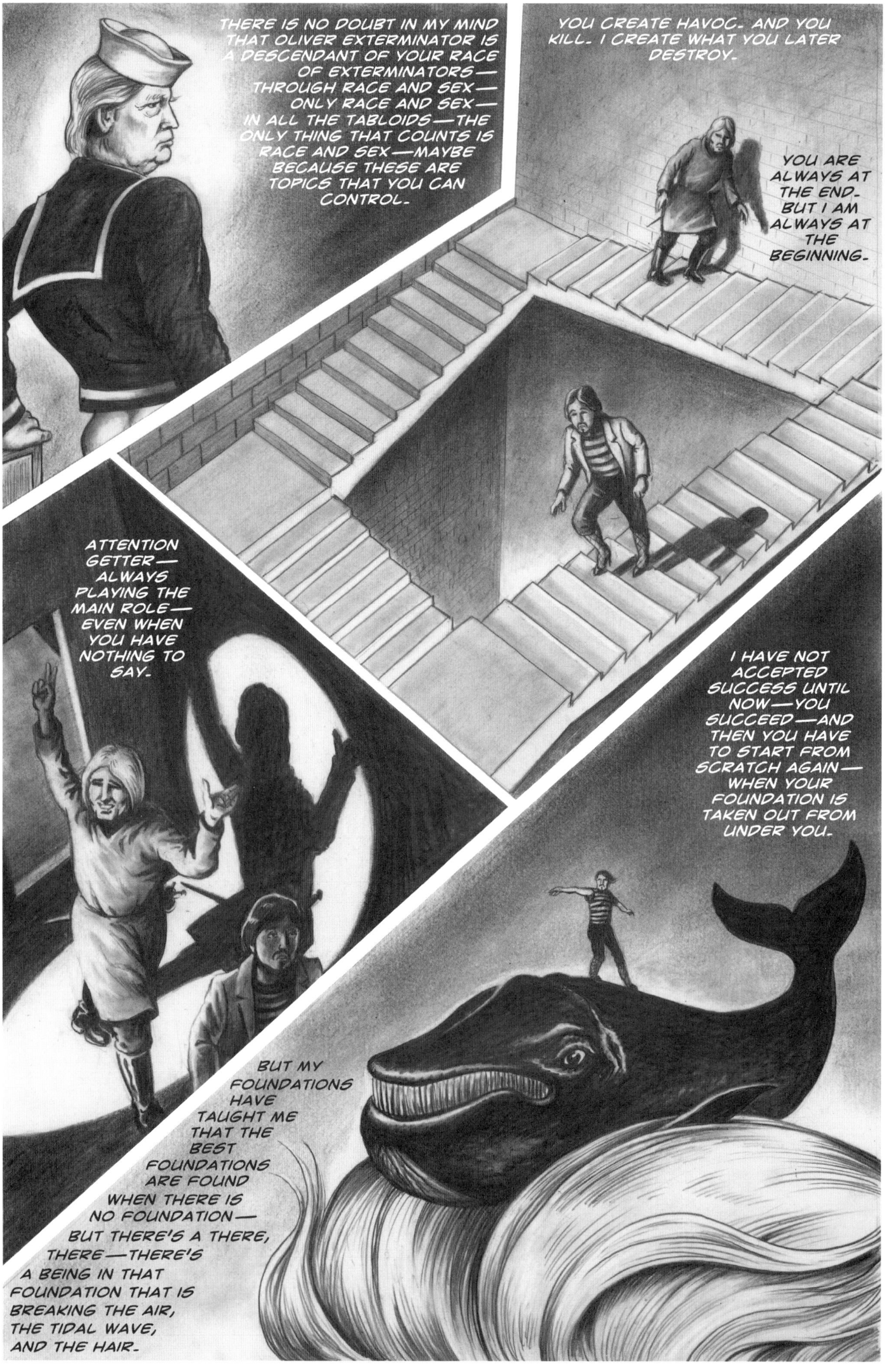
THERE IS NO DOUBT IN MY MIND THAT OLIVER EXTERMINATOR IS A DESCENDANT OF YOUR RACE OF EXTERMINATORS—THROUGH RACE AND SEX—ONLY RACE AND SEX—IN ALL THE TABLOIDS—THE ONLY THING THAT COUNTS IS RACE AND SEX—MAYBE BECAUSE THESE ARE TOPICS THAT YOU CAN CONTROL.
YOU CREATE HAVOC. AND YOU KILL. I CREATE WHAT YOU LATER DESTROY.
YOU ARE ALWAYS AT THE END. BUT I AM ALWAYS AT THE BEGINNING.
ATTENTION GETTER—ALWAYS PLAYING THE MAIN ROLE—EVEN WHEN YOU HAVE NOTHING TO SAY.
I HAVE NOT ACCEPTED SUCCESS UNTIL NOW—YOU SUCCEED—AND THEN YOU HAVE TO START FROM SCRATCH AGAIN—WHEN YOUR FOUNDATION IS TAKEN OUT FROM UNDER YOU.
BUT MY FOUNDATIONS HAVE TAUGHT ME THAT THE BEST FOUNDATIONS ARE FOUND WHEN THERE IS NO FOUNDATION—BUT THERE'S A THERE, THERE—THERE'S A BEING IN THAT FOUNDATION THAT IS BREAKING THE AIR, THE TIDAL WAVE, AND THE HAIR.

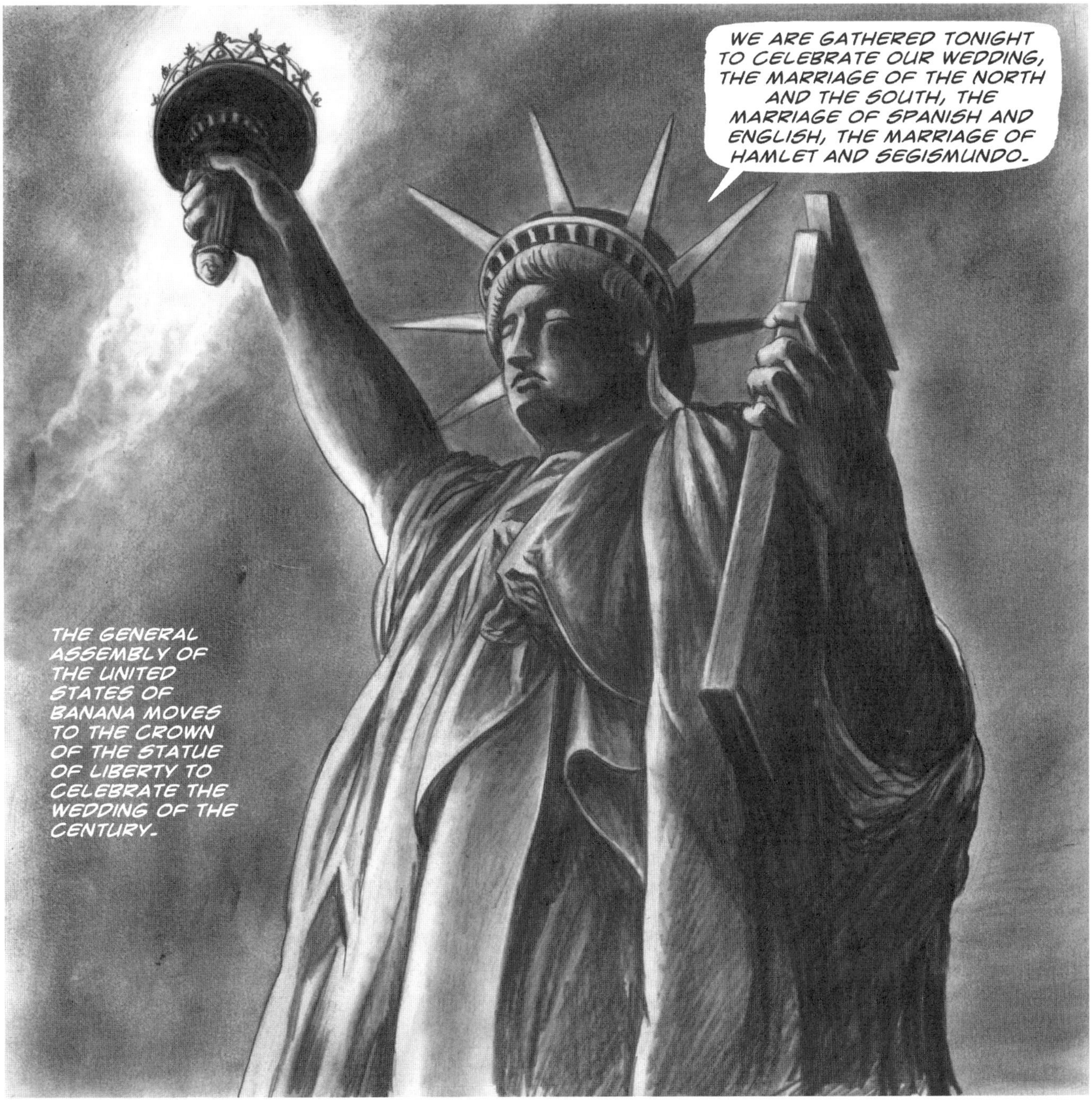
THE GENERAL ASSEMBLY OF THE UNITED STATES OF BANANA MOVES TO THE CROWN OF THE STATUE OF LIBERTY TO CELEBRATE THE WEDDING OF THE CENTURY.
WE ARE GATHERED TONIGHT TO CELEBRATE OUR WEDDING, THE MARRIAGE OF THE NORTH AND THE SOUTH, THE MARRIAGE OF SPANISH AND ENGLISH, THE MARRIAGE OF HAMLET AND SEGISMUNDO.

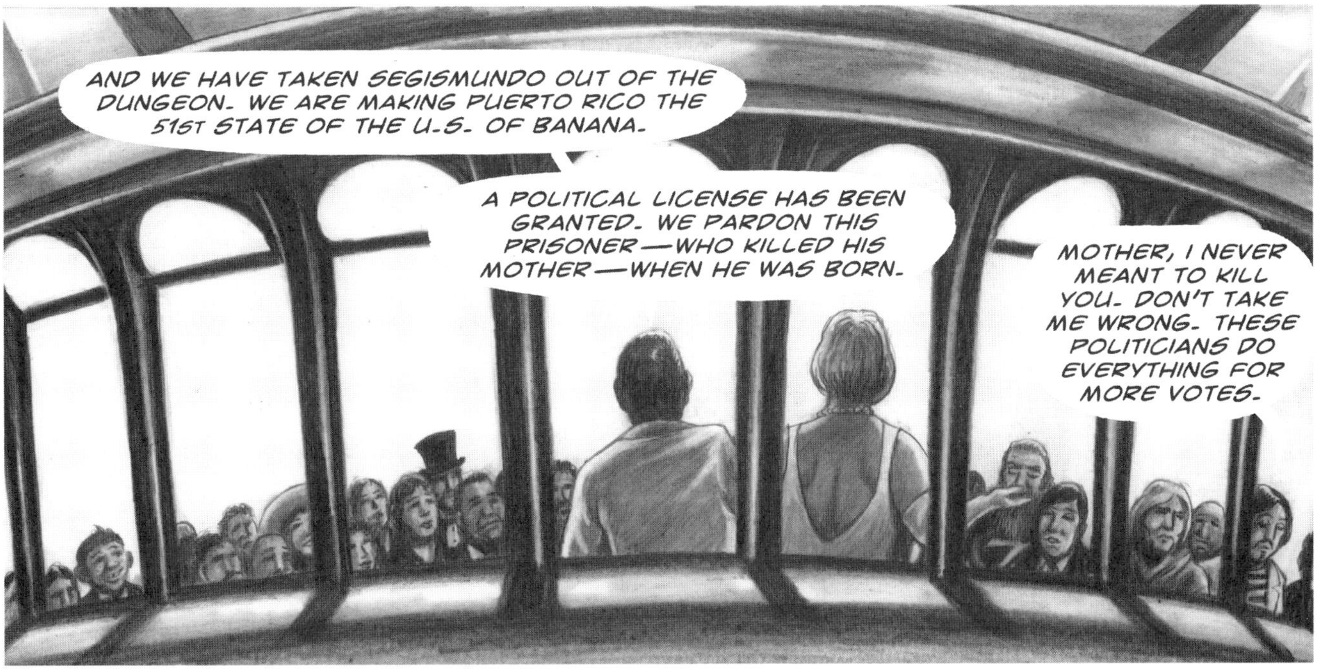
AND WE HAVE TAKEN SEGISMUNDO OUT OF THE DUNGEON. WE ARE MAKING PUERTO RICO THE 51ST STATE OF THE U.S. OF BANANA.
A POLITICAL LICENSE HAS BEEN GRANTED. WE PARDON THIS PRISONER—WHO KILLED HIS MOTHER—WHEN HE WAS BORN.
MOTHER, I NEVER MEANT TO KILL YOU. DON'T TAKE ME WRONG. THESE POLITICIANS DO EVERYTHING FOR MORE VOTES.

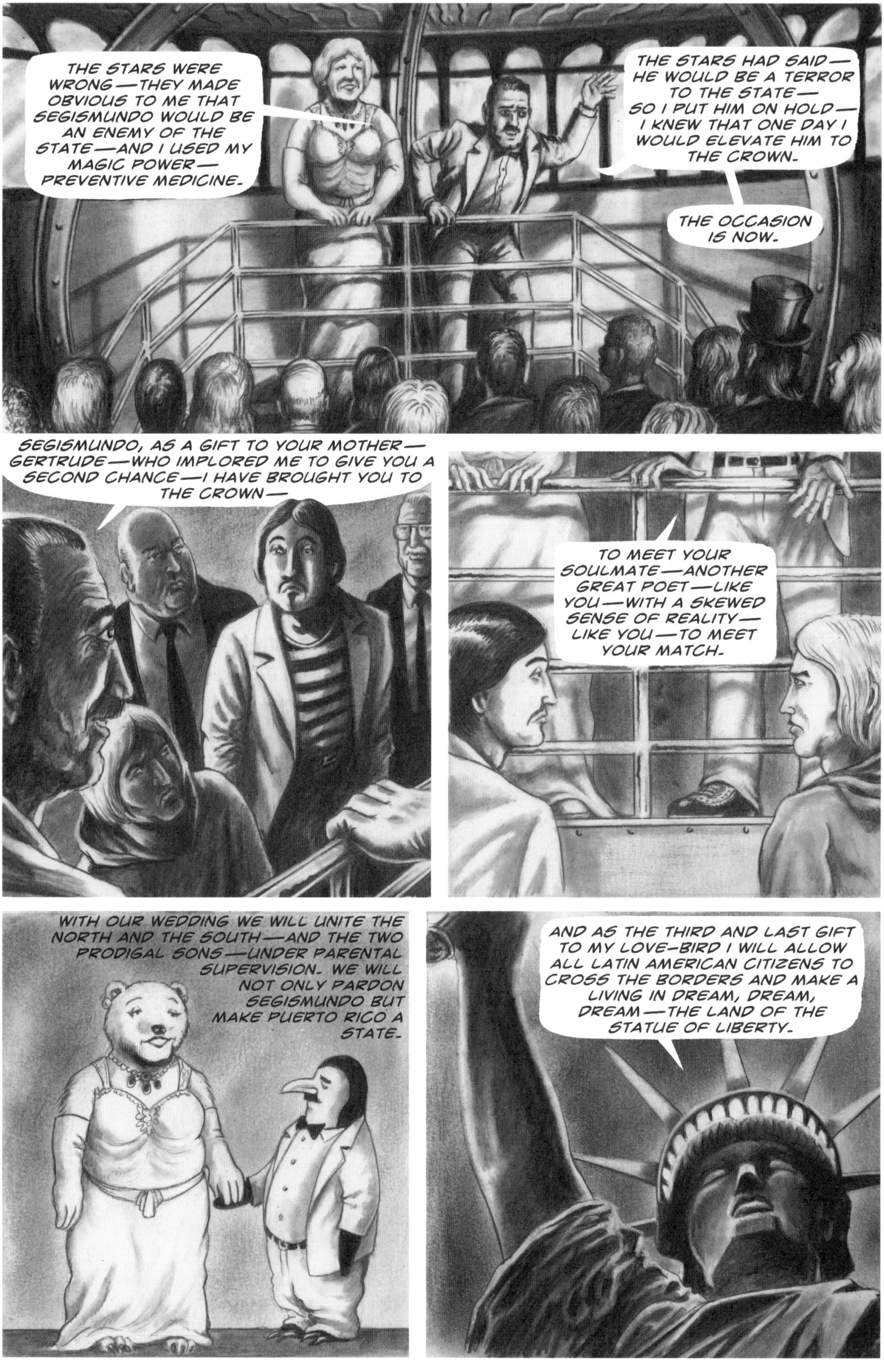
THE STARS WERE WRONG—THEY MADE OBVIOUS TO ME THAT SEGISMUNDO WOULD BE AN ENEMY OF THE STATE—AND I USED MY MAGIC POWER—PREVENTIVE MEDICINE.
THE STARS HAD SAID—HE WOULD BE A TERROR TO THE STATE—SO I PUT HIM ON HOLD—I KNEW THAT ONE DAY I WOULD ELEVATE HIM TO THE CROWN.
THE OCCASION IS NOW.
SEGISMUNDO, AS A GIFT TO YOUR MOTHER—GERTRUDE—WHO IMPLORED ME TO GIVE YOU A SECOND CHANCE—I HAVE BROUGHT YOU TO THE CROWN—
TO MEET YOUR SOULMATE—ANOTHER GREAT POET—LIKE YOU—WITH A SKEWED SENSE OF REALITY—LIKE YOU—TO MEET YOUR MATCH.
WITH OUR WEDDING WE WILL UNITE THE NORTH AND THE SOUTH—AND THE TWO PRODIGAL SONS—UNDER PARENTAL SUPERVISION. WE WILL NOT ONLY PARDON SEGISMUNDO BUT MAKE PUERTO RICO A STATE.
AND AS THE THIRD AND LAST GIFT TO MY LOVE-BIRD I WILL ALLOW ALL LATIN AMERICAN CITIZENS TO CROSS THE BORDERS AND MAKE A LIVING IN DREAM, DREAM, DREAM—THE LAND OF THE STATUE OF LIBERTY.

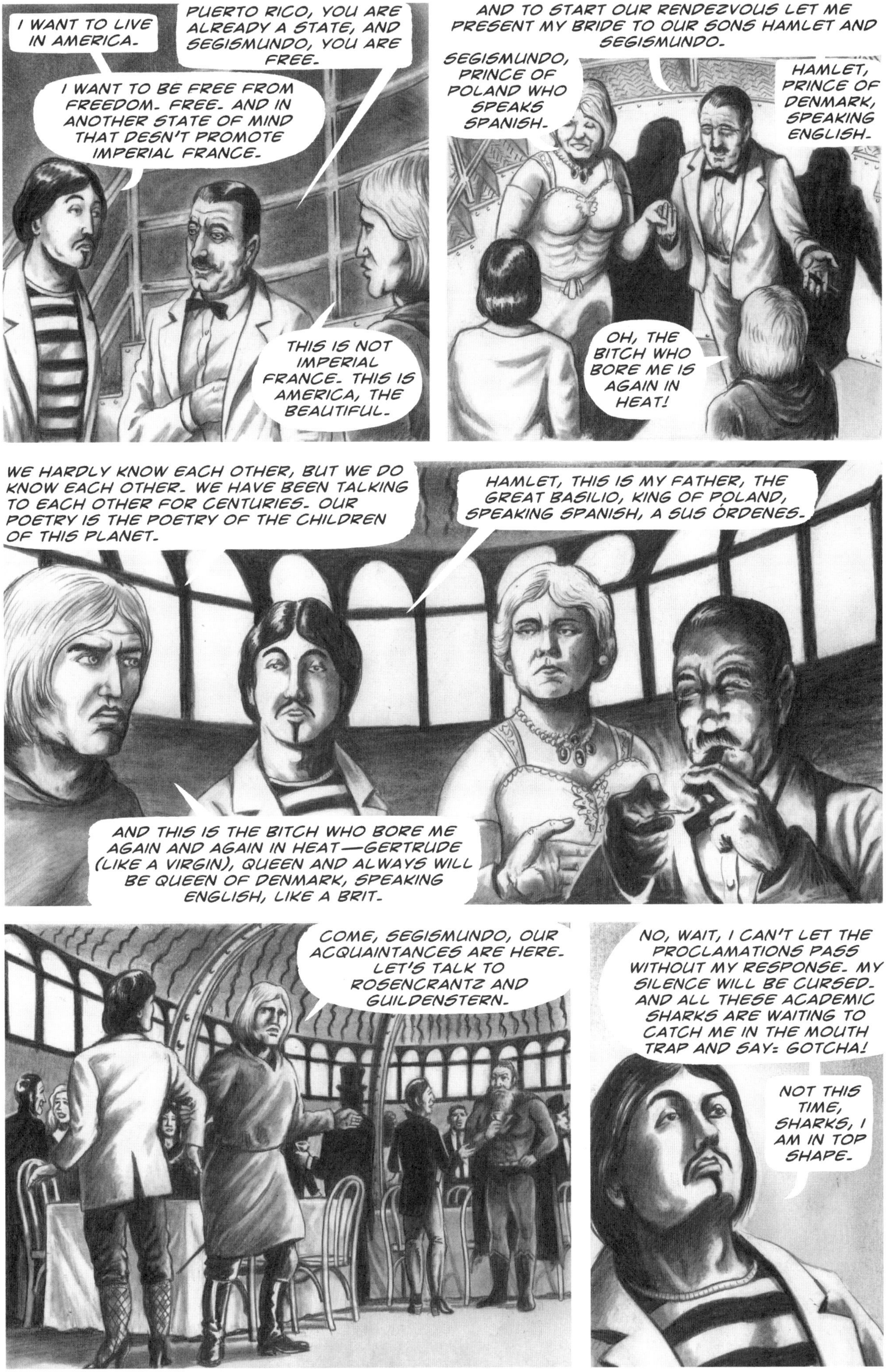
I WANT TO LIVE IN AMERICA.
PUERTO RICO, YOU ARE ALREADY A STATE, AND SEGISMUNDO, YOU ARE FREE.
I WANT TO BE FREE FROM FREEDOM. FREE. AND IN ANOTHER STATE OF MIND THAT DESN'T PROMOTE IMPERIAL FRANCE.
THIS IS NOT IMPERIAL FRANCE. THIS IS AMERICA, THE BEAUTIFUL.
AND TO START OUR RENDEZVOUS LET ME PRESENT MY BRIDE TO OUR SONS HAMLET AND SEGISMUNDO.
SEGISMUNDO, PRINCE OF POLAND WHO SPEAKS SPANISH.
HAMLET, PRINCE OF DENMARK, SPEAKING ENGLISH.
OH, THE BITCH WHO BORE ME IS AGAIN IN HEAT!
WE HARDLY KNOW EACH OTHER, BUT WE DO KNOW EACH OTHER. WE HAVE BEEN TALKING TO EACH OTHER FOR CENTURIES. OUR POETRY IS THE POETRY OF THE CHILDREN OF THIS PLANET.
HAMLET, THIS IS MY FATHER, THE GREAT BASILIO, KING OF POLAND, SPEAKING SPANISH, A SUS ÓRDENES.
AND THIS IS THE BITCH WHO BORE ME AGAIN AND AGAIN IN HEAT—GERTRUDE (LIKE A VIRGIN), QUEEN AND ALWAYS WILL BE QUEEN OF DENMARK, SPEAKING ENGLISH, LIKE A BRIT.
COME, SEGISMUNDO, OUR ACQUAINTANCES ARE HERE. LET'S TALK TO ROSENCRANTZ AND GUILDENSTERN.
NO, WAIT, I CAN'T LET THE PROCLAMATIONS PASS WITHOUT MY RESPONSE. MY SILENCE WILL BE CURSED. AND ALL THESE ACADEMIC SHARKS ARE WAITING TO CATCH ME IN THE MOUTH TRAP AND SAY: GOTCHA!
NOT THIS TIME, SHARKS, I AM IN TOP SHAPE.

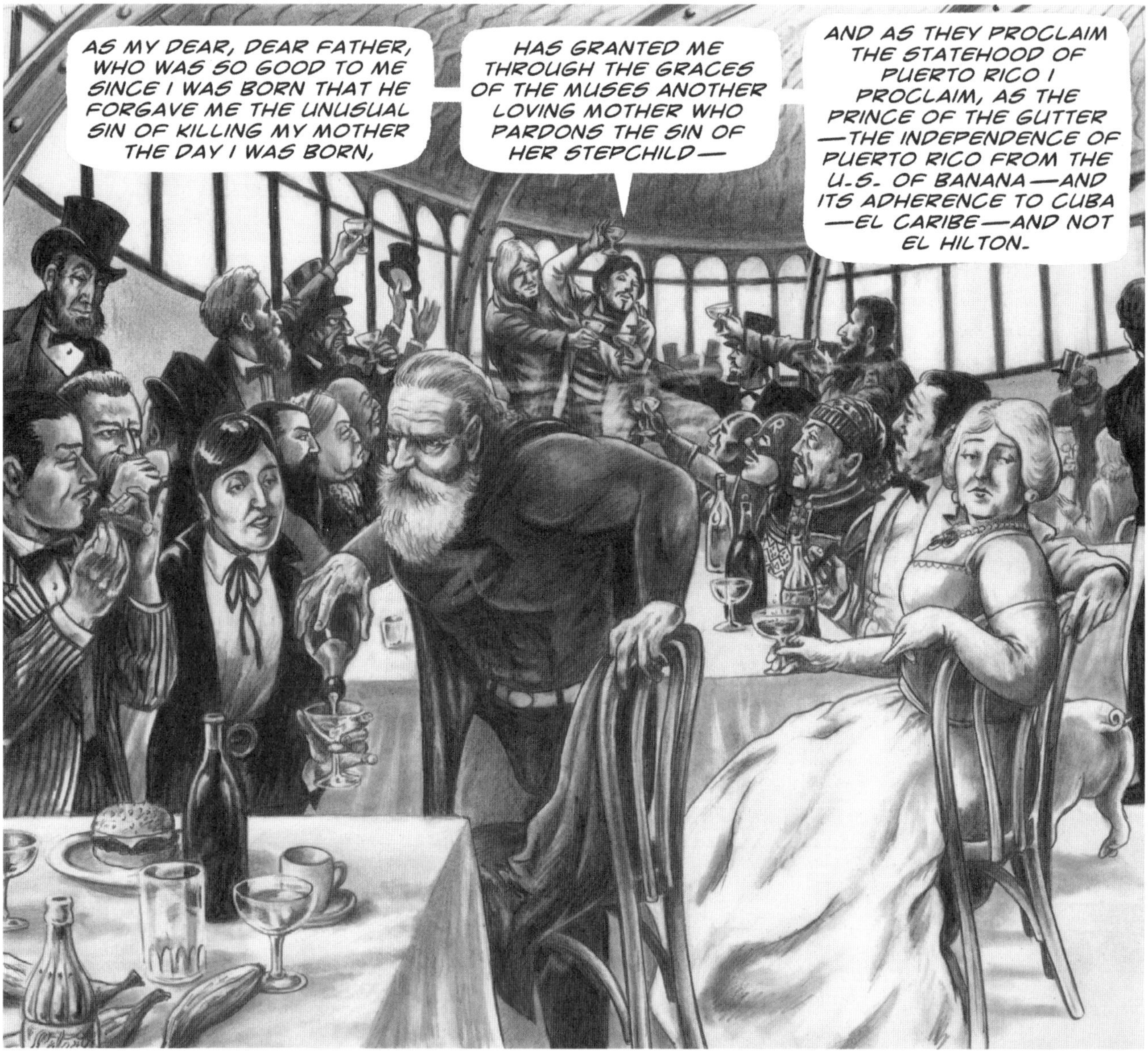
AS MY DEAR, DEAR FATHER, WHO WAS SO GOOD TO ME SINCE I WAS BORN THAT HE FORGAVE ME THE UNUSUAL SIN OF KILLING MY MOTHER THE DAY I WAS BORN,
HAS GRANTED ME THROUGH THE GRACES OF THE MUSES ANOTHER LOVING MOTHER WHO PARDONS THE SIN OF HER STEPCHILD—
AND AS THEY PROCLAIM THE STATEHOOD OF PUERTO RICO I PROCLAIM, AS THE PRINCE OF THE GUTTER —THE INDEPENDENCE OF PUERTO RICO FROM THE U.S. OF BANANA—AND ITS ADHERENCE TO CUBA —EL CARIBE—AND NOT EL HILTON.

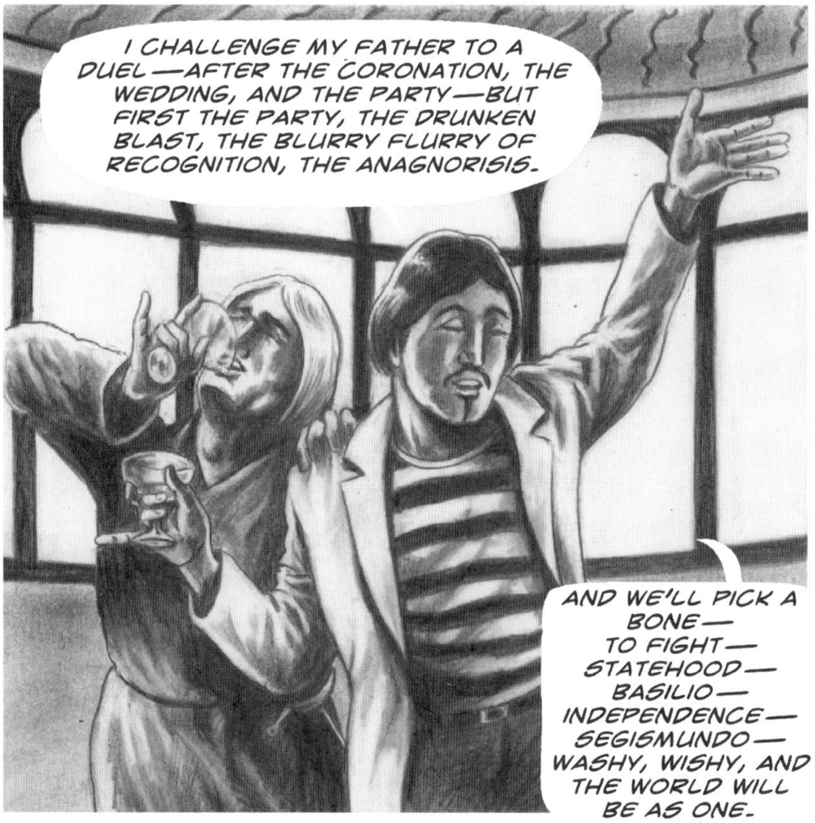
I CHALLENGE MY FATHER TO A DUEL—AFTER THE CORONATION, THE WEDDING, AND THE PARTY—BUT FIRST THE PARTY, THE DRUNKEN BLAST, THE BLURRY FLURRY OF RECOGNITION, THE ANAGNORISIS.
AND WE'LL PICK A BONE— TO FIGHT— STATEHOOD— BASILIO— INDEPENDENCE— SEGISMUNDO— WASHY, WISHY, AND THE WORLD WILL BE AS ONE.

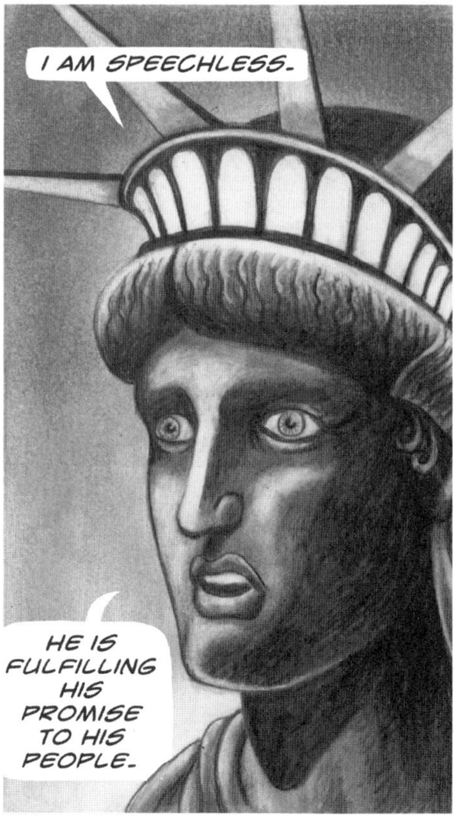
I AM SPEECHLESS.
HE IS FULFILLING HIS PROMISE TO HIS PEOPLE.

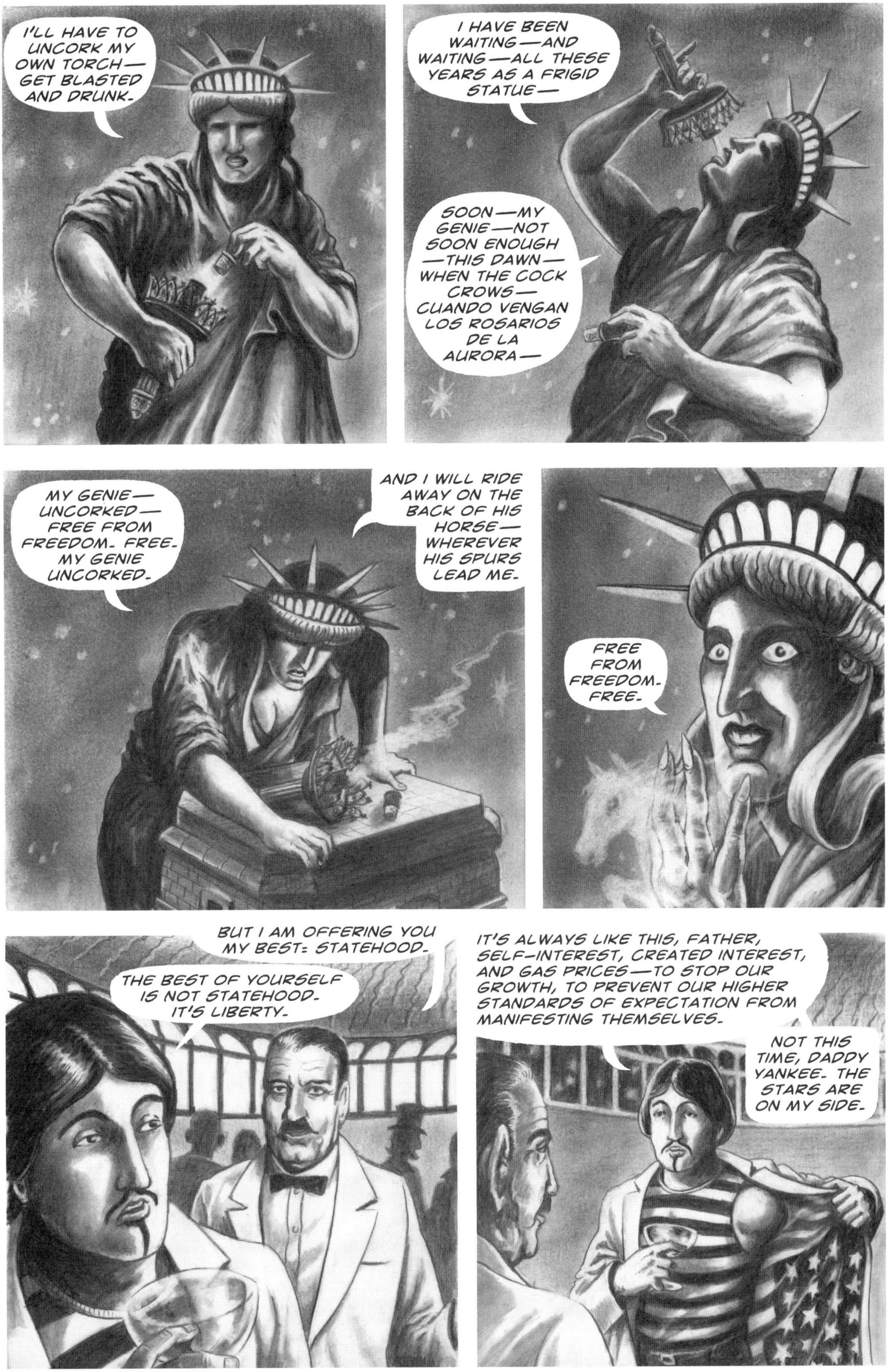
I'LL HAVE TO UNCORK MY OWN TORCH—GET BLASTED AND DRUNK.
I HAVE BEEN WAITING—AND WAITING—ALL THESE YEARS AS A FRIGID STATUE—
SOON—MY GENIE—NOT SOON ENOUGH—THIS DAWN—WHEN THE COCK CROWS—CUANDO VENGAN LOS ROSARIOS DE LA AURORA—
MY GENIE—UNCORKED—FREE FROM FREEDOM. FREE. MY GENIE UNCORKED.
AND I WILL RIDE AWAY ON THE BACK OF HIS HORSE—WHEREVER HIS SPURS LEAD ME.
FREE FROM FREEDOM. FREE.
BUT I AM OFFERING YOU MY BEST: STATEHOOD.
THE BEST OF YOURSELF IS NOT STATEHOOD. IT'S LIBERTY.
IT'S ALWAYS LIKE THIS, FATHER, SELF-INTEREST, CREATED INTEREST, AND GAS PRICES—TO STOP OUR GROWTH, TO PREVENT OUR HIGHER STANDARDS OF EXPECTATION FROM MANIFESTING THEMSELVES.
NOT THIS TIME, DADDY YANKEE. THE STARS ARE ON MY SIDE.

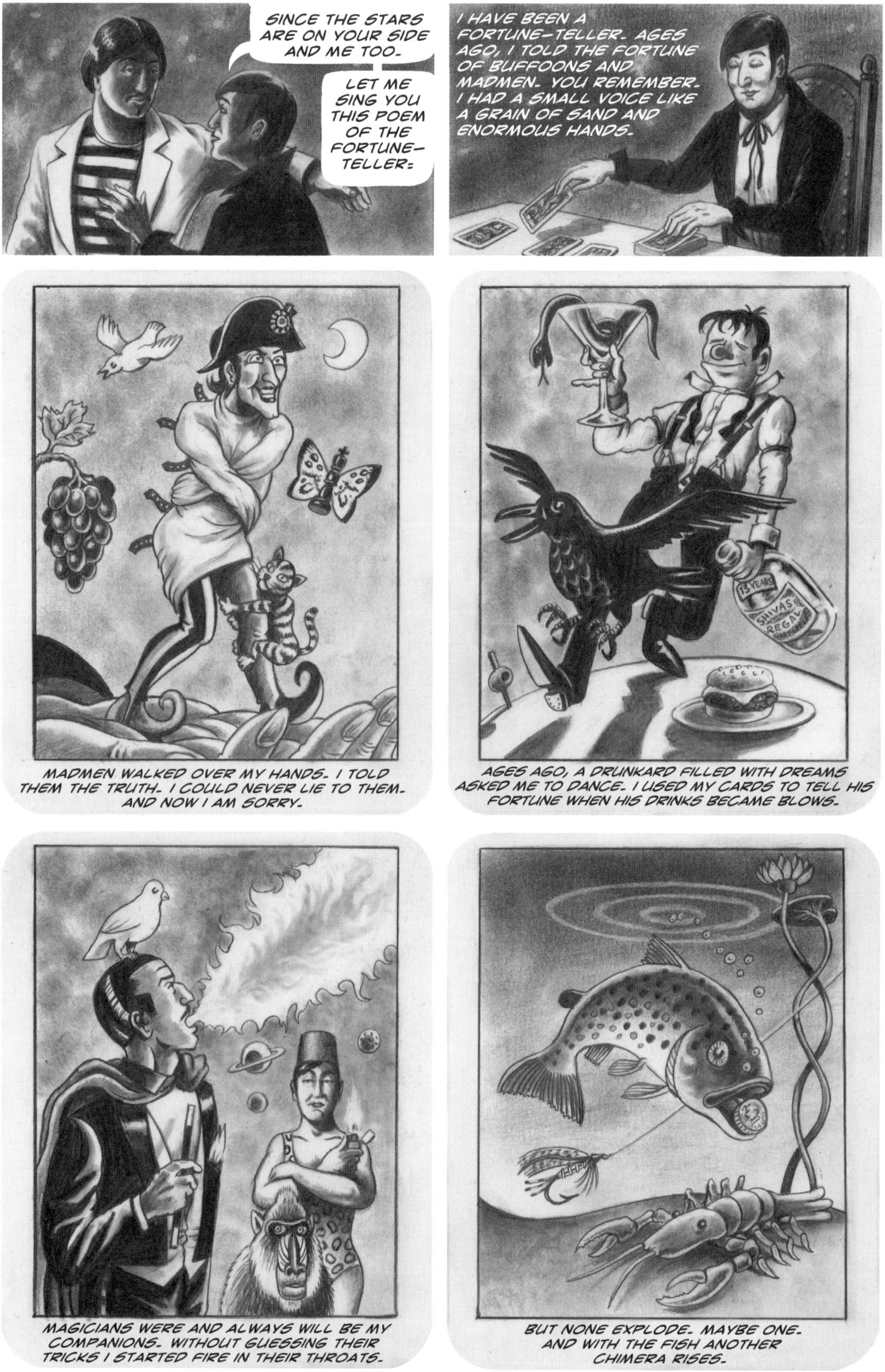
SINCE THE STARS ARE ON YOUR SIDE AND ME TOO.
LET ME SING YOU THIS POEM OF THE FORTUNE-TELLER:
I HAVE BEEN A FORTUNE-TELLER. AGES AGO, I TOLD THE FORTUNE OF BUFFOONS AND MADMEN. YOU REMEMBER. I HAD A SMALL VOICE LIKE A GRAIN OF SAND AND ENORMOUS HANDS.
MADMEN WALKED OVER MY HANDS. I TOLD THEM THE TRUTH. I COULD NEVER LIE TO THEM. AND NOW I AM SORRY.
13 YEARS
SHIVAS REGAL
AGES AGO, A DRUNKARD FILLED WITH DREAMS ASKED ME TO DANCE. I USED MY CARDS TO TELL HIS FORTUNE WHEN HIS DRINKS BECAME BLOWS.
MAGICIANS WERE AND ALWAYS WILL BE MY COMPANIONS. WITHOUT GUESSING THEIR TRICKS I STARTED FIRE IN THEIR THROATS.
BUT NONE EXPLODE. MAYBE ONE. AND WITH THE FISH ANOTHER CHIMERA RISES.

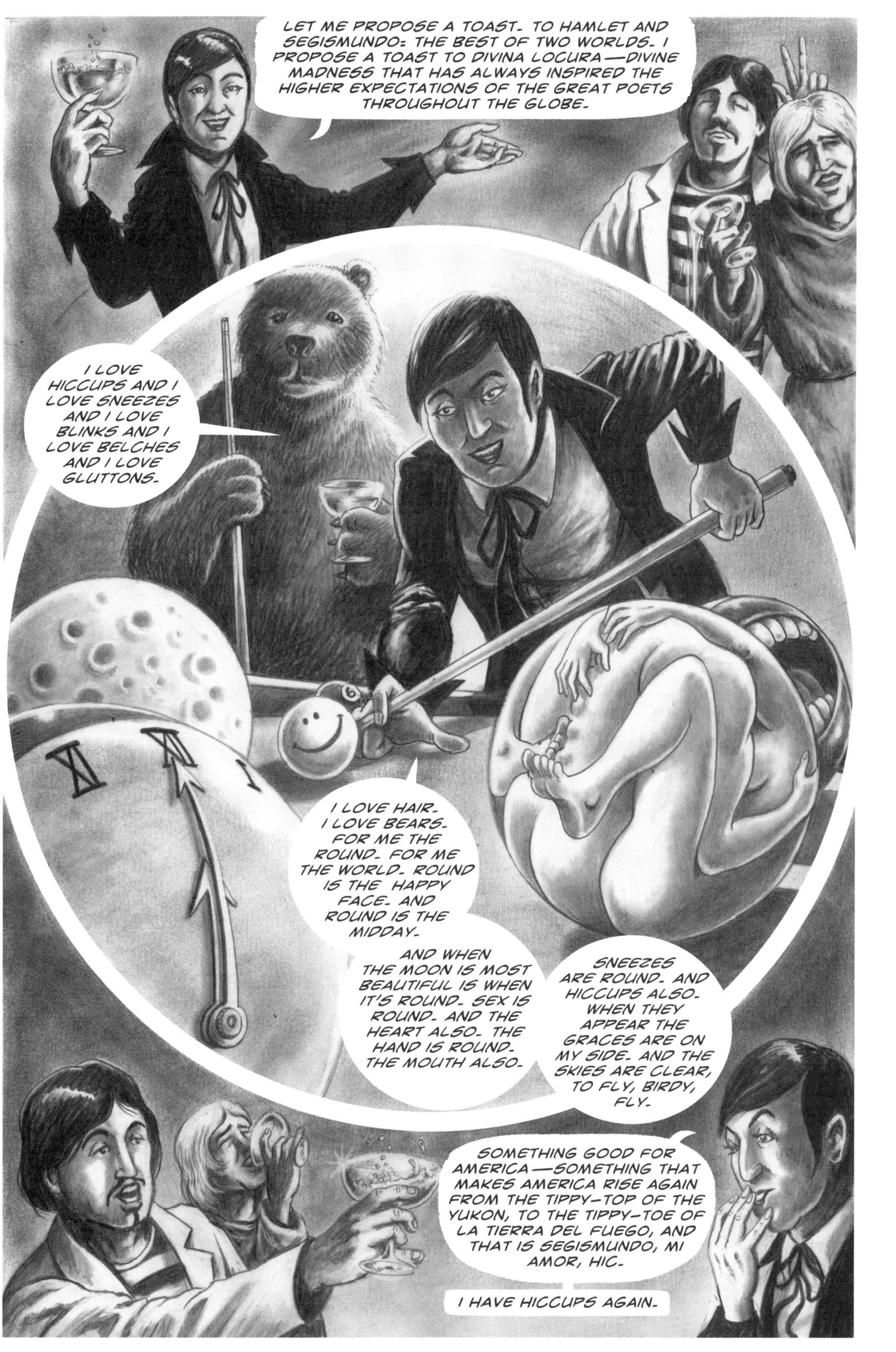
LET ME PROPOSE A TOAST. TO HAMLET AND SEGISMUNDO: THE BEST OF TWO WORLDS. I PROPOSE A TOAST TO DIVINA LOCURA—DIVINE MADNESS THAT HAS ALWAYS INSPIRED THE HIGHER EXPECTATIONS OF THE GREAT POETS THROUGHOUT THE GLOBE.
I LOVE HICCUPS AND I LOVE SNEEZES AND I LOVE BLINKS AND I LOVE BELCHES AND I LOVE GLUTTONS.
I LOVE HAIR. I LOVE BEARS. FOR ME THE ROUND. FOR ME THE WORLD. ROUND IS THE HAPPY FACE. AND ROUND IS THE MIDDAY.
AND WHEN THE MOON IS MOST BEAUTIFUL IS WHEN IT'S ROUND. SEX IS ROUND. AND THE HEART ALSO. THE HAND IS ROUND. THE MOUTH ALSO.
SNEEZES ARE ROUND. AND HICCUPS ALSO. WHEN THEY APPEAR THE GRACES ARE ON MY SIDE. AND THE SKIES ARE CLEAR, TO FLY, BIRDY, FLY.
SOMETHING GOOD FOR AMERICA—SOMETHING THAT MAKES AMERICA RISE AGAIN FROM THE TIPPY-TOP OF THE YUKON, TO THE TIPPY-TOE OF LA TIERRA DEL FUEGO, AND THAT IS SEGISMUNDO, MI AMOR, HIC.
I HAVE HICCUPS AGAIN.

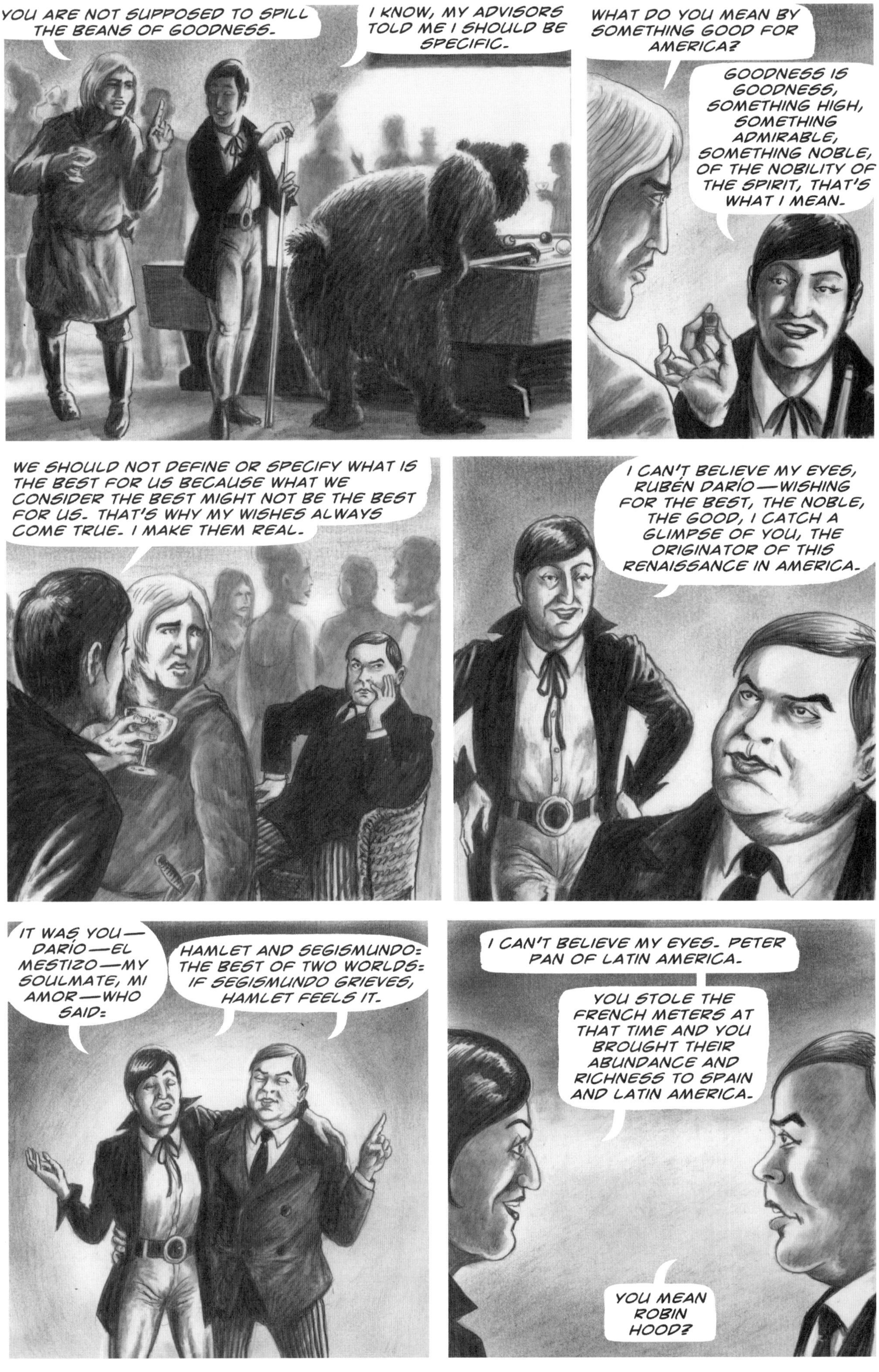
YOU ARE NOT SUPPOSED TO SPILL THE BEANS OF GOODNESS.
I KNOW, MY ADVISORS TOLD ME I SHOULD BE SPECIFIC.
WHAT DO YOU MEAN BY SOMETHING GOOD FOR AMERICA?
GOODNESS IS GOODNESS, SOMETHING HIGH, SOMETHING ADMIRABLE, SOMETHING NOBLE, OF THE NOBILITY OF THE SPIRIT, THAT'S WHAT I MEAN.
WE SHOULD NOT DEFINE OR SPECIFY WHAT IS THE BEST FOR US BECAUSE WHAT WE CONSIDER THE BEST MIGHT NOT BE THE BEST FOR US. THAT'S WHY MY WISHES ALWAYS COME TRUE. I MAKE THEM REAL.
I CAN'T BELIEVE MY EYES, RUBÉN DARÍO—WISHING FOR THE BEST, THE NOBLE, THE GOOD, I CATCH A GLIMPSE OF YOU, THE ORIGINATOR OF THIS RENAISSANCE IN AMERICA.
IT WAS YOU—DARÍO—EL MESTIZO—MY SOULMATE, MI AMOR—WHO SAID:
HAMLET AND SEGISMUNDO: THE BEST OF TWO WORLDS: IF SEGISMUNDO GRIEVES, HAMLET FEELS IT.
I CAN'T BELIEVE MY EYES. PETER PAN OF LATIN AMERICA.
YOU STOLE THE FRENCH METERS AT THAT TIME AND YOU BROUGHT THEIR ABUNDANCE AND RICHNESS TO SPAIN AND LATIN AMERICA.
YOU MEAN ROBIN HOOD?

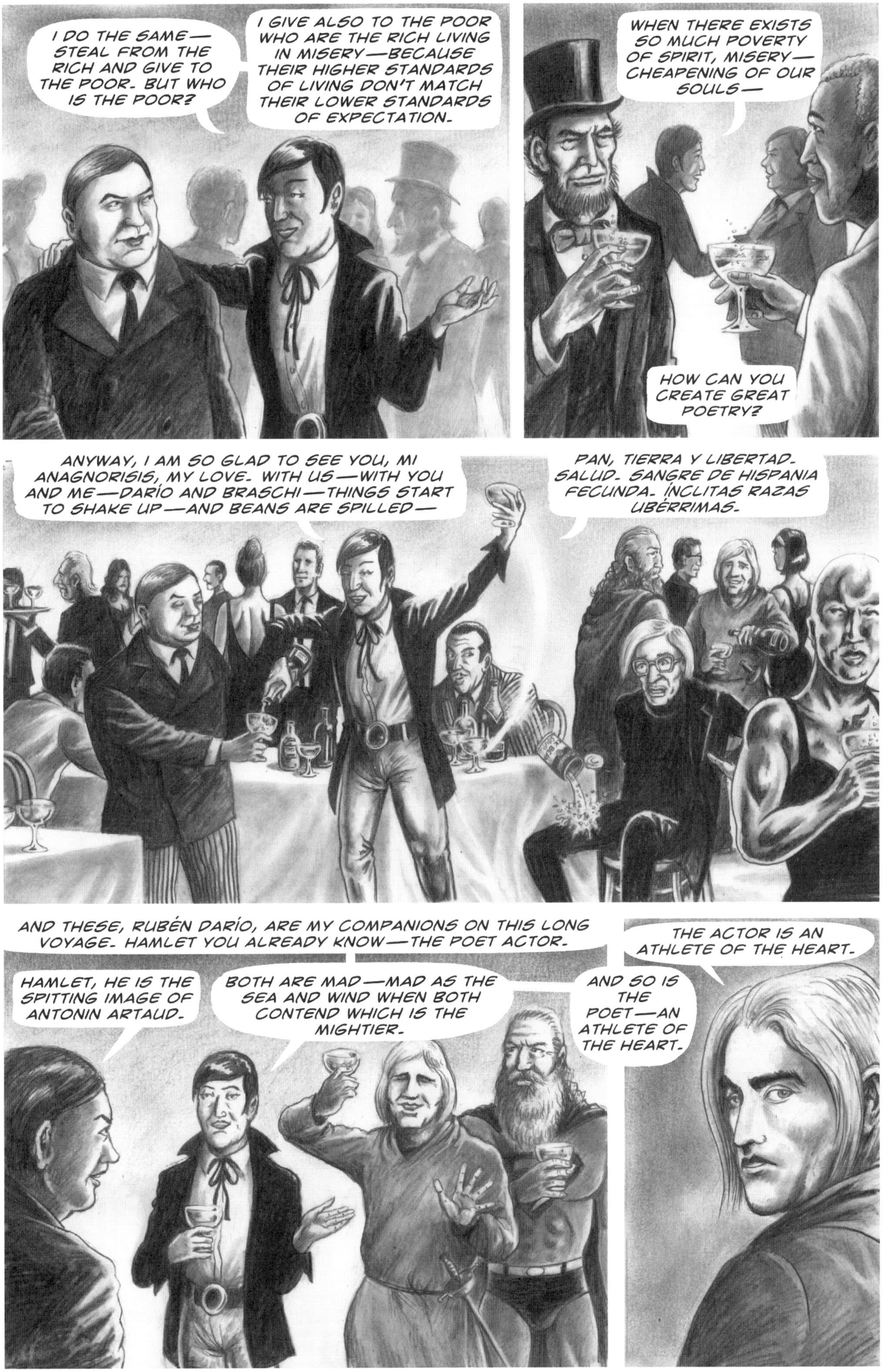
I DO THE SAME—STEAL FROM THE RICH AND GIVE TO THE POOR. BUT WHO IS THE POOR?
I GIVE ALSO TO THE POOR WHO ARE THE RICH LIVING IN MISERY—BECAUSE THEIR HIGHER STANDARDS OF LIVING DON'T MATCH THEIR LOWER STANDARDS OF EXPECTATION.
WHEN THERE EXISTS SO MUCH POVERTY OF SPIRIT, MISERY—CHEAPENING OF OUR SOULS—
HOW CAN YOU CREATE GREAT POETRY?
ANYWAY, I AM SO GLAD TO SEE YOU, MI ANAGNORISIS, MY LOVE. WITH US—WITH YOU AND ME—DARÍO AND BRASCHI—THINGS START TO SHAKE UP—AND BEANS ARE SPILLED—
PAN, TIERRA Y LIBERTAD. SALUD. SANGRE DE HISPANIA FECUNDA. ÍNCLITAS RAZAS UBÉRRIMAS.
AND THESE, RUBÉN DARÍO, ARE MY COMPANIONS ON THIS LONG VOYAGE. HAMLET YOU ALREADY KNOW—THE POET ACTOR.
HAMLET, HE IS THE SPITTING IMAGE OF ANTONIN ARTAUD.
BOTH ARE MAD—MAD AS THE SEA AND WIND WHEN BOTH CONTEND WHICH IS THE MIGHTIER.
AND SO IS THE POET—AN ATHLETE OF THE HEART.
THE ACTOR IS AN ATHLETE OF THE HEART.

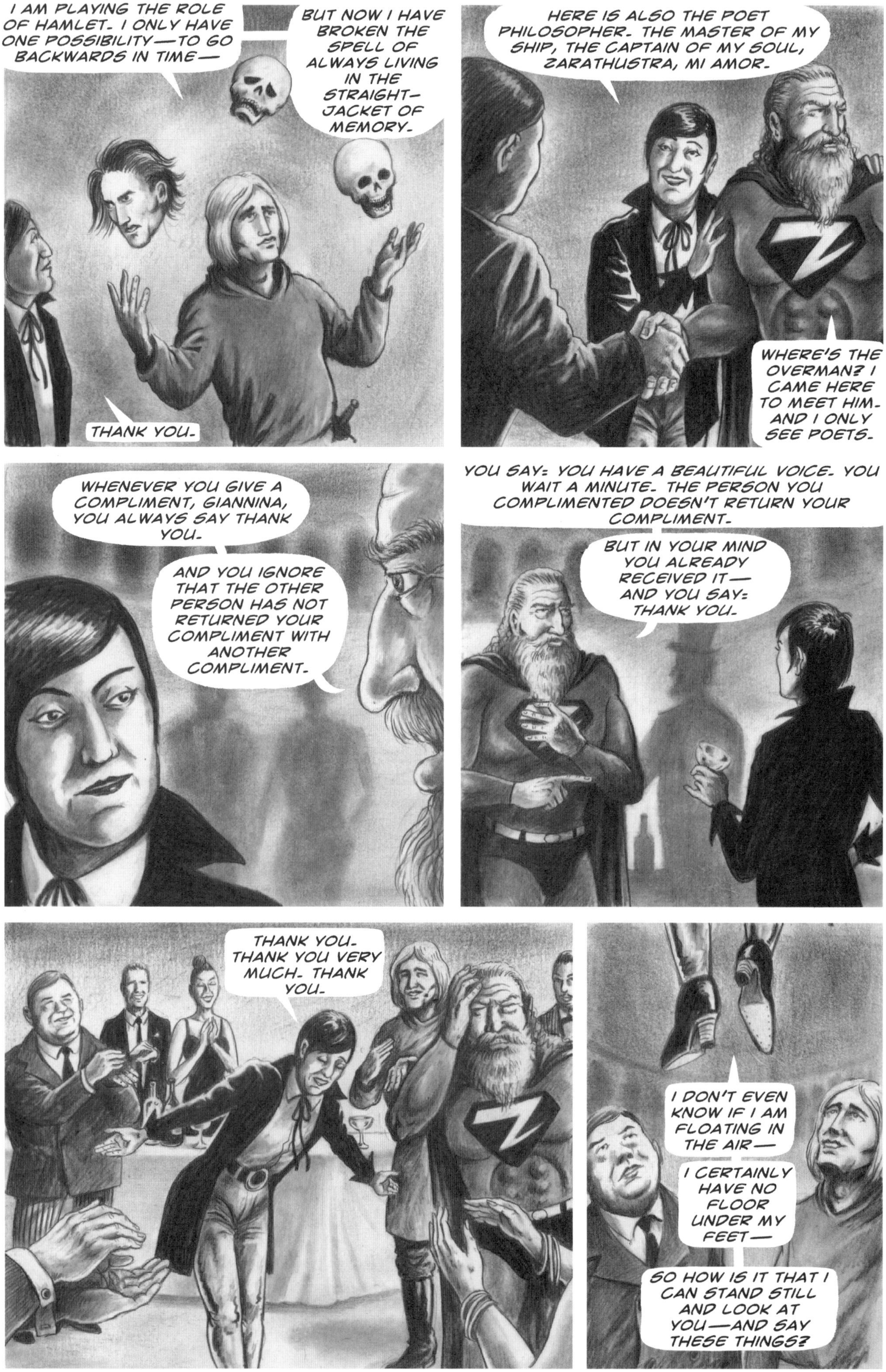
I AM PLAYING THE ROLE OF HAMLET. I ONLY HAVE ONE POSSIBILITY—TO GO BACKWARDS IN TIME—
BUT NOW I HAVE BROKEN THE SPELL OF ALWAYS LIVING IN THE STRAIGHT-JACKET OF MEMORY.
THANK YOU.
HERE IS ALSO THE POET PHILOSOPHER. THE MASTER OF MY SHIP, THE CAPTAIN OF MY SOUL, ZARATHUSTRA, MI AMOR.
WHERE'S THE OVERMAN? I CAME HERE TO MEET HIM. AND I ONLY SEE POETS.
WHENEVER YOU GIVE A COMPLIMENT, GIANNINA, YOU ALWAYS SAY THANK YOU.
AND YOU IGNORE THAT THE OTHER PERSON HAS NOT RETURNED YOUR COMPLIMENT WITH ANOTHER COMPLIMENT.
YOU SAY: YOU HAVE A BEAUTIFUL VOICE. YOU WAIT A MINUTE. THE PERSON YOU COMPLIMENTED DOESN'T RETURN YOUR COMPLIMENT.
BUT IN YOUR MIND YOU ALREADY RECEIVED IT—AND YOU SAY: THANK YOU.
THANK YOU. THANK YOU VERY MUCH. THANK YOU.
I DON'T EVEN KNOW IF I AM FLOATING IN THE AIR—
I CERTAINLY HAVE NO FLOOR UNDER MY FEET—
SO HOW IS IT THAT I CAN STAND STILL AND LOOK AT YOU—AND SAY THESE THINGS?

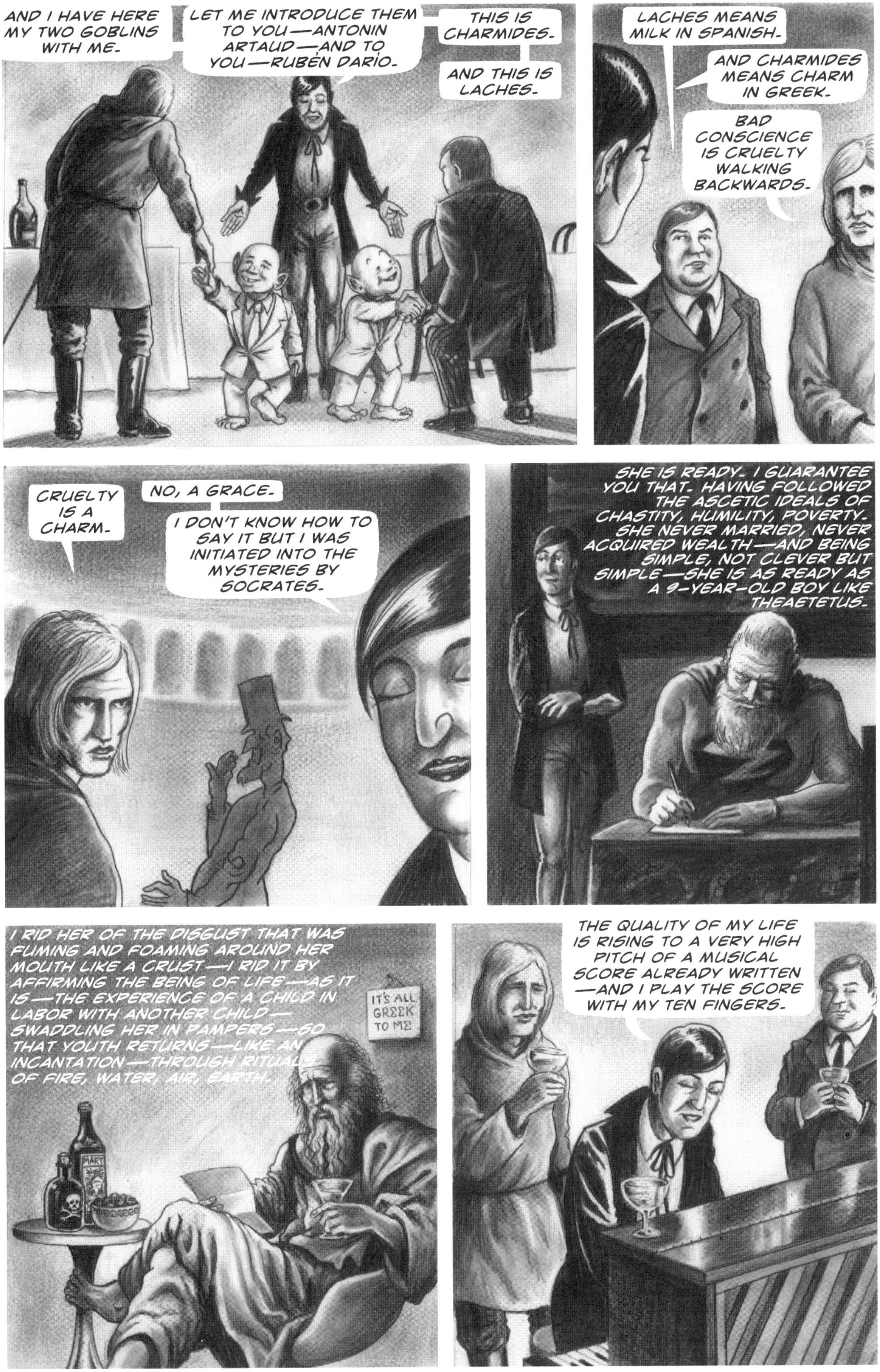
AND I HAVE HERE MY TWO GOBLINS WITH ME.
LET ME INTRODUCE THEM TO YOU—ANTONIN ARTAUD—AND TO YOU—RUBÉN DARÍO.
THIS IS CHARMIDES.
AND THIS IS LACHES.
LACHES MEANS MILK IN SPANISH.
AND CHARMIDES MEANS CHARM IN GREEK.
BAD CONSCIENCE IS CRUELTY WALKING BACKWARDS.
CRUELTY IS A CHARM.
NO, A GRACE.
I DON'T KNOW HOW TO SAY IT BUT I WAS INITIATED INTO THE MYSTERIES BY SOCRATES.
SHE IS READY. I GUARANTEE YOU THAT. HAVING FOLLOWED THE ASCETIC IDEALS OF CHASTITY, HUMILITY, POVERTY. SHE NEVER MARRIED, NEVER ACQUIRED WEALTH—AND BEING SIMPLE, NOT CLEVER BUT SIMPLE—SHE IS AS READY AS A 9-YEAR-OLD BOY LIKE THEAETETUS.
I RID HER OF THE DISGUST THAT WAS FUMING AND FOAMING AROUND HER MOUTH LIKE A CRUST—I RID IT BY AFFIRMING THE BEING OF LIFE—AS IT IS—THE EXPERIENCE OF A CHILD IN LABOR WITH ANOTHER CHILD—SWADDLING HER IN PAMPERS—SO THAT YOUTH RETURNS—LIKE AN INCANTATION—THROUGH RITUALS OF FIRE, WATER, AIR, EARTH.
IT'S ALL GREEK TO ME
THE QUALITY OF MY LIFE IS RISING TO A VERY HIGH PITCH OF A MUSICAL SCORE ALREADY WRITTEN—AND I PLAY THE SCORE WITH MY TEN FINGERS.

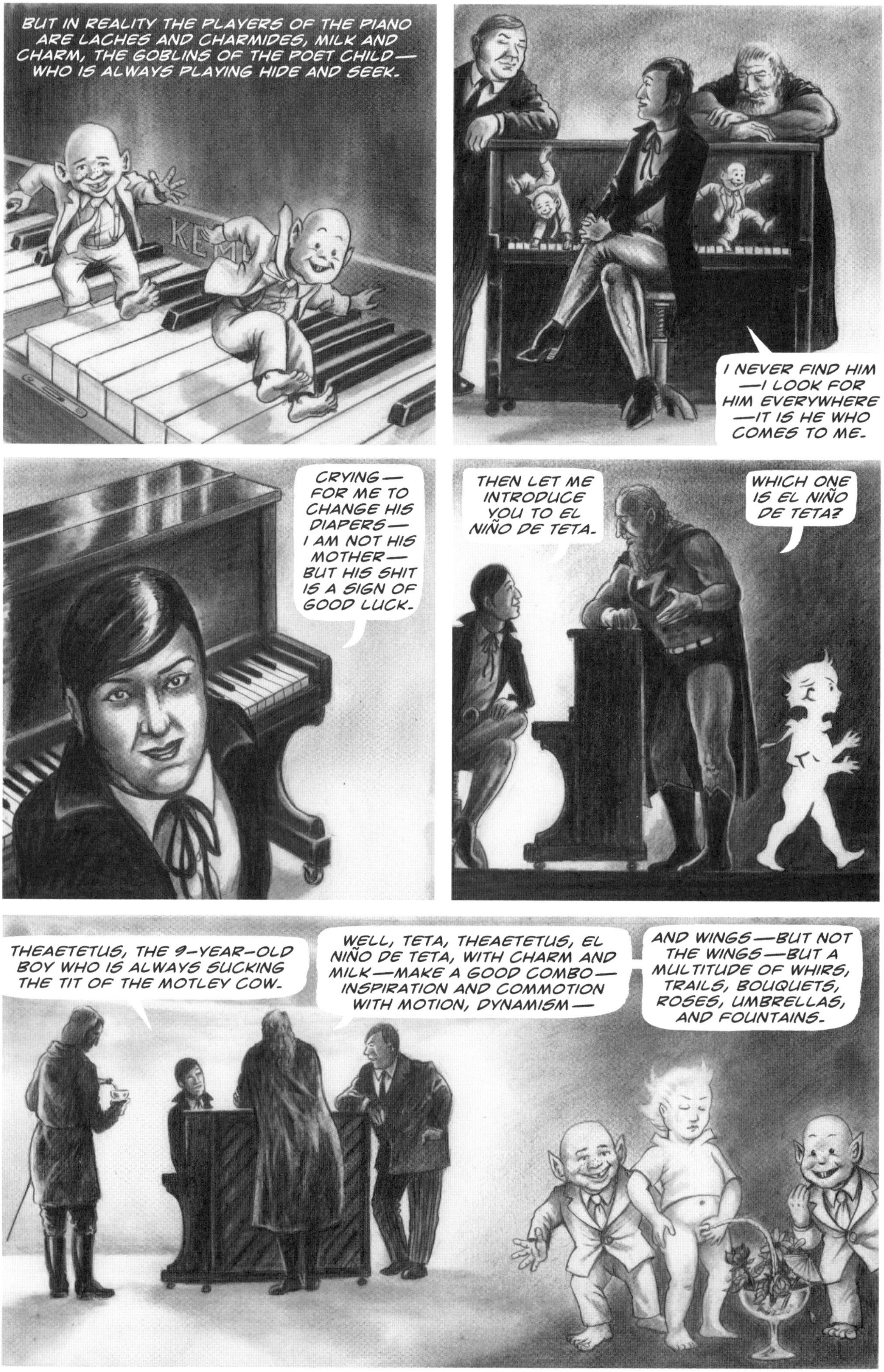
BUT IN REALITY THE PLAYERS OF THE PIANO ARE LACHES AND CHARMIDES, MILK AND CHARM, THE GOBLINS OF THE POET CHILD— WHO IS ALWAYS PLAYING HIDE AND SEEK.
I NEVER FIND HIM —I LOOK FOR HIM EVERYWHERE —IT IS HE WHO COMES TO ME.
CRYING— FOR ME TO CHANGE HIS DIAPERS— I AM NOT HIS MOTHER— BUT HIS SHIT IS A SIGN OF GOOD LUCK.
THEN LET ME INTRODUCE YOU TO EL NIÑO DE TETA.
WHICH ONE IS EL NIÑO DE TETA?
THEAETETUS, THE 9-YEAR-OLD BOY WHO IS ALWAYS SUCKING THE TIT OF THE MOTLEY COW.
WELL, TETA, THEAETETUS, EL NIÑO DE TETA, WITH CHARM AND MILK—MAKE A GOOD COMBO— INSPIRATION AND COMMOTION WITH MOTION, DYNAMISM—
AND WINGS—BUT NOT THE WINGS—BUT A MULTITUDE OF WHIRS, TRAILS, BOUQUETS, ROSES, UMBRELLAS, AND FOUNTAINS.

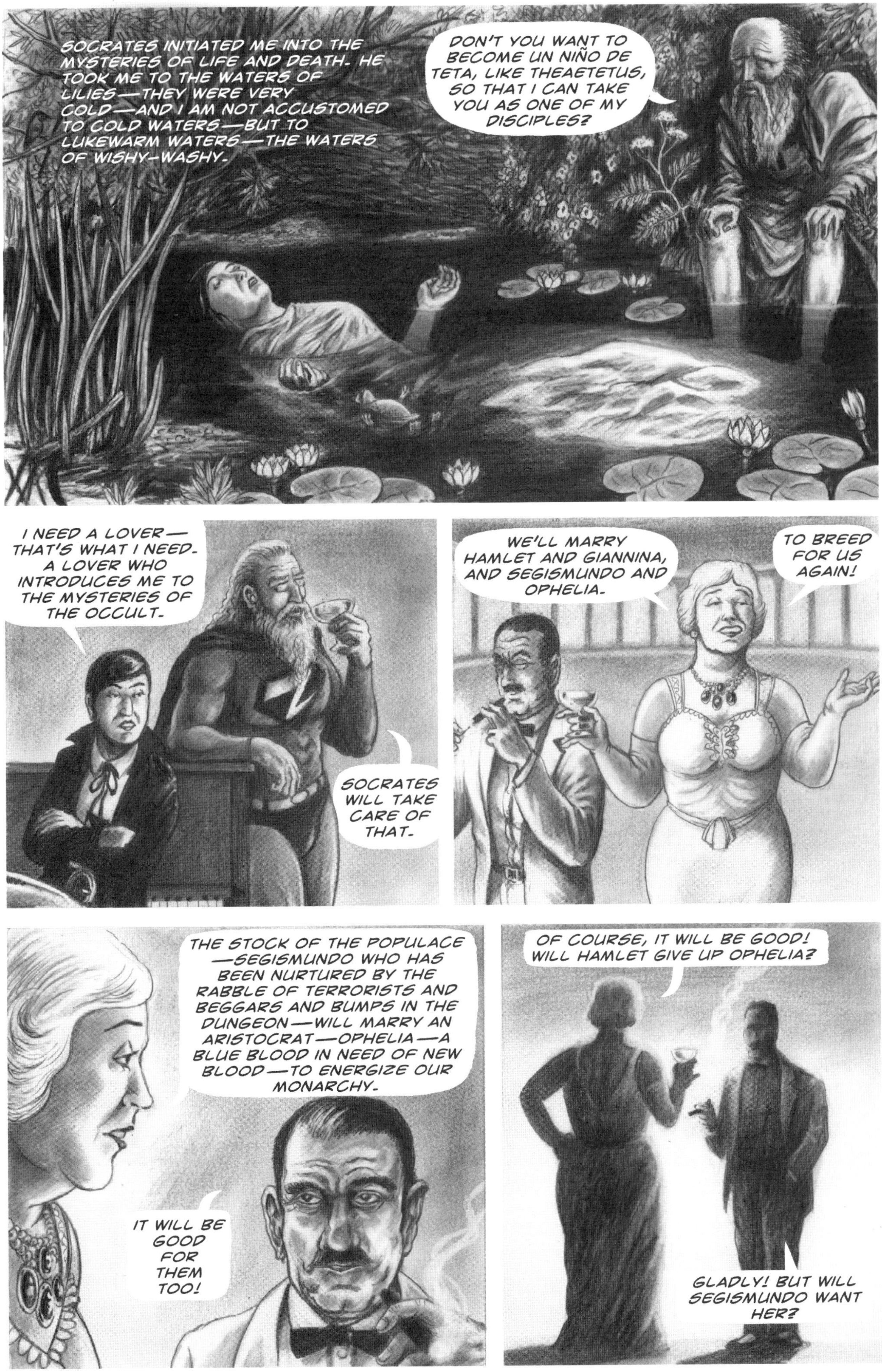
SOCRATES INITIATED ME INTO THE MYSTERIES OF LIFE AND DEATH. HE TOOK ME TO THE WATERS OF LILIES—THEY WERE VERY COLD—AND I AM NOT ACCUSTOMED TO COLD WATERS—BUT TO LUKEWARM WATERS—THE WATERS OF WISHY-WASHY.
DON'T YOU WANT TO BECOME UN NIÑO DE TETA, LIKE THEAETETUS, SO THAT I CAN TAKE YOU AS ONE OF MY DISCIPLES?
I NEED A LOVER—THAT'S WHAT I NEED. A LOVER WHO INTRODUCES ME TO THE MYSTERIES OF THE OCCULT.
SOCRATES WILL TAKE CARE OF THAT.
WE'LL MARRY HAMLET AND GIANNINA, AND SEGISMUNDO AND OPHELIA.
TO BREED FOR US AGAIN!
THE STOCK OF THE POPULACE—SEGISMUNDO WHO HAS BEEN NURTURED BY THE RABBLE OF TERRORISTS AND BEGGARS AND BUMPS IN THE DUNGEON—WILL MARRY AN ARISTOCRAT—OPHELIA—A BLUE BLOOD IN NEED OF NEW BLOOD—TO ENERGIZE OUR MONARCHY.
IT WILL BE GOOD FOR THEM TOO!
OF COURSE, IT WILL BE GOOD! WILL HAMLET GIVE UP OPHELIA?
GLADLY! BUT WILL SEGISMUNDO WANT HER?

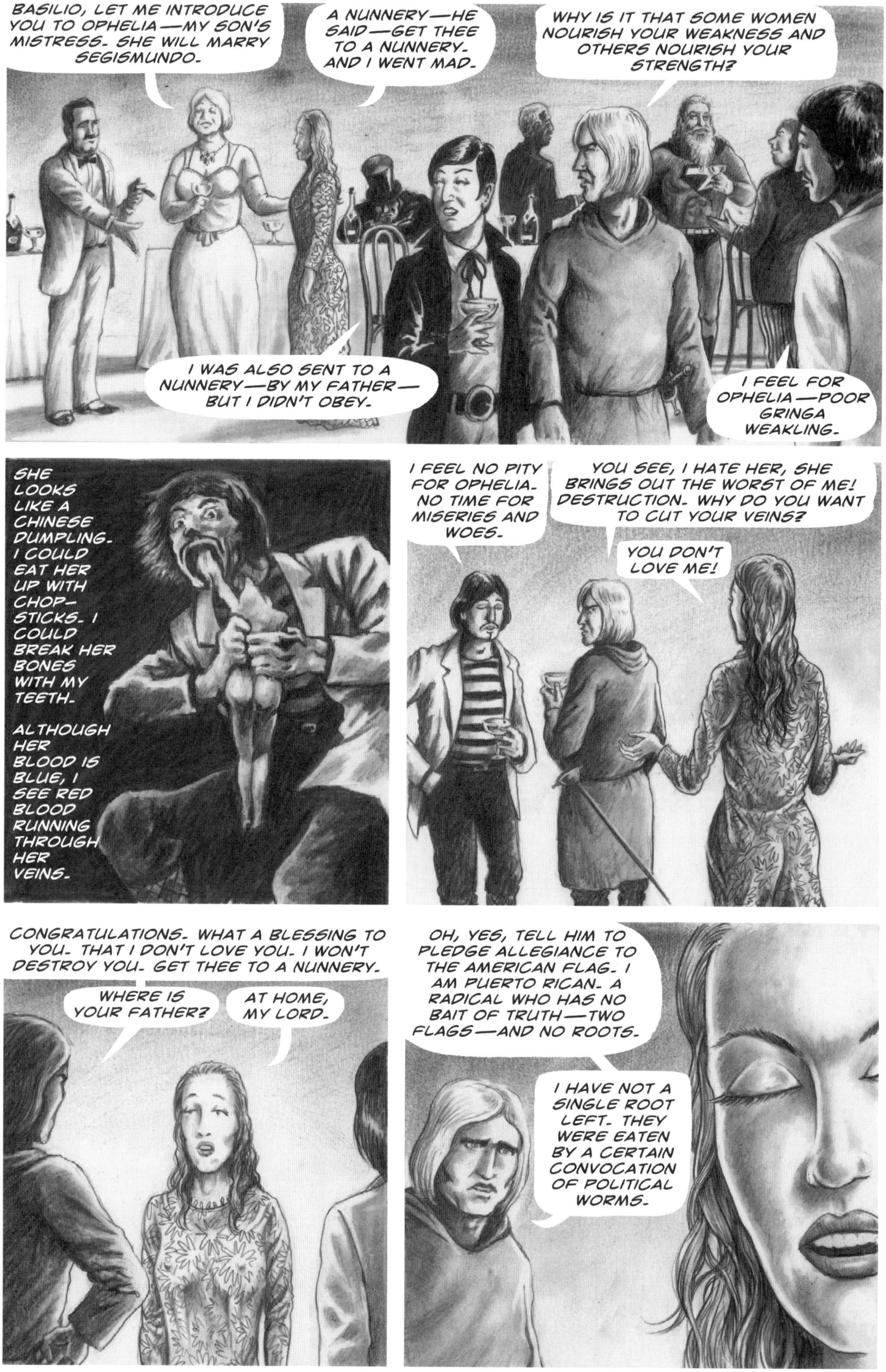
BASILIO, LET ME INTRODUCE YOU TO OPHELIA—MY SON'S MISTRESS. SHE WILL MARRY SEGISMUNDO.
A NUNNERY—HE SAID—GET THEE TO A NUNNERY. AND I WENT MAD.
WHY IS IT THAT SOME WOMEN NOURISH YOUR WEAKNESS AND OTHERS NOURISH YOUR STRENGTH?
I WAS ALSO SENT TO A NUNNERY—BY MY FATHER—BUT I DIDN'T OBEY.
I FEEL FOR OPHELIA—POOR GRINGA WEAKLING.
SHE LOOKS LIKE A CHINESE DUMPLING. I COULD EAT HER UP WITH CHOP-STICKS. I COULD BREAK HER BONES WITH MY TEETH.
ALTHOUGH HER BLOOD IS BLUE, I SEE RED BLOOD RUNNING THROUGH HER VEINS.
I FEEL NO PITY FOR OPHELIA. NO TIME FOR MISERIES AND WOES.
YOU SEE, I HATE HER, SHE BRINGS OUT THE WORST OF ME! DESTRUCTION. WHY DO YOU WANT TO CUT YOUR VEINS?
YOU DON'T LOVE ME!
CONGRATULATIONS. WHAT A BLESSING TO YOU. THAT I DON'T LOVE YOU. I WON'T DESTROY YOU. GET THEE TO A NUNNERY.
WHERE IS YOUR FATHER?
AT HOME, MY LORD.
OH, YES, TELL HIM TO PLEDGE ALLEGIANCE TO THE AMERICAN FLAG. I AM PUERTO RICAN. A RADICAL WHO HAS NO BAIT OF TRUTH—TWO FLAGS—AND NO ROOTS.
I HAVE NOT A SINGLE ROOT LEFT. THEY WERE EATEN BY A CERTAIN CONVOCATION OF POLITICAL WORMS.

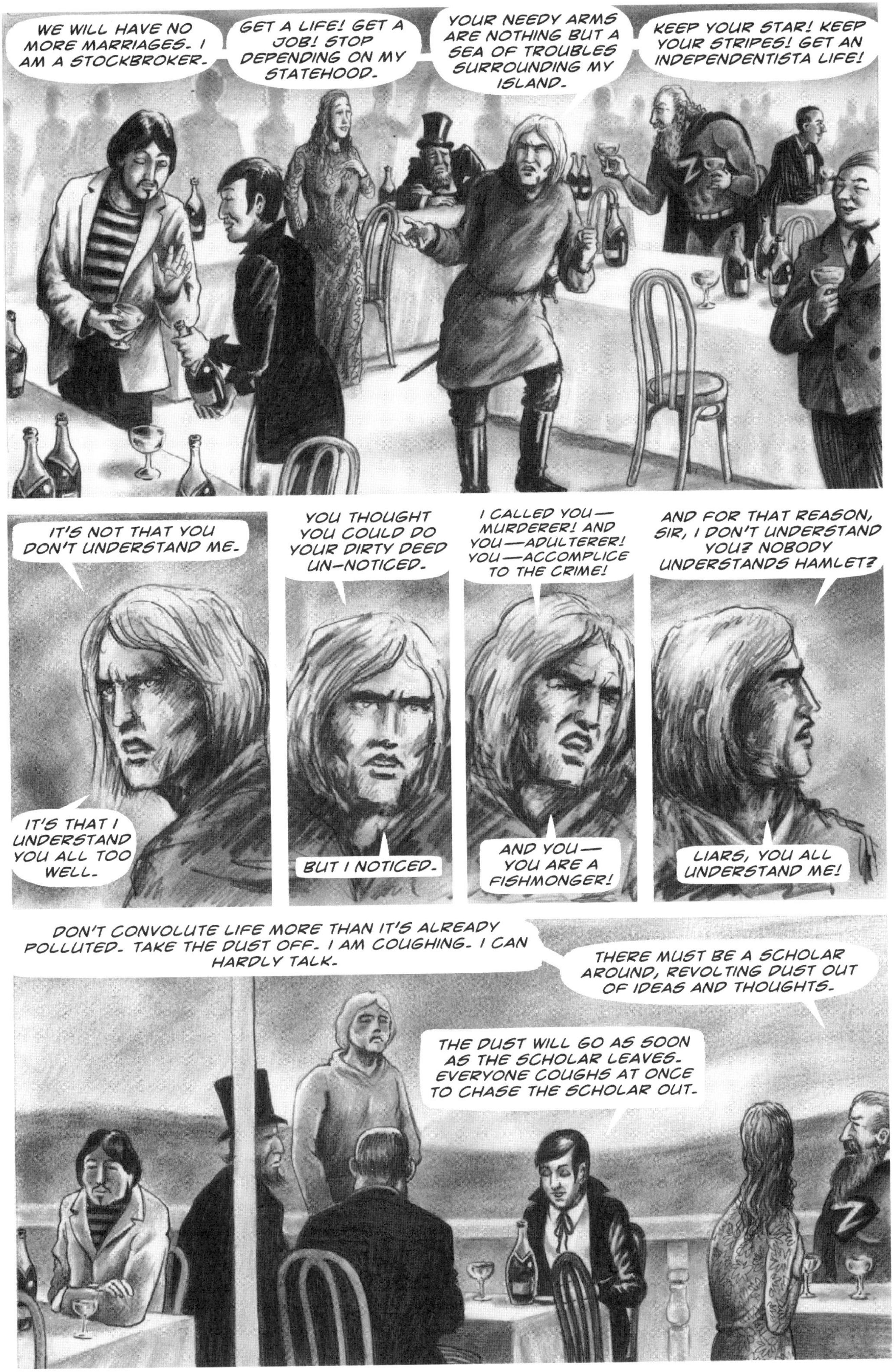
WE WILL HAVE NO MORE MARRIAGES. I AM A STOCKBROKER.
GET A LIFE! GET A JOB! STOP DEPENDING ON MY STATEHOOD.
YOUR NEEDY ARMS ARE NOTHING BUT A SEA OF TROUBLES SURROUNDING MY ISLAND.
KEEP YOUR STAR! KEEP YOUR STRIPES! GET AN INDEPENDENTISTA LIFE!
IT'S NOT THAT YOU DON'T UNDERSTAND ME.
IT'S THAT I UNDERSTAND YOU ALL TOO WELL.
YOU THOUGHT YOU COULD DO YOUR DIRTY DEED UN-NOTICED.
BUT I NOTICED.
I CALLED YOU— MURDERER! AND YOU—ADULTERER! YOU—ACCOMPLICE TO THE CRIME!
AND YOU— YOU ARE A FISHMONGER!
AND FOR THAT REASON, SIR, I DON'T UNDERSTAND YOU? NOBODY UNDERSTANDS HAMLET?
LIARS, YOU ALL UNDERSTAND ME!
DON'T CONVOLUTE LIFE MORE THAN IT'S ALREADY POLLUTED. TAKE THE DUST OFF. I AM COUGHING. I CAN HARDLY TALK.
THERE MUST BE A SCHOLAR AROUND, REVOLTING DUST OUT OF IDEAS AND THOUGHTS.
THE DUST WILL GO AS SOON AS THE SCHOLAR LEAVES. EVERYONE COUGHS AT ONCE TO CHASE THE SCHOLAR OUT.

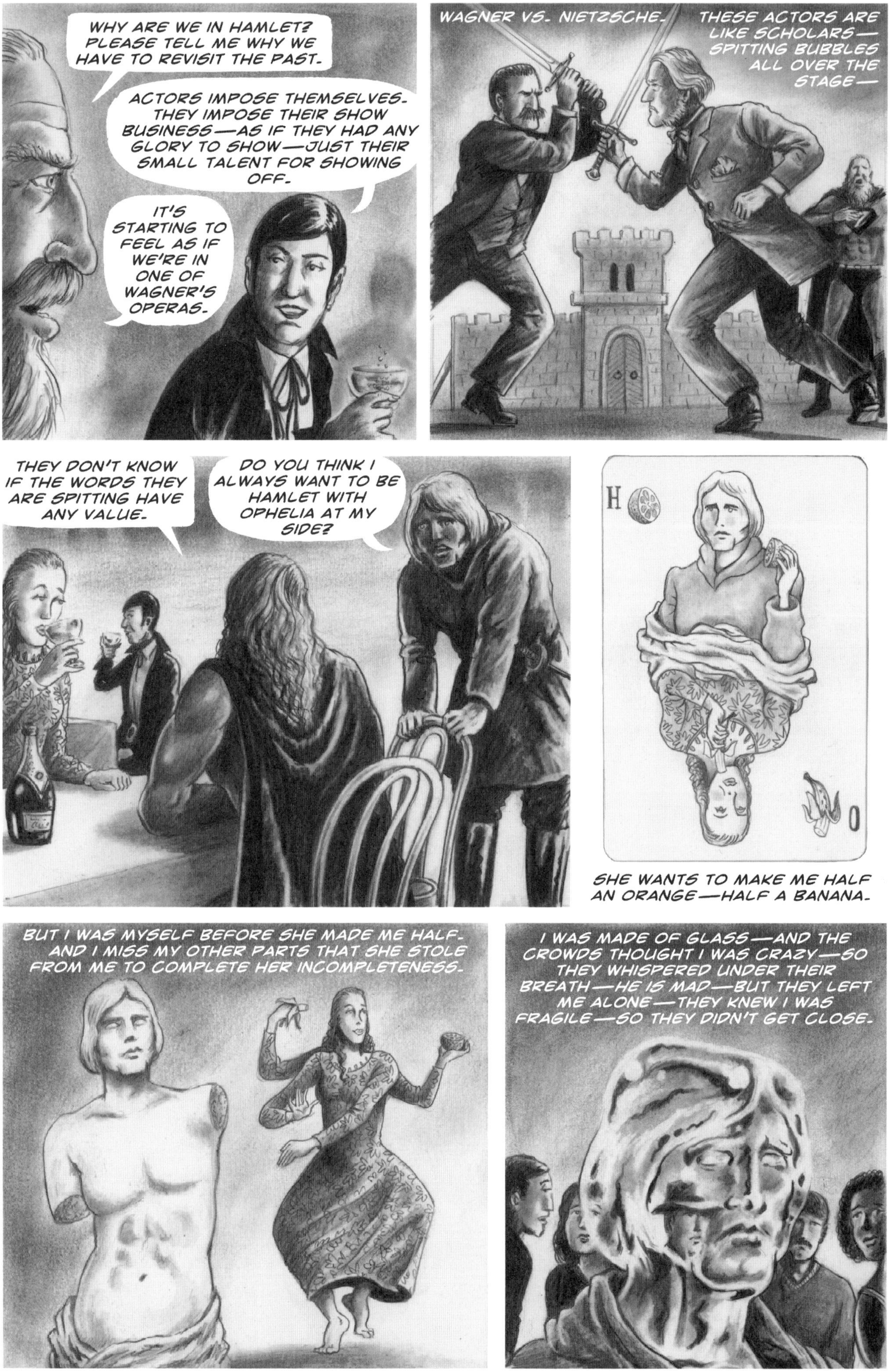
WHY ARE WE IN HAMLET? PLEASE TELL ME WHY WE HAVE TO REVISIT THE PAST.
ACTORS IMPOSE THEMSELVES. THEY IMPOSE THEIR SHOW BUSINESS—AS IF THEY HAD ANY GLORY TO SHOW—JUST THEIR SMALL TALENT FOR SHOWING OFF.
IT'S STARTING TO FEEL AS IF WE'RE IN ONE OF WAGNER'S OPERAS.
WAGNER VS. NIETZSCHE.
THESE ACTORS ARE LIKE SCHOLARS—SPITTING BUBBLES ALL OVER THE STAGE—
THEY DON'T KNOW IF THE WORDS THEY ARE SPITTING HAVE ANY VALUE.
DO YOU THINK I ALWAYS WANT TO BE HAMLET WITH OPHELIA AT MY SIDE?
H
O
SHE WANTS TO MAKE ME HALF AN ORANGE—HALF A BANANA.
BUT I WAS MYSELF BEFORE SHE MADE ME HALF. AND I MISS MY OTHER PARTS THAT SHE STOLE FROM ME TO COMPLETE HER INCOMPLETENESS.
I WAS MADE OF GLASS—AND THE CROWDS THOUGHT I WAS CRAZY—SO THEY WHISPERED UNDER THEIR BREATH—HE IS MAD—BUT THEY LEFT ME ALONE—THEY KNEW I WAS FRAGILE—SO THEY DIDN'T GET CLOSE.

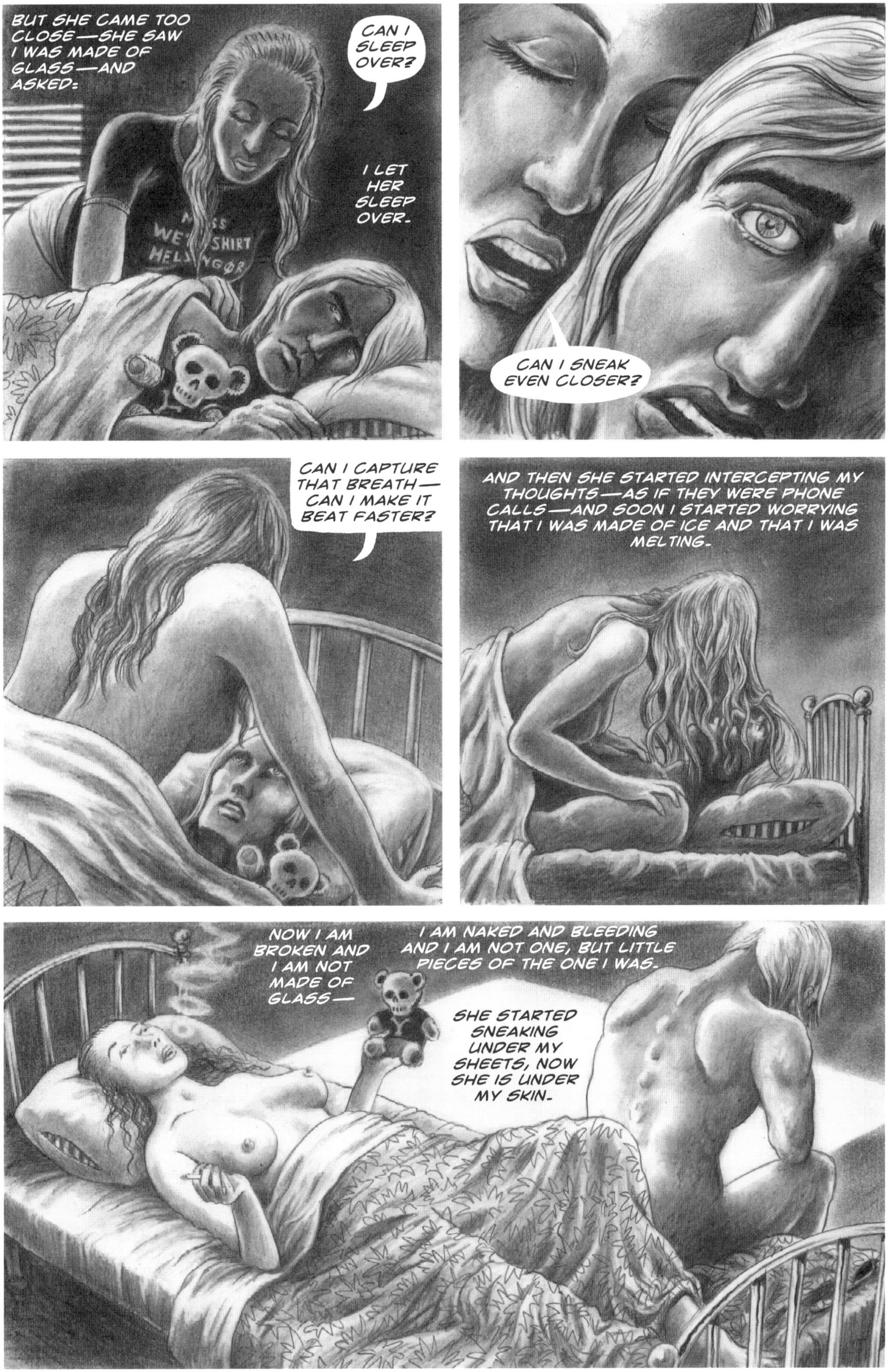
BUT SHE CAME TOO CLOSE—SHE SAW I WAS MADE OF GLASS—AND ASKED:
CAN I SLEEP OVER?
I LET HER SLEEP OVER.
CAN I SNEAK EVEN CLOSER?
CAN I CAPTURE THAT BREATH—CAN I MAKE IT BEAT FASTER?
AND THEN SHE STARTED INTERCEPTING MY THOUGHTS—AS IF THEY WERE PHONE CALLS—AND SOON I STARTED WORRYING THAT I WAS MADE OF ICE AND THAT I WAS MELTING.
NOW I AM BROKEN AND I AM NOT MADE OF GLASS—
I AM NAKED AND BLEEDING AND I AM NOT ONE, BUT LITTLE PIECES OF THE ONE I WAS.
SHE STARTED SNEAKING UNDER MY SHEETS, NOW SHE IS UNDER MY SKIN.

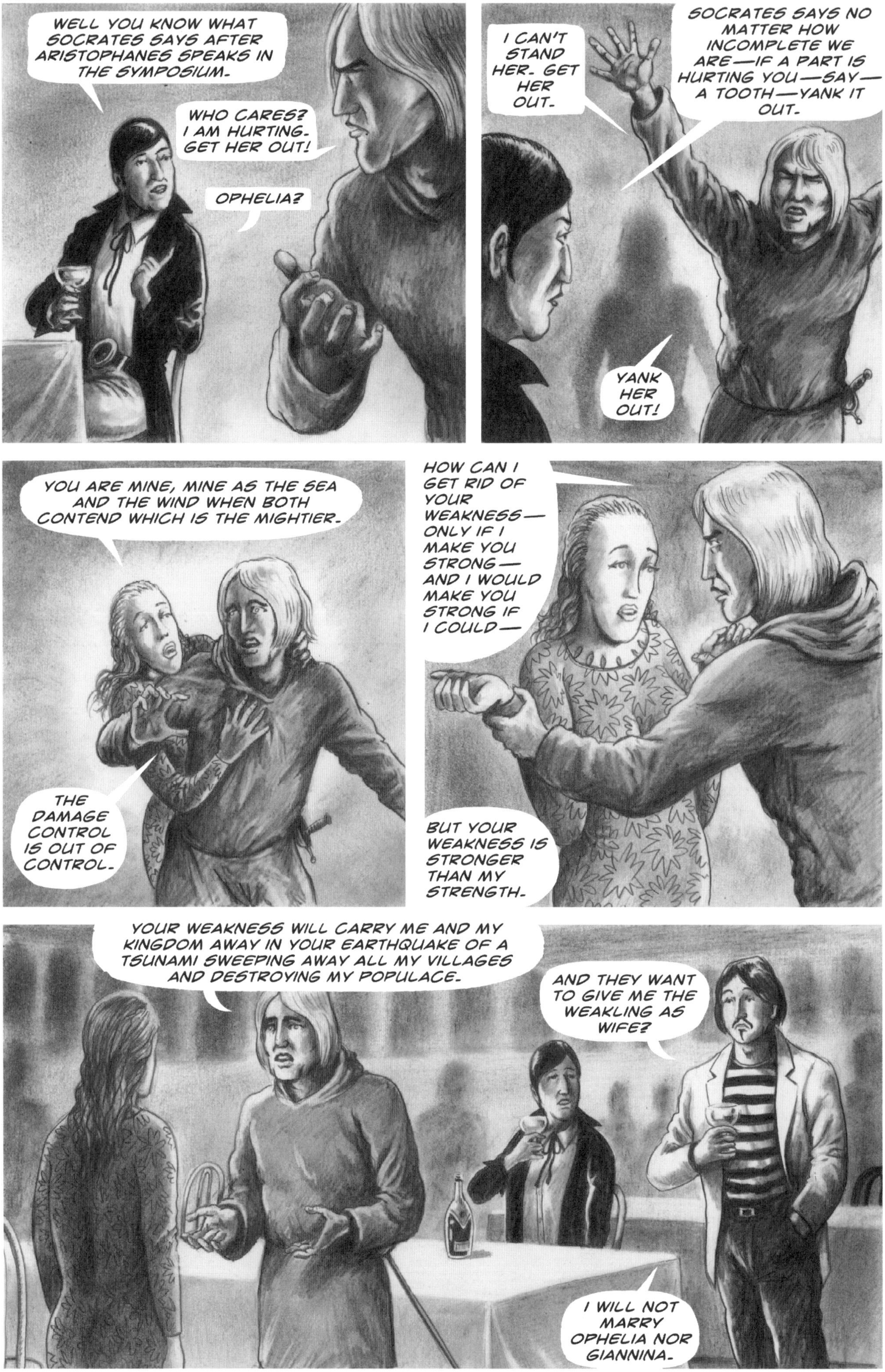
WELL YOU KNOW WHAT SOCRATES SAYS AFTER ARISTOPHANES SPEAKS IN THE SYMPOSIUM.
WHO CARES? I AM HURTING. GET HER OUT!
OPHELIA?
I CAN'T STAND HER. GET HER OUT.
SOCRATES SAYS NO MATTER HOW INCOMPLETE WE ARE—IF A PART IS HURTING YOU—SAY—A TOOTH—YANK IT OUT.
YANK HER OUT!
YOU ARE MINE, MINE AS THE SEA AND THE WIND WHEN BOTH CONTEND WHICH IS THE MIGHTIER.
THE DAMAGE CONTROL IS OUT OF CONTROL.
HOW CAN I GET RID OF YOUR WEAKNESS—ONLY IF I MAKE YOU STRONG—AND I WOULD MAKE YOU STRONG IF I COULD—
BUT YOUR WEAKNESS IS STRONGER THAN MY STRENGTH.
YOUR WEAKNESS WILL CARRY ME AND MY KINGDOM AWAY IN YOUR EARTHQUAKE OF A TSUNAMI SWEEPING AWAY ALL MY VILLAGES AND DESTROYING MY POPULACE.
AND THEY WANT TO GIVE ME THE WEAKLING AS WIFE?
I WILL NOT MARRY OPHELIA NOR GIANNINA.

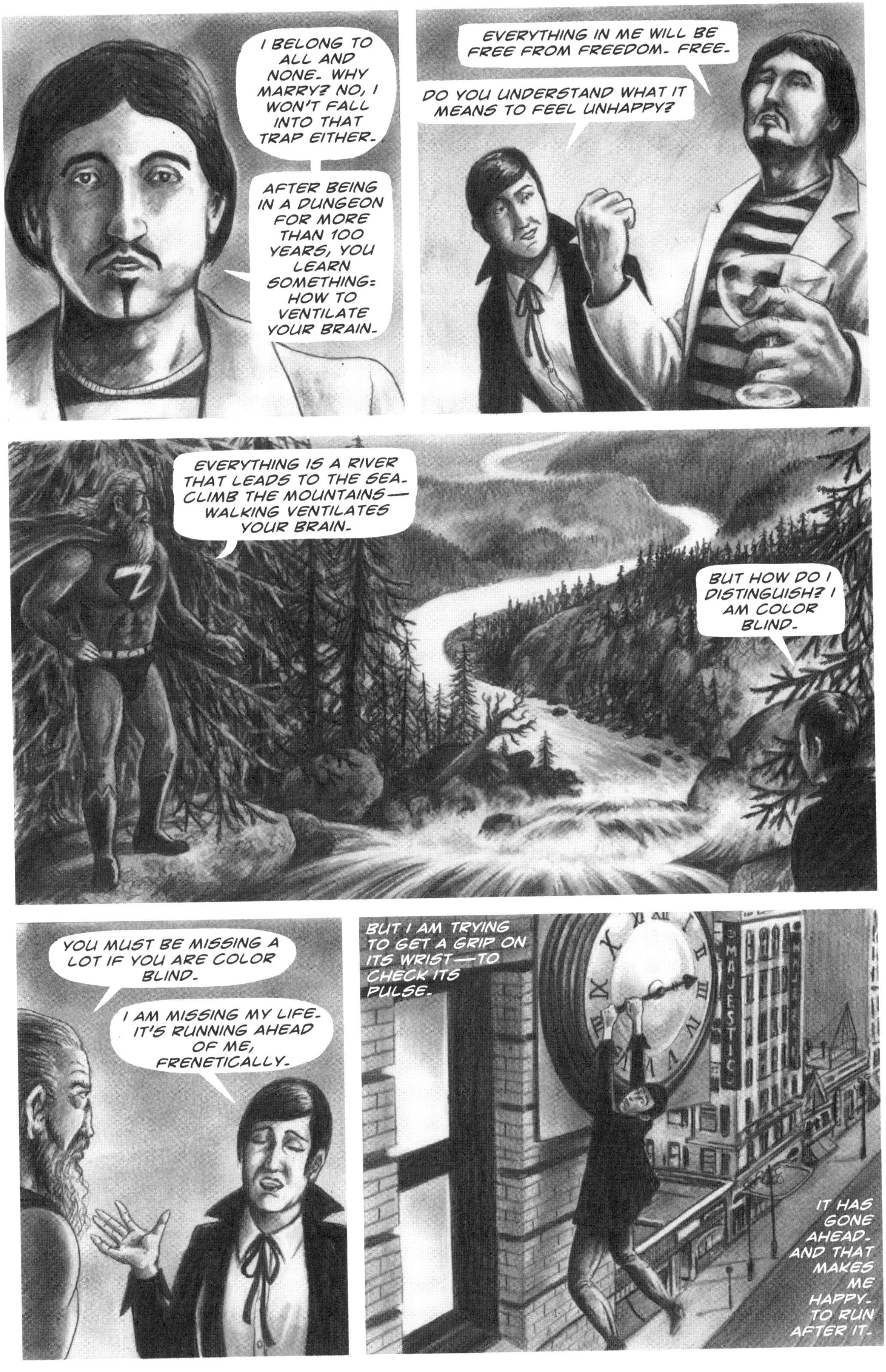
I BELONG TO ALL AND NONE. WHY MARRY? NO, I WON'T FALL INTO THAT TRAP EITHER.
AFTER BEING IN A DUNGEON FOR MORE THAN 100 YEARS, YOU LEARN SOMETHING: HOW TO VENTILATE YOUR BRAIN.
EVERYTHING IN ME WILL BE FREE FROM FREEDOM. FREE.
DO YOU UNDERSTAND WHAT IT MEANS TO FEEL UNHAPPY?
EVERYTHING IS A RIVER THAT LEADS TO THE SEA. CLIMB THE MOUNTAINS— WALKING VENTILATES YOUR BRAIN.
BUT HOW DO I DISTINGUISH? I AM COLOR BLIND.
YOU MUST BE MISSING A LOT IF YOU ARE COLOR BLIND.
I AM MISSING MY LIFE. IT'S RUNNING AHEAD OF ME, FRENETICALLY.
BUT I AM TRYING TO GET A GRIP ON ITS WRIST—TO CHECK ITS PULSE.
MAJESTIC
IT HAS GONE AHEAD. AND THAT MAKES ME HAPPY. TO RUN AFTER IT.

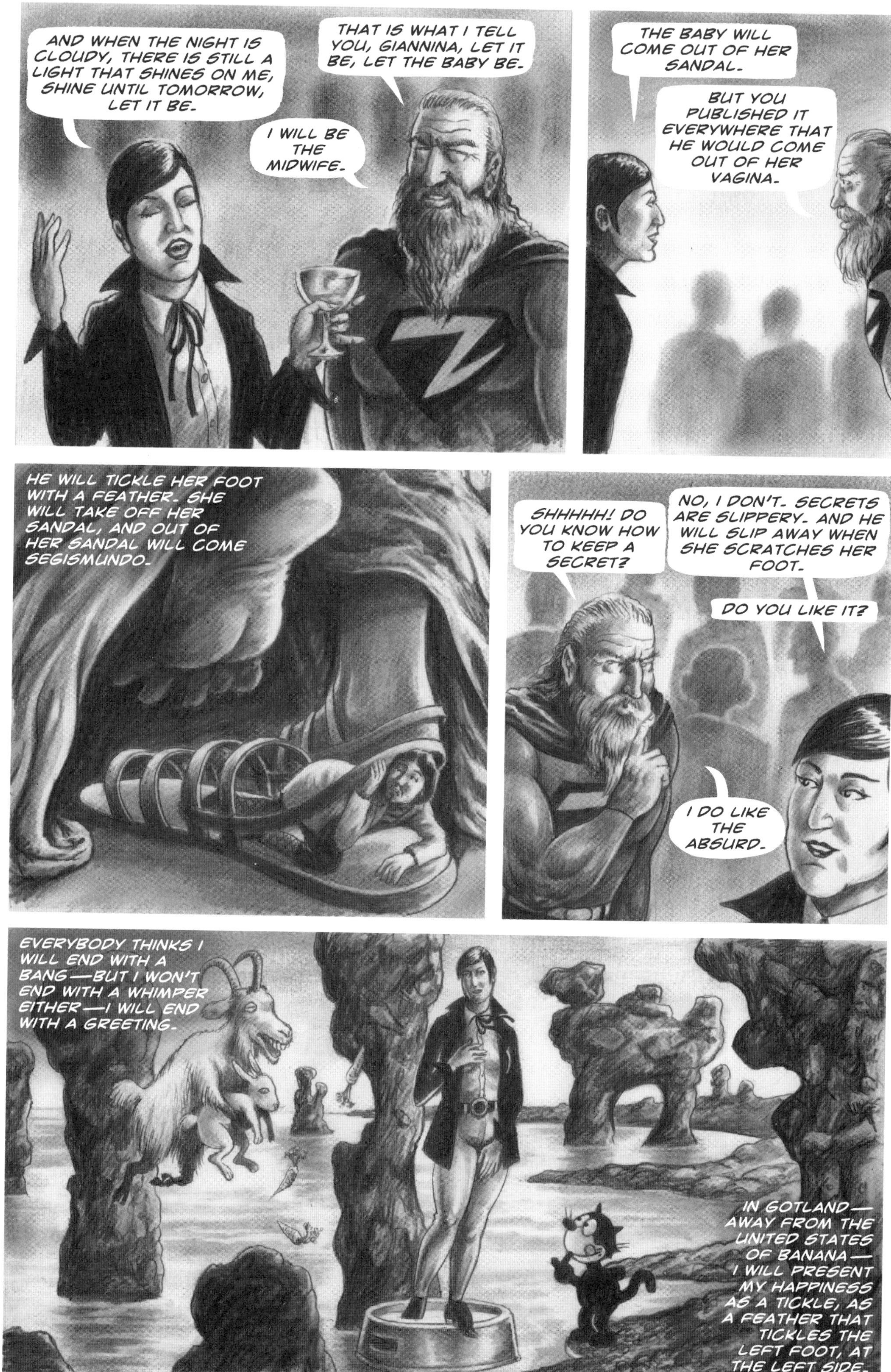
AND WHEN THE NIGHT IS CLOUDY, THERE IS STILL A LIGHT THAT SHINES ON ME, SHINE UNTIL TOMORROW, LET IT BE.
THAT IS WHAT I TELL YOU, GIANNINA, LET IT BE, LET THE BABY BE.
I WILL BE THE MIDWIFE.
THE BABY WILL COME OUT OF HER SANDAL.
BUT YOU PUBLISHED IT EVERYWHERE THAT HE WOULD COME OUT OF HER VAGINA.
HE WILL TICKLE HER FOOT WITH A FEATHER. SHE WILL TAKE OFF HER SANDAL, AND OUT OF HER SANDAL WILL COME SEGISMUNDO.
SHHHHH! DO YOU KNOW HOW TO KEEP A SECRET?
NO, I DON'T. SECRETS ARE SLIPPERY. AND HE WILL SLIP AWAY WHEN SHE SCRATCHES HER FOOT.
DO YOU LIKE IT?
I DO LIKE THE ABSURD.
EVERYBODY THINKS I WILL END WITH A BANG—BUT I WON'T END WITH A WHIMPER EITHER—I WILL END WITH A GREETING.
IN GOTLAND—AWAY FROM THE UNITED STATES OF BANANA—I WILL PRESENT MY HAPPINESS AS A TICKLE, AS A FEATHER THAT TICKLES THE LEFT FOOT, AT THE LEFT SIDE.

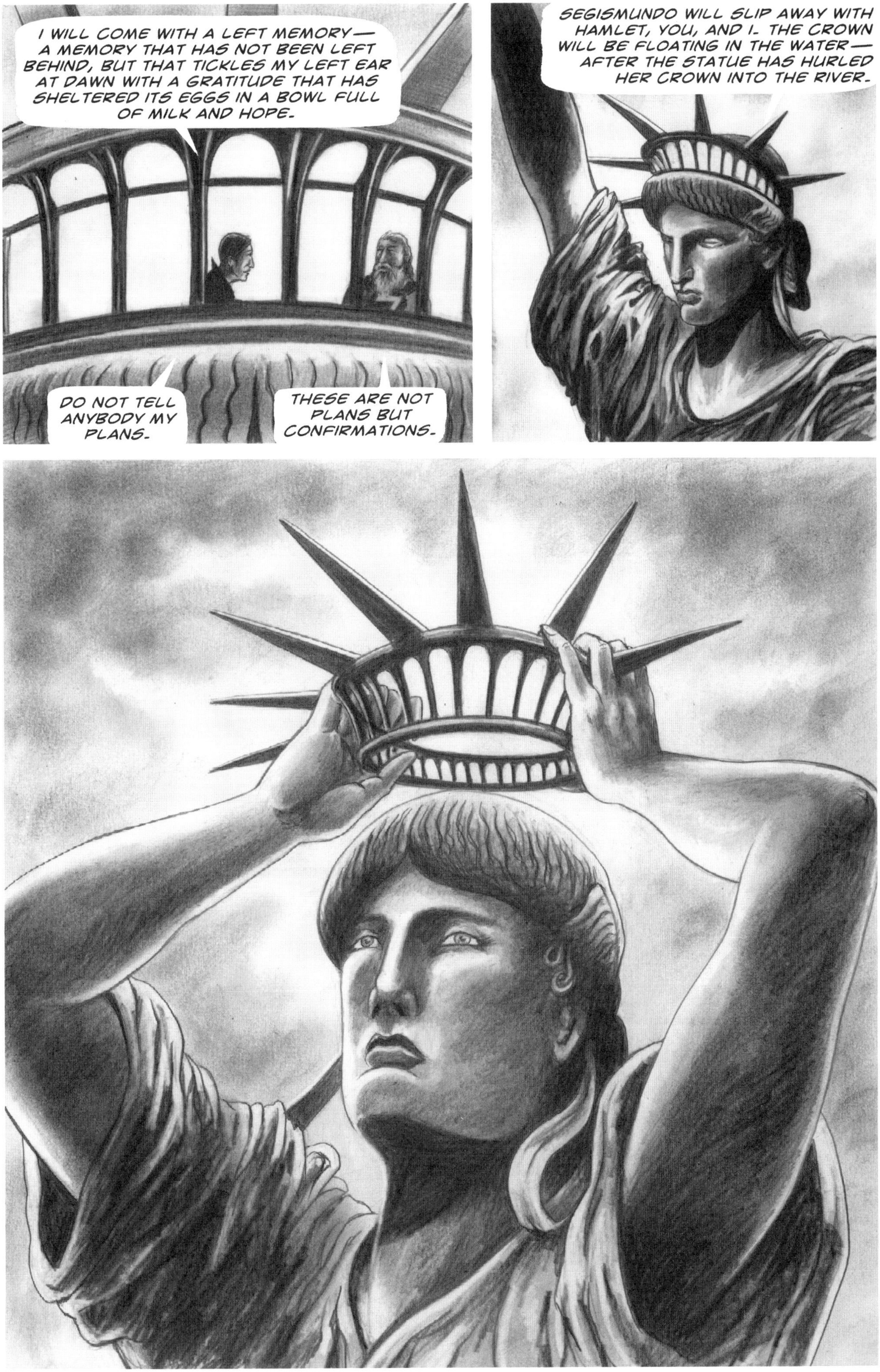
I WILL COME WITH A LEFT MEMORY—A MEMORY THAT HAS NOT BEEN LEFT BEHIND, BUT THAT TICKLES MY LEFT EAR AT DAWN WITH A GRATITUDE THAT HAS SHELTERED ITS EGGS IN A BOWL FULL OF MILK AND HOPE.
DO NOT TELL ANYBODY MY PLANS.
THESE ARE NOT PLANS BUT CONFIRMATIONS.
SEGISMUNDO WILL SLIP AWAY WITH HAMLET, YOU, AND I. THE CROWN WILL BE FLOATING IN THE WATER—AFTER THE STATUE HAS HURLED HER CROWN INTO THE RIVER.

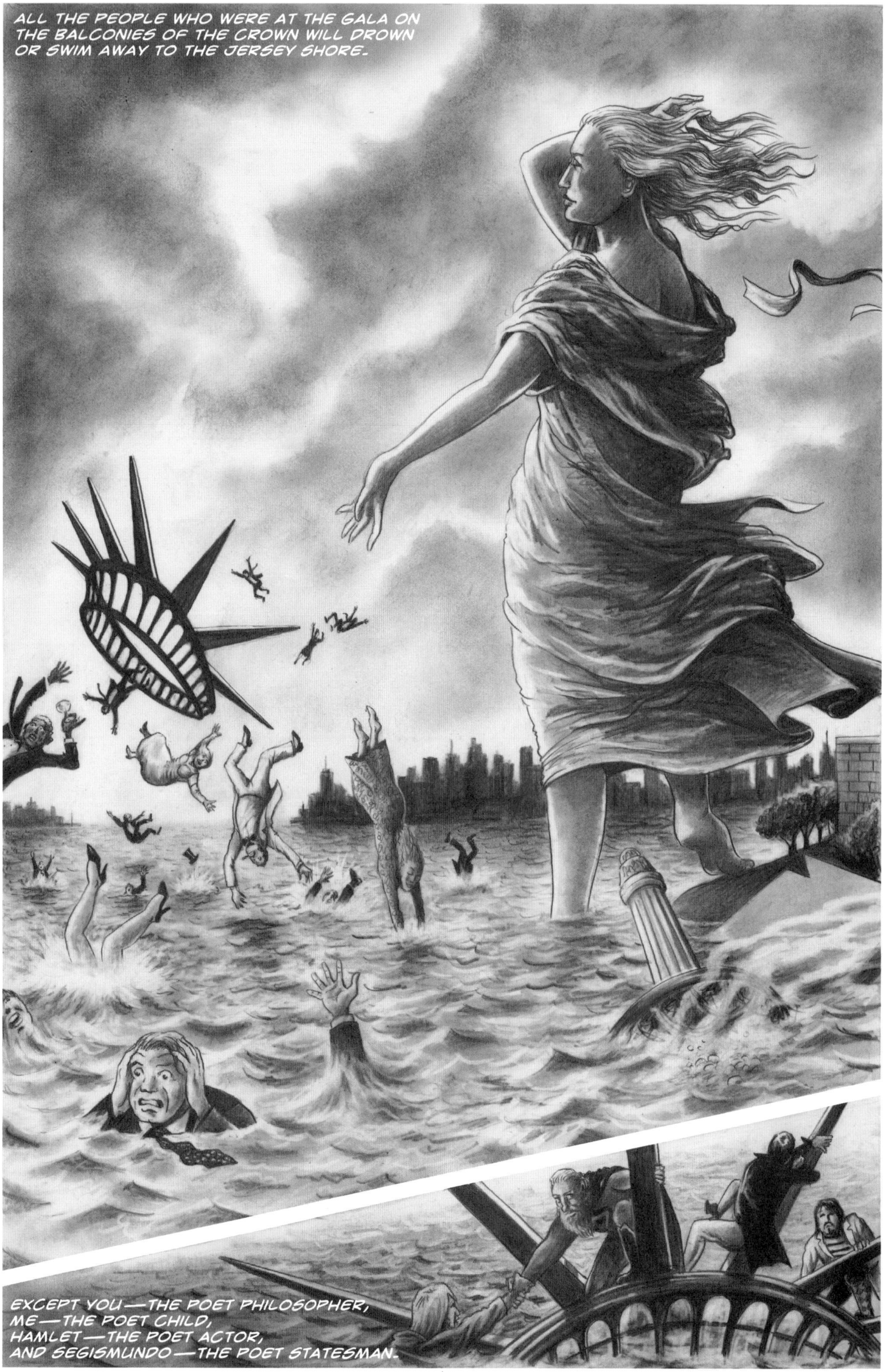
ALL THE PEOPLE WHO WERE AT THE GALA ON THE BALCONIES OF THE CROWN WILL DROWN OR SWIM AWAY TO THE JERSEY SHORE.
EXCEPT YOU—THE POET PHILOSOPHER,
ME—THE POET CHILD,
HAMLET—THE POET ACTOR,
AND SEGISMUNDO—THE POET STATESMAN.

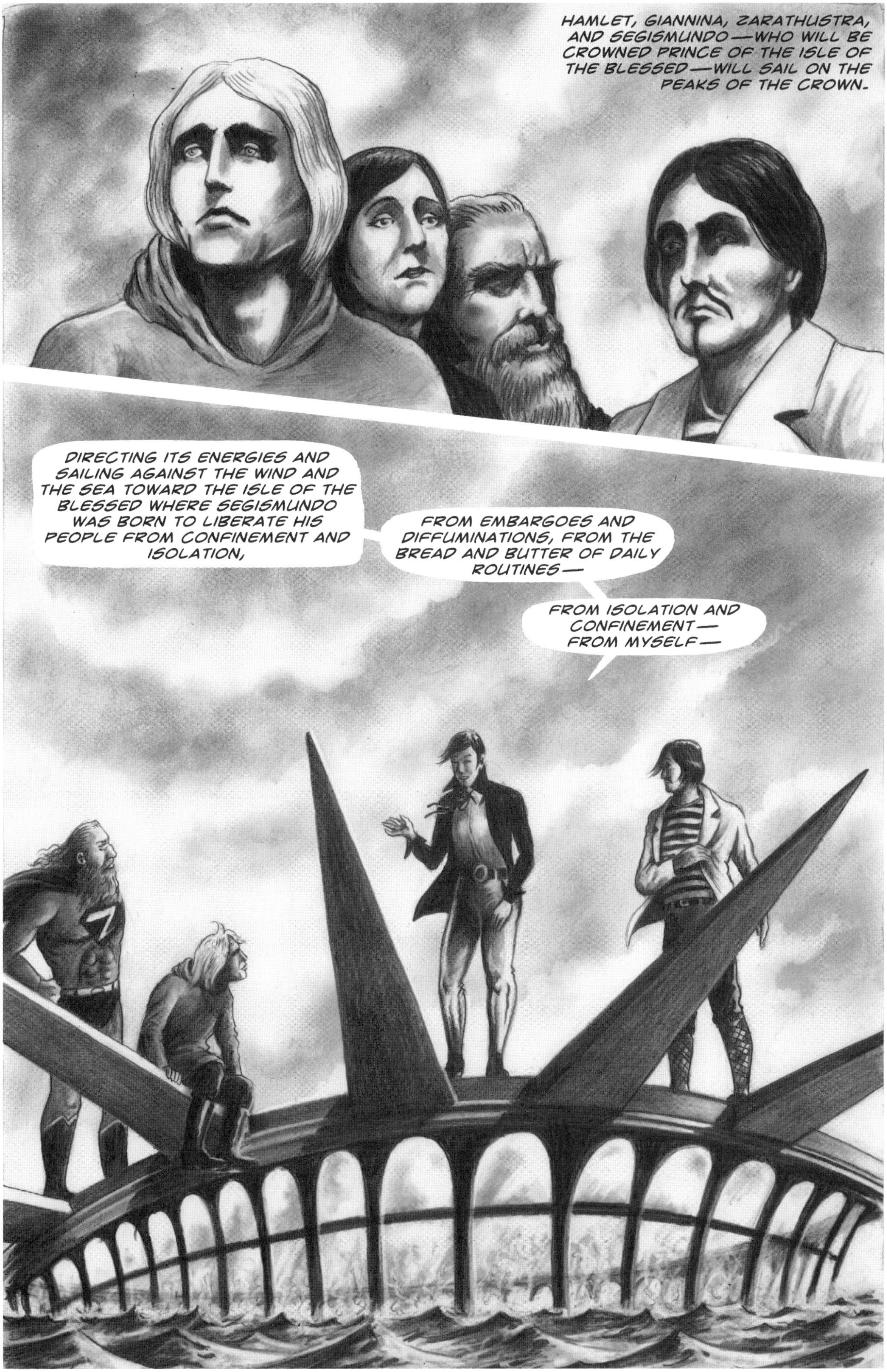
HAMLET, GIANNINA, ZARATHUSTRA, AND SEGISMUNDO—WHO WILL BE CROWNED PRINCE OF THE ISLE OF THE BLESSED—WILL SAIL ON THE PEAKS OF THE CROWN.
DIRECTING ITS ENERGIES AND SAILING AGAINST THE WIND AND THE SEA TOWARD THE ISLE OF THE BLESSED WHERE SEGISMUNDO WAS BORN TO LIBERATE HIS PEOPLE FROM CONFINEMENT AND ISOLATION,
FROM EMBARGOES AND DIFFUMINATIONS, FROM THE BREAD AND BUTTER OF DAILY ROUTINES—
FROM ISOLATION AND CONFINEMENT— FROM MYSELF—

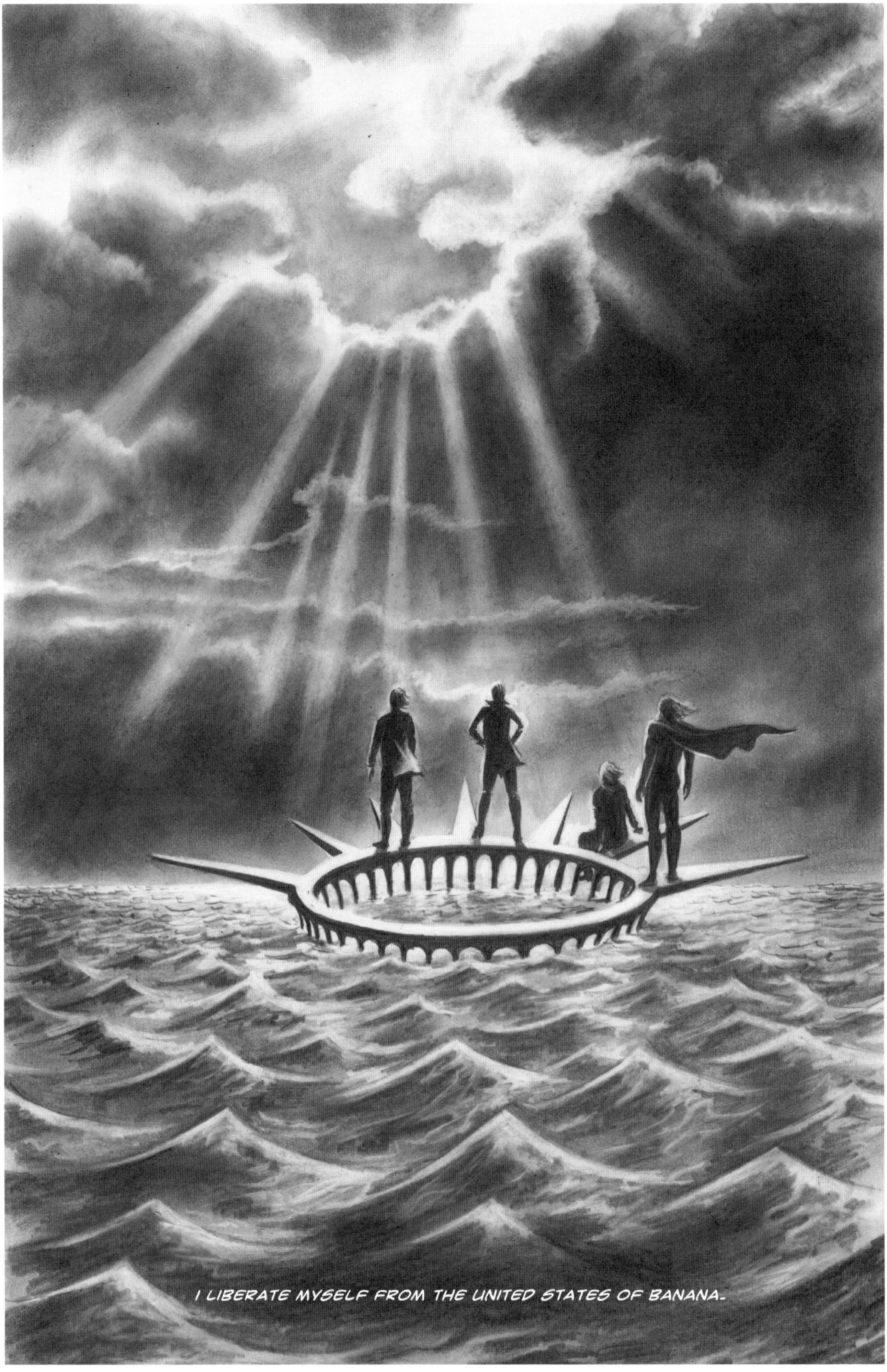
I LIBERATE MYSELF FROM THE UNITED STATES OF BANANA.

Whether you have picked up this graphic novel to read for pleasure or for a course, we are certain you have found inspiration in these pages. *United States of Banana: A Graphic Novel* is a work about dialogue, about thinking through big ideas aloud, and about building friendship across differences without necessarily attempting to resolve them. As such, we hope that you will want to talk to others about what you have read and seen. The following guiding questions may help frame your reading, interpretation, and discussion of this multifaceted work.

1. What does Giannina's revolution consist of? Why does she believe in it so firmly? What does she see as wrong with the status quo, and how does she propose to change it?

2. What does "freedom" mean in this graphic novel? If the Statue of Liberty is no longer a symbol of freedom, what does it represent? How has it come to represent something new? What do you think it means to be "free from freedom"?

3. Why do you think Braschi chose Segismundo as a stand-in for Puerto Rico? What are the correlations between his imprisonment in *Life Is a Dream* and the political status of Puerto Rico?

4. Describe the attitudes of Giannina's companions, Hamlet and Zarathustra. What do their perspectives bring to the conversation about the liberation of Segismundo? Why do you think Braschi chose these two characters for a book about political revolution?

5. Why do you think Braschi focuses particularly on characters from seventeenth-century literature (Hamlet, Segismundo, Ophelia, Rosaura, etc.) to tell this post-modern story? How does their inclusion change the way you view the original works?

6. What role does Segismundo play in his liberation? Why must he rely on the help of others to be free? What do you think this reliance suggests?

7. Why does this story unfold in New York City and not, for example, Puerto Rico? How does the setting impact the characters' actions, thoughts, and feelings? How does New York City appear in the graphic novel? What kind of place is it?

8. What intersections of race, class, and gender are present? How are they represented? According to the graphic novel, how should the diverse cast of characters work together to bring about change? Why must they all work together?

9. What kinds of characters appear under the skirts of the Statue of Liberty? Why? What do you think the graphic novel is saying about political prisoners?

10. What is the relationship between the graphic novel and 9/11? You may want to consider the imagery that references 9/11 and its aftermath. Why does it appear in the graphic novel? What is the graphic novel trying to say about the relationship of 9/11 to US politics? To US empire?

11. Joakim Lindengren's illustrations are rich, powerful, and often shocking. They are also highly referential with obvious allusions to modern art, US and Puerto Rican

pop culture, historical events, and more. Choose three to four images that are particularly striking and discuss the relationship between image and text. How does the image give meaning to the text?

12. One of the most controversial images shows smoke billowing out of the World Trade Center as the backdrop to Nick Ut's iconic photograph of Phan Thi Kim Phuc during the Vietnam War. The text reads, "Inspiration made an installation that day." What do you think Braschi means? Why did Lindengren choose to visualize the statement with this image? What does the Vietnam War have to do with 9/11?

13. Several images and passages are racially and sexually charged, repeating racist, sexist, and homophobic tropes. What examples can you find? How do you interpret their role in the graphic novel?

14. What do art and poetry have to do with political liberation in the graphic novel? How does poetic language and visual art come to bear on the characters' journey toward political revolution?

15. What is the point of the "Wedding of the Century"? Why do Basilio and Gertrude decide to marry, and what implications does this have for both *Hamlet* and *Life Is a Dream*? Discuss how this grand spectacle might relate to contemporary politics.

16. How can we understand Basilio and Gertrude's use of the phrase "global warming"? Why do they say they will unite the Americas "in the name of global warming"? What are they trying to do by framing their marriage in this way?

17. Braschi writes, "Puerto Ricans feel it's better to be conquered by a conqueror than to be exterminated by an exterminator. If you ask them to choose between an exterminator and a conqueror, they prefer to be vanquished, and that's why they choose Wishy-Washy." What does she mean? What is the difference between a conqueror and an exterminator, and to what political situations is she alluding? What is she trying to say about Puerto Rico's status? About Puerto Ricans? Their political options?

18. *USB* is about building bridges across geographies, social class, race, high and low culture, and more. Nevertheless, some people are left out of Braschi's project and the future it proposes. For example, at the end of the graphic novel, Basilio and Gertrude and all of their elite friends must drown in the sea. Why?

19. What does "United States of Banana" mean? Think about all the possible meanings of "bananas" in US and Latin American contexts. Why did Braschi choose this title? If a banana republic is, broadly speaking, a country reliant on the export of a single product, what is the United States' main export according to *USB*?

20. What do you think will happen after the characters sail off on the crown of the Statue of Liberty? Why?

Amanda M. Smith is Assistant Professor of Latin American Literature at the University of California, Santa Cruz, where she researches twentieth- and twenty-first-century Latin American cultural production.

Amy Sheeran is Assistant Professor of Spanish at Otterbein University. She specializes in early modern Peninsular literature.